TOWER OF BONES BOOK III

VALLEY OF SORROWS

I0610214

CONNIE J. JASPERSON
WORLD OF NEVEYAH

Connie J. Jasperson

FIRST EDITION
ISBN-13: 9781680630480
ISBN-10: 1680630482
Graphics & Maps © Connie J. Jasperson
Fantasy landscape with a tower © Unholyvault | Dreamstime.com

Special thanks to Eagle Eye Editors
www.eagleeyeeditors.me

Published by Bard Books
An Imprint of
Myrddin Publishing Group
Contact us at - www.myrddinpublishing.com

:

ii

BOOKS BY CONNIE J. JASPERSON

WORLD OF NEVEYAH, TOWER OF BONES SERIES:
Tower of Bones (Tower of Bones series book I)
Forbidden Road (Tower of Bones series book II)
Valley of Sorrows (Tower of Bones series book III)

WORLD OF NEVEYAH (stand-alone)
Mountains of the Moon
The Wayward Son (forthcoming in 2016)

OTHER BOOKS BY CONNIE J.JASPERSON:
HUW THE BARD
TALES FROM THE DREAMTIME

DEDICATION

This book is dedicated to the incredibly talented authors at Myrddin Publishing Group. I can't imagine any group of people I would like to be on this crazy journey with more than you. Thank you all from the bottom of my heart.

Alison DeLuca, you are a rock in the stormy seas of publishing, and nothing would ever get done without you! Irene Roth Luvaul, you inspire me daily. Greg Jasperson, you are the most patient of spouses—which is a blessing, as the book was five years in the writing.

ACKNOWLEDGMENTS

This book wouldn't exist without the hard work and sincere efforts of David P. Cantrell and Carlie M.A. Cullen.

And finally, many, many thanks to the Tuesday Morning Panera Writing Group--Lee French, Trish Nelson, and Shannon Reagan.

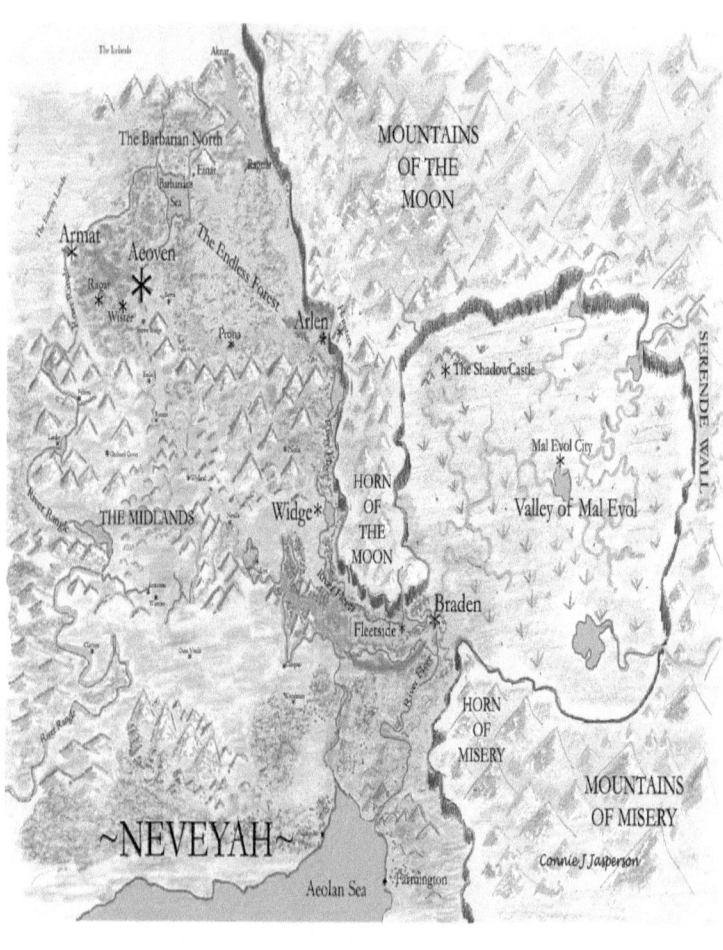

The Icelands

Aleut

The Barbarian North

Einm

Bargello

MOUNTAINS
OF THE
MOON

Barbarian
Sea

Armat *

Aeoven
*

The Endless Forest

Rogue
* *
Wister

Arlen
*

* The ShadowCastle

Prona

Mal Evol City
*

HORN
OF
THE
MOON

Valley of Mal Evol

Widge *

THE MIDLANDS

Red River

Fleetside *

Braden
*

Braid Range

HORN
OF
MISERY

SERENDIE WALL

~NEVEYAH~

Aeolan Sea

Parrington

MOUNTAINS
OF MISERY

Connie J Jasperson

PRELUDE 1
—14 Saggitus 3262—
Braden Temple

Edwin's nerves were strung so tautly that he'd woken after only a few hours. He'd lain awake, sunk in the morass of his misery. Unable to remain in bed he rose well before dawn and went down to the Temple kitchen, looking for a change of scenery to jolt himself out of his depression.

He lit the lamps and stoked the fire in the large stove. Filling the tea kettle, he sat at the big table the cooks used for preparing meals, waiting for the water to boil. Once his tea was made, he set the pot on the table and poured a cup, and then sat. Holding the cup, he stared into a corner, with nothing to distract him from the crushing weight of his troubles.

Abbott Garran's shadow loomed, cast by the lamplight. The big man's thick hair was uncombed, his night-shirt loose over his trousers, and he wore a pair of red, felted slippers. "You're going to break the handle off that cup if you don't relax, son." He found a mug for himself and sat opposite Edwin, who looked up. "I thought I heard you come down here."

Garran poured himself a cup of tea, stirring a large amount of honey into it. As he did so, he took in Edwin's haggard face, noting the shadowed eyes, and the worry lines deeply engraved across the younger man's forehead.

"What's *really* happening back home?" Edwin sat up straight, refilling his cup. "Dad wants to protect me from it, but I need to know."

"John and I disagree about how to handle this, but

he means well," replied Garran. "It's just that he and I both crumble under this sort of thing. He's trying to keep you from falling apart the way we would. I think he underestimates you."

Edwin forced himself to speak calmly. "Something's not right. I've studied Lorana's case notes extensively. I know exactly what she does—she specializes in treating Stefyn D'Mal's victims. I trust Lorana and my stepmother, Halee, to care for Marya and I'll do what I need to do here, but I have to know the truth."

Garran tried to keep a dispassionate tone to his voice. "She's frantic to kill whatever it is she believes lives in the walls. That hasn't changed, and every other day or so her obsession surfaces again. That first night she was convinced fire was the only way, and she took action."

Edwin set the cup down. "That's not at all the way Marya was when she was first freed from D'Mal's clutches. Nervous, yes. Skittish and afraid of everything, yes. But dangerous? No. Something else is going on there."

"You're right. We believe a mindbender is seeded into the population in Aeoven."

Edwin was silent, sorting things out. Red rage rose as he realized what Garran meant with those deceptively calm words. "Are you saying my wife has been tampered with? That some bastard has violated her mind?" He lowered his voice but his fists clenched so tightly his knuckles were white. With some effort, he willed himself to relax.

"We think so, yes. Whoever it is, they must be one of D'Mal's best because they haven't drawn attention to themselves yet. It's hard to pick them out. The ones we do discover nowadays are well trained and exceedingly good at remaining hidden. It takes a special mage to ferret them out. The problem is, only one mage currently in Aeoven has the ability to detect the presence of a mindbender and recognize what he is sensing, but he's without a partner in this search."

As Garran explained everything that had happened after the fire, Edwin's eyes widened. He tried to focus, to comprehend what he was hearing. The Abbott finished, and said, "I warn you, when you return home you'll have to make some hard choices for your son's sake."

"What do you mean?" Once again, Edwin clenched his fists to keep from hitting the table. "When Dad said Lorana was handling her case, I was afraid it was bad, but I didn't realize.... Before we do anything drastic, Zan needs to see her. He might be able to help her." Fear warred with bewilderment, fueled by helpless anger. "I'll do whatever I have to, for Jonny's sake." He wiped his cheek, but tears still stung his eyes. "My wife...my baby...it's difficult to accept."

Garran patted his shoulder. "Take comfort in the fact that Marya is in good hands. There's nothing you can do until you get your work finished here in the gap. We'll be home by Holy Day, which is the best we can do. That's when our task will really begin. We *are* going to find this acolyte of Tauron."

Visibly making the effort to pull himself together, Edwin was barely able to nod.

"Kalen Rallsson has been put on the hunt. He's been able to trace several crimes to one woman, but she disappeared at the same time Cayne Narvesson was murdered, just after you left."

"I hadn't heard about Cayne's murder. I didn't know him well, but it's…shocking."

"I'll bet Kalen will have found his prey before we get back home because it's personal." Garran grinned wolfishly. "Kalen always gets his quarry, and he's not gentle. But now that you're informed, what are you going to do?"

Edwin's head rested in his hands, but it didn't muffle his sharp response. "Serve Aeos, of course. Closing off the Braden Gap has to come first or Neveyah will fall. I won't allow that to happen, regardless of what Tauron does to my family and me. No matter how he tries to distract me, he won't succeed." He looked up. The murder in his eyes and venom in his voice startled Garran. "Whoever this acolyte of D'Mal's is, she'd better pray to her dread god that Kalen finds her before I do." Cold anger replaced helpless grief, filling him with the burning desire to get started on their quest. "If I catch her first, I'll dismantle her down to her last groveling tear."

The intense, deadly look Edwin now bore was one Garran had never seen in a healer, and it stunned him, again reminding him sharply of just how radically things had changed.

The kitchen door opened and the cook came in, clearly surprised to find the Abbott and a guest sitting in the kitchen so early. The two excused themselves and walked back to the guest quarters. Pausing in front of the door to the suite he and Friedr shared, Edwin said, "Thank you for telling me the truth. Dad means well, but I needed to know."

"You're stronger than John and me, in many ways.

We were never able to handle defeat or loss well."

"Maybe you're stronger than you give yourself credit for. You're both still here, prepared to face whatever comes along." Edwin's smile was strained, but he made the effort.

"You may be right." Sensing Edwin's desire to get on with things, Garran nodded. "We both have letters to write, and notes to make in our journals before you boys get on the road. I'll meet you all in the dining room for breakfast in an hour or so. We need to go over your route one last time, to ensure Moran and his squad can stay one step ahead of you in relocating the few hardy ranchers who're still hanging on inside the gap. We don't want to leave anyone on the other side."

"Agreed. And I need to write to Lorana, now I know what's actually going on. She needs to know she has my support, and that I will want a complete update when we return here to Braden, hopefully in two weeks."

Edwin channeled his anger into planning his next task, already visualizing how to build the wall and erect the final shield in as quick and efficient a way as possible. "I'm going to have to retrain myself to do Christoph's job, but if we can work as fast with Dad as we could with him, we'll have at least four weeks of work before we return to Aeoven."

After leaving Edwin, Garran continued on to his rooms, lost in his thoughts. The two sides of Edwin Farmer were disconcerting. The kind and gentle healer was somehow more frightening than the deadly assassin because now he knew what lay buried underneath the calm exterior.

PRELUDE 2
—14 Saggitus 3262—
Same Day in the Palace of Dreams

The door to Lourdan's study opened and Stefyn entered. "May I intrude? I have a guest I'd like you to meet, who's come all the way from Mal Evol. She's alone in our world and is in need of light company. You could use a lunch break—you've been studying too hard since you returned from the monastery."

"You're back! It's felt like an eternity, but I've made good use of my time." Lourdan closed his books and stood, embracing him. "Certainly, I'd like to meet your friend. I could stand a break as I'm researching some of most honorable Qarik's teachings, and making some minor corrections where his memory seems to have gone astray. Fortunately, it's all clear in the books you left me."

Stefyn's eyes hardened. "Qarik will be more assiduous in what he imparts to you from here on out, I assure you. But in the meantime, you must join us in the drawing room. I'm sure you'll find our guest most delightful. An afternoon spent socializing with a bright young lady won't hurt either of us."

"Have you just returned? You must be tired. Honorable Memschak told me you had to return to Mal Evol to resolve some problems. He mentioned a rogue priest attempted to seize your birthright from you, and vandalized your home—what next?"

"He told you? Good. Then you know what Lork did and how his actions will affect your path once you've been through the remaking. I've resolved it as well as I can for now. But on a positive note, I've just received word that one of our agents in Neveyah was successful in completing a task I was forced to leave unfinished several years ago. Linette should be on her way back to Mal Evol as we speak." Although the patch hid one eye, his good eye glittered with satisfaction. "She has a knack for removing Aeos's mages, and will be most helpful to you. We'll discuss all of this at length later. In the meantime, we arrived early this morning while you were at your lessons, and I've settled our guest in her rooms. She's had a chance to rest, but now we're perishing for our lunch." Stefyn held the door open. "Come—I've had starberries brought in from the country. I think our guest will enjoy them."

Yllene stood by the window in the opulent drawing room, gazing out upon the strange gardens, unsure what to expect. While on their journey, Stefyn had instructed her in every aspect of what she was to do, but she worried the man she was to be bonded to—*married*, he had called it—wouldn't fall in love with her and then she would die, sacrificed on Tauron's altar anyway.

Stefyn had somehow removed her augmentations and done something to her mind. She couldn't sense her gifts or speak anything of her own volition. At the inns where they'd stayed on their long journey, she'd been left unguarded, apparently free to come and go as she wished. But though she desperately wanted to tell someone that Stefyn had kidnapped her, she was unable to say the words. They wouldn't come, no matter how she tried.

She couldn't initiate a conversation. All she was able to do was give polite but non-committal responses to greetings or nod her head and smile. No matter what she planned during the night, she always found herself meeting Stefyn downstairs, dressed in the clothing he'd given her, and entering the carriage. She didn't know why she was going along with his charade—the man he intended her to bond with most likely wouldn't like her anyway.

It's so different in this world. It's too hot and too...too strange. And no one knows I'm here. Her lips trembled and she forced herself not to give in to her tears, knowing Stefyn would be angry if he found out she'd been crying again. She shuddered, remembering how the chi had gathered around him on their journey out of Mal Evol. His rage had manifested itself several times during the days before they'd arrived at the portal. And then, once they passed through the strange cave that was the portal, it had taken two days before his madness had completely worn off.

Several times she had inadvertently displeased him. He'd hurt her, calling her 'Marya,' but after he calmed down he'd apologized and healed her. She remembered hearing about a healer who was kidnapped before Yllene was even a novice—but that girl was rescued. It was likely no one even knew Yllene was missing yet, as it had only been two weeks. A tear formed and she quickly brushed it away.

The door to the drawing room opened. Stefyn entered leading a familiar-looking man and her mind ground to a halt...those augmentations...She knew him. Even with his curly, dark hair grown out far longer than she remembered it being, she recognized him, because

9

he'd been one of her instructors. He was Christoph—her lips refused to form his name, but she knew exactly who he was. None of her thoughts would manifest themselves as words.

Her eyes met Stefyn's. His smirk told her he knew what was going through her mind, gloating as astonishment registered on her face. He was fully aware of exactly who Lourdan was, how she knew him, and wanted her to recognize him. She saw it in his eye. In his twisted way, he was enjoying every minute of her shock and horror, feeding off it.

Stefyn beamed as she smiled and curtseyed, unable to stop herself. She was a puppet, and he pulled the strings. He crossed the room, and taking Yllene's hand, he introduced her. "Lourdan, this is Yllene, a young lady I met on my travels. She'll be studying at the University. I thought you would enjoy meeting each other—you have so few friends outside of the palace. She has a great deal of knowledge that will help you in your studies over the coming weeks before your remaking."

"I'm pleased to meet you, Yllene." Lourdan's smile was charming and welcoming. Clearly he didn't recognize her, which amazed her. "I'm studying to be a priest so, of course, I'm quite interested in our culture and history. Perhaps I can pick your brain as there are some things I'm just learning."

She wanted to say his true name, wanted to pull away from Stefyn, but instead her body did as he willed. Yllene smiled and nodded, weak-kneed and nearly unable to stand.

An expression of exultation crossed Stefyn's face. "Shall we have our lunch?" He placed her trembling hand in Lourdan's.

An intense thrill of electricity ran between them, connecting them. Yllene gasped as the current passed through her.

Lourdan's eyes widened in shock, and his grip tightened. Astounded, he raised her hand to his lips. "Yllene...your name is as beautiful as you are. I've never met anyone as lovely as you."

The instant her hand touched Lourdan's, new windows opened in her mind and old doors closed. Yllene forgot everything that had gone before, swept away by the momentous experience. She had no memory of Lourdan's true past or hers. Unbidden, answers to his artless questions tumbled out of her mouth, answers Stefyn had put in her mind, but she didn't notice—they were real to her.

Stefyn stepped back, watching as his spell settled over his pair of lovebirds. He'd been required to use a special charm to encourage Lourdan to desire her sexually as he wasn't attracted to women at all, but he'd prepared ahead for that eventuality. Discreetly following in the role of chaperone, he allowed them a small amount of privacy as they strolled in the garden after dinner, sensed their embrace in a secluded bower, and reinforced his spell of desire.

He just happened to be available when Lourdan came to ask his approval on their marriage, even agreeing to perform the ceremony himself that very night. "Why wait? When you find the woman you were born to love, seize the moment. She's a scholar and can help you with your studies as much as I can. I've many tasks to occupy me and you'll be happier studying in her company—for the next few weeks anyway."

He layered several subtle spells over them during the marriage vows, binding them closer, smiling paternally as the flames of the candles turned a deep purple, signaling their union had received Tauron's divine blessing.

A sacrifice was only worthy if the giver truly valued it, so it had to be this way. Stefyn would be there to pick up the pieces when Lourdan offered her up. He'd be observing as Lourdan performed his first ritual of sacrifice as an acolyte of Tauron. That would be when he would need his support.

Near dawn, as Lourdan and his bride slept in each other's arms in the rooms adjoining his, Stefyn opened his eyes and rose, calling for his manservant. He gave orders that High Priest Qarik should be summarily dragged from his bed and brought before him.

Qarik might serve on the ruling Circle of Six, but he was still Stefyn's servant. That point would be driven home most creatively. He would pay for deliberately feeding Lourdan misinformation and his penance would be an example to the others. When Stefyn was done with Qarik, any others who may have tried to sabotage Lourdan would be leaping to correct their errors.

VALLEY OF SORROWS

The Braden Gap and the Wall

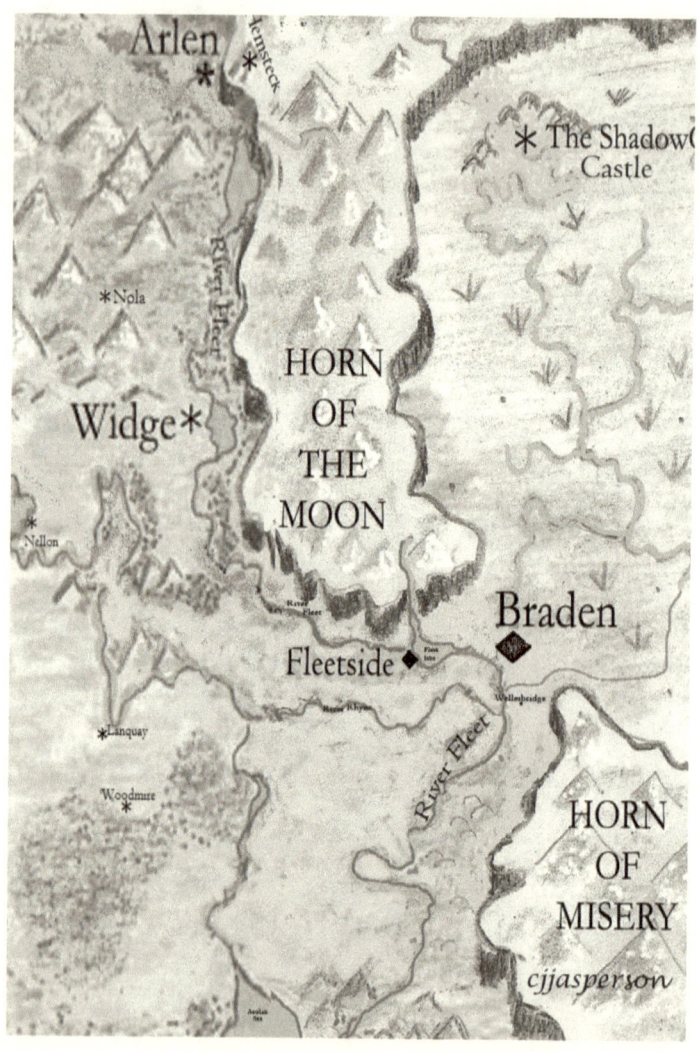

VALLEY OF SORROWS

Chapter 1

Moran, Abbott Garran's assistant, spoke to the four mages gathered around a horse-drawn wagon. "The wagon and team are yours to keep, Friedr, since you can no longer walk as quickly as you could before. There's plenty of room for them in the main stables at Aeoven, and folks to care for them. On this journey, stay at inns wherever you're able, as you'll rest better."

"With Edwin along, we won't be hanging about in common rooms," replied Friedr, winking. "He's a stick-in-the-mud, you know."

Edwin shrugged and rolled his eyes at Friedr's cliché.

"So I've heard," Moran agreed, chuckling at Edwin's expense. "Anyway, several farms along the way might put you up, but don't count on it. There may be trouble when they're told to move west or be cut off from Neveyah forever. Still, I'll be riding ahead of you, visiting them all and clearing out those whose lands are in the way of the wall or on the wrong side. I'll have several squads of mounted soldiers fanning out to help round up livestock in the gap and taking care of resettling people, forcibly if needed. Other squads will clear the farms north of us while you complete the southern half of this."

Looking up from checking the horses' hooves, John asked, "You have a list of the vacant homesteads in the Midlands for displaced farmers to move to?"

Moran nodded. "And I'll make sure to note who was assigned to each."

"Good—we don't want any accidental doubling up. Even without that complication, there's bound to be trouble, so don't let your guard down. If I may suggest, take Rohr Macsson's squad with you. I trained with them all this last Harvest. They're older and less likely to be rattled by angry farmers threatening them with pitchforks."

"Yes, Sir," Moran replied. "I'll take Div's unit too if Garran is agreeable."

"A good choice. They're experienced in dealing with back-country folk and can sort out the stubborn ones." John turned back to the horses, brushing the bay's mane. "There you go, Peta. You look a bit better."

Conversations drifted in the morning air. Before they went down to breakfast Garran admitted he'd given Edwin the complete story of what had happened back in Aeoven. Now, John was wary, unsure how his inability to protect Marya from herself would affect his relationship with his son.

"Dad." Edwin's voice so close to John's ear startled him. "Stop beating yourself up over what happened at home. You couldn't have changed anything, but you managed to keep my wife from killing herself. You kept my son safe. You and Halee— there's no need for you to feel this burden of guilt. Thank you, thank you, a thousand times over for being there when I was absent." He rested his hand on his father's shoulder.

Overwhelmed by his conflicting emotions, John changed the subject. "What's the plan for today, Son?"

"We're just going to raise a new shield and scrape up earth to build a wall for the next six weeks or so," Edwin said with a grin. "Not exactly glamorous work. The shield will be similar to something you've already done. All of my well-publicized, so-called discoveries came from examining your work on the Great Shield and copying your ties and workings."

"You've said that before, but I don't see it." Worry lines creased John's forehead, and he gazed into the distance. "It was desperation, not genius that raised the Great Shield. I think the only reason we were able to do it was because we didn't know what we were doing. I'm glad it succeeded, but I don't have any idea why it worked. I've looked at it since then and I'm mystified by it. It's as if someone else constructed it. I can't take credit for it because I have no memory of the experience." His eyes met his son's, and he shrugged.

Edwin nodded. "I think I understand. But this will be different."

Zan had finished loading their kits on the wagon and turned to Moran. "We can get a message to you if we run into any trouble we can't handle, and we'll keep you informed of what we're doing with a daily report if you're in the area. Edwin and I can drop it to you in this with our air-magic." He handed Moran a small, wooden box that would fit in his saddle bags. "Just check it in the morning and at night. Once you're out of our range, we'll just have to manage until we get back to Braden."

They climbed into the wagon and settled themselves. Edwin asked, "What made you decide to raise a shield? I always wondered where you got the idea and the chi. It took a massive amount—I can sense the strength of it every time I pass through." He wondered if he would get an answer. His father was notoriously unwilling to discuss the Great Shield.

Friedr flicked the reins and Beulah and Peta set a smart pace, heading south along the East River Road toward their first destination. The breeze off the wide river was cold and sharp, but the four men were well insulated against the chill.

"I guess I do owe you an explanation of sorts—at least, what I remember about those last few days of the war. I'll try to tell you while we're traveling because it's a long story. Several parts of it are gone from my mind, and some of my battle-magic is compromised—I lost the ability to call fire and it will never come back.

"I can't boast about something I feel was a miserable failure. It works, but only barely—the shield isn't what it should have been because we had no lightning mage in the mix."

The cart bumped and rolled down the rough road as, reluctantly, John spun the tale. His voice carried over the noises of the horses and the wagon. "It happened just after we escaped the siege at Ronan's Vineyard, an old walled citadel from the early days. We'd had the high ground there and under better circumstances, it would have been perfect for waiting out a siege. We'd held on for a full day longer than we dared to hope we could...."

>>><<<

John's story wound to a close. "Even though I'd been punished and my ability to raise magic had been taken from me, Riverbinder seemed to *want* to do what I was asking of it. The sword didn't fight me as it usually did. I know now we did manage to do something amazing, but I don't know exactly what. The memory of what the blade actually did was seared from me. My next memory is waking up in a field hospital. The healers told me that Halee, Garran, and I were the only survivors amidst a sea of butchery. All our soldiers, my brothers- and sisters-in-arms who trusted me to bring them home...were dead." John fell silent.

Edwin shuddered. "Dad, losing your gifts for all those years.... What a terrible burden to bear alone."

Friedr agreed. "But I understand your reluctance to confess your problem. You probably thought your gifts would come back."

John nodded. "I hoped they would. I kept it secret from everyone, until just this year. I partially regained the use of magic, but that's why I couldn't duel with it, and why I had to go to such lengths to never use it offensively."

Friedr shook his head, grinning ruefully. "You had me completely deceived. I think you even had your son fooled."

Edwin nodded. "I knew you were hiding something. You have more secrets than Father Rall—you always have had, so I don't press you."

"I'm sorry for not being honest with you about my problems—I'm just so used to carrying them alone that I don't know how to share them anymore."

Edwin reached out and embraced his father. "Thank you for telling us about that day. I know you hate to talk about the war, but it helps me to know what happened to you. The things we went through don't seem as bad, knowing what you endured."

Zan agreed. "Whenever I think I've seen too much, remind myself that some people have seen far worse." The wagon swayed over the rutted road and he gazed into the distance. His grim profile sharply emphasized the changes the last few months had wrought.

"It's just perspective, Zan," John said wryly. "Sometimes I—I can't think about it without freezing up. I don't know why."

Zan turned, meeting John's eyes with a hint of his old self. "Many of the patients I've seen in some of the most rural areas are former soldiers, people who're unable to live a normal life now they're no longer on the front lines. They can't take being around crowds of people for very long, so they prefer farming. They're still reliving the war, as you are. I've been able to help many of them." Zan grinned at John's skeptical expression. "The people I can't help are those who're afraid to let go of their fears. Their terrors are familiar, and they cling to them because that familiarity comforts them. They dread the unknown more than the demons they know."

The look of shocked comprehension on John's face would have been comical, had it not been such a serious moment.

Hiding his grin, Friedr reined the horses to a walk. "This is where we should make the first stop. We're going to follow a fairly well-traveled road along on this eastern side of the River Fleet today, but tomorrow we'll enter the open prairie."

Chapter 2

The wagon rolled to a stop. Edwin said, "We're going to start the wall here so fewer people in Braden will know it's going up."

John replied, "Good idea. That will give us more time before the enemy discovers what we're doing."

Edwin nodded. "We'll connect it to the city walls when we return this way after we've finished the first leg of this task."

Friedr had halted the wagon at a wide, grassy place beside the river. "I camped here many times as a journeyman doing my time in the militia while Aeolyn was still in the novice barracks." He grinned at John. "This first time will show us what the limits of our abilities are once we add you and your sword to the mix. Maybe the next stop will be further, or not."

They climbed down from the wagon, stretching. Zan took a low stool from the wagon, thickly padded to enable Friedr to sit more easily than he did on the ground. He sat, not completely comfortable, but in less discomfort than was usual for him. Edwin cast a spell for pain relief on him and winked at the big man's affronted glare.

"I'm becoming quite spoiled." Disguising his resentment of his situation with a wry grin, Friedr drew Dragonstorm from its sheath.

Edwin unsheathed Leviathan. "Dad, you're not the only one learning something new here today. We've never done this without Christoph leading before. Earthbinder was always the hub, uniting us and channeling our magic." He looked away, unable to disguise his sense of loss.

"I assume you have a plan for building this wall." John's statement caught Edwin by surprise. "A few drawings or such? Something to go by?"

"I do, sort of. It's all up here." He tapped his head, grinning at his father's consternation. "The wall will be the simplest part, but it's going to look spectacular. I'm going to make it like the walls of Arlen, except flashier."

Numbly, John asked, "Flashier? How so?"

Edwin grinned at his father's comical expression. John's whole life had revolved around careful planning and preparation. "Don't worry, Dad. I know what it should look like, and once we have the first section built, I'll know how to do the rest. I'm making it as tall as the walls around Arlen, and smooth as glass."

"I don't know, Son." John's strangled tones made Zan and Friedr grin. "Wouldn't some drawings be useful?"

"There speaks the instructor," said Edwin. He winked at Friedr, who also disliked improvising. "I know what we're doing. Honest."

Friedr chuckled at Edwin's jab. "I know what you mean, John. I hate doing things by intuition, but it seems to be Edwin's best talent. Fortunately, we aren't going to worry about tolerances, gradients, or soil compression ratios because the wall is just for appearances. No one will ever come near enough to touch it."

"You'll see," Zan agreed. "We're raising the shield first because nothing will be able to cross it. Once it's up, we'll build the wall."

Edwin sat opposite John. "Considering the amount of soil I'll need to scrape up to do this right, we'll have a good deep moat. Add the magic shield to it and nothing will ever cross this barricade, not even insects. It's just a variation on what most earth-mages do when they're repairing dikes and building retaining walls, except larger and with a barrier against D'Mal's empathic magic. I think we can do it the way I envision by linking and using the swords to magnify the magic."

John nodded. Reluctantly, he reminded himself it was Edwin's project. He had to have faith in his son's ability to visualize what he wanted. Setting aside his worry, he said, "I've linked before, but it's different for animal healers. I don't see into the patient the way you do. When we delve a sick horse or other creature, we can only sense areas of heat and cold where disease or infection is. You actually see lights, so I hear."

"Your empathy is different but more than strong enough. You can do this, or Aeos would have sent someone else. Are you ready?"

"I'm nervous, of course." John exhaled heavily, his rueful expression more telling than his words. "I never could make this finely-wrought bar of steel function the way magic swords are supposed to. It stubbornly refused to transform into the fiery weapon of terror against the legions that I wanted, indeed that I desperately *needed* it to be. It makes my spells far stronger than they would be without it. But instead of having an appreciation for that, I became arrogant, sure I could do more than I was able to in reality."

"Ours never did much more than that either," agreed Friedr. "I was a bit disappointed, but perhaps it's all there is to them. They do increase the power of our magic, and we'd never have survived any of our battles without them. I'd have died after my injury if it weren't for Edwin and Zan drawing chi through their blades to support the surgery."

John said, "When I went back to Markett, I put Riverbinder in the trunk with no regrets. It has great magic, but none I'm able to use. The failure is not in the sword but is in me. I was never able to consciously unlock it although my father insisted I would. He died believing I could, swearing he'd seen it in a true-dream when I was just a babe. I've never lived up to that promise." With a self-mocking smile, he handed the blade to Friedr.

Awed, Friedr examined it, holding it up to the light, seeing subtle engravings under the smooth surface, runes only visible when the blade was held at a certain angle. "Yes...there is deep magic within it and great power. But I don't think it's what you think it should be—don't ask me why because I'm not a smith. Glass is easier for me to sense." He handed it back to John.

Despite his obvious skepticism, John gripped his sword and positioned it the same way as the others had theirs. Opening the gifts for veterinary healing wasn't difficult. A feeling of warmth and completion settled over him as he was drawn into the link.

Once inside, the difference was clear. It wasn't at all like linking had been with the other veterinarians and for a moment, he was caught up in the wonder. He *saw* the earth beneath them, all the way back to the walls of Braden through Edwin's eyes and felt the presence of the others, realizing the blades were what made the difference.

First, Edwin called the element of earth, holding it uncast. At his request, Friedr contributed the component of fire, holding and sustaining the spell as Edwin wove the two elements together. When asked, Zan added lightning.

At Edwin's mental request, John called his element of water, holding it as if preparing to cast it, doing as he was asked, and then slowly pouring it into the mix. An undercurrent of surprise rippled through the link. For a moment, a startled look crossed Edwin's face, and he faltered, but firmed up his barriers and continued.

John was completely unprepared for what happened as he let go of the magic. The feeling was tremendously physical, growing more extreme with every moment, rising to a nearly sexual peak. He inhaled, trying to separate from the sensuality of it. He'd always found calling his element to be gratifying, but this was an erotic intensity he'd never felt before. The power of the experience threatened to sweep him away in a tidal wave of carnal pleasure. Trembling, he was barely able to remember who he was or what he was doing. He wanted nothing more than to fall into the water and never come up.

"John, you forgot to buffer yourself against the magic." Dimly, John heard Zan's mental voice, bringing him back to unwilling awareness. "I didn't realize you'd be affected this way although I should have. Your connection to your element is too deep." Sensing John's embarrassment, he added, "We each deal with this distraction too, so don't feel uncomfortable about it."

"Distraction…is too mild a word for such an extreme experience." John felt rather than saw Zan's agreement.

Control of John's magic was gently taken from him and this time, he felt panic as if Edwin pulled the magic out of him despite his will to the contrary. Friedr said, "I found that aspect of this difficult at first, too. You'll get used to it." Friedr's thoughts had a droll tone to them.

The power Edwin wielded intimidated John, and he was grateful to be but a passenger, contributing only what he was asked. His hearing and other senses were enormously expanded. It occurred to him that, yes, their magic had been magnified by the link, but then it was enlarged exponentially by the swords. The elements had been melded into a power of which he had only ever dreamed.

He had yearned for such power in the last days of the war. Somehow he knew beyond a shadow of a doubt this magic was never to be used as a weapon—it was domestic magic at its most extreme.

Gradually, John became aware of a low hum emanating from Riverbinder, something he'd never noticed before. On the heels of that realization, he saw strong lines of force through the link, almost like intensely colored lightning connecting Riverbinder to the three other swords. The four blades were linked as if communicating with each other. Riverbinder generated both the blue energy of water and a strange glowing element he didn't recognize. Dragonstorm gave off the orange-red of fire, and Stormbringer the white-yellow he'd always associated with lightning. Leviathan was the connection through which the power was gathered and then expressed, emitting both a dusky red energy which John knew was earth-magic and a glowing, spectral force like that of Riverbinder, only stronger.

The ghostly force wrapped the four elements. His son's willpower twisted them, compelling them to do his bidding, creating a spell, unlike anything John had ever imagined possible.

Inserted into the lace was the ghostly element. With a shock, John understood Edwin had intertwined healing spirit so intricately it appeared not to be there at all. Edwin realized it at the same time, his elation rippling through the link.

Friedr spoke through the link. "Riverbinder's power is healing chi or spirit. Now we know."

Edwin anchored the spell to both the soil and the water flowing underground, using the ambient chi that lay within the earth to power his spell of aversion. Once they had set the ward, he guided them in tying it off.

When at last Edwin broke the link, there was a profound sense of stillness, as each man considered what had just occurred.

It was Zan who broke the silence. "Something new happened. The swords recognized Riverbinder." He looked at Friedr for confirmation and received an answering nod. "Stormbringer hummed. They were linked, just as we were."

"The others welcomed it as if it were a long-lost brother." Opening his journal, Friedr noted down his observations. "I certainly don't recall that sort of—well, *power* is the only word I can think of—when we were shielding the heart of Neveyah against Tauron's poison. Christoph's staff, Earthbinder, was the nexus for the link."

John managed not to look shaken. "I completely

overlooked the buffer. I forgot everything—like a rank journeyman." His son's next comment left him speechless.

"I didn't know if we could do it—but I hoped so. It was a lot worse than I expected, yet it was easier because Riverbinder was in the link." Edwin stretched. "That was startling, to say the least. I thought I was losing control at first, but once I remembered to firm up my buffer, I was able to cope." Sadness overcame him briefly, as he thought about Christoph and his magic staff. "But now we know the Goddess long ago foresaw the need for the fourth sword."

Edwin stood up, and the others followed suit. "Dad, this is the first time our swords have shown their true power. Like you, we were never able to figure out what they did beyond drawing chi and increasing our elemental magic. But today they revealed themselves to us."

John looked away, unable to meet Edwin's eyes. "I was pretty disconcerted by it. I've never felt the magic that way. If I had, I promise you I'd have died from letting it run wild. We're fortunate you are dedicated to preserving Neveyah, Son. The power you wield is certainly beyond me." He colored as he glanced at Zan. "Thank you for pulling me back. I know now how our young mages get lost in the magic, and what we need to do to prevent it. I'll never forget to buffer myself again."

"Experience is a good teacher," Zan agreed, grinning.

"Surviving it is the trick," replied John, rolling his eyes. "It was too much of a surprise—I was completely unprepared. I don't know how to explain this to the

Abbacy, but I have to get it across to them somehow."

"Spirit is empathy and battle-magic is sensuality. The two combined is deadly unless a mage can learn to buffer against it," Edwin told his father. "I couldn't use my air-magic without getting lost at first, and I was desperate. I had to come up with some way of not dying when I began using my abilities. Air and earth were especially difficult for me. Christoph kept me from getting lost during those first months until I figured out the buffer." A wry grin lightened his drawn features. "The problem is you desire nothing more than to let it kill you."

Mutely, John agreed, shuddering. Finally, he said, "Perhaps we should teach buffering *before* we begin training novices in the elements, especially now battle-mages are being given more healing-empathy. It could prevent problems when a young mage has latent empathy that hasn't shown itself."

"Good idea," Zan agreed. "The senior instructors will understand when *you* tell them what happened and why. They just didn't get it when *I* tried to explain it— but I'm a lower journeyman."

"Not anymore, Zan. You're an adept in both healing and battle-magic. You'll get those pins before Holy Day, I promise." John was pleased to see a startled smile lighten the younger man's melancholy expression.

Friedr finished writing in the quest log and looked up. "About the Great Shield—when you raised it, the three of you each had small amounts of latent healing ability. You and Garran both had one star, and Halee had three. It was just enough to enable Riverbinder to take over and create the link. When you constructed the elemental part of the shield, your spirit became woven in with it though you were unaware you'd done such a thing. I confess I've been unable to figure out how such a monumental thing was constructed by three battle-mages when no healer was present to contribute the healing-chi." His sharp, blue eyes were thoughtful as he added, "I'm convinced your blade enabled the link for you three. Its primary virtue is this: it allows you to use and control spirit as if you were a full healer adept. More than that, it increases the available spirit the way our swords enlarge the elements."

John sat back. "Until today, I was never sure." He exhaled heavily, and his voice caught. "My dad...I wish I could tell him." After a moment, he burst out, "I'm a fool! I was never able to make it work because I was trying to use it for the wrong purpose. All that time, I was trying to make it do something it was never designed to do. My *father* saved Neveyah when he made this sword. Without it, we'd never have built the Great Shield."

Edwin handed John some bread and cheese, and sat back down, grinning. "We never understood our blades either. Usually, I just muddle around until something goes right, then I keep doing whatever that was. But we've only completed half of our task here. Now we must build the physical wall so we can move on to the next place. Time is short. We need to eat and finish our work. Also, we have to do several more lengths today if our cart can carry us fast enough. We'll definitely have to eat more often, though. At least, I will. This kind of work takes it out of you."

"You've never handled that much magic before," Zan agreed. "My father was always the nexus, and we didn't generate half that much power."

VALLEY OF SORROWS

Chapter 3

Edwin stepped away from the camp and stood to gaze at his creation, seeing his reflection with the sun setting behind him. Dark as polished obsidian, the wall was everything Edwin had hoped it would be and, judging from his comments, much more than his father had ever imagined.

John walked up to stand beside him. "Before I came back to Neveyah after Holy Day, I dreamed of this wall nearly every night. It drove me mad trying to figure out what Citadel it could belong to."

Edwin said, "I don't recall dreaming of it, but Zan did, and he told me what it had to look like."

In actuality, raising the wall had been the simplest part of the task. It was just a matter of the four of them linking, channeling earth-magic to excavate soil, compacting and shaping it, and hardening it with Edwin's skills. The construct was slightly taller than the walls of Arlen, averaging fifteen meters tall and rooted twice as deep within the earth.

As he'd planned, a wide, deep moat of varying depths gradually filled with groundwater on the Mal Evol side of the wall, formed by a great trench. The depth and breadth of the moat demonstrated the immense amount of soil that had been magically compressed into the densest rock possible to form the wall.

Unlike the fortifications of Arlen, there was no parapet at the top, only razor-sharp shards of knifelike flint, standing like deadly sentinels, glinting whenever the sun struck them. The face was as smooth as polished glass, with no handhold to be found anywhere on it. No one could approach that wall as they would be repelled by the ward. The enemy would look at it, yearning to cross, and be forever unable to do so.

The wall was ominous, but like fireworks, its intimidating appearance was mostly for show. Part of its menace was enhanced by the spell of aversion woven into the shield.

They created four lengths of the wall on the Neveyah side of the barrier John had raised just after the war twenty-five years before, east of the River Fleet. The new shield cells were layered against the leading edge of the honeycomb-shield they had erected over the heart of Neveyah with Christoph several months previously, which Edwin felt would strengthen the new wall.

"It looks pretty fancy," said John. "It's funny, how scary it is when all you did was compact the earth into rock. You might think it simple and ungraceful magic, but I don't think even Halee could do that four times in one day."

"If she had the four swords to work through she could. She has that much strength." Edwin's voice was quiet, his mind on the strategy for getting as much built as possible before they attracted unwanted attention. "We should build the barrier as high into the Mountains of Misery as we can. It will sort of swoop up for the last few leagues until it joins the top of the cliff."

"You should do that at the Horn of the Moon too," John agreed. "I don't think anyone will try to scale the escarpment at either end, but you never know. The southwestern escarpments of the Mountains of Misery are even higher than those we know as the Mountains of the Moon. The cliffs are just as sheer. There are no paths and believe me; I've checked. They rise straight up in precipices that are easily two leagues high at the lowest points. The children of the Bull God can't breathe well up there. In fact, once they undergo the change and become minotaurs, they're less able to survive the heights than we are."

"That's what I needed to know," replied Edwin. "The Horn of Misery seems higher than the Horn of the Moon, but I thought it was just my perspective."

"So the valley really is surrounded by impassable walls." Zan sat near the fire with his sewing box out, mending Friedr's spare shirt by the light of the flames. "From the part where we've been skulking about, you can't see the eastern walls except as a smudge on the horizon. It's hard to picture it as a valley."

"I can't explain how high the Mountains of Misery are at the point where they now touch Serende. Those mountains were the center of the god Ariend's world of Cascadia. You can imagine how vast the valley is, that those eastern mountains should appear as only a smudge on the horizon. Mal Evol is indeed a valley, and the only easy entrance to it is in the Gap, which Aeos created when she saved what remained of Ariend's world," replied John. "She left only one way in and out since it's bordered on the east by Tauron's world of Serende.

"But D'Mal and his black carriage.... How does he ride to Serende in *that*, going over Mountains such as you are describing?" Zan's question was echoed in Friedr's expression.

John forced a smile, feeling sadness at the thought of the friends who were guarding the outpost at the Serende Wall when the legions overran it. "If you know where the portal is you can use it. His portal is inside a cave at the base of the eastern escarpment—and in the old days, we had an outpost there, making sure no people or *things* came through it. Our portal to the world of Ariend is a pile of rocks that were originally an altar to Aeos, before the dividing of the world and long before we were civilized by Aelfrid Fire-sword."

"Now I know why I was attracted to playing at the rock pile," Edwin said. "I felt at peace and didn't feel like I lacked friends when I read my books out there."

Zan had been listening intently. "John, Feia always said your father was the luckiest mage in the history of the Temple." Wynn Farmer had long been one of Zan's heroes.

"It's true that my father was blessed with an inordinate amount of luck," laughed John. "He was certainly the craziest man I ever knew." John stopped and stood as if he had something he didn't want to say but felt compelled to speak anyway. "Edwin, I hoped against hope that you'd never be called to Neveyah. I didn't want you to go through what I did, losing your friends and losing faith. I wanted you to be happy."

"I'm not happy at this time in my life, Dad, I admit that. How could I be? But I'm going to try to be as content as possible under the circumstances. I do know that I'm happier here than I ever was in Markett. I love my life in Aeoven and wouldn't change it for anything, no matter how disrupted it is when I *do* get back there." A hint of darkness flickered in his eyes. "I'm not going back to Markett anytime soon, especially now. Marya needs to be cared for properly, and that can only be done here." He lifted his hair, exposing the stealth rune. "Besides, I have this. Garran tells me I can't leave

Neveyah until there are no rogue-mages."

"And that will never be." John pulled his cloak around him, blocking out the chill breeze. "Would you have changed nothing? Not even if it would bring Christoph back?" His eyes searched his son's face as he asked the question, "Or your daughter?"

"Realistically, nothing I could have done would have saved the baby. I couldn't have altered Christoph's lot or Marya's situation. I feel certain I couldn't have changed anything in Aeoven, no matter whether we were there or not, because Tauron worked his will all those years ago when she was D'Mal's captive. We who serve Aeos are all that protects Neveyah against him. I will face his attacks. His attempt to destroy our family from within won't stop me." There was steel in Edwin's gaze. "If anything, it's made me more determined to stand against him."

John saw a lot was going on beneath the unruffled surface his quiet son showed the world. The knowledge that Edwin would be a bad enemy made him proud. "I know what you mean. But I hate this feeling of helplessness, of having no control over our lives, just because we're descended from a legendary man who was cursed with an impossible, flaming sword."

Edwin laughed. "Dad—we're bound to this wheel, whether we wish it or not. Christoph's destiny was written in the stars long before we were born, as was yours and mine. The prophecies all tell us that. My fate is to be your son, to follow in your footsteps, and build a new wall against him. I don't fight it because I saw what that did to you." He reached out, clasping his father's arm. "I don't mean to tell you it was easy, what we've endured, because it wasn't. It broke us for a short time, but Aeos gave us strength and we survived. Now we're stronger."

"My father would say you're tempered steel now, Son," John said, wiping a tear from his eye. "I broke—I shattered." He dropped his head to his hands. "And then, for the last week, riding in the mail-carriage, I've been terrified I'd have to go through it all again." He looked up, emotion raw on his face. "Only this time I was afraid I would lose you. When we left Aeoven, all Garran and I knew was that we were once again put in charge of some hopeless military campaign against the endless legions. I was terrified that once again I would fail to get it right and you'd be taken from me."

Edwin replied. "You love so strongly, Dad. You see that love as a weakness, but it's not. It's a strength you were able to use when the time came."

John had no answer for that, just shaking his head. Finally, he asked, "How did you go on after what happened at the Shadow Castle? What gave you the reason to keep going?" He was asking more than the obvious, of that Edwin was certain.

"It was hard. When Christoph was grabbed and pulled through the portal, we nearly went mad. The look on his face...I can't even describe his terror." Edwin was a mass of emotions John knew too well, things he'd keenly felt for far too long. "We were helpless to save him because D'Mal had planned exactly that, and maneuvered us into the position we found ourselves in. He wanted Christoph in his clutches. He knew Christoph had healed the throne and broken it free of Tauron's poison. Now Stefyn D'Mal can't read the throne through a minion as he has been able to do until now. He has to return to Mal Evol, something he's loath to do because of the madness he suffers when he is here."

"I'd have thought he'd have recognized you—after all, he held you captive in the dream-world." John smiled as he added, "I'm glad he didn't."

"Our armor was specially created for stealth, and the Baron's vision is compromised now he only has one eye. He may believe I'm dead because he *did* stab me in the heart when I was his captive. Besides, he assumed we were just soldiers with minor gifts, guarding Christoph and lending him our chi because that's the way Tauron's priesthood works."

John absorbed what Edwin said. Suddenly the enormity of it all was more than he could bear. Clenching his fists and raging helplessly, he jumped up and began pacing back and forth. "Gah! Poor Christoph—he was a pawn in their great game like you were six years ago, and as we were. Pawns!" John's pain and frustration burst like a dam breaking. "I never wanted to be fated to do anything. I *fought* my destiny the way you fight those poor rat-people, with just as much chance of changing it as you have of eradicating them. Fate? No, not fate—pawns! That's what you are when destiny is pushed on you by forces outside of your control. And the more I fight it, the more I find myself going down this preordained path of glory. I want no part of it!"

Edwin stood solidly under the onslaught of his father's pain and frustration until John's emotional storm subsided and he was once again calm, and faintly embarrassed.

"Yet here you are, Dad. You're doing exactly what you were born to do, saving the world again. What does that tell you?" Edwin's ironic smile brought an answering one from his father.

"It tells me I'm a fool, Son. I'm a fool who knows it, and probably won't stop being one." His temporary storm of angst had passed. John laughed at himself as he said, "Zan frequently tells me I should just try to go with the currents of the river of fate, but my natural inclination is to swim upstream as hard and fast as I can."

"That's why I love you, Dad. You taught me everything I know about *really* fighting. Staying in the fight until it's done is only part of it." Edwin clasped his father's shoulder. The two sat talking by the light of the fire, choosing to share the first two watches between them.

As they made ready to bed down, Zan and Friedr looked at each other and silently nodded. "They have a lot to bury between them. John has spent a long time healing from the war, and the things that happened in Aeoven weigh heavily on him." Friedr's voice was quiet, for Zan's ears only. "Aeolyn's letters tell me it's bad there—very bad. Edwin has lost his dream girl forever."

"In their letters, both Anna and Dane have told me some of what's been going on." Zan nodded, worry stark in his dark eyes. "I know a lot of what happened there, and we may not be able to resolve it in a way we'd like. If it's something set into motion by D'Mal himself, I know *I* won't be able to unravel it, even though I've been trained to work with mind-healers. I don't know anyone who can."

"I know. But we'll cross that river when we have to." Friedr sighed, as he settled into his blankets. "We'll be there soon enough."

VALLEY OF SORROWS

Chapter 4

Friedr brought down the first bridge on the old, abandoned trade road that crossed the River Fleet into Mal Evol.

Edwin grinned as the long, wooden construction collapsed, assisted in its failure by Friedr's magic. "That was flashy. You've set the mark high—we'll have to work to beat you." Zan and John agreed, watching as the bits washed downstream.

"That was my intention." Friedr had a glint in his eye. "It was a challenge."

"And it was fun. Don't say it wasn't." Edwin's comment drew chuckles from the others.

Friedr's glee at his success was hard to contain. "It was. We should have a little fun, to keep us from making mistakes out of boredom."

That night they stayed at a farmhouse where they were welcomed and well-fed. The older man who owned the farm was already packed up and ready to move west. He hoped to leave the next day for the farm he'd been granted near Hyssop and was expecting the squad that was to escort him and guard his herds.

"It's a bit closer to a town than I prefer, but it's a new start. This place has been failing for years, but I didn't have any idea of where I'd go." He shrugged. "A few days ago, I could swear I saw the rainbow glints of something like a thunder-cow in the distance. I was fixing the fence in my easternmost field so my pacas wouldn't escape. A waste of time now, wasn't it?" He laughed. "That's why I wasn't as surprised as you might think when Moran and his men came around telling us border-landers to move on. He didn't have to tell me twice to quit while I'm ahead. But I didn't expect to have a place to go, and I'm grateful."

He looked closely at John and grinned. "I know you. Ain't you the man who was my boss out in Bardon's Hollow during the war? John Farmer? I heard you quit the magic business, but I guess I heard wrong."

"I did go back to farming for a while. Now I'm teaching and doing a little veterinary work here and there. But I'm still a mage when they need me." John nodded, wracking his mind for the man's name. "Ganner...I do remember you. You were one of the best archers we had, a dead-eye. You went south to Wellesbridge with Bryson Sorensson's army just after the fall of Mal Evol City."

"That was then. Nowadays I can't hit anything unless I have an ax in my hand, and even that's iffy." He shrugged at John's puzzled look. "It's just that my arms aren't long enough for me to read a book anymore."

"I can fix that for you," said Friedr. "It's a common thing, something we see a lot of. It won't take me ten minutes."

"I haven't wanted to bother the Temple over something so minor." The old man's grin was gap-toothed but jovial. "I figgered as long as I could still tell the difference between day and night, I was doing fine."

The wall that had risen during the day, cutting his land in half diagonally, amazed him. Over a simple supper of bean soup and fresh-baked bread, Ganner admitted he was impressed by how quickly they were able to construct it. "If you hang around mages long enough, you sort of expect miracles, right? But that wall reeks of Aeos's deepest sorcery." He looked at

John. "You always were the one, though. You had the magic and the balls to use it like no one else."

John coughed, turning red. Everyone laughed as he tried to get his breath back. "Well, this time, it's not me—it's my son who's in charge of this venture, and he's pretty good at what he does. I'm just a hired hand on this quest."

The next morning, a squad of Temple soldiers arrived to escort Ganner and his livestock to his new farm. Edwin, John, and Zan packed the last of the old man's dishes and his few remaining possessions while Friedr healed his eyes.

The last thing they heard Ganner say to the squad leader as they drove out of sight was, "Blessed Aeos—I really let this place get run down. I had no idea how shabby it was looking. That fire-mage healed my eyes...never knew a battle-mage could heal a person that well before. But it seems like miracles are happening right and left around here."

"Yep," replied the lanky squad leader who rode beside his wagon. "They're happening on all sides nowadays."

After they had left Ganner's place, Zan brought down the second bridge. As it quietly sank below the surface of the river, his mates applauded his finesse. "Very smooth, Zan." Friedr's compliment pleased him. "You had plenty of flash and noise with the lightning, but exercised complete control with the actual sinking of the bridge. Not a drop of water splashed on us."

The tall mage thanked him. "Working with John when we were repairing the sewers in Aeoven taught me that true finesse is being able to exercise absolute discipline over your magic."

>>><<<

As the wall grew ever southward toward the Horn of Misery, they diverted several small creeks and made sure plenty of deep, shielded channels to the river maintained the growing moat at the size Edwin wanted it to be. The River Fleet originated high up in the Mountains of the Moon but was also fed by many creeks and smaller rivers that came out of Mal Evol and he didn't want to turn the valley into an inland sea.

Two days after leaving Ganner's place, John noticed something odd in the distance to the east, a strange-looking cloud hanging low to the ground, approaching them. They'd managed to create two lengths of the wall, and were on their way to the third stop of the day, hoping to get it done before midday. "Look at that. It looks odd to me."

Zan peered at the horizon in the direction John pointed. "Could it be dust? I've never seen a cloud like that." Edwin and Zan sent their spirits out to investigate but returned to their bodies quickly.

Edwin said, "Thunder-cows—a lot of them. At least, I've never seen that many in one herd. Something has spooked them and it looks like we're squarely in their path."

"What could spook something like thunder-cows?" John's astonishment was echoed by the others. "This can't be natural—they don't form large herds. A minor beastmaster, perhaps? One who's seen the wall and knows what it means."

"I wondered when D'Mal's minions would get wind of what we're doing and try to stop us." Friedr unsheathed Dragonstorm. "We don't want these things escaping into the Midlands, so we need to turn them around somehow."

Edwin agreed. "I don't want to have to kill them if we can avoid it." He thought for a moment. "I think we need to funnel them in some way."

John shook his head. "How? They're not like sheep or pacas. They're independent and liable to hare off in any direction, more like moose. They're running from something that frightens them, but they don't seem to have a mental picture of it…it's something terrible they can't identify…or each one is afraid of something different, I can't tell exactly. But whatever it is the leader is panicked and must escape it…he seems to have their minds…." John's eyes refocused and he turned to Edwin. "Since they're spooked we'll be lucky if we don't end up zapped to death. The charge they're carrying isn't a fun thing—I know firsthand. Getting zapped by two at once could kill you."

"Could you somehow link with the chief bull?" Zan's question startled John. "You just sensed them."

"I did?" John looked startled. "I thought you three could hear them too." He tried to hide how disturbed he was by that revelation.

"Not me. I only hear people." Edwin and Friedr both nodded at Zan's admission.

"But I've seen you work with injured draft animals and horses. They all obey you. I thought it was one of your healing gifts."

"Nope. This is your gift, so maybe you can turn them around." Edwin grinned. "You've always had mental conversations with horses and dogs. Why not other intelligent creatures? Perhaps it's part of your gifts that came along with your blue stars and crescent moon."

"Maybe. Riverbinder has the power if I have the ability." John shook his head. "They're not cattle, though, despite their name. They're completely different and wild. I don't think they belong in this world. They seem to communicate telepathically with each other, so…maybe I could if you were linked with me." He squinted at the dust cloud, trying to gauge their speed, and how long he had before they got close enough to where he could deal with them.

"What's the catch?" Zan sensed John's concern.

"It's just we'll have to wait until they're almost on top of us. I'll have to be pretty close to their leader to be able to drop into his mind enough to influence him. I have to make him understand he must turn around."

"Fire," said Friedr. "Make them think they're running into a fire."

"I can't." His sudden panic beat at their barriers as did his desire to flee. "I don't…fire is my…."

Zan cast a soothing spell. Edwin looked alarmed at his father's sudden terror, wondering what had triggered it.

Friedr scrambled for words, wondering what he'd said wrong. "It just has to be a mental image, not the real thing. Make it huge and as scary as you can."

"Project the terror you just experienced into the leader's mind, John. I'll be there to help you get through it." Zan locked eyes with John. "I won't let you get lost in your flashback if it's triggered by this."

"How did you…? Never mind." John nodded, still uncertain. "Maybe I can try to project a prairie fire, but you must all link to me. I hope Riverbinder will cooperate, or I won't have the chi to do this.

Riverbinder won't help me with some things." It was clear to the three healers he couldn't speak of the incident and that his sword had been involved in whatever it was.

Friedr agreed. "The swords are touchy, that's true. At least, mine is." He shrugged. "How come we always have to do things the hard way? Hopefully, they won't bust up our wagon when they get here. I doubt a thunder-cow would be easy to tame if we need to find new transportation."

John's nerves had him laughing just a little too much for the joke. "Those spines along their backs might do some serious damage if you were to leap on one!"

Friedr gazed at the approaching herd, considering the possibilities. "There's an idea." Eagerness lit his face. "I think I could do it if I were to leap from the wagon at just the right moment. It's merely a matter of landing at the right angle to not castrate yourself on those knives along their spines."

"Think of the ride. I'll bet no one has ever done that before!" Zan laughed as hard as John at the thought of Friedr leaping on a passing thunder-cow.

Edwin glared at them. "Don't encourage him, you idiots. All we need is to have Friedr turned into a eunuch and his good leg broken at the same time. I'm not going to be the one explaining that to Aeolyn."

John and Zan both put on ludicrously sober expressions.

"Oh, dear goddess. Save me from you two. This is serious."

"You're a stick-in-the-mud, farm boy." Friedr grinned at Edwin's angst. "You know that, right? If you're looking for it, your sense of humor is lodged up your backside." Edwin's sudden flush made John and Zan burst out laughing again.

Edwin grinned and sighed. "I know. Your joke...it was something Christoph would have said."

Friedr nodded. "And we'd have laughed." He clasped Edwin's shoulder. "I miss him too."

Drawing their swords and grounding the points to the bed of the wagon, the four mages faced the approaching herd. The wagon vibrated as the pounding of their hooves shook the earth, the drumming growing louder with every passing second. Effortlessly, John calmed the horse's minds, sending them into a deep sleep, soothing their dreams.

Then he extended a mental hand to the others and they fell into the link. As the herd raced nearer, John attempted to single out the king bull's mind, trying to get some sort of a fix on it. So many minds and all of them terrified. It was difficult to find the king. One stood out, powerful...different...forcing them all to listen....

Shaking with the effort, John merged with the king and was assailed by the weight of hundreds of panicking minds, wild with fear. Overwhelmed by the urge to flee from some indefinable miasma of evil, John cried out in blind terror, compelled to join in their mad flight. Friedr's large hands on his shoulders pulled him back and his son called to him mentally, bringing back his awareness of *self*. Wrenching his consciousness above the herd-mind, he projected the idea that the grasslands ahead of them were ablaze and safety lay behind them.

Nothing happened. The ground shook as the herd

was upon them, parting on both sides to stream past the wagon and the sleeping horses as if they were a large boulder in a rushing river of gleaming one-horned beasts. The razor-sharp horns flashed by, and the reflected light from the rainbow scales covering their immense bodies dazzled the eyes of the men who stood in the wagon.

This time, John raised Riverbinder, turning and pointing it at the king bull. He put all his will into projecting the image and scents of a grasslands wildfire, trying to force it upon the leader's conscious mind. He felt the surge of energy as Zan raised Stormbringer, touching the tip to Riverbinder, and then Dragonstorm, and Leviathan...a tidal wave of power flowed from John as he visualized the image, strengthening it...felt the shock of horror as the leader "saw" the flames and scented the smoke...knew the others' confusion...terror behind them, fire before....

Intent and focused, controlling but not submerged in the all-encompassing herd-mind, John inserted into the king bull's mind a memory of the safety of the thorn forest and the comforts of the valley they had come from. Slowly...slowly... the idea rippled through the herd as he sustained the image of the fire they were running into.

Unbidden, from John's own buried experiences, came the scent of burning flesh and the overwhelming horror as waves of unbearable heat rolled toward them. Terror overtook him, and with that, the herd panicked. Once again, Edwin and Friedr kept him in the wagon, each gripping him with one hand and maintaining the contact through their swords with the other. As he had promised, Zan was there in his mind. The horrors receded as John regained control of himself, but Zan remained tightly linked to him, keeping him grounded in reality.

At last, the running mass of glittering, rainbow-hued beasts thundered around and passed the wagon again, returning the way they had come. Myriad shafts of multicolored light reflected off their scales and horns in uncountable, disturbing patterns, confusing the eyes and minds of those who watched, spellbound.

Maintaining the mental image of the savannah in flames behind them, John remained with the thunder-cows for as long as he was able. He sagged to sit on the wagon bench as he lost contact with the herd-mind and fell out of the link.

The others were silent, watching the dwindling dust cloud.

"I can't do that again. I did the only thing I could, but it went so wrong...oh, goddess, you have no idea how bad it went, and it was my fault." John's face had paled and he trembled violently. His words came out in a strangled cry, "It was *all* my fault!"

Zan took John's face in his hands, inserting a loop of forgetting into his mind. "You don't ever have to do it again. You can leave it behind. You did the only thing you could do under the circumstances." He continued inserting small loops that would be triggered each time John began to panic, to enable him to speak calmly of whatever the incident was, if and when he chose to. "You are feeling relaxed now...everything is fine, everyone is safe."

After several moments, John began talking as if nothing had happened. The others had worked with Zan before, knew that was to be expected, and behaved accordingly.

"Dad, you just projected a seeming. That illusion was equal to anything Beryl could do, and she's really good at it. I can't do anything like that." Edwin was shaken by the horrific memory triggered in his father's mind and tried to hide it from his dad. He pried the lid off the water barrel and dipped out a cup of water, handing it to John, along with an apple and a chunk of cheese. "That took as much out of you as a major healing. Maybe you should draw some chi through your blade."

John shook his head. "I did what? No. I'm sure it wasn't that sophisticated. I just planted the illusion of a prairie-fire in their minds."

They finished their quick lunch and then Zan cleared his throat. "John, can you wake up the horses now? We've got to stay moving if we can or we won't have the wall done before Lourdan's army arrives."

John winced. "I can't believe I forgot they were still sleeping. I was afraid they'd wake in the middle of the herd, so I used a spell normally used for surgery." Centering himself, he woke them, making sure they were alert. The two horses shook themselves, clearing the sleepiness, whickering to each other.

John looked at his companions, feeling an overwhelming sense of camaraderie with them, for what they'd just been through. "I almost lost myself several times back there, in more ways than you can know." He saw Zan's raised eyebrow. "Well, maybe you do know. Anyway, thank you for bringing me back, all of you. Thank you for whatever it was you did, Zan. Beryl has been trying to help me, but once the memory gets me, I can't get out of it."

Friedr said, "I've seen Garran in the same state and Kalen too—different triggers, but the same reaction. You all made sacrifices for us, and we'll do whatever it takes to keep you glued together." He chucked the reins. Lurching forward, the wagon once again rolled toward their next destination. "What was it like, running with the herd?" His sardonic grin drew an answering smile from John, who, now the adrenaline had left him, was trembling from exhaustion.

"Stranger than anything I ever imagined. The peculiar nature of the thunder-cows' herd-mind is…I can't describe it. Horses are simple, to my way of thinking. Those creatures are something else entirely. They really *are* alien to our world." Drained, John leaned back against the rails of the wagon bed. "I don't know why that made me so tired, but I think I'll nap for a while if you don't mind." He chuckled softly. "I think that stunt just might have been dangerous enough even for Halee. And *she* likes dangerous things." His eyes closed and exhaustion overtook him. He slept, heedless of the jostling of the wagon's bumping along over the trackless prairie.

Edwin covered his father with his cloak, his expression unguarded, a look of tenderness mixed with pride warming his drawn features. "You did something pretty amazing just now," he whispered to his sleeping father. "It was as insane as the barbarian's notion of riding them bareback." He climbed over the bench and sat next to Friedr.

Friedr laughed. "You have to admit, that was fun. Who knew your dad was a beastmaster?" He grinned at Edwin's surprised look. "That's what he is, you know. He just proved it and managed to resolve that situation with his usual flair for style. Traveling with your family is just one surprise after another."

Sitting opposite John, Zan had been staring into the distance, lost in his dark thoughts. Now he turned his gaze to Friedr and his grim features broke into a wide smile. "You're right. He's the only beastmaster I've ever heard of who is a Temple mage. Usually, it's a trait mindbenders develop, but John *is* known to be rather unconventional in his approach to things."

Friedr offered the reins to Edwin. "Would you take these? I need to get that down while it's still fresh in my mind." Pulling out his notebook, he updated their quest diary. The wagon's rumbling, creaking noise and the faint jingle of the horses' harnesses mingled with the occasional calls of birds that punctuated the cool solitude of the late Harvest day. Going more slowly than they had been while traveling the trade road, they made their way across the trackless prairie.

VALLEY OF SORROWS

Chapter 5

It was Sunnaday morning and the seventh day of their task. The mists rose over the prairie, lending a fleeting beauty to the day. They were a silent group as they prepared to leave their camp, each man thinking of home, feeling fatigued and not fully rested. But still, they broke camp every day as soon as it was light.

They sat around a fire, drinking tea and eating a large breakfast of bread and cheese, along with substantial servings of nut-porridge from their rations. Friedr broke the silence. "You three look terrible. This is far more exhausting than what we did with Christoph. I'm starving all the time, no matter how much I eat." His slender frame had grown even leaner, and all three of the younger men wore leathers that were loose on them.

John nodded. He'd become slimmer, but was not as thin as the younger men, who had been working hard and existing solely on packets of dried rations for a season. "I noticed how exhausting it is, but didn't want to complain. I've never used magic as intensively for such prolonged periods as we're doing with this." He thought for a minute. "Maybe we need to keep jerky or toothbreaker out to chew on while we're riding from spot to spot, in addition to eating more often."

Officially called Temple-sausage, toothbreaker was a perennial staple that kept even the poorest families in Neveyah from starving during the winter. A chicken sausage, it was highly spiced and then smoked so dry it had to be shaved thin, or cubed small and dropped into soups to make it soft enough to chew.

Friedr finished his tea and said, "I think you're

right. I don't know how much jerky we have, but we can get more in the next town. I'm not that fond of eating toothbreaker by itself. It's too fiery for my delicate tongue." The others laughed.

The four rose and began breaking down their camp.

Edwin washed up their dishes and the porridge pot, preoccupied. His thoughts were dark, revolving around what could be happening with his wife, thinking about the way he'd always cooked a Restday breakfast, unsure if Restdays would ever be the same, wondering if Marya would recover. There were too many "ifs" for him to think about, so he tried to imagine what Jonny might be doing and hoped he was having fun with Freylin and Rynne.

Zan stood at the rear of the wagon, focused on packing the large canvases they fixed to both sides of it, stretched out as a pair of lean-tos for them to sleep under. The arrangement was easier to set up and tear down than a tent, and they slept dry for the most part. As always, he was privately obsessing about what he'd done, setting the truth geas on his father, Christoph, burdened by guilt and the terrible cost of that action.

Friedr was quiet too, wondering how his wife, Aeolyn, was coping back in Aeoven. Their two children were active, and with Jonny added into the mix it had to be trying for her. Aeolyn was better organized than any person he knew, but still, managing three small children while pregnant had to be difficult. She was Father Rall's assistant too, so her days were packed.

He didn't know why he was fretting—Rall and Jules would help her, and Dane would too. They were like grandfathers to all the children in their little group. Friedr set the last of their cooking gear into its place behind the seat and climbed up on the running board, balancing on his good leg so he could shift some of their gear to make room for two to ride there.

John finished laying turf back over the fire pit, smiling to himself, thinking about Halee. He savored the sense of amazement he always felt when he thought about her. His wife was the strongest woman he'd ever known. Surely she was dealing with Marya's situation. But Halee was fragile in ways no one but he knew. What she faced with Marya wasn't something she was emotionally equipped to deal with.

Still, she could face down a minotaur with her bare hands, and win the fight with not a hair out of place. She had done so twice—those memories made him shake his head in wonder that they'd survived. He put the shovel in the wagon and walked back to get the horses from where they were picketed, noticing they were edgy, whickering to each other. He peered around trying to see what was making them nervous. A brief flash of silver caught his eye.

John shouted, "Chimaera! Watch yourselves!" Drawing Riverbinder, he was just in time to defend the now-terrified horses. His blade moved swift and fast as liquid lightning as he kept the creature away. Edwin and Zan raced to join him, but the beast flicked out, reappearing behind them.

Creatures of magic, chimaeras had the ability to transport themselves a few feet, flickering from place to place like a stone skipping on a pond. They were deadly and difficult to fight because they were never where you thought, and were equipped with a poisonous tentacle that they used as a whip. They always returned magic with lightning, and the few records of battles with them said they were notoriously difficult to kill.

Lightning crackled off Edwin's shields, and he slashed at the beast, which vanished before his sword met it. The three men were hard pressed to protect the horses, and also to avoid being stung by its tentacle.

Edwin and Zan had read about chimaeras but had never seen one before. John called, "Mind its sting! Block it, whatever you do."

The silvery creature reappeared beside a startled Friedr, who was trapped on the wagon's step, unable to reach his blade. The silvery tentacle whipped through the air toward him, as if it was a line cast by a fisherman, only far more quickly. His staff flashed, tangling the deadly appendage and temporarily halting the creature in its tracks. Moving with even more speed than he'd ever demonstrated in the dueling arena, John used that moment to run the creature through.

Riverbinder sizzled as it stabbed deeply and sliced downward, and John leapt back, avoiding the blue blood that sprayed.

With a shriek, the chimaera promptly flickered in and out, traveling several feet in an attempt to flee. When it emerged the last time, the creature remained, as if it could go no farther. Strange hissing sounds emitted from the beast as it staggered. The whipping had halted too, the tentacle withdrawing into its body, then extruding as if it had no control over it.

Edwin, Zan, and John surrounded it, and careful of its poisonous sting, they hacked it apart until it lay dead. Once the life left it, the creature rapidly began decomposing, turning gelatinous before their eyes.

"Is everyone okay?" Friedr hobbled over, grabbing first one man and then another and delving them, making sure no one had been poisoned. "Hold still, John. Let me have a look at you."

John stopped trying to twist away. "I'm okay. I just want to make sure the horses are safe. It was trying to steal one of them."

"The horses can wait. They can't build the shield, but you can, so you're more important right now." Once Friedr was satisfied everyone was all right, he returned to loading the wagon, grim-faced and silent.

Edwin stared at his father. "I've never seen anything as fast as you, Dad. You could beat my arse in a duel any day."

"I'm good for short bursts," John said, still breathing hard. "I'm not that good for the long haul. You have speed and endurance, and it's impossible to predict your moves, which is why *you* would beat *me*."

Shaking his head, Edwin squatted down, peering at what was left of the chimaera, hoping to see what it looked like now that it was in one place. "Where did this thing come from? It can't be a creature Aeos created." Edwin's nose wrinkled at the odor of the fast-decaying corpse.

"I've heard they're from Serende, same as thunder-cows." Zan fought down his nausea at the smell. "I couldn't get a good look at it."

John had finished checking the horses. He said, "Don't touch that tentacle—it can still kill you. You never really do get a good look at them, Zan. They move too fast, skipping in and out the way they do, and they rot too quickly once they're dead." Having found the horses unscathed, John hitched them to the wagon.

Edwin gave up trying to examine the creature and used his magic to bury it deep, hoping to be rid of the stench. "I'd like to know what they actually look like. All I could see was a flash of silver and then the whip."

John said, "I've only encountered a chimaera once before."

"What do you think? Did that beastmaster send it after us? He must have known his thunder-cows didn't stop us," Edwin said.

John agreed. "Probably. It's too much of a coincidence that a chimaera was hunting so far to the west of the thorn forests. It could have been following the herd from the other day, but I think it was set on our trail." He shuddered. "I can't even imagine trying to control the mind of one of those things." He saw Zan's wry expression. "And no, I wasn't even tempted."

Once the others were settled, Friedr climbed into the driver's seat, flicking the reins to get the horses moving. He remained silent as they rolled south across the grasslands.

Seated next to him, Zan spoke. "What's wrong? You aren't your usual cheery self."

"It's nothing." Friedr could feel Zan's eyes boring into the side of his head. "It's just something stupid."

"What? Tell me."

"You aren't going to leave me to just wallow in my misery, are you? All right, since you insist." Friedr glared at him. "I was useless in that melee. I could barely defend myself, and my staff was all that saved me long enough for John to draw it away from me. We were ambushed, and my sword was nowhere near to hand. I couldn't get to it. I'm a liability."

Normally buried frustration sparked in his blue eyes. "And now I'm a self-pitying liability who can't accept the fact that he's lame. I can't depend on my sword. I know now how Christoph felt when everyone was fighting all around him and he was unable to do little more than defend himself. I was in danger of being killed back there because I couldn't reach my sword without dropping my staff. The staff saved me—it seemed to *want* to deflect that whip-like thing."

"It's not an ordinary staff, Friedr. Edwin made it—who knows what it's capable of?" Zan looked back over his shoulder. Edwin sat in the rear, staring out the back, lost in his own dark thoughts, not even aware of their conversation. He turned back to Friedr. "I wouldn't worry too much. You're still deadly. Trust me."

John spoke from behind them. "You just have to get used to fighting differently, that's all. I never saw anything move so fast in my life as that staff when he tried to sting you. You're a master when it comes to fighting with the staff, as much as you are with any other weapon. You just haven't had a chance to get used to this change in your life. You'll figure it out."

"I suppose you're right." Friedr nodded but said nothing further. With each day that passed he felt increasingly alone, but didn't want the others to know the extent of his depression.

The others also fell silent. The noise of the horses plodding across the prairie and the creaking of the wagon broke the stillness of the misty, gray morning.

VALLEY OF SORROWS

Chapter 6
Serende—The Palace of Dreams

Stefyn D'Mal entered Lourdan's rooms through the adjoining door. They had just completed Lourdan's first sacrifice as a true acolyte on the path to the priesthood. With the obligatory congratulations from his tutors out of the way, a coldly grim Lourdan had retired to his quarters, saying only that he needed to study.

Lourdan had been magnificent, performing the ritual flawlessly as he was required. He had concealed his emotions well from the Circle of Six, who now agreed he likely did have the horns to be a priest of Tauron despite having been born a child of Aeos. Two were firmly on his side, and the four rebellious priests who had the power to block Lourdan's ascension to the final step of initiation into the priesthood were in check. None of them could find a legitimate reason to do so, as he'd just proven himself to be utterly ruthless in his worship of Tauron.

Stefyn's nerves jangled. He was filled with anxiety for a multitude of reasons. Fear for Lourdan's sanity was a large part of it, as the connection to the god was as dangerous as it was powerful. He paused for a moment, passing a hand over his eyes.

Whatever had made him think he could manipulate things in such an outrageous fashion and not be affected by it? The ritual that day had been the culmination of events he'd set into motion while Lourdan was still in seclusion. Stefyn had created Yllene just for that one crucial purpose.

But through the process of forming her for Lourdan, he'd grown to cherish her, loving every fiber of her being as if she was his daughter. Despite knowing what her fate *had* to be, he desperately hadn't wanted Lourdan to do it. He'd had to force himself to watch as Lourdan did as he was required, several times having to restrain himself from begging him to stop before it was too late.

Yllene wouldn't have allowed her husband to stop. Stefyn had shaped her too perfectly. She'd done exactly as he'd originally intended, insisting on going to the altar, swearing it was her path to heaven, and Lourdan's only way to the priesthood.

Stefyn wondered why he'd thought her sacrifice wouldn't affect him. It was as bad as when Max...dear god, his own brother....

And what had he done to Lourdan by choosing that path?

After a moment, Stefyn pulled himself together. It had to be done. She was all Lourdan had, just as Max had been all Stefyn had. Without a worthy sacrifice, one couldn't be considered for the priesthood. It was written that the acolyte must give to the god that which he held most dear, or it was not a worthy offering.

The door to the servants' passage closed behind Relf, Lourdan's valet. Alone at last in the privacy of his own rooms, Lourdan dropped the cold, stony expression that had hidden his true emotions from the other acolytes and priests who would have seen them as a weakness. Heartache burst from him and he fell to his knees, sobbing and clawing his face until bloody furrows marred his handsome features.

Eventually, he sat at his desk staring out the window, wounded and unseeing. In trembling hands, he held the lock of golden-brown hair that was all that remained of his dreams, his happiness.

Stefyn allowed Lourdan his grief. When he was calmer, he slowly approached him, healing his ruined face so that no scar remained. Then he knelt beside Lourdan. "You're grieving. She was a daughter to me— we loved her. She was worthy." He put his arms around Lourdan, comforting him.

Lourdan spoke rapidly as if to drown out his thoughts, his voice high-pitched, verging on hysteria. "I had to, Stefyn. She made me do it. My worthy offering…. She forced me to do it. My first sacrifice as an acolyte to the one god…and she demanded the privilege!"

Holding him, Stefyn murmured comforting words, none of which Lourdan heard.

"Six weeks of bliss—of heaven—it wasn't enough." Lourdan's voice had risen to a wail, and then subsided. A hint of madness crept into his eyes. "I don't regret offering her up to Tauron, no, no, no—only the best is worthy of his love. She was all I had to give, but…but…. What now? I can't live with this emptiness. No past. No future…no children for me now, and no wife. All I have left is my god and the hope he will treasure her as much as I did!"

Lourdan's screams tore at Stefyn, his pain beat on him. His earth-magic shook the palace, sending servants scurrying for cover, causing the priests who knelt in the chapel far below to look up in fear.

Stefyn knelt there, holding Lourdan and sobbing. *Forgive me, my love—I did it for you.*

VALLEY OF SORROWS

Chapter 7

Edwin had chosen to camp near a creek, where the four tired mages bathed and did some laundry. "Clean underwear—who'd have thought such a luxury could make me so happy?" Edwin's comment sounded from the bank where he wrung the water from his shirt.

"Yes, and thanks to John's foresight we can actually hang them up," said Zan. "That's far better than when we were in Mal Evol. They never really felt clean when we had to lay them out on the dirt to dry."

"After drying so near the fire, our socks will smell like smoked trout," replied Edwin, laying his wet clothes over the makeshift clothes line. "But they'll be clean trout!"

Friedr snorted. "Barbarian laundry always smells like the campfire—at least, in my village it does. You get used to it."

Edwin laughed.

That night John stood the first watch. His eye was drawn to a torch that bobbed in the distance, making its way across the prairie toward them. He woke the others. "We're about to have company."

"Friend or enemy?" Friedr dressed quickly, as did the others.

"Friend, I think—they light their way with a torch to let us know they're coming. We'll make tea and offer them soup. There's plenty left from supper." As the light approached, they made ready to receive guests but were armed and ready to fight.

An immense, heavily shrouded figure stood just outside their camp, leaning on a crutch. Speaking in a deeply accented voice, he said, "I'm not your enemy though you might think it once you see me."

Zan said, "Sit by our fire and be welcome minotaur." The others stared at him. "You're Zirik. Did Nal change huts? Is she your woman now?" The minotaur had been in one of the squads that had kept them from escaping the Valley of Mal Evol, forcing them to take to the underground river. In his boredom, Zan had spent hours spying on them, curious about their habits.

"Don't know how you know 'bout that." He smiled, his sharply filed teeth gleaming in the firelight. "But you're priests, and you're building the wall of magic, so nothing you do surprises me. I'll have to send a note to the chancellery in Mal Evol City telling Honorable Dalgek of your wall. But my note won't get there for a week, and it'll take a few more days after that to filter up the chain, so you should have time to get this end of it done, fast as you're working. If I don't send a note, they'll wonder about my loyalty."

The minotaur limped into the light of the fire and lowered his hood. His bovine face was wreathed in a smile. "Nal hasn't agreed yet to my offer, son of Aeos. But I've hopes. Yark is dead now, so perhaps. She remains in Mal Evol City and looks kindly on me. I've survived many terrible wounds, lost my left foot, so I'm mustered out now." He raised his peg leg for them to see. "It's an honorable wound and won't harm my chances with her, but they've put me to pasture. They won't be sending me back to Serende cuz they want farmers here, and none of the young bulls are fit to do it. All they know is fighting. Still, us old bulls who can't fight no more, but who're too stubborn to die can do it just fine, and it's better than begging on the streets back in Serende. With my leg like this, that's my only other choice, joining those who've been cast aside."

Zan nodded. "What brings you to our fire tonight? It was a long walk on your bad leg."

"I've my own bit of land now, and that's what I need to talk to you about. I'm just now claiming it, right? Had it for two weeks, Neveyah time."

Edwin smiled, handing their guest a cup of soup. "I think we understand. How can we help you?"

"Something happened to me just after I was healed. I had a visitation, you might say, from a lady all dressed in blue."

The four mages sat back, stunned. "Aeos?" John's voice shook.

"Yeah. I know that feeling—shocked-like, right?" Zirik nodded, his huge rack of horns casting shadows around the fire. "I'm no longer a son of Tauron, but I can't be on your side of the wall, cuz folks will be afraid, with the mark of the remaking still on me. So, if you could just build your next two stretches a mite wide of my pastures, I'd be grateful. I don't want my herd to run afoul of your magic shield, which I won't be mentioning in my note."

"Of course," replied Edwin, as the other all agreed. "Are there other neighbors like you out here?"

"Not too many yet, maybe three. But there will be, soon. I got to choose the homestead I wanted when I looked at Dalgek's map. I picked the one farthest away from anything his lot is doing. He thought I wanted to be close to the front line, so he gave me a big chunk, but that's not why. The blue lady told me to ask for this one." He cocked his head. "There's another thing you need to know. There's a new overseer coming to the valley, and rumor has it he's one of your own. But they also say he's the heir to Baron D'Mal, and second only to him.

"When I was in the infirmary, I heard he's to be remade very soon. Something about him terrifies Honorable Dalgek, and he's still only an acolyte, so he must be as strong as the baron. Time runs differently there—you have four weeks at the most to finish this, lads. The blue lady said to tell you, *'The gap must be closed three weeks before Holy Day.'* I'm not sure what she meant by that, but by my reckoning, the new overseer will be ready to take his place here within a month. Winter is nearly over there. The remaking will happen on the first day of spring."

Edwin looked at Friedr. "Winter...spring...that's two seasons. I thought she meant two of *our* seasons. This is bad."

"How do you know this timeline?" John's sharp question got Zirik's attention.

"I was in the healing camp when Dalgek came and selected those of us cripples he thought he ought to give a second chance at life. They were talking among themselves and I overheard." Zirik sighed, a strange rumbling sound. "This new commander will undergo the full remaking cuz he's to be a priest. It won't be the easy one like I had, which most lads don't survive if you want to know the truth. His remaking will require two weeks for the required sacrifices, which have already commenced, and then the ritual itself. Then it'll be two or three weeks to assemble the legions and march them here. With too many soldiers for the Highest to make a portal, they must go the long way, but the Overseer will be leading them. That's all

Serende time—it'll be half that for us here."

The four mages shifted nervously, looking at each other. Edwin said, "Thank you for this warning."

"Dalgek's quaking in his boots already, and he's one of the Circle of Six—if *he's* afraid, you should be too."

"How many soldiers will he bring?" John mentally calculated what forces Garran would be able to muster if they couldn't close the gap in time.

"Five thousand of the best, if he don't hear about this wall too soon and has the time to muster them all. Probably less, though, cuz he'll be sure to try and stop you once he learns of it." Zirik's soulful eyes fixed on John. "I remember you, sir. You're the Blue Death. You're just a legend now, but I saw you. I was a nipper of sixteen summers, just got my horns when they sent us to a place called Ronan's Vineyard. I'll never forget you standing on that wall. You're burned into my heart."

John had no idea how to respond to such a pronouncement.

"You did what no other son of Aeos could ever do—you spawned a secret cult of warriors within the ranks. I've been one since we got back to Serende after the war, and we started talking amongst ourselves. We have to remain secret for obvious reasons, but as the boys from Khelen go home, the Warriors of the Blue Death will ask to take their places, and they'll be allowed. None of the others want this soft land—there's no honor in farming as our folks see it and it's too far from Khelen and the royal court. But when Aeos takes this land back, our children will be hers. Our sons won't be faced with going through the remaking because they'll be farmers in a land no one else wants."

John slowly shook his head, astonishment stark on his features. "I don't know what to say. I'll never be right over the…citadel. I was out of my mind. What I did was unforgivable."

Not sure what he was referring to, the three younger mages glanced at each other and back to John.

"No, Sir." Zirik's eyes met John's, comforting him as best he could. "A warrior uses the tools he's given to get the job done. They'd seen you on the wall and knew you commanded the waters. They had felt the force of your magic. When they chased you into the sewer, they knew you'd not go down easy. They were stupid, and in Serende stupid gets you kilt."

"But you see, I'm a water-mage." John struggled with his words, feeling the full weight of his guilt. "Fire was my weakest element, and I was arrogant. What I did was unpardonably cruel. The fire-mage who was with us could have held them back if he'd had any chi left and he wouldn't have been out of control the way I was. He'd have used it to drive them back and give us the chance to get away, but I…. When they killed my wounded friends, I drew chi through my blade and then channeled my anger and hatred through a sword that I've only lately discovered was meant for healing. It was an improper use of my gifts. I paid the price—I lost the use of *all* my battle-magic until just before this last summer. I'll never be granted the use of fire again. It's my punishment."

Zirik's enormous hand rested on John's shoulder. "War is the great evil and we were caught up in it. Those of us who must do the fighting pay the price for our deeds, eventually. But when it comes down to the root of things, a man has to protect his own however he can."

Edwin, Friedr, and Zan each nodded, as the answers to their unasked questions of the last few days fell into place.

They shared soup and bread, and talked with Zirik until dawn, finding much in common with him despite their obvious differences. All the while, Zan had his sewing box out, working on a project as he always did, and the five men enjoyed themselves immensely.

"Pardon me, but I was wondering how you were injured?" Zan's curiosity had overcome his manners. "It's rude, I know, but will you indulge me?"

"It's no secret. About a month ago we were on patrol. Yark knew I was going to kill him and thought me an easy target, but I ended up roasting his heart. Of course, his blade was poisoned with bear-dog saliva, so I found myself cutting my own foot off in the healers' tent. They don't bother healing that sort of thing cuz there ain't no cure, but once my foot was off, they healed the stump with their magic. I still came out ahead, though." Zirik grinned, his pointy-toothed smile managing to make him look merry despite the serious nature of the conversation. "I walked out of the legions with a decent land grant and no young bull on my borders trying to steal it from me. I'm gonna have Nal in my hut before the end of the year, so I've done well, better than I ever thought I would."

Zirik set them all laughing when they discovered how he was building his herd. He'd taken advantage of a windfall two days before, snaring fifteen yearling thunder-cows that had been spooked by something and strayed across his land. He intended to raise them for meat and leather to sell in Mal Evol City to supply the legions.

Before they parted ways, Friedr healed Zirik as he'd developed sores on his stump from the cup of his peg leg. "I know what it's like. My brace chafes sometimes, but my friends are kind enough to keep me healed."

Zirik's smile was broad as he thanked Friedr.

Zan handed the minotaur a sock he'd altered to fit over his stump to provide some protection from the cup. "This will ease things for you I think—I made it so you shouldn't feel the seam. And here's a spare, so you can have one to wear while you're washing the other."

Zirik's pleased smile lit his face. "These are wonderful gifts. I've been meaning to do something like this myself, but I've been too busy to worry about a little pain."

"Pain is a warning you shouldn't ignore too long." Edwin grinned, looking almost like his old self. "Nal can't be your wife if you're dead."

"I've often wondered how that love triangle was going to go," said Zan as they rolled toward their next destination in the early light of dawn. "Zirik always was much smarter than Yark, in my opinion. And now we know why thunder-cows are in the valley—they're the legion's cattle."

Edwin started chuckling softly, at first trying to contain himself, but soon was slapping his thighs, roaring. The others eyed him warily, although they were familiar with this side of him. In between hoots, he gasped, "A minotaur walks up to our campfire and Zan asks him how his love-life is going. Now we're going out of our way to protect his flock, which just happens to be made up of thunder-cows, some of which we most likely met the other day. And to cap it off, the minotaur knows my dad, and is a member of a cult that reveres him and secretly worships Aeos." He howled with laughter. "There is justice in this world after all."

VALLEY OF SORROWS

Chapter 8

The team arrived at the River Lian and crossed over on their way to Wellesbridge, hard against the Horn of Misery. Having started just south of Braden, they were now approaching the halfway point of their task.

They came to a stone bridge that crossed into Mal Evol. It was Edwin's turn to bring a bridge down, but as they approached it, he realized it had been built by a master earth-mage, and he'd have to unravel the spells first. "This was constructed by Biann D'Braden, but I can sense she had a water-mage helping her. This won't be easy to take down."

While Edwin considered the problem, John walked out, stopping center-span to examine something. The bridge was built of large blocks of smoothly dressed stone, each fitted tightly against the other. Centuries of heavy use had worn ruts into the deck. It was now seldom used, but tracks in the dust covering the bridge deck gave mute testimony to the fact that someone did travel into the land controlled by Tauron. "Hoof-prints going east—whoever is now in the valley will be stuck there. It's probably for the best." John shrugged. "Whatever they're up to is likely not in the Temple's best interest." He walked back to the group as the others agreed with him.

Friedr said, "We should eat first since this isn't going to be as simple as we thought."

John and Friedr set a small camp, so they could rest and have a quick lunch. The fire was a welcome addition to the cold, clear day.

After they'd eaten and warmed themselves, Edwin

walked to where the bridge joined the road, examining it one last time to make sure what he planned was feasible. He turned back to the others, and said, "I'm going to need your elements for this as if we were raising the wall." The others agreed and drew their swords.

Once in the trance, Edwin called a massive steam explosion under the piers anchoring it into the bank on either side. At the very moment when the blocks were lifted by the force of the explosion, he used his and Zan's air-magic to urge the massive stones to follow the path of the explosion, landing them on the Mal Evol side, forming a levee the river would never wash away. They landed stacked against each other as if giant stonemasons had laid them.

As his final touch, using his earth magic he engraved in the center of the wall:

> *Christoph Berryman, Healer*
> *Died for you 4 Scorpius 3262*
> *Remember the One Who Fell.*

Dust drifted, settling at the base of the levee.

One by one his companions dropped out of the link. They stood silently, looking at the tall letters deeply engraved into the stone wall across the river. "Now we have a little memorial to our Christoph." Edwin's smile was reminiscent of his old cheerful self.

A strange, choking sound came from Zan. As Edwin turned to him, he saw tears coursing down the younger man's cheeks. He laid his hand on Zan's shoulder, comforting him while he wept, gazing at his father's memorial.

"How long did you plan it?" John asked, wiping a tear of his own. "That memorial will be there forever."

"I knew we'd eventually bring down a stone bridge. Zan deserves that the world should know his father gave up his life to keep them safe."

For a few moments Zan looked like the carefree young mage he'd been only a few months before, but that faded as he gazed at the memorial. Once again his face settled into the habitually grim expression he never seemed to be without.

The team made the last two cells in the southern end of the shield before making camp. The wall connected hard against the escarpment of the Horn of Misery, completely blocking the entrance to the valley. A lake had been created at the southern end of the moat where the soil for the wall had been excavated, and it took an extra hour to make it drain deep underground into the River Lian, so it wouldn't flood the valley. Where the wall connected to the escarpment, it swept upward to the top of the cliffs, rising to dizzying heights. At that point, it was visible for leagues, and while the area was sparsely inhabited, they knew they were in danger of being discovered.

As they settled into camp at dusk, a group of rat-people attacked them. Only Edwin and John had their sword belts on and quickly dispatched them. "We should stand watch in pairs," John decided. They drew straws and Edwin and Friedr drew the first watch.

In the damp darkness, Edwin sat hunched in his cloak, stirring the fire. "We'll need to hurry. It was foggy today and even when it lifted, the top was still shrouded in the clouds. But when the clouds lift higher.... Someone will realize what we're doing. That's when whatever minotaurs who are in the valley, and not in Zirik's cult, will be sent to stop us." His face was hidden, but Friedr sensed his dark mood.

"I know. We'll have to push the horses to get us back to Braden as quickly as possible." Friedr shrugged. He too was shrouded for warmth but felt the damp all too keenly in his bad leg.

When they took their place on watch, John and Zan had nearly the same conversation as Friedr and Edwin.

Zan rarely complained, but the chill and seemingly eternal fog they were working in was difficult to endure. "I don't want to sound like a whiner, but I'm looking forward to a dry bed. I hope Wellesbridge has a good inn. It's a mail-stop, but that doesn't mean much."

John nodded. "I'm looking forward to it. The food there was always good, and the bathhouse used to be quite decent. I hope it's still the same family running the place."

The only bridge they'd left standing was at the town of Wellesbridge, in the shadow of the Horn of Misery where the River Lian joined the Fleet. It didn't cross into land now falling to Mal Evol, but instead served the farms and villages that carved out a living along the Southern Escarpment.

Wellesbridge was a tiny town with no Temple, but there was an inn. It had clearly been a hard year, as the levees had been breached in several places. The four mages stopped and repaired the earthworks where they'd failed, which took very little time or magic compared to raising the shield.

John said repairing the levees would be their cover

story for being so far south. "Safety lies in secrecy. No one who is an agent for Tauron would think four lone mages would be responsible for something as massive as the wall, so we're here on the usual sort of business the Temple has us doing." The others agreed.

They arrived in town just after noon and quickly stowed their kits in their rooms. The innkeeper, a man named Norton, recognized John, remarking he hadn't changed much, except for the long, braided tail under his left ear that was all he had left of his waist-length hair. "I heard you went out west, took up farming. With that short hair and tail, you look like a mercenary." His gap-toothed smile was jolly. "I'm expecting a small caravan from the south. By dark, we'll be full up, so I only have two rooms to spare for you."

"That's fine," replied John, grinning. "I did go back to my family's farm out west of Armat to raise sheep while my son was growing up. But the Temple needed my skills again, so here I am. You had some broken levees this year. We've been sent to repair them."

"Good thing—we were nearly flooded out last year."

"We heard it was a bad year. But your fields are safe again for now, so we're heading back north," replied John. "I hope the food here is still as good as what your dad used to provide."

Norton laughed. "The old man passed on, but my ma did all the cooking here and she's still running the kitchen, so don't worry. It's biscuits and her special lamb stew tonight."

"Good. I'm looking forward to it." John grinned, rubbing his hands together. "My son is with me on this trip. We're heading back to Braden now that we're done here, but I remembered this place so I brought him and his friends into town just so they could taste her cooking."

Chapter 9

Friedr took full advantage of the unaccustomed luxury of hot baths, as did the others, also enjoying the fact there was a laundryman to clean their clothes. After updating their journals, they napped until hunger drove them downstairs a little earlier than the usual dinner hour.

Friedr and Zan came down first, drawn by the aroma of good food, glad to find there were no friendly-girls. They settled at a table near the fire, followed by John, who looked relieved at the mostly empty room. "I like a glass of ale now and then. I was looking forward to this." His confession made Friedr chuckle.

Zan looked up and nodded, suddenly aware his mind was wandering again. It had been going in circles since they'd arrived in Braden almost two weeks before and he read his mail. After reading the last letter, he'd sat for the longest time, unable to write and powerless to think of anything except that his action had been the cause of his father's sacrifice. Finally, he had dashed off something saying he was well and would be home before Holy Day. Now he made an effort to pay attention.

Edwin finally sat down, and their food was placed in front of them. "What are we discussing?" he asked, seeing his father's rueful grin.

"Ale," replied Friedr, as he tasted his stew. "This is really good. I've missed this kind of cooking."

Edwin savored the first bites of his meal. "You were right about the food here, Dad. And yes, good ale is well worth talking about." He raised his glass. "Thank the gods and goddesses for this invention!" The others agreed and raised their glasses.

John finally broached an apology he'd been putting off, with a slightly embarrassed smile. "I know it sounded like I have no appreciation for Aeos the other day when I was ranting about fate and I apologize for that. I'm glad I'm allowed to be a part of this. In some strange way, it's a chance for redemption."

Zan's dark eyes focused sharply on John. "You maintain a relaxed demeanor, no matter what you're feeling. All anyone ever sees is a man going about his tasks calmly and deliberately. But you're a true water-mage. Underneath the face you show the world is a river running fast and deep. Sometimes you're swept away by it. For you, nothing is ever truly settled because the undercurrents are constantly stirring things up. You shouldn't fight it so hard. You can't help being who you are."

John laughed. "Sometimes you remind me so much of my dad. He would sit there, apparently not paying an ounce of attention to what was going on around him and then out of nowhere he'd say something that cut right to the center of things. He skittered from topic to topic the way you do too. It drove me nuts when I was a kid, but I missed it when I left home and found myself gravitating to lightning-mages for my best friends. I like the trait in you."

"Oh. Well, I was recently told I'm somewhat like a fart in a skillet." Zan shrugged and sipped his ale. "I've been trying not to sound too idiotic. I hope Anna will bond with me and I'd like to be fairly settled when I get back so she'll consider my offer. I need to believe I might have a chance."

John had choked and Friedr pounded on his back, roaring with laughter at Zan's remark. "Oh, I think she'll definitely bond with you."

"Really?" Zan's somber face lit up. "I can't get her off my mind. The memory of her is what kept me going when we first discovered we were in trouble." He smiled faintly, lost in his thoughts.

Abruptly Friedr said, "So tell Uncle Friedr what's really bothering you, Zander Christophson."

"What? Oh…." Surprised, Zan looked at Friedr and then looked away. "It's just a personal thing. I'll have to settle this when I get home and I don't know how to do it."

"Tell me," Friedr commanded. "You can't go on like this. You're so distracted you can't carry on a conversation. It's very unlike you. Normally you carry on two conversations at once, even when talking to one person. Lately, you speak only when spoken to, unless it's business."

"It's nothing. It's stupid." Zan felt sick to his stomach. "Please, don't press me like this."

"It's Dane, isn't it?" John peered intently at him. "You're worried about telling him what really happened in Mal Evol. Now you're getting close to going home it's preying on your mind."

Zan's eyes met John's and he nodded, reluctantly. "It was my fault. Chris was right behind me and I was too slow to grab him. But how did you know?"

"I lost two men who were like brothers to me, Pauli and Wiley, and Frannie, a woman who was like a sister." John managed to speak calmly. "I'd rather have swallowed broken glass than send the news of their deaths to their families, but I had to do it myself because I loved them."

Friedr's sigh exposed his own feelings of guilt. "Don't take such a burden on yourself, Zan. We were there too. We were exhausted, too injured to be able to stop it, and completely burned out. With my broken arm and the poison, I was worse than useless. All we could focus on was trying to make our escape as quickly as possible."

Zan just shook his head, clinging firmly to his own sense of guilt.

Edwin met Friedr's eyes and an understanding passed between them. Edwin spoke sympathetically, but with firmness. "Think about this for a moment. If Chris had been in front of you or any of us, D'Mal would still have had him because he planned it so we'd be unable to protect your dad. The moment Christoph sat on the throne a connection was forged between them, so D'Mal knew exactly where he was at all times."

Edwin looked around the room, seeing that, for the moment, they were the only patrons there. He said, "D'Mal is nothing if not a genius at manipulating and maneuvering people. You can't take this guilt home with you. It's not yours alone. We all share the responsibility to some degree, but Dane won't blame you. I'll tell him everything that happened, from the day Chris healed the throne until the day he was kidnapped."

"But *I* set the geas on my own father so he could only speak the truth." Zan's guilt burst forth in a torrent. "It was me, not you. I couldn't take any more of his small lies so I set the geas on him. I made it so he was forced to sacrifice himself to save us, don't you see?" Tears poured down Zan's face. "*I* caused my father to have to make such a terrible choice."

John was silent, unable to hide his astonishment at hearing Christoph had been under a truth geas.

"We all intended to do that, Zan." Edwin leaned forward, trying to make him understand. "I had him by the throat, remember? The knowledge that my rage was one of the last things to pass between us is my burden, and I don't know how I'll ever get over it. I know how badly you feel. But you should also remember that Friedr threatened him with a geas too. You set it first, but I most certainly would have if you hadn't. He understood why and was the first to agree he deserved it." Edwin shook his head, and his voice broke. "Oh, goddess. He was such a good man and we loved him so. But he was difficult and stubborn when he wanted to be, and no one knows that better than Dane."

John looked at his son, trying to imagine what would drive him to violence against a man he loved like a brother. All three younger men were deeply disturbed, and suddenly he realized he was being affected by it. He firmed up his barriers. "I wasn't there, Zan, so I don't know exactly what happened, but I can guess. Something bad happened that Chris was responsible for, or you three wouldn't have been forced to set a truth-geas on him."

Mutely, Zan nodded.

"And knowing Chris, it was a sin of omission, one that jeopardized the quest, but was something he felt compelled to do anyway."

Zan just stared at his hands, trembling.

"It was his healing of the throne, wasn't it? He did

it on his own without first telling you he was going to do it. That was when everything went wrong, am I right?"

Again Zan nodded, and against his will tears leaked from the corner of his eyes.

"I don't know what happened between you four. But I *do* know about Stefyn D'Mal. Look at me, Zan." Unable to disobey the note of command in John's voice, he did. "I've seen how he works. Too many times I've seen what's left of a healer when he's done with them. He destroys them, just because he can. He feeds on their suffering and twists them until they're nothing but weapons for his dread god. What Marya endured as his hostage is partly why she had the breakdown when the baby died. He deliberately placed traps in her mind, things we couldn't see until one of his acolytes sprung them."

Edwin's face blanched at the mention of his wife. Still, he said nothing, knowing his father wouldn't bring it up without a good reason.

"When he first brought Marya home, Edwin told me Aeos was only able to partially heal her when she was freed, because the work was done by the mad god, through his priest. The gods are limited in the way they deal with each other, so that meant Aeos couldn't undo it all." John's compassion was clear though his words were hard. "D'Mal had treated her more gently than I've ever heard of him doing. But it was only because his god needed Marya to bond with him of her own free will to win Aeos once and for all, so his madness was reined in somewhat. Even so, she was destroyed by the experience."

Friedr sensed Edwin's sudden, deep despair at the

mention of his wife, wondering if he should cast ease on him.

Realizing Friedr hovered on the edge of interfering with Edwin's natural grief John placed his hand on his arm and shook his head slightly.

Instead, Friedr said, "The baron would have completely and utterly broken Christoph before the end of his first night, even without the geas. Stefyn D'Mal takes immense delight in breaking people, especially healers. Chris was lost to us the moment that portal closed."

John said, "Christoph knew that too, Zan. He did the one thing he could under the circumstances, and it was the bravest action anyone could take. And I'll tell you this: the man I knew as your father would have done what he did solely to shield you three from D'Mal's attentions. *Because* of the choice he made, D'Mal will never know he only had one-quarter of what he needed to take down the shield."

"I just keep thinking I could have done something, anything, and how will I explain to Dane that I didn't? I lost Christoph and I'm afraid I'll lose Dane." Zan sat hunched in on himself. "And I'm afraid what I did will turn Anna away from me."

"Anna is not stupid. You did everything you could to keep him safe," Friedr clasped his shoulder. "We were in trouble from the moment he sat on the throne. Don't do this to yourself. I've known Dane since I was a young novice and out of everyone who ever loved Christoph, Dane knew him best. He always told me Chris would die from his own stubbornness, and that's exactly what happened. We have to face the facts, Zan. We didn't have a chance of saving him once the connection to D'Mal had been made. He sealed his fate at that moment."

"I know, and you're right. I guess I'm still trying to get over the whole horrible mess, which surprises me because I thought I was handling it well." He looked around the table. "And I'm sorry I ruined the evening."

"I think it was something we had to discuss," replied Edwin, forcefully pulling himself out of his own well of misery. "We've all felt some degree of guilt and we all worry about how we're going to face Dane. But we'll do it together."

"You know, Zan, I'd be more worried Dane will want to 'make it all better' if I were you." John's wry comment was echoed by Edwin and Friedr, who chuckled knowingly. "You're the center of his universe now. He's likely to come unglued trying to make sure you feel no pain whatsoever."

"You're probably right," Zan said with a smile, feeling immensely better at having shared his burden.

>>><<<

Later that night, after Edwin and Zan had given up and gone to bed, John and Friedr stayed downstairs. Both men enjoyed being in a common room again and were getting a little deep into the fine ale Norton, the innkeeper, brewed. The room had begun to fill up.

A few locals had come in, and the small caravan had arrived from Bramington, in the southernmost corner of Neveyah, hard upon the Aeolan Sea. The southern merchant was guarded by hard-faced men wearing old-fashioned plate-armor, something rarely seen in the northern parts of Neveyah. He carried a precious cargo, rare dyes destined for the clothiers in Arlen.

They listened while a trader who was heading south talked about the immense wall, wondering how such a thing could have been created so quickly. He thought the goddess had done it. When the other customers saw the two mages in their common room and heard they were there repairing the levees, they asked their opinion about the wall.

John and Friedr agreed it was indeed the work of the goddess, which was not a lie, as she had granted them both the magic and the blades to achieve her task.

"Aeos has our best interests in her heart," said John. "She won't allow the heart of Neveyah to fall to Tauron's thorns."

The locals felt it was about time something was done to lock Baron D'Mal in his valley. Anjem, the swarthy tradesman who owned a small general store, said, "Minotaurs are settling just east of here, maybe thirty leagues inside the gap. They come here to my shop, trying to buy supplies because it's closer than their nearest town."

John and Friedr nodded. John said, "Abbott Garran did tell me this, last spring. But they aren't causing any trouble, are they?"

Anjem snorted. "Only the sort of trouble that knowing you have a minotaur for a neighbor might cause."

A local townsman agreed, saying, "Their faces are enough to curdle milk." The others were of the same opinion.

Norton said, "The Red Abbott, up there in Braden, says to sell them food but not ale, which makes sense to me."

Anjem nodded. "So we do, but we don't make

them too welcome."

A townsman said, "Yep. Don't need any drunken minotaurs here, that's for sure. Some of our own soldiers are bad enough to deal with, once they get a bit loose." Everyone laughed.

After a little more discussion, the locals went home and the other guests drifted up to their rooms.

Friedr and John sat in the empty common room, tired, but too wound up to sleep. Talk of minotaurs had reminded them of Lourdan and driven any thoughts of sleep away. "Lourdan should be just about ready for his remaking."

Friedr's words chilled John. "Are you sure?"

Friedr nodded. "From what Zirik said, yes. That's when things will get sticky for us. We've had it easy up to now." In the firelight, he looked old and tired, his face lined with pain. "We haven't met with much resistance. I suspect that will change."

"I know. Everyone seems to know something is happening. This end of the wall is really visible, even from great distances. I think the second half, from Braden to the Horn of the Moon, is going to be a race to the finish." John looked into the darkened corners of the room, suddenly feeling out of step with everything again. "I hope we can win it." He sensed Friedr's discomfort. "Are you in pain? I can cast ease if it would help you sleep."

Friedr's hard expression broke into a smile. "I'd appreciate that, thank you. I get a little better every day, but it hasn't been long since the injury and I've been forced to put a lot of stress on it when it should have been healing."

Chapter 10
Serende—The Palace of Dreams

The guards stiffened as a strange procession approached the room housing the portal in the palace barracks. Three men approached. One was the Highest, Stefyn D'Mal, accompanied by the Honorable Memschak, followed by an acolyte leading a woman bearing the faded tattoos of a priestess of Aeos.

The woman's hair was matted and her face was fixed in a grimace, a perpetual smile born of madness. Clad only in a short shift made of rough sacking, she crawled beside the acolyte on bloody hands and knees, as if she were a dog.

The acolyte, Lourdan, spoke. "Rise, Bekki-dog. You can walk like a woman now."

Instantly obeying him she stood, swaying on wounded feet. He steadied her, supporting her.

"But I'm not a woman anymore. Now I'm your loyal dog. You hurt me, Master, but I want you to do it again. You can hurt me and hurt me until you kill me."

"Kort, support her for a moment—gently." Lourdan passed her to a minotaur guard, ignoring the look of horror on the guard's bovine face as he took her.

The woman, who had once been a senior healer named Bekki, leaned against Kort, putting her arms around him and rubbing herself on him suggestively. "Wouldn't you like to kiss me? I'll let you up my dress and lead you to Tauron's arms…heaven on earth just for you. I'll hurt you like you want me to."

Finding humor in the guard's terrified revulsion, Lourdan bowed low before the minotaur high-priest. "Thank you, Honored Memschak. Your guidance enabled me to complete my task today. I am humbled and grateful you have chosen to instruct me."

Memschak inclined his head, a high honor for a mere acolyte. "You've come far in your studies." He turned and bowed deferentially to Stefyn. "If I'm not needed, Highest, I'll return to the chapel. Much needs to be done to prepare for the next stage of this child's journey. He has proven himself well." The priest's horrific face broke into a smile, his sharply filed teeth yellowed with age. Still, for a bull as old as he was, Memschak radiated power. "This one will dine on at least one high priest's heart before those old fools learn to look beyond what they can see with their eyes."

Grinning viciously, Stefyn said, "Yes. He may well do just that."

Lourdan remained bowed until the Honorable Memschak had completely departed. "All right, Kort. I can take her now."

The minotaur shuddered, carefully disengaging her arms from around him and handing her back to Lourdan.

Bekki's crazed, singsong voice rose and fell, taunting Lourdan, her eyes pinioning him. "I know you—but he won't let me tell you—you're my master but I knew you. I knew you, knew you, knew you...."

"Stop." Lourdan's calm voice halted her midstream, her eyes bulging and mouth lolling open.

"Good, Bekki-dog. What a good dog you are." Lourdan patted her head and she quivered with gratitude, her glittering, demented eyes worshipping him.

Stefyn gestured and the mirror-like surface of the portal cleared. A room appeared on the other side, a chamber in the barracks that housed the legions at the Keep of Mal Evol. Lourdan maintained tight mental control of his thrall as he guided her through the doorway. Stefyn held it open, and once the drooling madwoman had passed through, Lourdan stepped back, watching as Stefyn allowed the portal to close.

The two turned and began walking back to their private quarters.

"You did well, making your first thrall." Stefyn smiled sardonically, thinking about the mayhem that was about to ensue among the bored legions guarding the Keep of Mal Evol. "She'll stir things up in the barracks for an hour or so until they get smart and send for Dalgek to deal with her. It's the sort of thing that keeps the guards on their toes and weeds out the stupid ones." Turning from the portal he put his arm through Lourdan's, companionably leading him away. "Shall we have some wine in the garden? The roses are exceptional this year and I thought perhaps we could have a quiet dinner there."

"I'm honored, Highest," Lourdan replied.

Stefyn sighed. "Lourdan—surely we are friends. We are cousins. You've no need for formality with me."

"Ah, but you *are* the Highest. That position, combined with your abilities, demands my respect, although I will concede we are more than merely friends. I simply don't want my low status to compromise you in any way—that would be fatal for Serende." Lourdan grinned mirthlessly. "Dinner in the garden would be pleasant. I confess I find court dinners stressful. They pull me away from my studies for too long, and I become boorish. Those acolytes at my end of the table have little of interest to say, and are less than eager to discuss our craft as if by discussing it I'll somehow steal their knowledge."

"Which you would do, if you had that skill at your command."

"Of course, I would, and I *will* do exactly that once I figure out how. And on that note, if you don't mind, I have some questions about the procedure we just finished. I know what I did wrong and why she's completely unhinged now. I think I can do it next time in such a way that the subject isn't left completely demented." The dark, chilly smile was the one Lourdan had worn in public since the day of Yllene's sacrifice. "I'll have to keep trying, to see if my ideas are correct."

Stefyn laughed. "We don't exactly have a supply of kidnapped priestesses of Aeos on hand for you to play with—they're well-guarded and hard to come by. But something can be arranged. We have other prisoners available for such purposes. Practice is certainly required for you to develop control and gain strength in the magic arts, so I'll assist you in that." He saw his companion's concern. "Don't feel downcast. You passed this test admirably."

Lourdan said nothing, seeing her only as a flawed creation. "I'd hoped to create a weapon, but she'll be lucky if she survives the rest of the day there."

His mentor shook his head. "That will come later, when you've had more practice—and she's bound to eliminate several of the less intelligent guards there for us before Honorable Dalgek has her put down. Honored

Memschak and I both observed and checked your work. She is utterly your creature now—you severed her connection to the Temple of Aeos without her permission and it didn't kill her. Memschak agrees that none of the others could have broken her so quickly, and they certainly couldn't have kept her alive through the whole ritual. It's a marvelous achievement, and you managed to do it in only two days, succeeding where even seasoned priests frequently fail."

As they walked Stefyn wondered if Lourdan would return to sharing his bed soon. He wanted to seduce him without resorting to magic, but would do what he had to if Lourdan's grief dragged on for too much longer. To that end, Stefyn had carefully arranged a special, celebratory meal in his private rose garden to mark yet another successful step in his acolyte's path to the priesthood, hoping the serenity and a little wine would remind him that they still had each other.

Servants halted and bowed low, waiting unnoticed as the two men made their way through the ornately furnished, heavily carpeted halls. Lourdan said, "I've been considering the homeland. I realize the barrier raised after the war inhibits you from simply sending in the legions and taking over beyond the Gap. But you do keep some detachments in that valley." It was a statement, but Stefyn heard the question hidden within.

"We keep the worst troublemakers there, and never more than two companies. Dalgek has the ability to control those who guard the keep and he governs the city, but his skills lie elsewhere."

Lourdan nodded. "That explains why he's in Mal Evol. You need his father, Dalgon of Mektec, on your side, but his son is not as talented as a scion of his bloodline should be. Thus, Dalgon's son is High Priest of Mal Evol—a high and honorable title befitting a family as exalted as his, giving him a position as one of the Circle of Six, and a sinecure for one of his bloodline."

Stefyn smiled. "You understand perfectly. Dalgek barely survived the remaking with horns large enough to be accepted into the priesthood. Had I not intervened he would have been relegated to the path of a petty church official in a smaller town, or perhaps a tax collector."

"But that isn't an acceptable occupation for Dalgon's only male heir. The province of Mektec may fall when he succeeds his father." Lourdan's comprehension pleased Stefyn. "For now, Mektec follows you the way Khalmec does, and those two provinces tip the balance of power in your favor. You need him, but a warrior who doesn't understand battle will lose everything his father has fought to gain."

"If Dalgek were from a lesser family, he would be given a lesser task. He runs the Church in Mal Evol well. He's efficient but not brilliant. He's no leader and he knows it, but he does have something we can use in our favor. His sister, Elkendrak, is a born leader, but as a female, she must advise him behind the scenes. However, if she proves as canny a strategist as her father, she'll unobtrusively keep Dalgek on the throne when the time comes. Otherwise, I'll have to interfere and wed her to someone who *does* have the horns to rule."

They entered the garden and Stefyn led Lourdan to his favorite place, shaded by graceful feathertrees, near a fountain. Songbirds hopped from branch to branch, and the scent of roses filled the air. Near the bower, a table was laid for two and a tea cart stood to one side, laden with wine and appetizers: an artfully arranged platter of cheeses, clusters of starberries, and slices of nectarfruit.

Pouring an amethyst liquor into a goblet, Stefyn handed it to Lourdan. "You're still depleted from the ritual. Once you've regained your chi, I'll pour the wine and you'll sample the cheeses—you don't eat regularly enough. Then I'll assist you with your studies while we relax in this pleasant atmosphere." He seated himself on a cushioned bench under the rose-covered bower.

Lourdan drank the liquor, feeling his hair standing on end and relishing the intoxicating sensation of the chi as it filled his veins. Alive with the power, he rose and selecting a small plate, filled it with a selection of fruits and cheeses. He carried it over and sat next to Stefyn, holding it out to share with him. "Wine, cheese, and studies...how very romantic!" His mischievous grin completely charmed his mentor. "Is seduction my reward for doing well today?"

"Perhaps. If it's your choice. I'd never pressure you." Stefyn's pulse quickened beneath his cosmopolitan veneer. "I confess I've missed your delightful company, but I didn't blame you for deserting me. Yllene was incomparable—a woman that comes along only once in a lifetime." His charismatic smile betrayed his hope.

Lourdan's answering gaze was warm. "I can never refuse you when you look at me like that and you know it. And you *would* force me if you felt it necessary. We both know that. But, to honor her sacrifice, I must live and make the most of what my wife did for me. Yllene was a dream, a brief, essential part of my life. She often said passion was fleeting and we should enjoy it while we had it. From the day we met, she made clear her intention to go to Tauron's arms before our desire waned, using that emotion to make me a stronger priest. She believed that would be *her* immortality. She was right."

Stefyn said, "She was wise beyond her years." He sipped his wine, and listened to the birds in the garden, letting the peace of the afternoon seep into his spirit.

Lourdan raised his eyes to meet Stefyn's. "When I was lost in the depths of despair, you held me back from the edge of the abyss. You understood what I lost *and* what I gained by agreeing to such an audacious thing. You're more to me than a distant cousin, more than a mentor, and far more than merely a lover. You are and will always be my anchor, my solace. I cherish your open acceptance of the impact those days with Yllene had on me, and am comforted by my secure knowledge of your love for me, no matter what fancy takes me. And fancies *will* take me—I know this is true of me despite my lack of memories."

"Constancy in a marriage is laudable but true, abiding love does not require it. I too have fancies and brief passions—it's the nature of strong leaders to seize what they want." He spoke the truth, risking everything in his moment of trust. "You've become the center of my world. At the strangest moments, I find myself worrying over your deep grief, wondering how I could ease it—*if* it could be eased."

"Only time will do that—Relf assures me of this each morning as he prepares me to depart my darkened rooms. I must consider my valet's insight as I have only a brief span of time to call 'my life,' and little or no wisdom to offer. I'm a newborn infant barely five-months-old and already in that short time deep grief and intense joy have left their marks. Who knows what will happen tomorrow?" Lourdan looked away and fell silent. Stefyn sensed him gathering his thoughts.

After a few moments, he turned back to Stefyn. "The one thing I've learned is that this moment is all we can lay claim to, and we should enjoy this garden and the time we have in our grasp." He leaned toward Stefyn, kissing him gently.

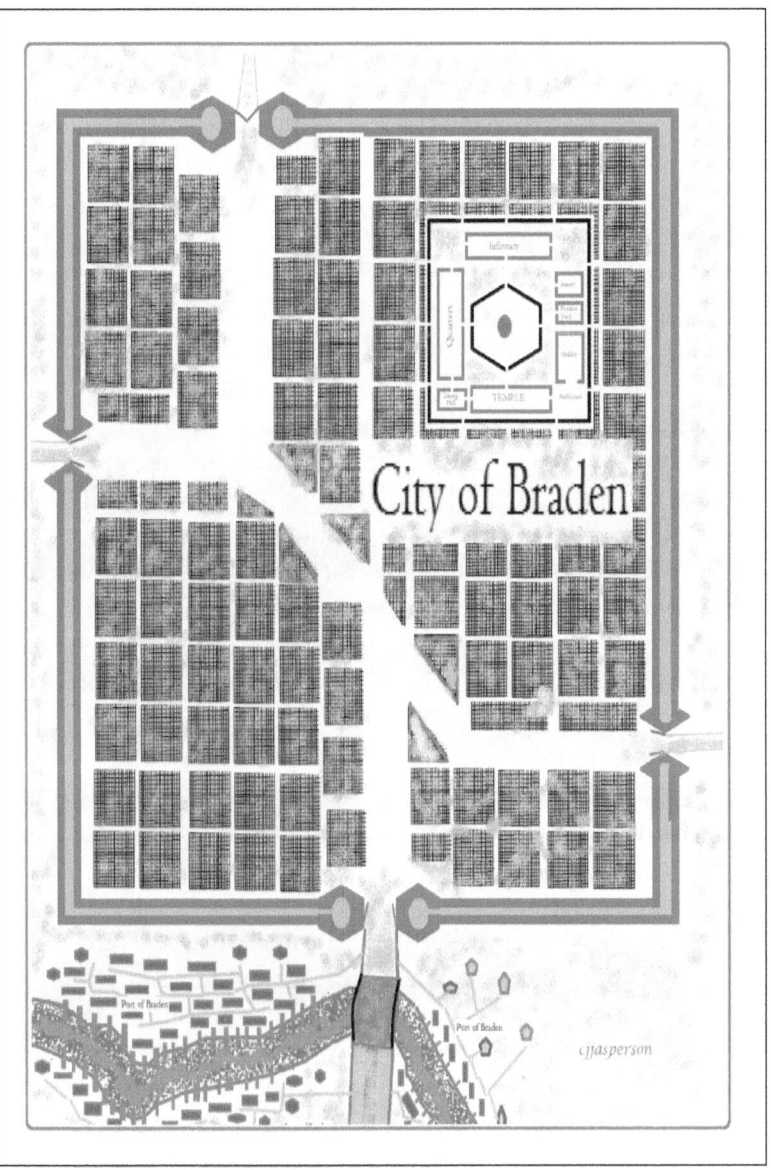

City of Braden

Chapter 11

The return trip to Braden only took two days. On leaving Wellesbridge, Friedr guided the cart up the main trade road far to the west of the River Fleet. It was wide, paved, and straight, unlike the ox-road that followed along the west bank of the winding waterway, all the way north to the city of Widge. Despite its winding path and muddy condition, they regularly observed oxen towing the heavy barges upstream, whenever the river crossed their path.

They pushed the horses as hard as they dared, spending only one night on the road, traveling until well after dark. The second day was clear and cold. Usually, the road on that side of the river was heavily traveled, but they saw relatively few people.

"Folks aren't traveling much. Things must be jumping in Braden." John's voice was quiet as he drove.

Zan was seated beside him and said, "Each time the road crosses the river we've seen barges being pulled north, so they're heading toward Braden. The last one was heavily laden, as it had a team of four oxen towing it, instead of the usual two." He shrugged. "We've seen none riding the currents south, though."

"I'd bet all available barges are being used to ferry things to Fleetside," replied John. "I suggested to Garran he use his authority as Abbott of Braden Temple to conscript any barges in the area, and he agreed it would be the fastest way to empty the city. It's only for a few weeks and it's for everyone's benefit."

"Besides, the Temple will pay the bargemen well," said Friedr, tucking his notebook into his pocket.

As they neared the city, the finality of what they were attempting had begun to dominate their thoughts and conversation. Zan broached the subject. "Even though the wall has been prophesied since the day they laid the first stone of Braden Temple, it still feels wrong. But I know we have to do it, and we're going to ensure Baron D'Mal is kept out of Neveyah forever."

John was unhappy about abandoning the valley to the Bull God, but masked his concerns, as always. "Tauron will still have his chance to make converts just as he always has. We'll be dealing with rogue mages forever, or until the Hero Foretold is born and does whatever it is he's supposed to do."

Friedr grinned wolfishly. "But Aeos also has the same chance—look at Zirik. Through people like him, she tells us she won't abandon the valley to Tauron and she'll never give up on her husband's world. Tauron may have temporary custody of Ariend's bones and part of his world, but Aeos has no intention of letting him keep them."

Zan said, "I like that Aeos is using Tauron's tactics to subvert and claim as many of his as she can."

"Maybe his minotaurs are ready for a kinder religion," said John.

Edwin closed his sketchbook and put his pencil in his pocket. "Zirik and his fellow cult members are the only hope for the people of Mal Evol. They care about the valley and will do what they must to keep the faith alive. They've belonged to Aeos since the war, so they know how to stay undetected." He changed the subject. "Three more weeks and we'll finally be on the road home. I'll be glad to get this over with."

Friedr nodded. "I feel the same way, my brother. This has been a long journey—in more than just the length of time we've been gone. I want to get home, but...I'm not who I was six months ago. Even if I weren't lamed, I wouldn't know how to fit in at Aeoven Temple now. I have no idea what my role will be."

The darkness under Friedr's eyes seemed unusually pronounced against his fair skin, but when Edwin delved him, he could tell his friend was only tired and depressed, as they all were. "I know what you mean." Edwin masked his own morose thoughts. "I hope...I hope many things."

John slowed the wagon as they approached the crossroads where they would turn east to cross the river and enter the city. They waited while a column of people marched across the intersection, led by an older earth-mage and friend of John's, Gorden Narvesson. Gorden taught mathematics and was the Temple's head of engineering.

He told his people to keep marching and broke away to step up on the wagon's running board. "Edwin—Garran took me south to see that wall— damned amazing. The Temple will be discussing it forever. When you get back, I want you to tell me all about it. I know you didn't have time to draw up any real plans, but I need to get the gist of how you built it into the archives." He looked around at them all. "You're the only group of mages I would trust to improvise on something so critical and so grand." He grinned at John and clasped his arm before he leaped down, running back to the head of his column.

John stared at Edwin. "That was high praise, Son."

Friedr nodded. "High praise, indeed." Gorden was a stickler for proper procedures and detailed blueprints that took in every aspect of the terrain any magic construct would be built on, as people's lives depended on the safety of the buildings, bridges, and walls they built.

Zan said, "I never thought I'd be included in that sort of compliment."

The others laughed. Friedr said, "I know. Your pranks were hilarious, but we despaired of you ever making journeyman."

Gorden's group finally cleared the intersection and the wagon was able to continue, turning east toward the wide stone bridge that crossed the River Fleet.

They passed a knot of shouting people, all wanting to leave with a later group. Vint, a journeyman mage of Zan's age, ran back, forcing his group to stay together. Soon his people were back in line and heading west up the main trade road, albeit reluctantly, just as he wanted them to. The young mage ran back to the front. There was more grumbling and John grinned, hearing Vint shout, "Don't make me come back there. We have to be at our first stop by dark, and we're going to keep to our schedule. Grumble all you want, but keep marching!" Two soldiers closed in behind the complainers, who quieted down and marched as ordered.

People were in discord everywhere along the road, but mages and healers kept the peace with force when necessary—it seemed as if every member of the clergy had been pulled out of their usual work or retirement and was now involved with the evacuation. Even old Henley was out, shouting orders from his perch on an ox-drawn wagon filled with toddlers and elderly people.

He kept his group in line as they came out of the city gates, heading toward the river.

The crowds were such that John could only maneuver the horses slowly, edging past the soon-to-be-abandoned quays. Every dock swarmed with laborers, barges were jammed into any slot available, being laden with goods and people bound for Fleetside, Dervy, or Widge. Friedr said, "It's hard to think these are the last barges that will ever leave the river port of Braden." Harried people cast angry, resentful looks at them, reluctantly giving way.

Half a league further on, the street just inside the west gate was in an uproar. John stopped to ask a Temple soldier what the problem was. "Just some old fool, sir. He'd rather go to the altar of Tauron than give up his rundown shack. And he has a fine home waiting for him, too."

"Do you need help?" John gazed at a knot of soldiers surrounding the struggling man. "He *will* end his days on the altar, if he doesn't move, now."

The crowd parted as the man was carried out, bound hand and foot and placed in a wagon, screaming his protests. The soldier grinned. "Thank you, Sir, but no. I've been dealing with this sort of thing all day. I don't even argue now. If they aren't too violent, I just have my lads bundle them up and haul them down the road. Once I get them about halfway to Morton, they forget they were ever angry. If they're too aggressive, I leave 'em for the Red Abbott to deal with."

John was taken aback, hearing Garran referred to as "The Red Abbott" and grinned. "I see. A mindbender has been at work here."

The soldier shrugged. "We think so, Sir. Abbott

Garran is pretty effective, though."

"I'm sure he is. Carry on then." John chucked the reins, carefully negotiating the wagon through the throngs.

At last, they pulled into the stable, got the team settled, and checked in with Garran. He directed them to their guest rooms and said he would see them at dinner.

"At least the mail should be a little more cheerful this time," muttered Friedr as he limped to the rooms he and Edwin were assigned to share.

"I hope so too," replied Edwin, a pall of gloom settling over him at the thought of facing his mail. "Although I don't see how it will be. Nothing will bring the baby back. And Marya...I don't know what to hope for."

His bitterness was sharp. It was the first time he'd voluntarily mentioned Marya and the baby since they'd left Braden on the first leg of their journey. The only times he'd discussed them had been in response to others bringing the subject up.

Friedr clasped Edwin's shoulder in commiseration. "I can only imagine the pain you've felt, my brother. You're a strong man, to continue the quest as you have, despite the losses."

"What else would I do?" Edwin looked away, trying to hide his grim thoughts. "I'm sworn to serve and protect, no matter what the cost. I'll somehow deal with Marya's situation when we get home. What's done is done and I can't change it now. Abandoning the quest would do no good to anyone."

"A dip in the baths will cheer you up," suggested Friedr. "I'm looking forward to it."

"It will definitely help." Edwin placed his kit in his tiny bedroom and then returned to the sitting room to wait for Friedr, carrying their clean clothes. Dropping into an easy chair, he closed his eyes and rested his head against the back. *This place is a madhouse. How does anyone get anything done here?*

Friedr limped into their sitting room. "Firm up your barriers. You're so tired you've let them slip." Chagrinned, Edwin sat up and did as he was told. Satisfied, Friedr asked, "Are you ready to go to the baths? I think your dad and Zan are already down there."

With an embarrassed grin, Edwin stood up. "Let's go." Picking up their clean clothes, he followed Friedr down the hall, his sense of balance mostly restored.

Edwin's mail held nothing hopeful. His wife hadn't improved and had, in fact, suffered several severe setbacks. There was no letter from her, which troubled him. He wrote his responses to the letters he'd received from Lorana and Halee, telling them the next Temple he would be able to get mail at was Fleetside, and that if all went well, he and his team would be in Aeoven well before Holy Day.

Zan, John, and Friedr were pleased with their mail for the most part, although the news regarding Marya worried them.

After dinner, John and Garran commandeered a vessel for the infirmary and spent the evening refitting it to carry patients. Leaving them to their task, Edwin, Friedr, and Zan assisted the healers in preparing the most critically ill of their patients to be moved to the new infirmary at Fleetside Temple. The journey would take one day by river, rather than two or three on the road, which would take too long and endanger them even more.

The healers at Braden Infirmary were glad to see the three adepts, as they had three gravely ill patients, men who'd been injured fighting a house fire only a day before. The more experienced healers had already departed for Fleetside when the fire occurred, and the journeymen who were left had no experience in such terrible injuries. The men could only be moved once they were in a deep sleep.

Edwin, Zan, and Friedr linked and with Friedr carrying the healing spells, they repaired and regenerated skin, teaching the other healers as much of that skill as they were able to learn. Then they guided the journeymen in casting and sustaining the deep sleep spells.

Once the journeymen were confident they could keep the patients safely in the deep sleep they each monitored the process. Senior healers would help wake the patients once they were safely in the new infirmary at Fleetside. Zan promised he would see each of the injured men when he arrived in Fleetside in two or three weeks.

It was well after midnight when they finally made it to bed, but having patients to care for again went a long way toward restoring Edwin's serenity, and improved the mood of the others too.

The next morning, they rose after only a few hours' sleep. The dining hall was full and with the cooks gone, John and Garran now bustled about the kitchen, making sure everyone was fed. John said, "Edwin, you and Zan man the buffet and serve everyone while I flip pancakes. I've had a lot of experience feeding large appetites."

"He did kitchen duty more often than any other novice in our group," agreed Garran. "Of course, I regularly found myself washing dishes beside him, but the crime was usually worth the punishment."

"I do enjoy a good breakfast, truth be told," Edwin said, taking his place as a server. "It's my favorite meal of the day. Put some blueberries in those, Dad. You've no idea how I've missed your breakfasts, and you playing the fiddle at night."

"When we finish up our quest, I'll be doing a lot more of both. I love to cook, and a little fiddle music makes a winter's evening cozy."

Garran took the opportunity to rib John. "Yes. Next to entertaining friendly-girls, fiddling around was always your dad's best talent!"

Grinning, John made his own jab. "You were no slacker, lover-boy. I'd play the music and you'd keep them dancing until the landlord threw us out at closing time."

Friedr chuckled at their exchange, and said, "I'll keep the tea urn full, and the tables wiped down." Despite his lame leg and having to lean on his staff, which made him mostly one-handed, he lifted the heavy tea kettles onto the tea-cart. After a little trial and error, he found a way to push the heavy cart out to the dining room, but for a moment, he was overcome by the frustration of it all.

Having lost so much of his muscle and flesh to the bear-dog poison six weeks before, he reminded himself he was lucky to be alive and walking.

Friedr filled the urns with boiling water, stretching

his limits and finding more things he could still do, albeit more slowly than before. He regularly chivvied the diners to clear their own dishes. "Anyone who leaves here with their dishes still on the table will find themselves in the kitchen doing the washing up!"

News of Friedr's disability had quickly percolated through the crowded dining hall, but even lame, no one doubted his ability to enforce his edict. The many mages and soldiers who knew him were disturbed, seeing him so permanently crippled, and many didn't know what to say. He understood their uncertainty and greeted them as if everything was normal, which set the tone for the morning.

By the time it was fully light out, the dining hall had emptied, and the kitchen was clean. The team turned to a task Garran required their help with—that of getting the last of the unwilling population out of Braden and on the road. "I'll need you for a day or two. Once I've got the last of these stubborn folks out of here, you can finish the city walls the way you've done the southern half.

"We know a mindbender is embedded in our population, perhaps more than one. They are always healers, but nowadays they're trained in Mal Evol City by D'Mal's priests. This means they're extremely difficult to spot, because these acolytes of Tauron look like any other person, and they've found a way of avoiding the madness, even though they don't have augmentations."

Friedr said, "I've frequently wondered how they handle the mage-talented who must emerge in the population of the conquered cities and towns. They must have some method of keeping them sane because they aren't as visible as Stefyn D'Mal." Edwin and Zan nodded. "No one speaks of it, so I wasn't sure if it was something I should be discussing."

"You've attained a high enough level within the clergy now to be told of this because you'll be dealing with this problem. We can't find all the young mages though we find most of them. So some do end up in Tauron's service," replied Garran. "I'm told the priesthood of Tauron has developed a method similar to the one that mages in Neveyah employed before Aelfrid Firesword."

Zan asked, "How well does that work? The legions despise us and all children of Aeos."

"They might despise us, but the priesthood of Tauron is regarded with suspicion and dislike by the immigrants from Serende. Although they fear and obey the minotaur priests, for healing they only trust those acolytes who remain physically unchanged. Stefyn D'Mal insists the mages gifted with the magic of Aeos are acceptable to Tauron, and apparently the god himself agrees. In Lunne, just before the summer solstice, the chancellor in Mal Evol City announced they're the emissaries who'll bring the children of Aeos to the Bull God."

"What? That's unheard of." John's shock was echoed by the others.

Garran nodded. "We've never been able to get the information we need to confirm this, but we know they're part of the priesthood of Tauron and have authority within their ecclesia. We need more facts, but the last three teams that went into the valley before you perished."

"I know about two of them. They were friends of

ours." Edwin's stomach clenched.

"This is what a select group of mages augmented with a certain rune handles very quietly," admitted Garran. "It's been determined that despite being healers, Edwin and Zan are members of that brotherhood. The problem has been kept a Temple secret for obvious reasons."

John agreed. "If this news got out, there would be trouble. In the bad old days, just after the war, there were riots and public executions of suspected traitors, by vigilantes. Time and again, the so-called spies were just ordinary people who weren't as well liked as they should be, and mobs of otherwise decent citizens committed atrocious crimes in the name of weeding out the enemy's minions."

Zan said, "Perhaps the hysteria was instigated and supported by the very people they were seeking to ferret out. Surely a true mindbender could easily avoid being hanged by a mob."

Garran nodded. "That's exactly where it becomes sticky. We'll talk about it later. We had intended for you to speak with Dario, but his wife, Bekki...passed away suddenly. As you can imagine, he's in a bad way."

The three younger mages were shocked. "What happened?" Friedr asked.

"We're not exactly sure, only she was found dead." He glanced at John, who shook his head slightly.

"She was very young," said Edwin. "My age, I believe." He could see Garran was hiding something, and exchanged a glance with Zan and Friedr. They knew it too. Seeing the set look on Garran's face, he declined to pursue it, deciding he would probably learn more later.

"These things sometimes happen." Garran shook his head. "But for now, we need your assistance as healers. We need you three to help my people get the last of our citizens out of town by the simple expedient of stepping in and removing the suggestions placed there by the mindbender. Then you place in their minds the idea they planned to go to Aeoven all the time."

At first, they were reluctant to do such an invasive thing. "That will delay us finishing the wall—and surely it's an improper use of our skills," objected Edwin.

Zan agreed. "We can't just seize the minds of people wholesale and bend them to our will. We'd be no better than the rogue-mages we fight!"

"Under ordinary circumstances it would be wrong and I wouldn't ask it of you. But this is the only way we've ever found to counter a mindbender's work." Garran reached into one of the pockets down the side of his leather trousers and withdrew a list of addresses they would visit. "I can order you to do it if it would make you feel better. It'll only hold you up for one day."

Friedr said, "I don't like it. It goes against everything we were taught. But this is war. We'll do what we must."

John stood up. Grinning he said, "Today is your lucky day, peacocks—you need to gear up in your flashiest armor, or the citizenry won't be at all impressed. Fortunately, it's all still here in the armory." He winked at Garran. "We need to gear up too. If we're hunting mindbenders, I'm not doing it naked."

Garran laughed, as John had hoped. At the three

younger men's quizzical expressions, he said, "I'll tell you the story while we're gearing up. Suffice it to say John has a storied past, and leaping out of a creek naked to keep a pack of rats from stealing our clothes is just the beginning."

John rolled his eyes.

Chapter 12
Serende—The Palace of Dreams

Stefyn D'Mal paced the luxurious sitting room that joined his rooms to Lourdan's suite. A dark aura surrounded him. Nervous, the servants blended even more into the background, hoping to avoid attention. He rarely noticed them unless he needed one, which was never a good thing.

The day had arrived for Lourdan's remaking. He considered the looming event, obsessing over the crucial ritual he would view but have no control over. Stefyn despised being denied control over even the smallest thing, and this particular rite was critical on so many levels. Everything he'd worked for to this point now hung on the outcome of the ritual that would commence in less than two hours.

Because of his small stature and low birth, the priesthood had assumed Lourdan to be weak, gutless. Lourdan had quickly proven himself to be otherwise, and he was now regarded with speculation behind carefully flat glances. Private discussions obliquely mentioned that the man of such slight build might have the horns to rule them after all.

Lourdan had been the epitome of gracious nobility as a few priests subtly continued their attempts to undermine him with each lesson. Even though he was chosen by Tauron himself, the four would-be renegade patriarchs on the Circle of Six gave him no respite. They'd harried and tormented him, mocked and derided him with the most politely phrased taunts. The fact he was personally favored by the Highest had meant his path to the altar was harder than that of a normal acolyte.

Lourdan's gaze disturbed the sons of Tauron, as did Stefyn's. The minotaurs' thoughts were easy to read—the intentions of the sons of Aeos were too difficult to decipher, too subtle even for their jaded taste. Now the priesthood collectively wondered how having two of them so highly placed would change their own hard-won positions in the hierarchy of the church.

Since his first days negotiating the shoals of noble society as just another prince in the Palace of Dreams, no one had dared to physically harm Lourdan. But if he should falter during the ritual they would tear him to shreds and devour his heart, as would be their privilege. If Stefyn wanted to maintain his own position of power, he'd be forced to kill Lourdan himself, immediately. It was a thing he would do only so the others wouldn't have the pleasure of drawing his death out.

If Lourdan survived, he would be changed and Stefyn didn't know how it would affect their relationship. In the months since his arrival, he'd become hard, as a priest of Tauron must be. After his wife's sacrifice, he'd developed a cold interest regarding medical matters, demanding to know how different the anatomy of a remade warrior was, compared to a person not changed. The priesthood could not answer that question satisfactorily, as they didn't know, but the fact he'd asked made them uneasy. They were aware that he'd carried out some...examining...of men unfortunate enough to land in the dungeon.

Stefyn planned that when Lourdan survived his remaking, he'd be lodged in the Keep of Mal Evol for most of the time. There, he'd have the time and plenty of troublemakers upon which to assuage that curiosity, out of sight of the Hierarchy. Because they were lovers again, Stefyn would open a portal for him every other day. They would have time together every evening by Neveyah time.

Stefyn's nerves jangled with apprehension, his mind roiling with fear and doubt. Woe unto the priesthood, if it came to light they'd deliberately left out a crucial bit of information and Lourdan died as a result. If he lost him during the Rite of Remaking, he didn't know how he would go on. *I've given up everything and everyone for Tauron. I'll give him up too if I must. Please god, don't ask it of me!*

When he'd calmed, he entered Lourdan's rooms, seeing him standing at the window looking out at the courtyard below. His manservant was dressing his hair. With his emotions carefully shielded, Stefyn waited while Relf finished his duties.

Lourdan's empathy made him peripherally aware of Stefyn's turmoil, but he felt only hope and longing for the ceremony to be over. Knowing the pain he would suffer during his remaking would be nearly unendurable didn't worry him unduly. Stefyn had shared his memories of his own remaking mind-to-mind. It was no longer an unknown quantity so there was no need to fear it. The sharing had been difficult—excruciating—but he knew the ritual would last a finite length of time, exactly three days. His life was about to change, forever.

The Rite of Remaking would give him nearly all the powers and privileges Stefyn had. Tauron would live within him and he would feel whole instead of half-empty as if some immense part of him was missing.

After arranging Lourdan's dark, curling hair and adjusting his collar one last time, Relf bowed and silently withdrew. Only then did Stefyn cross the room to stand beside him. Lourdan smiled as Stefyn embraced him, his arms going around him in response.

"The Circle is ready," Stefyn said. "Are you sure you're prepared? When Tauron enters my body, it won't be me anymore. I'll be a witness only, and the god himself will perform the ritual. For three days you will be bound to the altar. For three days, you'll receive no sustenance, only water." *Only pain.* His thoughts were shielded, but Lourdan knew he was afraid.

"You worry too much. It's necessary. It is written that the one who would preside over the altar must have endured the altar. Once I am remade, we'll be a force no one can stand against." His cold features warmed as they always did for Stefyn. "I'll regain my memories, filling the emptiness that wounds my life. I must succeed."

"You'll be even more changed than you are now, as I was. I fear I'll lose you, either way." Lourdan was so fragile, so physically weak, and if he *should* survive the touch of the Dark God.... "When this is over, you'll no longer be my own good, kind Lourdan. You'll be the High Priest of Mal Evol and your heart will be His." Stefyn's embrace tightened as if to protect his lover.

"I'm no longer good or kind, if I ever was. My heart is his already—life as an acolyte of Tauron precludes anything else. I was chosen by you.

Therefore, if the nobility sees me as less than strong, it will weaken you, and that must never happen. Unless you remain here in the Palace of Dreams, striving to force the clans to work together, Tauron's great plan can never be realized and Neveyah will remain just outside his grasp." Lourdan took Stefyn's hand and led him out to the balcony overlooking the shining spires and onion-domed towers of the golden city of Khelen. "This is what you must concentrate on—this world and these people. And, no matter how changed I am in the eyes of the world, I will always love you. I *know* some things and this is one of them."

Even the skyline of the fabled city couldn't completely soothe Stefyn's fears. "You'll still love me, but despite that love, you'll desire to kill me and take my place. It's the natural way of things. It's the way of the priesthood. The weak are weeded out and only the strongest and best survive."

"Tauron foresaw the possibility of conflict between us and in his wisdom he created me lesser than you. He withheld the ability to wield fire and lightning when he granted me the Goddess Aeos's magic, to ensure I can never rise up to challenge you. He gave me great strength in his magic and made me stronger than the others so I may be your right hand in Mal Evol, but without those elements of her magic, I'm a lesser mage. I'll rule as your regent, implementing his plan on your behalf, creating the lush valley that Tauron desires. Because he placed the tattoos on me as her mages are marked, I won't suffer the madness in that land." Lourdan's lips brushed Stefyn's cheek. Affection and confidence radiated from him, and also joy that his day had finally arrived. "In this way you'll be able to accomplish the task Tauron has set before you—that of ruling the rebellious children of Serende and, through me, you will still rule the Valley of Mal Evol as is your birthright."

"What if...never mind. You'll do brilliantly. I should be reassuring you, but instead, you're consoling me," said Stefyn. "You have three days ahead of you that will be hard. Despite Tauron's affection for you, you may not survive the ritual, for nine of ten who attempt it die in the process, and they are born his children. Their physical strength far outstrips yours. Also, you'll be tested far more harshly than they— they've never endured the full Sharing of Ecstasy, having only had the merest hint of the god's true touch. If it kills you, I'll wish to die myself."

He roughly gathered Lourdan to him. "I can't prepare you well enough for the third day—you can't imagine the pain and the ecstasy of the Joining with the God."

"I won't die. I've seen my future. This is the only way. The retired legions, who are even now being resettled to Mal Evol to farm the land, will only accept me if I've undergone the full ritual. I must be proven to be stronger than they are, or I won't be able to rule them for you." Lourdan's grief surfaced as he said, "Yllene offered herself up and I know exactly why she did it." He met Stefyn's gaze.

Warily Stefyn held his lover, his thoughts shielded as closely as if he faced the Circle of Six, wondering what he knew or guessed.

When he spoke, Lourdan's voice was tight. "It was love that made her so certain she had to do it. She was a being created of love and was so wise. I was never meant to keep her when her soul was so near to heaven. Tauron gave her to me to make me stronger, and because of her, I am. Now *I* am to be the sacrifice. I must endure the pain, or I'll never have the holes in my mind filled. My body is weak, yes it's true, but my heart is strong. No lesser priest will dine on it."

Stefyn's pulse settled to a normal rate. "I know. I just wish.... Are you ready then? The acolytes are waiting to begin the purification." He put aside his uncertainties.

"I'm ready." Stepping away from Stefyn and bowing, Lourdan spoke the words Stefyn dreaded. "Take me to the altar. Let the God of Fire and Darkness feel my agony and taste my ecstasy. Freely, willingly I give my life to him. Let him understand all that I am. Let him remake me in his image as he remade you." With those ritual words, the Rite had begun.

That is what I fear. In what way will you be altered? Masking his thoughts beneath a smile, Stefyn knew Lourdan would lose the last shreds of compassion that were so much a part of him in the terrible Rite of Remaking. How it would affect their love for each other, Stefyn didn't know. Still, Tauron demanded a sacrifice, and this time, Lourdan was the offering. "Then let us go."

VALLEY OF SORROWS

Connie J. Jasperson

Chapter 13

Edwin and the others geared up in the armory, preparing to go out to help speed the evacuation. Friedr was disgruntled as he couldn't quite get the leather trousers that matched his red armor on over his lame leg. "I can't tell you how happy I'll be when you get my red leathers altered, Zan," muttered Friedr as he geared up. "But at least, I can wear my red armor again. That excellent brown armor is not as fine-looking as this is."

"The brown ones you've been wearing don't really show once you have everything else on. The brace hides it on your left leg, and your boots cover it to your knees, so really, it's only the right thigh, and that's mostly covered by your vest," Zan replied, looking him over critically. "I'll work on your red ones this evening if I have a chance."

"You two are worse than novices sneaking out to their first midnight garden party." Garran rolled his eyes, and Jase, the fire-mage who was the armorer at Braden, shrugged. Both men were also fire-mages and wore armor in varying shades of red. Garran's distinctive red armor had the people of his city referring to him as "the Red Abbott." Zan's white and yellow gear was a sharp contrast to Edwin's midnight-blue and green armor. John's armor was the flashiest, in varying shades of turquoise with slashes of white and earthy red.

The four accompanied Garran, Jase, and a company of soldiers, which included their old friends, Benn and Div, to the moneylenders' quarter.

Soon, they were walking through the oldest section

128

of Braden. The buildings there were only two stories tall at most. A rather grim air seemed to hang around the area, unlike the rest of the city. "This is where the problems mostly are, now. We've cleared the rest of the city, but close to a hundred families are still holding out in this area." Garran's voice was rough with annoyance. "We definitely have a mindbender at work here."

Well-shielded, Edwin opened his senses to the area. "I see what you mean. Something is undeniably wrong."

Sure enough, the first door they knocked on was opened by an angry man who refused point blank to be relocated to Aeoven. "You perverts get up to who knows what. I'll not have my children exposed to your sort!" He slammed the door in their face.

Garran blew the door to splinters and cornered the man, telling him he'd be relocated whether he wanted to be or not. Zan stepped in took over the man's mind, calming him and gently removing the negative suggestions that had been crudely placed in his mind. Soon he was docilely helping to load his family and all their possessions onto the cart. "I can't imagine what happened to the door," he said, looking at the wreckage. "It was just fine last night!"

"Don't worry, sir. You won't be coming back here, and the houses in Aeoven are much sturdier," said the squad leader, Benn, consoling the confused homeowner. "It was a fragile door."

That was how the whole day went, with small variations. Once the suggestions had been removed, there was no more trouble. Unfortunately, the task took one day longer than Garran thought, putting the team even further behind.

The next afternoon, after they'd gathered all the remaining troublemakers into a docile group, the four questers walked to the western gate with Garran and Jase as they shepherded them down the road toward Aeoven. "We'll just get this last group across the river to their first stop in Morton and then I'll leave them in Jase's hands and return to finish emptying the Temple and deconsecrate the altar. We'll be back the day after tomorrow."

It felt a little strange to be the last people in the abandoned city. As they walked back to the Temple, they discussed their plans for reinforcing the western walls of the city and blending them into the rest of the wall so it would appear seamless.

"Gorden will be proud—I may have to commit this part to paper to figure it out." Edwin laughed at the look on his father's face. "The shield will have to repel creatures and people just as the rest of it does, but this one area must have ramparts to allow Lourdan to see what lies beyond the wall," Edwin said. "I'm just not sure how to make it approachable."

"I just wish I knew why he has to be taunted like this. It doesn't seem fair," muttered Friedr. "I know what the prophecies say—I just wish I knew why."

"You're suffering from the same old problem I've always had," replied John, grinning at Friedr. "I hate to be the one to preach the Temple's sermon, but there must be a reason. It may not become apparent until long after we're gone. How many things have you all done since Christoph fell that are actually signs for the Hero Foretold to read? We must accept the fact that we can't win. We can only build a strong fence, and it's our job to see to it that the one who ultimately triumphs has all the tools he needs to do just that."

That night John prepared their dinner in a strangely empty dining hall. The echoes of their footsteps and conversations felt ghostly in the cavernous room. Edwin sat with his pencils at the ready, listening as John explained where he thought the points of weakness would be, and how they might reinforce those places.

Edwin agreed, taking notes which he turned into drawings. He drew the walk up to and along the ramparts as he thought it should look, saying, "We need to make this look as majestic as we can. I want to impress Lourdan with Aeos's power."

They discussed how to weave the current gates into the walls once the Temple was completely vacated. Edwin felt they would offer a point of weakness, and after much discussion they had a plan.

For once, they went to bed early. Friedr set wards on the main doors, just in case there were any strays who had returned intending to loot the Temple. If someone entered, they would immediately know.

"Strange how empty the place feels." Edwin's comment broke the silence as they walked to their quarters.

"Someone else was still in town a few minutes ago," replied Zan, after a moment. "I felt a resonance, like a healer and some other mages were still somewhere near. I didn't recognize them and they're gone now."

"Why didn't you say something earlier?" asked Friedr, in pain, tired, and exasperated.

Zan flinched. "It was only a few minutes ago, and I wasn't sure. Besides, I thought you could feel them too.

I'm sorry, but it wasn't until just now I realized what I was sensing."

"Relax, Friedr. We're all tired and nearly out of chi." Edwin tried to take the sting out of his words. "You're really good, Zan. You sensed the three novices we found after we left Aeoven. I'm not as sensitive as you." He sent his senses out, searching the city, trying to find the mages Zan had sensed. "I can't find them," he finally said, frustrated at the effort. "Maybe they're Temple mages and they've left the city now. We'll search again after we recover our chi."

"I don't sense them anymore either," Zan replied, his brow furrowed. "I did sense them earlier, though, and they're not anyone I'm familiar with. I don't like it."

"I believe you." Friedr tried to ease his aching leg, regretting being short with Zan. "It could be they are Temple-mages who've been posted away for most of the last ten years, and you wouldn't know them."

"That's true. There must be a lot of mages who've been posted in the south with the army for a long time, and I've never met them. It's just these felt different. I can't explain it." Zan cast a spell for pain relief on Friedr. "Here. You're getting to be as bad as Edwin, you idiot. When you're in pain, you don't rest. Then you're grumpy and we have to put up with you."

Shock that Zan could say such a thing was clear on Friedr's drawn features. "I'm never grumpy," he sputtered. "I have the patience of a saint. I have to, dealing with you two." He harrumphed. "Calling me an idiot—look who's talking! And thank you. I did need it."

VALLEY OF SORROWS

Connie J. Jasperson

Chapter 14
Serende—The Palace of Dreams

Torches lit the Holy Sanctum. Golden candelabras
stood at each end of the sacred altar, upon which the
broken body of the acolyte, Lourdan, lay. The Ritual of
Remaking was well advanced, and now began the third
and final day of the ordeal. The witnesses knelt before
the altar, all of them members of the almighty Circle of
Six, each priest the highest of the priesthood, save for
Stefyn, who was above them all. All who knelt there
were naked, as they should be. It was written they
should appear thusly so the god would see they had
nothing to hide.

More than one kneeling priest wished with every
fiber of his being for Lourdan to fail. His existence was
an affront to them because he wasn't a true son of
Tauron, and their resentment of him was palpable. Still,
he survived, with more stamina than was shown by
those who observed his ordeal, and whose trials had
been less. This shamed them.

Only two of the six patriarchs, Dalgek and
Memschak, prayed fervently for his success.

Once again the god entered the body of his highest
priest, who found his mind shunted to a small corner.
From his position as First Observer, Stefyn prayed that
on this most grueling and important day of the
remaking, Lourdan would be successful and survive.
He reflected that his lover had done well so far.

On day one, Lourdan had correctly answered every
question the Circle of Six put to him, no matter how
obscure the subject or the lack of respect with which it

134

had been asked. Naked, blindfolded, and bound to the altar, he was questioned closely. They mocked him, hounding and harrying him, beating him with special ceremonial whips while meticulously questioning his knowledge of the history and culture of Serende and Mal Evol.

Even Honorable Memschak and Dalgek, knowing what their responsibility was, questioned him closely. They also beat him as mercilessly as the others as this was one area Lourdan had to be proven worthy in, or he couldn't be their master.

The other four asked deviously phrased questions regarding the most obscure concepts of doctrine and theology, but despite the pain of his wounds Lourdan evaded their traps. Those four priests were openly disdainful, seeing only a weak child of Aeos attempting to seize a position of power in their hierarchy.

At the end of the first day when Stefyn regained the use of his body, he gave Lourdan the only comfort he was allowed to offer, holding a cup of cool water to his lover's parched lips. "Drink this." Lourdan sipped and then Stefyn laid his hand on his forehead. "Sleep." Still blindfolded and bound to the altar, Lourdan immediately fell into a deep slumber from which he would only awaken at Stefyn's command.

On the second day, he was questioned by Tauron himself. Forty times the question was asked, "What would you have me do?" Forty times the god's hands hovered, waiting for his answer. Each time the answer was rewarded by eternities of torture as his body was remade. Gradually a difference in the acolyte's appearance emerged, one that was invisible to the naked eye, unlike the alterations that had been wrought in the priests who watched his form being contorted into grotesque, agonizing positions.

Lourdan's change was far more radical, a transformation clearly visible to the god-sight of each child of Tauron who watched in fascinated horror.

At some point, he lost the ability to hear the question, but his answer remained the same. "Remake me, O my God. Remake me so I am fit to be your faithful servant." No matter he was gasping or even screaming, Lourdan embraced the agony because as long as he suffered, he still lived. The pain meant he was winning. "Ask of me what you will, and my answer will be the same." Once more, his body was twisted impossibly, as only a god could do.

His agony was without beginning and without end. Still, the Dark God's hands hovered over him and again he was asked, "What would you have me do?"

With each question, Lourdan teetered at the edge of the abyss. Waves of the most excruciating pain wracked his body and shuddering he answered the Dark God, "Remake me, O my God. Remake me so I am fit to be your faithful servant." He remained conscious, knowing he must, for to lose consciousness was to die, and he refused to die. The Dark God had promised him answers, promised his memories would be returned when he'd been remade.

Promised his sacrifices had not been in vain.

From his place as First Observer, Stefyn watched and willed Lourdan to endure. He had to live. He *had* to. Stefyn knew he wouldn't succumb to death's release as long as he had the hope of gaining the memories he lacked. He also knew the god would honor his promise, and Lourdan would be supplied with memories to fill the emptiness of his past—yes, that would happen.

But what those memories would be only Tauron himself knew. Stefyn had kept two secrets from Lourdan, one of which was the true story of his origin and the other was the complex truth about Yllene. Those two secrets he would take to his grave.

And because of those two secrets, he knew that the memories Tauron chose to give Lourdan would be the ones that best played to the god's needs.

Eventually came the absence of pain—the release was indescribable, and it was all Lourdan could do not to moan from the sheer pleasure. The god retreated, and again a familiar, beloved voice said, "Drink this." He managed to sip the water. Stefyn passed his hand over his eyes and told him to sleep. Tied to the altar, Lourdan immediately fell into a deep sleep.

On the morning of the third day, Lourdan woke to find himself immediately plunged back into hell. Three times more, the question was asked, and three times he was rewarded with pain. Each time the pain was double that of the previous time. He was given a moment of ease before the question was asked again. Still Lourdan answered "Remake me, O my God. Remake me so I am fit to be your faithful servant." In the long moments of agony, his world narrowed to the task of surviving. After the third answer, the suffering was replaced with the blissful absence of pain. Once again the Dark God's hands hovered over him and again a beloved voice asked, "What would you have me do?"

Fully believing the answer would plunge him back into the abyss of pain, Lourdan answered, "Remake me, O my God. Remake me so I am fit to be your faithful servant."

This time, the god's response was different. "I would be your lover and share your ecstasy."

From somewhere in his memory the proper words came. "I am yours. Taste my ecstasy as you have tasted my pain."

Tauron gestured to the altar, and the bonds were released. Raising Lourdan to a sitting position, he embraced him. His lips touched Lourdan's, and instead of pain, he was suffused with pleasure, pure carnal ecstasy, unending and exquisite to the highest degree. Wrung by the erotic release that was the gift of the god's kiss, Lourdan waited for the question he knew would follow, his breath coming in short, ragged gasps. Though he knew it not, the six priests who observed had only experienced the god's kiss in their ordeals. They hadn't experienced the full Joining, and every one of them knew this would be the place where he would either fail or survive and become their master.

"What would you have me do?"

"Remake me, O my God. Remake me so I am fit to be your servant."

Hours passed and the day became night. Somehow Lourdan held on to consciousness until at last Tauron spoke again.

"Who are you?"

Dazed and wounded, Lourdan managed to say the words Yllene had taught him. "I am your faithful servant. I am yours, now and forever."

With those words, the third and final day of the Ritual of Remaking had come to the closing phase, the ritual cleansing. Tauron abandoned Stefyn's body and hovered over the altar; a darkness filled with stars, slowly rotating, observing Lourdan as he lay dazed and unmoving on the altar, examining him with the patient consideration only a god could muster.

Coming to awareness of his body and in a haze of pain, Stefyn knelt before the altar, disturbed by the memory of what he'd witnessed, praying his lover had survived it. *I lived through the remaking younger than he is. Surely he lives. Surely....*

Opposite the altar, steps led down into the hammered-gold bathing pool, known as the Fount of Purification, used only for the ritual cleansing. Two heavy ewers stood on the table before it.

Stefyn stepped to the pool for the ritual of purification using one of the heavy pitchers. His body was the chosen vessel of the god so he was scrupulous in purifying himself, washing away all evidence of the god's frenzy. After the purification, he once again knelt before the altar in prayer.

Lourdan sat up and slipped from the altar table. His features were battered and unrecognizable. He swayed, nearly losing his balance, but remained on his feet. With the utmost determination, he staggered to the fount, his pain-wracked limbs barely supporting him. Bloody and covered with lash marks and contusions, he now had one final test to pass.

With his heart in his mouth, Stefyn watched as Lourdan completed the ritual, terrified he would stumble and fall when he was so close to success. To fall would be to die, for only the strongest could survive. Four of the watching circle of witnesses wanted nothing more than to see him fail now when he'd endured far more than they had in their pathetic remakings.

Those priests bore the horns visible to the uninitiated, where the final change in Lourdan would be as Stefyn's—visible only to those others who were children of Tauron.

Somehow the fragile, broken man made it to the pool and stood, raising the heavy ewer of holy water over his head with trembling hands, offering it to Tauron. Holding his breath, Stefyn willed Lourdan to say the Words of Completion.

Through his cracked and bloody lips, Lourdan spoke. "I wash away the past." He poured some of the water over himself. "Cleansed of what was, I am reborn in your love." More water poured over Lourdan's head, reviving him, making him stronger. "All I am, all I ever was, and all I will ever be, I offer to you, my god." Again and again, he poured the water over himself, sluicing away the filth. "You remade me, making me fit to be your servant. You tasted my essence, my pain, and my ecstasy." He poured the last of the water over himself and purified, he stood in the pool. "With this water, my body is cleansed, as you cleansed my soul. I ask you to accept the gift of my life as my offering, God of Fire and Darkness. I am remade, and wish only to be your servant." He stepped out and knelt before the altar, beside Stefyn, head bowed, praying.

Now was the moment Stefyn feared most, the Sifting of the Soul. The star-filled darkness hovered over Lourdan, revolving as the true essence of Tauron examined him, body and soul. If, after all of Lourdan's suffering, the god decided he wasn't pleased with the remaking, Lourdan would die. Silently, Stefyn willed that there be no flaws found in the soul of the man who knelt beside him, remade.

The Dark God spoke in the minds of all who were gathered before him. "Lourdan. Rise. You are my beloved servant. Serve me for all of your days and I will reward you with your deepest desire. Name your reward."

Obediently Lourdan stood, his head bowed before Tauron with all his desires as bare as he could make them. Also exposed was his complete acceptance of whatever the god chose to give or require of him. "You know all my desires, oh my god. I need no reward. To serve you for all my days is my reward."

A tendril reached for Stefyn, raising him to stand beside Lourdan. "And what would you have of me, most devoted servant?"

"God of Darkness and Fire, you know all my desires." Stefyn answered as he always had and always would. "I need no reward. To serve you is my reward." No matter what the cost, he meant it with all his heart.

The darkness that was the god surrounded and wrapped them both, becoming a whirlwind. A shriek was torn from Lourdan's throat, and bloody tears streaked his face, but he didn't sob or whimper. Abruptly the god was gone.

With his god-sight wide open Stefyn saw the final Sign of the Remaking, invisible to the naked eye, but perfectly clear to any child of Tauron.

Lourdan's spirit-self towered above the groveling priests. The horns of the Bull God, wider than any save those Stefyn bore now graced his head.

In a pain-infused fog, Lourdan wondered where he was and what he was doing. His vision cleared and six forms came into focus. He saw the faces of the four high-priests who'd taunted and tormented him for weeks in preparation for this ordeal, and also the two who had tried to help him. He raised his right hand and five of the minotaurs voluntarily fell forward, faces pressed to the floor, swearing by the Dark God they would serve him as faithfully as they served the highest priest. With his god-sight Lourdan saw it was so.

The sixth glared at him resentfully, and his thoughts were as clear as if they were spoken.

This one. This one plots rebellion against me. Lourdan's hand beckoned the recalcitrant priest to come. Against his will, the priest found himself crawling on his belly to kiss Lourdan's feet. Now the priest knew the fear he should have felt before.

"You despise me because of my small stature and my birth as a child of Aeos," Lourdan's voice was harsh. "You have never endured the god's touch as I have. This tells me *you* are weak." He raised the priest off the floor with the merest line of stasis. Five priests stared as the stasis spell, which they could scarcely see and could never manage to use with as deft a skill, was employed to bind and gag the rebellious priest. With a look of horror, the now-penitent priest tried to beg for mercy, but his voice was stopped. No sound emerged.

With his right hand, Lourdan tore open the minotaur's chest and clawed out the living heart. Taking two bites, he tossed the rest to the kneeling priests. "Share this celebratory meal among you. Tomorrow we begin the true work for which we've been called. You're released until then." He flung the corpse into a corner, the magic of the stasis spell crackling in the air.

Five Minotaur priests, three with the whites of their eyes showing their terror, scrabbled for the heart, shredding it amongst themselves. Then they crawled backward out of the sanctum, bowing and touching their foreheads to the floor all the way. The doors closed after them.

Clutching his head Lourdan fell toward Stefyn.

Weeping with joy, Stefyn caught him as he fell. Slumping to the floor before the altar Stefyn held him, comforting and easing his pain, oblivious to his own wounds. Pouring a massive healing spell into Lourdan's broken body, Stefyn blessed the dark god, fervently thanking him for the gift of Lourdan's life.

Chapter 15

The next morning the team commenced connecting the long barrier-wall to the actual walls of Braden, which took half the morning. Immediately they went outside the city and began rebuilding the western wall of the city itself, connecting it seamlessly to the section they'd built south to the Horn of Misery.

Over the next two days, in the course of reinventing the walls of the abandoned city, they altered the old town nearly beyond recognition. Using the combined forces of the swords, they leveled entire neighborhoods that had once butted against the battlements. From there they excavated the earth to make the restructured wall.

The main boulevard through Braden ran west to east. The old city had been built with high, stone ramparts guarding all four cardinal directions. Edwin created immense culverts that passed through and beneath the old south and north city walls, allowing the moat to flow along the length of the barrier. If anyone were brave enough to cross the moat and attempt to scale the walls, the shield would either repel them or, if they persisted, kill them.

Outside the wall, half a league to the west where it had always been, the River Fleet flowed—a silver ribbon in the distance running past verdant fields. But now the river rolled swiftly past where the port once stood. New banks climbed to meadows as if they had never known the levees, piers, or warehouses that had lined the road outside the western walls of Braden. The immense stone bridge was gone, leaving no trace.

When viewed from the river, the wall was black and menacing, stretching as far to the south as the eye could see.

Once they arrived at the end of their task, Edwin intended to anchor the shield and the new wall to the southernmost tip of the Horn of the Moon, at a place ten leagues east of the village of Fleetside. That way both river traffic and local commerce to and from the port of Fleetside wouldn't be affected by the wall. The city would become a more important port, picking up the business that had always been done in Braden, and the Abbott of the new Temple there was preparing accordingly.

On the morning of the third day, they created the ramparts and the winding stairs along the inner wall which led to it, making the one place someone could see beyond it. Edwin felt the tricky part would be leaving both the ramparts and the way up to them unshielded without compromising the purpose of the wall. After much contemplation, he hit upon the idea of making the shield extend only inches from the wall along the wide stairwell and along the outer wall of the ramparts. He made the shield deliver a severe shock of lightning if it was brushed against, so the stairs would be rather tricky to negotiate. One would have to stand at least a foot back from the battlements. "No sense making it easy for him. After all, Lourdan *is* the enemy." Edwin's grim smile was a caricature of his old self.

John agreed with Edwin and then gestured at the wall. "This shield will stand forever. But hopefully, it won't take that long for the Hero Foretold to be born and set things right." He looked at his son. "Perhaps you'll live to see the day, although I'm sure I won't." His wry grin lit up his face. "I'm an old man, by Temple standards. So many mages of my age have succumbed to the effects of the magic. I have a much smaller group of peers than I ever would have thought. For some reason we believed we were all going to live forever."

"Dad, you're only forty-eight. Old Mr. Legg was ninety-four when he passed away." Edwin laughed. "If you didn't tell folks your age, no one would know. The same goes for Halee. A lot of the younger mages think you're my brother."

"Wait until you're known as 'Granddad,'" John teased Edwin. "Then tell me you don't feel old!"

They managed to finish up just as full dark fell. Weary and drained of chi, they drove back to the Temple through the dark, haunted-feeling streets, lighting their way with a mage-light in the lantern.

They'd just got the fire going in the stove when Garran returned with Jase and two squads of Temple soldiers, bringing twenty wagons. He intended to completely empty the store rooms and move everything to the other of the two new Temples, the one in the northern city of Arlen.

Supper that night consisted of vegetable soup made heartier with tiny, cubed chunks of toothbreaker. With bread and cheese, it was a good, filling meal, and was ready in half an hour.

"If this is what rations are nowadays, I'm staying in the militia," quipped their old friend, Div, as he came back for a second helping. "This is better than anything my ma ever fixed. She never quite got the hang of softening the toothbreaker before she served it. She always swore by it for my little brothers when they were cutting their teeth!"

Garran grinned wickedly, glancing at John, who'd prepared the meal. "Well, it really helps that John points his sword and 'magics' it into submission before he drops it into your soup!"

John laughed.

"Don't surprise me none," replied the laconic squad leader, taking a large bite. "Ain't no other way to make that sausage eatable without simmering it for a day or two."

The next morning, the new arrivals stood in awe as they got their first good look at the walls that had changed so dramatically during their absence. "And it'll be just like this, unbroken from horn to horn? Tauron's hordes will be completely penned up!" The soldiers' astonishment pleased the four mages, who'd begun to wonder if their great creation was really as miraculous as they needed it to be.

"I knew things were changed when we rolled up in the dark last night, but this—it ain't the same place at all." The soldier's comment was echoed by the others of his squad. "You boys leveled half the town. What do you need an army for? You could just bury the enemy."

Edwin laughed. "Truthfully, what we've been doing isn't too different from digging irrigation ditches—just on a larger scale."

"Having four magic swords to magnify your spells doesn't hurt you any, I'd wager," said Jase, with a thunderstruck expression. "I doubt I'd be able to do a wall like that."

Zan said, "For fighting, it helped that our battle-magic was magnified by the blades, which made an immense difference in Mal Evol. But the strength of destructive magic channeled through the blades is minimal compared to the strength of creative magic. Aeos doesn't like destruction. Her gifts work best when used with compassion."

As the others talked, Garran and John walked along the shore of the wide moat, examining the wall. "Amazing...utterly amazing. You never cease to amaze me, farm boy."

"This is Edwin's circus—I'm just one of the clowns. Tomorrow, after you've departed with the last of the wagons, we'll seal the western gate, making it look as if it was never there," John said. "Every time we cast these spells the wall goes up a little faster than the time before, so with luck, one week, perhaps two should be all the time we'll need. After that, we'll firm up the shield along the escarpment to Arlen. Then we're going home as fast as Friedr's cart will roll. I'm really looking forward to getting back to Halee."

"I like seeing you behaving like a man in love again. It makes you more human," Garran's chuckle rumbled. "Well, as human as any mythical hero ever is."

Reddening, John made a rude noise at Garran. "You should talk. The people here call you 'The Red Abbott' and think you can do no wrong. They like your fancy armor!"

"You aren't going to get me with that old trick, you jealous thing. I'm not Friedr or Zan, worrying all the time about my wardrobe!" Still laughing Garran changed the subject. "The first wave of pilgrims should arrive in Aeoven today. Now the seneschal's teams will be getting them settled and preparing for the arrival of the next group, which should be tomorrow."

"Have you received any news about their journey?" asked John. "How did they fare with the rats?"

"So far as I know, there've been no serious attacks by the rats, only minor feints. The squads have been well able to protect the columns of refugees," replied Garran. "Either the rats are being frightened off by the large numbers traveling together, or they're unable to enter the lowlands." He changed the subject again. "I finally had time to read Friedr's report last night. You boys had some adventures while you were south of here."

"Not as many as I thought we would—I really expected more. But I think we'll find ourselves drawing a lot more unfriendly attention soon if we haven't already. I expect we'll be deep in it on the next leg of this quest."

Garran said, "You're likely right. I'll send a squad back for your protection once I make it to Fleetside."

>>><<<

The rest of the day and into the night they helped Garran and his men load everything that was left in the Temple store-rooms onto the wagons and pack horses. With that done, they gathered in the sanctuary, and kneeling before the altar, prayed to Aeos, asking her permission to move the holy vessel to the new temple in Arlen. In answer, the holy flame winked out. They deconsecrated the altar and the Vessel of the Flame, in preparation for dismantling the sanctuary.

The altar and sacred objects were carefully packed in a wagon, which Garran himself would drive.

At dawn the next morning, the four questers prepared breakfast for Garran and his men and then packed the last of the kitchen gear onto a pack-pony that was tied to Garran's wagon. Waving goodbye, they stood on the steps and watched the last line of wagons roll out of the courtyard.

John and Edwin latched the Temple doors wide open. "We may as well make Lourdan welcome," said Friedr, leaning on his staff and hoisting their kits into the cart one-handed. "I wonder what he'll make of this place. We've gone to a great deal of trouble to modify it for him."

Zan tightened the straps on their water barrel. "I'm sure he expects us to be taken by surprise. It'll be interesting to see if Lourdan is as good at thinking on his feet as Christoph was. Somehow I doubt it since their life experiences are so vastly different."

VALLEY OF SORROWS

Chapter 16

The dreary streets of Fleetside were packed with refugees from Braden, just as they had been for the past week. Every day, as soon as one group departed, a new group arrived. They stayed for one night and then moved on. Teller gazed through his curtains, watching the throng setting up tents on the street, preparing to camp for the night.

"The world has gone mad. I don't know how they're doing it, but that black monstrosity means we're never going home. So what are you going to do now?" Teller asked his sister, who'd arrived with the most recent caravan of refugees. His voice was an oddly high tenor, almost womanly, yet not. "Your work is done in Aeoven. Why don't you go back to Mal Evol while you can?"

"I was trying to do just that." Linette's eyes flashed, always a dangerous sign. "That's out now. I had only been back in Braden for three weeks and was taking up my new task when everything went to hell. I told the guards I had to help my father close up his farm, but they refused to let me out the east gate. They said I couldn't go east, not for any reason, and that the militia would help him. Then those Temple freaks turfed me out of the bakery, 'helping' me load the wagon and putting me into a convoy. I had to comply or draw attention to myself. The best I was able to do was sneak away once I arrived here. I thought you might still have a route into the valley."

"I managed to alert most of our people to the problem. Hopefully, Ferol and his brothers can stop whoever is working the goddess's magic. I was trying to rally the Gap, but the Temple commandeered my wagon, along with everyone else's. I'm supposed to have it back tomorrow. Then I'll finish getting the word out."

"Don't waste your time. Have you actually seen it? Words fail me. Aeos must be doing this herself. Nothing short of a miracle will stop it. By the time you've notified everyone, the wall will be complete and you'll be on the wrong side. The priesthood gave you the one chance, but only if you remained in exile. They'll kill you if they find you in Mal Evol."

Teller looked away, unable to meet her eyes. "I know. What are you going to do? I'm not able to support myself, much less another mouth to feed. Even a junk-man must pay the tithe to the Temple." He turned back to her. "Why are you here? What happened to Oren?"

His expression was easy for Linette to read—he had plenty of gold tucked away, but desperately didn't want her in what he saw as his patch. "Oren died. Dalgek was done with him. He might have been our cousin, but he failed to attract new acolytes for the priesthood. He paid lip-service to god, but his heart wasn't in it. I regularly had to subsidize Oren's tithes to the Temple of Aeos with my wages when I was working out of town just so he wouldn't draw unwanted attention to our shop." Linette shrugged. "Dalgek insisted I resolve that mess, so I did. I'd just gotten things worked out when the bloody Temple decided to evacuate the city."

Teller said nothing.

Linette peered through the curtains and then returned to her chair. "The street is full of mages. It's clear Fleetside isn't safe for our sort anymore. You have a new Temple here, if you hadn't noticed. Ordinarily that would be no problem, but your Abbott is Noli Rainesson. Trust me, he's not as thick as the Red Abbott was in Braden. In a town this small, nothing will escape his attention. We're safer in a large town where they can't keep such a close eye on us."

Both jumped as a loud knock sounded on the door.

Teller looked at her. "Who could that be?"

"Open it, fool. It feels to my senses like a mage is on your doorstep. You're a devoted follower of Aeos, and don't forget it."

Teller opened the door. His eyes widened. Two battle-mages and a healer stood on the stoop.

"Good afternoon, sir." The younger battle-mage in yellow and white greeted him. "You are Teller? The rag-and-bone man?"

Teller nodded. "I am. I take other folk's broken junk to the reclaimer's yard. Have you need of my services? I'm supposed to have my wagon back tomorrow."

The healer said, "My name is Healer Anders and these are mages Vint and Allyn. We're tracing the movements of a healer who was last seen in this neighborhood just over two weeks ago. Her name is Bekki. Do you recall seeing her?"

Concentrating on telling the absolute truth, Teller replied, "I do. She treated me for an infected hand. It had me nearly crippled, but she fixed it." He held up his hand, showing a thin white scar.

"What day was that, sir?" Anders stood with his pencil poised over his notebook.

Teller thought for a moment. "That was Lunaday,

two weeks ago. She said she was on a circuit, from Braden Temple. I do know she planned to see another patient after me."

"Do you know who?"

"She didn't say, Sir Mage," replied Teller.

Allyn, the older battle-mage in blue and white, said, "Thank you. We may need to check back with you again later. Will that be a problem?"

Teller laughed. "Only if you expect me to feed you! Otherwise, not at all."

After her brother had closed the door, Linette peered through the curtains. The two battle-mages and the healer stood on the curb, conferring. The younger mage, Vint, glanced up at the house and then back to the healer. He said something and the healer made another note.

After the Temple mages had progressed down the street, Linette turned back to her brother. "What was that all about? What did you do?"

"My duty." Teller looked at her, scorn radiating. "Honorable Dalgek had a task for me. Someone very high up needed a Temple healer, preferably female. The under-priest who contacted me didn't say who she was intended for, and I didn't ask. I just made sure she met the escort and was safely on her way to the Shadow Castle, as was my duty."

Linette stood with her lips pursed. "We have to leave Fleetside. When I was evacuated from Braden, I was offered a new bakery in Aeoven. I'm going to take them up on their offer, and you're going with me."

Teller was aghast. "But you're known there. You said you were done with your task there. What if there are repercussions?"

"What repercussions? Unlike you, I do neat work. I never leave any loose ends for them to follow. They know the woman is dead and are investigating her murder." Linette's laugh was harsh. "Those mages who just left here suspect you're hiding something, Brother dear. At this point, they don't think it's serious, but they're coming back later this week with a trained mind-healer to question you again, just to be sure."

"What? How do you know?"

"Trust me. That's what they were discussing while standing on the curb. They added your name to the list of people to be seen when someone who is better at truth reading arrives." Teller started to speak, but Linette cut him off. "Don't argue with me. I could see that in their surface thoughts, just like I could read your guilt."

Teller burst out, "But you're well-known in Aeoven. What about that?"

"Linette the friendly-girl is dead. I look nothing like her and am far too respectable to behave like a friendly-girl, so why would they connect me with her? The only man there who knew my secret is dead." She glared at her brother. "As you will be too, if you don't do as I say. We need to be on the road to Aeoven tomorrow, as soon as you regain your wagon."

"So. You finally disposed of your Temple boyfriend," Teller said. "He was so far gone when I saw you last spring that I wondered how long it would be before he lost his usefulness."

Linette glared at him. "Cayne was addicted to a nasty drug. He was weak for turning to daze-spice in the first place."

"And you exploited that weakness to the fullest. I

just wonder how many years you wasted trying to break his geas and turn him." He enjoyed the hateful look she gave him. "You should know that battle-mages are nearly impossible to break except on the altar. Healers are far better for our purposes."

Linette's voice could have cut steel. "Honorable Dalgek directed me to attach myself to him, and I did so. Whether or not it was a waste of time is not up to you to decide—Dalgek found the information I gleaned from him useful. Through my association with Cayne, I was able to complete a task for Baron D'Mal." There was no disguising the pride she felt. "I finished setting the mindtraps he'd previously placed in a healer's mind. This woman was somehow rescued before he could finish his work. They were old, so it must have happened before the Baron left Mal Evol." Triumph animated her coldly beautiful features. "His work is completed now."

Unwilling to allow his sister that victory, Teller said, "Are you sure you did it right? Mindtraps are tricky. You're nowhere near his caliber and messing with his work could cause us more trouble than it's worth." He clutched his head, falling to his knees. "Stop! I know you have the ability, but do you have the training? You weren't trained for the priesthood. I was. The results from continuing someone else's work are never satisfactory. That much I do know."

"You're right that I don't have Tauron's magic, but I'm a full priestess and that counts for something. You've forgotten I was trained by Graylor himself in all the many nuances of Aeos's empathic magic. I have both the ability *and* the skills, Brother dear. Don't ever doubt me again." She stood over her brother, raising the pain level until he cried out. "I might not be quite as sane as you'd like me to be. Fortunately, I'm able to bleed off the excess chi when it builds up too much, but there's no telling what I'll do."

"All right. I believe you. For god's sake, make it stop!" At last, the pain in Teller's head eased. Getting back to his feet, he staggered to a chair. "What really happened to cousin Oren? The agreement was that he'd run dad's bakery in Braden for us while we carried out our tasks. He was perfectly healthy when I saw him last month."

"Cousin Oren died and I took back our bakery. That's all you need to know." She glanced out the window. "Better get packed, Brother. As soon as you get it back we're going to load your wagon and join a convoy headed north, like good little refugees."

VALLEY OF SORROWS

Chapter 17

Friedr drove the wagon through the empty lanes, past the vacant buildings, turning onto the main street heading toward the western gate. The pale sunlight of the late harvest morning filtered down through leafless fruit trees to the deserted gardens. The larger shrubs had been hedged and formed intricate mazes where lovers had once trysted and children had played games of hide-and-seek, but no sounds other than those of their wagon or the occasional call of a bird broke the silence.

The emptiness was eerie as they drove past the many lush parks the city had been famous for, plots thickly planted with winter herbs and colorful aromatics brightening the landscape even on cold, gray days. Already wind-blown leaf litter and small debris dotted the once-pristine landscape, contributing to the abandoned air.

As they approached the center of the city, Friedr said, "We just have to seal the western gate, and finish the wall to the escarpment and then we can go home." He hunched in his cloak, feeling the chill of the wind that presaged rain. "I can't tell you how much I want to be home. I've many things to settle once we get there, and I can hardly take worrying about it." Though he tried not to show it, he was again obsessing that his horribly scarred leg would turn his wife away from him. Part of him knew it wouldn't change their relationship, but the worry was always there, nipping at the edges of his thoughts, and had been growing since he woke up in the cavern, maimed.

"I feel the same way." Zan's somber tones carried in the silence of the morning air.

Edwin nodded and said nothing, gazing into the distance. His stomach roiled, thinking about the mail that would be waiting for him in Fleetside, once they finished their task.

They rounded the corner. As the wagon made the turn, they sensed the raising of magic and immediately shielded against it.

This wasn't the wild, unfocused magic of the rat-people. It was familiar but different. Zan, Edwin, and John drew their weapons, rolling off the wagon and hiding in doorways. Fire suddenly rained down around them

"Rogue-mage...make sure you weave your barrier into your shields, Dad. I don't want him taking you over and using you against us." A sad look crossed John's face at his son's words, but he nodded his acceptance and Edwin didn't pursue it. Just as John's barrier snapped into place, fire rained on them again from one side and lightning from another.

Looking around for some sort of shelter, Friedr was an easy target, perched in the cart as he was. He raised his staff, deflecting a bolt of lightning, and with his shields up he was at last able to abandon the wagon, drawing his sword. Moving as quickly as he could, he leaned in the sheltered corner of a doorway. With both hands free, he was able to use his staff with his left hand, as well as to defend with his sword. He opened his senses, searching for his attacker, finding a single mage closing in on him.

The elements flew from alleys and around corners. Edwin and the others deliberately drew attention away from Friedr, but one remained, casting spells targeting him, likely because he was lamed and appeared the weakest.

The styles of the mage's volleys were unique, nothing like the way the Temple mages were trained. Using Dragonstorm to conserve his chi, Friedr seized the magic and used it to harass his foe. He sensed the volleys weakening and leaning out of the doorway, he caught a glimpse of a dark-haired youth of about fourteen. *Ah hah...got you, ignorant child....* As if he were teaching a novice, he used just enough strength to tease the boy into overcommitting, and drained the boy's chi.

Shouting something in an unfamiliar dialect, the boy raced at Friedr, swinging a sword and attacking with all his might.

On a side street, Edwin and Zan crouched in a doorway. Zan concentrated on locating the positions of at least three attackers, finding them strung out in various places throughout the neighborhood. "I count five of them. Friedr is dealing with one right now. I sense a healer with strong empathic abilities, in one of these buildings," he whispered.

"I see what you mean. He has a strange...I guess 'signature' is what you'd call the way he feels to me...and he's preoccupied."

"He *should* be preoccupied. I don't see how, but he's linked with all of them, guiding their every move. I can't figure out how he's doing it. Battle-mages can't link unless they have healing empathy, and not one of them feels like they could be latent healers. They must be in his thrall, bound by a geas to obey him." Zan cocked his head, stretching his senses. "A mage is approaching, just around the corner in this alley. I warn you, he's not in control of his mind."

"I'll deal with him," replied Edwin, switching his senses to the new attacker. "You discover where the lightning is coming from and deal with it. Let's try to save these children for the Temple. You have the skill to do it, and we need them." Nodding, Zan moved off, staying low.

A ball of fire flew around the corner and splashed off Edwin's shields. Easily catching and balling it up, he sent it back toward the caster and ran toward the pile of junk he was hiding behind. Water sheeted off Edwin's shields as he leaped over a pile of refuse. The water was followed by lightning. He snatched the lightning, and making a needle, cast it back at the crazed mage. The minute the shields went down, Edwin cast a spell on the thin, ragged young man, placing him in a deep sleep.

Edwin followed the sounds of spells being traded back and forth, creeping along the side lane and staying close to the walls of the buildings. He paused, feeling the mental-probing of the strange healer who desperately tried to break through his barrier. His ever-present anger flashed to the surface and he gave the mindbender a severe headache for his efforts. Smiling as he felt the man's agony, he kept moving toward the sounds of battle.

John's voice said, "Over here."

Edwin darted to his father's side in time to see a girl of about sixteen go down under a neatly placed water spell, her feet sliding out from under her. As she slipped, her shields faltered and Edwin quickly invaded her mind, sending her to sleep. He felt a mix of consternation overlaid with an almost parental concern from the hidden mindbender as the girl in his thrall lapsed into unconsciousness. Now the mindbender's awareness was colored with a deep fear for the safety of his—children? Edwin definitely sensed frantic worry for their welfare.

The sound of Friedr's sword ringing against steel caught their attention. John and Edwin ran to Friedr's side, arriving just as a very young mage slid off Friedr's sword and into a bloody heap.

Edwin swayed and clutched the wall as the mindbender felt the death of the boy and panicked. Grief and rage combined with desperation now colored the man's emotions. With the realization of the boy's death, the mindbender suddenly lost control of his senses. The link to his two remaining thralls surged and appeared to strengthen, and the man seemed to regain his mental balance. Sorrow and disbelief tinged the strange healer's thoughts, sending...gratitude? Yes, Edwin definitely sensed him thanking them through the link for helping him recover his sanity.

"I think I know where he is—the mindbender, I mean." Edwin shook his head, trying to clear it.

"This was a child!" Friedr's horror-stricken voice sounded loudly in the street. "He should have been an upper-level novice, not lying dead at the end of my sword!" The big man's hands shook as he wiped his sword. "He wouldn't stop firing his little spells at me, and when he ran out of chi, attacked me. I disarmed him of course, but when that happened he ran himself onto my sword! The young idiot killed himself!" The color had drained from his face.

Casting ease on Friedr, Edwin glanced at John who knelt beside the dead child. "Dad, you know about these rogue mages—why did this boy commit suicide?"

John looked up at his son. "They're under a geas to kill themselves if they're caught." He rose to his feet, no longer merely a soldier. He was in charge and radiated authority. "Edwin, you said you may have located the mindbender. You two use your combined talents to deal with him." John grabbed Friedr, forcing him to look at him "This is an order. Whatever you do, don't kill the bastard! He has knowledge we need." He pinned Friedr with his eyes. "You *will* keep him alive. Pull his fangs, but don't let him die."

John towered and before his presence Friedr felt small and inconsequential. In the rush of a moment, he understood why the soldiers they'd met all followed John Farmer as if he was a holy icon and why Zirik had worshiped him—John *commanded* and you were compelled to obey. Agreement was torn from Friedr's lips, although he wanted nothing more than to kill the mindbender and John knew it. He drew himself up and gave the salute used by the Barbarian Elite. "As you command, Sword of Aeos."

Shaken to the core by what he'd just been through, with the boy killing himself and then seeing the other, normally hidden side of John, Friedr linked with Edwin and they began homing in on the mindbender.

Edwin had nothing to say. He'd seen that side of his father on occasion and knew there was no disobeying him.

Chapter 18

Running through the streets and staying close to the buildings, John followed the sounds of magic hissing in the morning air. He found Zan one street over, shielded behind a stone wall, trading spells with two young mages.

"I don't want to kill them," Zan said as John settled in beside him. "I could take them out easily with a two-pronged thunder-fist, but I want to save them for the Temple."

"You won't be able to, Zan. The mindbender has them under a geas. A boy just ran himself onto Friedr's sword when he ran out of chi and lost his blade." John's voice sounded raw. "Rall won't accept them. I guarantee it. They're a danger he won't want to risk. And something you need to know—during the war we were *never* able to save any mage who'd been taken over by a mindbender, whether they were Temple trained or not."

"I'm going to save them. I can undo his work." Zan saw John shake his head over his obstinacy but didn't care. "I'll break their shields and put them to sleep. While they're asleep, I'll do what I can to save them."

John caught the look on Zan's face and sighed. "What do you want? I have no element of fire."

"Throw me a cat-zapper. *They* will give me the fire I need."

John picked his way over to where he had room to toss Zan a little lightning, allowing the enemy's spells to slide off his shields. Immediately Zan took John's lightning and snatched the enemy mages' fire, separating it, creating two lightning needles which he aimed at the bases of their shields. Simultaneously both sets of shields went down and Zan pounced, placing both mages under a deep sleep spell before they knew what had happened.

As the two slid to the ground unconscious, John said, "You've been practicing."

"I have indeed," Zan said, grinning rather smugly. "They're big fellows, close to my age I would say. Maybe we should get the cart to move them."

Linked to Friedr, Edwin drifted on the breeze, searching the street for the mindbender. At last, he found their quarry hiding in an abandoned flower shop. They observed as the man realized he'd been discovered, watching as he sorted through his options when he was unable to penetrate either of their barriers. He quickly jumped back into the shadows when Friedr flung the door open. "I want to talk to you, mindbender. You're good at letting others do the fighting and dying for you, aren't you."

"Spare me your self-righteous anger, fire-mage. I've anger of my own and sorrow aplenty, thanks to you." The healer cast a compelling. Friedr's healer's barrier was strong, and he stood unaffected by his effort.

Having no effect on Friedr, the man shifted his attention to Edwin. "Sir Mage," he said, "I know something about the new regent. He is to be here soon. Will you be ready to meet him with your magic? I've heard what his strengths are. Would you like to know them?" He backed around the corner to where he was shielded from Edwin by the wall. "Just hear what I have to say. It's for your own good." A wave of compulsion rolled off Edwin's barriers.

When Edwin didn't answer, the mindbender spoke to Friedr. "I can heal your crippled leg, fire-mage. You'll be able to fight again as you once did. Will you allow me to heal you?"

Edwin felt the man poking at his barriers and reached out to place a barrier around him. Suddenly the mage clutched his head, moaning, "No...you can't...you don't...." He staggered out of his hiding place and to Edwin's amazement the man's eyes rolled up in his head. He collapsed in a crumpled heap, fully under a deep sleep spell, one suitable for performing surgery, and lay there comatose.

"John said to pull his fangs." Friedr stared down at him, eyes cold as slate. "They are now pulled."

"Right then," Edwin replied, feeling stunned by Friedr's abrupt handling of the situation. Looking first at the fallen mindbender and then at Friedr's flat expression, he shook his head. "I'll see what's happening. He's not in communication with his thralls, so maybe things are settling down." Sending his senses out, Edwin discovered there were no young mages left awake, and saw Zan and John were walking back toward the cart. "It looks like Dad and Zan have taken care of the other two. I'll go and meet them. Remember—don't harm him."

Friedr shrugged, his face unreadable. "I promised I wouldn't kill him."

Leaving the flower shop Edwin headed to where he'd left the first young mage. The boy still slept, and Edwin reinforced the spell to hold him until John and

Zan could help him load the boy into the cart.

With them in the wagon, Edwin and Zan searched their pockets and John went inside the flower shop to see what, if anything, Friedr had learned.

Friedr sat on a chair, staring into a corner. The mindbender still lay slumped where he had fallen. Friedr looked up as John entered the store. "A boy killed himself today because this man placed the thought in his head that he must kill me, or die. The others will be under the same sort of geas. When they awaken, they'll kill themselves no matter what Zan thinks. There must be a reckoning."

"I fear you're correct. Zan or Edwin will have to get a message to Garran, telling him to return with a healer who can control him. We'll have to place the inhibitions on this man. He must be taken to Aeoven to be tried for his crimes," John replied. "There are procedures for this and I'll ensure they're enforced."

"Then I shouldn't be allowed anywhere near him. I wish nothing more than to shred his mind and leave his empty body for the crows." Friedr's bitter tones grated and using his staff, levered himself up, ready to leave the room. "I have the ability, you know. After this morning, I can't be trusted not to use it."

"Sit back down."

Again, Friedr obeyed John's command, unable to do anything else.

"Before you leave here feeling disgusted with yourself, let me tell you a story. It's my story and I've never told anyone. Halee knows because she stumbled upon me and witnessed the end of what had happened. Garran suspected something because he saw the way the blood had splattered on me. In my experience, only one act could have produced such a blood splatter as the stains on my armor and leathers were that day." A peculiar, haunted look came over John's face.

Friedr had to firm his barrier against the onslaught of John's emotions; a mixture of sorrow, anger, and guilt. Momentarily taken aback by the turbulence lurking beneath John's composed surface, his curiosity was piqued.

As John finished his tale, Friedr sighed. "No one would call the woman's death a crime, John, no one but you." His wry grin lit up his tired face. John shrugged as if he'd heard it before. "You have too high a sense of morality. You and Edwin have this idea one must be noble at all times." His grin faded as his eyes slid to the unconscious man by his feet. "In this business, it's just not possible to maintain such high moral standards. Incidents such as these come along, and then what can you do? We can't take this vermin with us. We aren't going to be able to care for those mages out there who're now at risk of killing themselves if they should wake unattended."

John nodded. "It's a problem. But I warn you as I did Zan that if by some miracle, they do survive, Rall won't accept them as mages. He'll insist they be cut off from their abilities and have Beryl place a deep forgetting on them so they aren't dangerous. That's all we can do because they can't be retrained as mages, and they belong to Tauron, heart and soul." John shrugged again and changed the subject. "Mindbenders run in covens. If this man has accomplices within the population who have gone with the refugees to Aeoven, Zan will peel the information out of him. I could almost pity this creature. I wouldn't want Zan rummaging about in my mind, in the mood he's in just now."

Friedr rolled his eyes. "You know how he is once he gets his teeth into a mystery." They both laughed harshly.

The door flew open and Zan came in, followed closely by Edwin. Zan was livid, his rage battering their barriers.

"Settle down. You need to calm down." Edwin was clearly unsure of what Zan would do next.

"What is it?" asked John, fearing he knew the answer.

Zan's voice fell harshly in the quiet of the abandoned flower shop. "They're dead. Their hearts have stopped."

John stood between Zan and the unconscious mindbender, calm in the face of his fury. "I warned you this could happen. We'll wait for Garran." He turned to Edwin. "Call for him now. He's less than an hour away, as slow as those carts were going. Use your air-magic to send him a message." At his father's command, Edwin nodded.

A cold light played in Zan's eyes. "I'll peel the information from him, using the skills I have. I swear I won't injure or kill him."

"No." John stood firmly where he was. "The Temple has laws regarding his trial and punishment, and we're going to follow them. This falls under my command. You won't touch this man until Abbott Garran returns. Stand down and cool off, Zander Christophson, or you won't be allowed anywhere near him at all. This requires a calm head, and right now you don't qualify."

Chapter 19

By the time Garran arrived, Zan had calmed down, apologizing to John for his irrational behavior. "I swear upon my vows to Aeos it won't happen again. A healer can't allow his personal feelings to cloud his judgment."

Sending the wagons on, Garran had taken a horse and galloped back immediately, arriving in less than half an hour. A squad followed behind him bringing an empty wagon and Arren, the only healer they had who could handle the prisoner.

Once he was apprised of the situation, Garran agreed Zan should interrogate the man. "But I'll allow this only if Edwin and Arren are linked to you during the process, and if John and I witness the interrogation."

Arren agreed. "I'll take notes for the official record. I don't have the kind of skills for mind-healing that Edwin and Zan have, but I can lend my chi and verify everything was done properly." He sighed, gazing at the sleeping prisoner. "He has immense ability—he could have been one of the great ones. What a shame he was lost to us. Once Zan has cut him off from his powers, I'll be able to manage him for the journey to Aeoven."

>>><<<

Garran and John sat in the abandoned flower shop, unwilling witnesses to Zan's relentless dismantling of the mindbender, whose name was Graylor.

It had grown dark, and Zan's questioning had been

going on with no rest for hours. "When is he going to let up on him?" Garran's whisper was for John's ears only. "I don't see how he could possibly have anything more to tell him."

"I don't know. Edwin said the man's mind is like an onion," whispered John in reply. "Layers and layers of spells, each concealing the center. When Zan reaches it, he'll release him to you, unharmed. He'd honor his vows even if Edwin weren't monitoring the situation. Besides, this is Zander Christophson we're talking about. Do you really think he's going to give up before he's gotten what he wants? He has more tenacity than anyone I've ever seen."

"True. He did sit in a cave for two weeks, observing the enemy's every move, day and night," agreed Garran, glancing at Zan out the corners of his eyes.

They continued observing the questioning of the prisoner. Graylor sat in a chair, apparently free to go if he wished. For all intents and purposes, he was physically unharmed, but in truth, he was bound to the chair as if held by chains of iron. His frustration was clear. "I told you. We were to prepare the faithful in Braden for the arrival of the new regent. We arrived late yesterday. When I saw what you'd done, I had to find a way to stop you. You people are so misguided. You amaze me."

He referred to Stefyn D'Mal as either "the Highest" or as "the Baron." "Please, let me go! I've told you everything. I'm a dead man now, and you've left me with no defenses." The thin man wept. "Why? Silence in my head…why? I only wanted to help you. Please let me go. Dalgek can't reach me now, so I have to go to him."

"Ah yes," responded Zan, "the high priest of Tauron, whom you report to. Tell me about Dalgek."

"He has the charge of the priesthood in Mal Evol City. He's a son of a highly placed noble family and while he is devout, he has the soul of a bureaucrat. He gets things done, but he wouldn't have an original thought if it walked up and slapped him. What more is there to know?" Graylor leaned his head back. "Please, let me rest. You murdered my family. Let me grieve in peace." Exhaustion and misery exuded from him.

"I'll let you rest soon, but I need more clarification on some things we talked about earlier. You knowingly set a geas on each of your acolytes that caused them to kill themselves, and I'm beginning to understand your reasoning, but let's talk about that a little more. Tell me again why you did it?"

Exasperation colored Graylor's voice. "I told you. Without some form of control, the magic makes you go mad—surely you know this. Those of us born with healing talents have to maintain control somehow and that's how we do it."

"And you're under a geas too?"

"The geas was set on me when I became a mage. It's set on all mages in Tauron's Mal Evol. I'm a healer, so I'm the one who controls when and how my counterparts use their magic and they, in turn, anchor my mind. The system works well."

Friedr asked, "What is your role in the lives of your thralls?"

"Thralls?" Graylor glared at him. "That implies slavery, and nothing could be further from the truth. We're bound to each other, and when one of us is injured, we all suffer." Graylor began weeping again. "*You* killed them, fire-mage. Don't you dare talk to me." He turned his face away from Friedr, tears streaming down his face. "You should kill me too because the minute you free my mind, I'll go mad and you'll all die. I don't want to hurt you, but it could happen because I have no one to chain my empathy."

Zan said, "I've resolved that problem—you're severed permanently from your gifts."

Graylor looked ill. "I wondered...I sense only my own mind and I am empty...now I'm nothing. I thought it was because they were...dead. But to lose my gifts too...." His face crumpled and he burst into gut-wrenching sobs. "Please, let me die."

After the man had calmed, the questioning continued. "Tell me again what your role is in your coven." Zan's voice was calm, detached. "I'm having trouble understanding it." With each question, he loosened the geas inhibiting the speaking of that knowledge, and each time he asked the question, he received a clearer answer.

Between sobs, the man answered questions. "I've told you and told you. I ensure the excess magic gathering around them is vented safely away. In return, they keep my mind anchored when the empathy becomes too much."

"What else did you do for them? Young battle-mages are dangerous, left unchecked."

"I was their parent. I raised them, nurtured them, and loved them. It was my task and my joy to make sure they were happy, and also that they couldn't accidentally use their magic by thinking wrong, or being angry."

"And you did this how?"

"I keep telling you. We were joined, always. They could only use their magic when I allowed them to. Without the protection of our closed link, they posed a threat to society, as did I. The priests of Tauron set that geas on us to protect the public." Graylor's lips quivered and he closed his eyes against his tears. "When I was rendered unconscious, they were a danger to themselves and to the world." His voice broke and he began weeping again. Waves of genuine grief rolled from him. "I loved them. I can't believe they're dead when they were so young and so special. You can't imagine how lonely it is, without them in my head."

Zan allowed Graylor a moment to collect himself, disconcerted at the depth of the bond between the mindbender and his acolytes. Glancing up, he saw the same consternation in the other Temple mages observing the interview.

Friedr's expression was somber, his remorse palpable. "We feel their deaths keenly too. Please believe me. I wasn't aware they would die if you were rendered unconscious, or I would never have done it."

"It's done. You can't bring them back, no matter how sorry you are. You're a fool to rush in, randomly casting spells when you don't know the consequences. No healer can afford to be hasty, fire-mage. That gift is the most dangerous of magics and the healer must be both cautious and meticulous with its use. If you were one of mine to train, I'd have you doing penance for a year." He nodded toward Zan. "I take comfort in knowing your master will devise a fitting punishment for you. He's not a gentle or forgiving man." Graylor leaned his head back with his eyes closed, raw grief making his voice harsh.

The others looked thrown at hearing Zan referred to as the master, but Friedr nodded. "You're right. He should, and I will accept my punishment."

Zan ignored the comments but waited a moment before he asked his next question. "Who were they and where did you acquire them?"

"Each was sent to me when the priests of Tauron discovered they had the talent." Graylor's halting words were thick. "Maleeia came to me when she was barely nine and began having moments of anger with instances of fires happening around her. She was my first and was a daughter to me, the joy of my life. Then I was given Ald, Sevryn, and Raj. What will I do?" Edwin layered a spell for ease on him so he could continue speaking.

"How long have you been an acolyte of Tauron?" asked Zan. "It seems a strange vocation for a child of Aeos."

"I'm *not* an acolyte." Graylor's indignation elicited smiles from the observers. "I'm a full priest of Tauron and proud to be so. Aeos abandoned us when I was but an infant. Tauron is our god now. I was twelve years old. I was taken to the priests when my empathy began to develop and trained to be the Leash for the Hounds of Tauron."

"Hounds of Tauron?" Refusing to be diverted, Zan continued unraveling the many spells binding the man's mind. "I'm unfamiliar with this term. Who are the Hounds of Tauron?"

"I thought everyone knew. The priesthood of Tauron has declared it a great honor to be gifted with the magic of the Goddess, and parents are rewarded for bringing their talented children to us. The Hounds of Tauron are the mages whose parents were born children of Aeos before the great ascension. We've been given this gift of her magic to serve god. Healers are the 'leash', the one who binds and controls the 'hounds'—those gifted with the elements. The gifted are a terrible menace unless they're bound. You sons of Aeos know this, too. Why else do you bind yourselves with a geas? Before you cut me off from my ability, I could easily see it upon all of you who are from your Temple."

The room was quiet, as the witnesses to the questioning digested that bit of information.

Zan smiled, comforting the man. "Yes, it's true that we bind our magic to serve Aeos and Neveyah. We didn't realize young mages in Tauron's Mal Evol were also bound. We didn't know what happened to them and were concerned for their safety. Are there many of you? We're familiar with only one, and he's completely mad."

"Baron D'Mal, the Highest of the high priests." Graylor nodded his comprehension. "He was the first and is bound by Tauron himself. He's sane when he's in Serende and can't remain in Mal Evol for any great length of time. But through the very soil of the land, his hand is ever upon our hearts."

Zan continued his examination. "What can you tell me of him?"

"He embodies both sides of the magic, as does the new Overlord, so I'm told. It's a great honor, I'm sure." Graylor sounded doubtful. "But it's one that few mages survive, as your fire-mage can attest to. Other than you three and the new Overlord, I know of only one so gifted, and he is the Highest. Most Holy Tauron doesn't like to see mages wasted and the survival rate is very low even for mages not cursed with both magics. So the priesthood instituted the new way of saving us. I was the first so chosen, to be a leash."

"Are there many groups like yours?" The questions had begun to upset Graylor again, a sure sign Zan was nearing another critical nexus as he unraveled the intricate net of spells.

"We are very rare. Fewer children with the gifts are found each year and none at all this year or last. With each generation, we're becoming more and more children of Tauron, and the curse of Aeos's magic is gradually being lifted from us. Soon we'll have only the magic of Tauron, a much safer magic."

Zan nodded. "Tell me who's in Aeoven." His voice was warm and compelling as if he were the man's only friend. "I see a woman with red hair whenever you think of her. What's this red-headed woman's name?" He loosened a tightly wound loop.

Against his will, Graylor's mouth betrayed him. "Linette..." Groaning, Graylor clamped his teeth shut. As he had throughout the interview, Arren made a note of both the question and Graylor's answer.

"See? You can't hide your secrets from me. I know you know more than you're saying. What is Linette's position in the community of Aeoven?" Zan inserted his presence into the mind of Graylor, now releasing and adjusting the primary layers of loops and geas' that had been placed in the man's mind from the day he'd become an acolyte of Stefyn D'Mal.

Tears leaked from the corner of his eyes as Zan began working on a loop that was particularly tightly entangled in the man's psyche. "No...don't do it. Please don't do it. It'll kill me. If you cut that and he feels it, the god will kill us all."

"I won't sever it. You can rest now and feel at ease. Let me help you remember. It will help you to tell me these things." Now that he'd arrived at the core of Graylor's mind, Zan began layering his own spells, replacing the ones that had been there before with a new binding, applying a delicate compelling, commenced by his spoken words. "It will relieve your mind to know my curiosity has been satisfied." With those words Zan spun a spell for ease and wove it into the net that now became the framework controlling the man's thought processes. Working precisely, he resumed loosening the final loop of the old geas and let it untie itself, drifting away.

"How does Linette hide her abilities?" Zan knew the answer but had to keep the man talking and focused on his words to ensure the new spells wouldn't fade. "She must be very clever."

"Oh, yes, very clever, one of the best at casting seemings. She can hide in plain sight…many healers around…can't tell an extra healer is there who shouldn't be." Graylor's head drooped forward from exhaustion. Edwin strengthened him so he could continue answering questions. "My idea, really. When so many are gathered in one place, no one stands out."

"That was a very good idea, very smart. Does Linette have any acolytes such as you had?"

"No…the madness had a grip on her when we found her…not suitable to train others…works best alone."

"What was her task?"

"She is Dalgek's to command, not mine."

Zan felt Graylor's resistance and changed his tactic. "Do you know where Linette is now?"

"Dalgek had a task for her." Graylor's eyes unfocused and glazed over as if he were in a waking dream.

Again Zan asked, "You keep thinking of Aeoven. What was her task in Aeoven?"

"Shepherd for one of your own...mage who fell from grace."

Friedr, John, and Garran exchanged looks.

"One of ours?" Zan's gentle question received a nod. "Do you know a name?"

"No. I was never told."

"Cayne," Garran whispered to John, feeling ill.

Friedr stared at him, his eyebrows raised.

John nodded. "I'll explain later, but he must be talking about Cayne." He remembered the pain of the knife in his back. But more than that, he remembered Cayne had been his friend before the mindbender had twisted him around so badly. "He's dead now, and his handler was surely his murderer."

Zan now asked the question Garran was most interested in. "Who might be secretly marching with the group to Aeoven?"

"Perhaps Teller, if he was here when you emptied the city."

"Who is Teller?"

Graylor replied, "A failed priest who couldn't be trusted around children. He had family connections, so he was unmade, gelded, and exiled."

"What is his skill?" Zan finished removing the last of the spells binding the man to Tauron.

"I never asked."

"Where is Teller now?"

Graylor shook his head. "I don't know. I don't like him."

"Why don't you like him?" Zan began layering his own spells on the man.

"He abused a child. They should have offered him up on the altar, but they let him live."

Zan persisted. "Why did they let him live?"

"Dalgek finds him useful here."

"What does he look like?"

"Brown hair, tallish. He's been castrated, so he has that high voice."

Garran's eyes met John's. He said, "Teller could be anywhere. But, at least, we have a name."

John said, "As chaotic as things are right now the Temple won't be able to find him, even with that description."

"I know. Kalen will have to deal with it."

Friedr asked, "What happened to Cayne?" His eyes demanded an answer.

John shook his head. "It's a long story, and I haven't told Edwin yet."

Garran said, "I told him what happened. He was shocked, but not surprised that you hadn't told him. You need to be more forthcoming with your son."

John had the grace to blush. "I know. I didn't want to upset him, and I don't want Cayne's name tarnished."

Friedr shook his head. "We thought we were in the thick of things while we were in Mal Evol, but it's clear you were up to your neck in it back home."

The three fell silent as Zan continued to question Graylor.

VALLEY OF SORROWS

Chapter 20

It was near dawn when Zan finally reached the end of what he could accomplish with Graylor. No one could sleep, so they brewed the tea stronger than usual and prepared to continue on their journey.

Garran selected messengers from his squad, one to ride to Fleetside, and one to Aeoven, bearing letters regarding the spies in their midst and what to look for. To the man sent to Aeoven, he said, "Ride as hard as you can. Change horses at every inn or Temple along the road, but make as much speed as you are able. Kalen Rallsson must have this knowledge as soon as possible and you can go much faster than the mail coach. Once Kalen has that message, take this letter to Father Rall."

Dismayed by the previous day's incident, Garran refused to leave the team's safety to chance. He took John aside, overriding his argument that Garran needed every soldier. "No. You were ambushed yesterday. The priesthood of Tauron knows something is going on here. Even though D'Mal is still in Serende, he has a long arm, and will try every way possible to stop this wall from being completed. You'll be attacked again before this is over. I wish I could spare you a company, but you'll have to manage with a squad and a half. I'm permanently assigning you my journeyman, Lenn, whom you might remember. I just sent the paperwork to Aeoven so it's official—*you* now have a journeyman. He remains yours until he promotes to adept, which will be at your say-so. I can make do without a journeyman until I get to Arlen."

John laughed. "I do remember him. He's quite

promising if you want to know the truth. But I don't know what I'll have him do—all I'm doing is building a wall."

"Right. You're just building a wall. He's a capable journeyman, but all *I* have him doing is paperwork. He could use a little education in the advanced magic arts." Garran shrugged. "You might as well handle that since you're actually working with magic. Besides, you did so well teaching him the art of dueling."

John's embarrassment made Garran chuckle. "He'd have learned a little humility eventually. I was in a bad mood that day."

"You're in a mood every day." Garran snorted. "Anyway, Lenn's a good soldier and I've taught him all I can. You need an extra mage protecting your group now. He's sharp and will sense an attacker raising magic nearby if it occurs when you're tranced." He grinned and turned toward the knot of soldiers. "Lenn! I have new orders for you." Lenn hurried over to Garran, greeting John with uncertain respect.

Garran said, "Lenn, you're now attached to John Farmer. You'll assist him, guarding this team while they complete the last half of their task. Once you arrive in Aeoven, you'll remain with him as his journeyman unless Father Rall has a different task for you."

Lenn nodded and made appropriately agreeable noises, but privately he was dismayed and both John and Garran knew it.

Unable to argue with Garran's logic, John acquiesced. "Lenn, I'm glad to have your assistance. Get your things into the back of our wagon, and let your squad know they've been transferred to our team. We'll need two more pack ponies to carry the supplies for the extra horses." He and Garran then turned to the list of tasks Garran still had to accomplish, trying to ensure nothing had been omitted.

Feeling a bit stunned at the way things had changed, Lenn did as he was told. When he and his squad had arrived in Braden with Garran to deconsecrate the Temple, he'd examined the great, black wall that stretched south as far as he could see, reportedly all the way to the Horn of Misery. In his opinion, rumors didn't do it justice.

After getting the supplies he thought they would need, he requisitioned three pack ponies for carrying supplies, making a total of four. He decided to err on the side of caution, getting the fourth to carry the several large tents and other gear Garran was equipping them with, as the food had to go in the wagon.

Before Garran departed once again, he drew the group of mages off to one side.

Zan greeted Lenn, who clasped his shoulder and grinned. "John's really easygoing. You'll like working with him." He didn't notice Lenn's look of shocked disbelief. "I'm Edwin's journeyman. This will be fun, just like old times."

Speaking to Edwin, Garran quietly explained his conviction that the Temple had to have a secret access to the valley, even if it was never used. "I don't care where you put it, although this seems like as good a place as any. I know you want to seal it off, but how else will the Hero Foretold be able to sneak into the lost city when his time has come?"

Reluctantly, Edwin agreed. "This place is too obvious, so perhaps not actually at the old gate. What it will be and what the key to the new entrance is must remain a secret known only to the six of us and to the Holy Father and his successors. I have an idea, and it won't be too hard, but it'll take more time than we originally planned today." He'd had no sleep and was tired, as were the others, but they were all determined to press on as far as they could that day. "If it works, I'll drop a note to you tonight using my air magic."

Garran and his soldiers headed for the gates. The others mounted up and followed him, bidding him and his squad goodbye in the early light. After the Abbott had disappeared into the mists that hugged the river, Edwin's group stood outside the western gate.

Lenn and his men shut the gates, and closing their eyes, Edwin and Zan concentrated and dropped the large wooden bar inside, locking them out of the empty city. Working about four furlongs back from the wall, and employing his earth-magic as carefully as he could, Edwin knit the new spells into what they'd done previously.

Lenn felt like he didn't know Zan anymore. It was as if the man who'd been his roommate in the novice barracks had been replaced by a much older stranger. He wondered if Zan knew how much he'd changed.

He was utterly intimidated by John Farmer, but somehow he was stuck as his assistant. How that was going to go, he didn't know, because John had a reputation for being hard to work with. Then there was the fact that John had been reinstated as the commander of the Temple militia, which made him doubly his boss. The man had rather sharply handed him his ass in a hat when Lenn had gotten cocky with him in the dueling arena. Everyone who'd witnessed it was still laughing at his expense.

Friedr, the man acknowledged as the Temple's finest warrior, had been grievously injured, his crippled leg now encased in a heavy brace. From the corners of his eyes, he watched as the warrior struggled to walk even with the assistance of his staff. That in itself was difficult for Lenn to grasp—what could have happened to him that an adept healer like Edwin couldn't heal? Clearly, the story that the four had been on a standard healing journey had been a cover for a more covert quest.

And Christoph, Zan's father, had died on that journey. Having witnessed his father's death was likely the cause of Zan's perpetually serious expression. Lenn couldn't imagine what such an experience would be like—it must have been hell. He suddenly realized it might have occurred in the same battle during which Friedr had been so gravely injured.

Friedr's voice, talking to Edwin, startled Lenn out of his ruminations. "Let's get this over with."

Lenn stationed his men so that no approach was unguarded, his senses on alert for anything, man or beast, that might want to stop them completing the task. As he observed the surroundings, he also watched the group who now worked in a trance.

About fifteen minutes into the spell, the hairs on Lenn's arms stood on end as the air around him changed. Intense magic eddied around the four working mages. From what he could tell, the whirling mass of power was focused on the four swords. The thought of handling that much power made him queasy.

Lenn observed in silent disbelief as the four mages

wove their magic into an even larger spell. He was unable to follow half of it, as it was healing magic. The elements he *was* able to sense were woven so rapidly he couldn't follow how it was done, other than Edwin was leading it.

After a while, the outline of a door the size of a normal entryway formed. Visible only to Lenn, it was north of where the West gate-towers had once stood. The new entry was dwarfed by the wall but was clearly defined to his mage-sight by the elements of fire and lightning. It appeared just as the air around him changed, manifesting as a glowing orange-red line that flared, then faded and vanished as if by command. Immediately, three brick-sized shapes of the same orange-red formed within the space where the door had been, also created of fire and lightning, emerging in a deliberate sequence, and then also vanishing. Lenn realized that what he was witnessing was the creation of the magic key to unlocking the secret door.

In less than an hour, the new wall stretched flawlessly where a gate wide enough for four large wagons to pass through abreast had once stood. No sign of the old opening remained, although it was likely within the new wall.

When it was completed, the four mages raised a shield, interwoven with magic Lenn couldn't quite sense, but the shield took longer than closing up the hole in the wall had. Once again, the hair on his body rose as the elements swirled and the unseen shield fell into place over the now seamless expanse, making it unapproachable.

From his point of view as a mage, the shield was the most miraculous part of the ramparts. Lenn couldn't look at the other mages, feeling as beneath their notice as a bug.

Dropping out of the link when they'd finished, Edwin rose and crossed to stand beside Lenn, gazing at his handiwork, followed by John. "This took much longer than usual. We usually do the shield first because it takes so much chi to raise it, and the wall is nothing too special, just a glorified dirt fence. But this time, we had to seal off the old gate and create the secret entry. I made it so it opens into what was the old muster-room for the gate guards, a place that should either go unused or become a storeroom, as there are no windows." He turned to Lenn. "It looks as it should to me. I don't sense any weak spots. Do you?"

Edwin was so unpretentious about it that Lenn stared at him. He pulled himself together and opened his senses fully to the shield, examining it meticulously, answering as if an instructor was testing him. "There's no weakness that I can sense. I can't sense healing chi, but I know it must be in there because a force binds the elements, one just outside my grasp."

John said, "Good. You have dependable sensing ability, which is why you can predict an opponent's moves in the dueling arena. I need you to open those senses every time we do this, and if you detect even a hint of any weakness in the shield, ever, we need to know before we move on."

Edwin grinned at his dad's seriousness, his somber face lighting. "I hope you won't, but you may notice something we don't. We need every eye on this."

"This seems solid and unbreakable to me. I can't imagine what I could sense that you won't."

Edwin turned back, surprised. "Every mage sees

VALLEY OF SORROWS

things a little differently. When it's something we've created, we see what we want or expect to see. We're doing it on no sleep, and have to make up two extra days that we lost here."

John agreed. "We could inadvertently leave a weak area where the shield could be breached. Having your fresh eyes along to inspect our work is a huge relief."

Lenn asked, "Sir, about the secret doorway. It's composed of fire and lightning. Why is it made of only those two elements and not all four?"

John nodded. "Good. You were paying attention. We met a friend in the most unlikely of places, one who must remain in the valley to minister to those who remain children of Aeos in secret. He told us the new governor can't sense those two elements of Aeos's magic, but he does have full use of Tauron's magic."

Edwin said, "We hope we've done this in such a way that he won't be able to find the secret gate. We used spirit to weave the rune for stealth into the shield for the door along with the healing chi. At least, I hope the rune works to keep it hidden."

Lenn thought for a moment about the person John had mentioned, wondering who it could have been. "I should have realized some of our people would have to remain there, risking their lives to continue their work for Aeos. It only makes sense. What a sad day—we're abandoning them."

John laid his hand on Lenn's shoulder, surprising him. "We haven't abandoned them. They've chosen this task and they do it with all their hearts. We each serve Aeos in our own way."

The squad mounted up, and the four mages climbed into the wagon. Standing on the running-board,

Lenn said, "I'll continue to ride my horse, if you don't mind sir, unless you need me in the wagon. I'm going to ride ahead with Reni, my sergeant. We've six soldiers to add to our roster, so we have some recalculating to do. Extra rations have been accounted for and also extra feed for the horses."

John agreed. "I saw you commandeered four pack-ponies. Good work. We'll have to watch the footing in some places, so pass that along. The road we're taking is not well used and it's likely to be rough, which will slow us down quite a bit." Lenn jumped down and John chucked the reins to get the team moving.

After they'd traveled a while, John said to Friedr, who sat beside him, "We need to finish this wall and get back to Aeoven. I suspect I'm not the only one here who'd like to sleep in my own bed for a change." His smile, as he glanced back at his son, was tentative.

Edwin held his sketch pad but sat staring into the distance with a false smile plastered on his features. Zan had insisted on taking Lenn's second-best shirt to mend. He'd collected all the mending from the squad, earning smiles all around.

"No," replied Friedr. "You're not alone in that desire." He was tired and had nothing to divert himself with while he rode along like so much cargo, lamenting the fact he wasn't able to walk or even ride a horse with his leg in the brace. Edwin had cast ease on him so he wasn't in pain, but his mind would give him no rest. His sense of guilt regarding the young, dead mages was overwhelming. He desperately wished Zan had punished him as Graylor thought he should.

From the rear of the cart, Zan looked up, as did Edwin, unable to block out Friedr's misery. Linking,

Zan sent a thought to Edwin. "It was a mistake any of us could have made. They were casualties of this disgusting war." Edwin agreed, and still linked, they inserted several loops into Friedr's unconscious mind, making him "forget" his terrible mistake.

Abruptly Friedr started, wondering what he'd just been thinking of. "Sorry John. I must have dozed off for a moment. I think I'll use this time to organize my notes." He pulled out the quest diary, making notes regarding the morning's work and the new additions to the team. Thanks to Zan's intervention, his eyes skipped over certain passages, not seeing them.

John glanced from the corners of his eyes at Friedr and then looked back to Zan, who nodded, confirming his suspicion.

The cart rolled down the muddy, rutted road, inching toward the Horn of the Moon, swaying and lurching in the cool, damp, grey of the late harvest morning.

Chapter 21
The Keep of Mal Evol

"Wish me luck." Lourdan embraced Stefyn one last time before stepping through the gateway. "I'll be waiting here tonight when the portal next opens."

"I do wish you good fortune. More than you know. Everything depends on this." Stefyn stepped back, unable to pass through the portal because he was carrying the spell. "I'll have the strength to open it again tonight your time since I'll have rested for a full day by our time here. Seven o'clock—we'll have dinner here and you can tell me all about it then."

Lourdan paused, gazing back at him with one eyebrow raised. "You'll already know all about it. You'll be watching my mind as you always do, and as you think I'm unaware of. But we can talk about it later if it pleases you." His smile was warm as the portal closed. The image of his rooms in the Palace of Dreams faded, and the chamber he now stood in was reflected, as if in a large mirror.

The room he'd stepped into had been created from a large storeroom just for him. His valet, Relf, had created a private place where he could come and go without the legions knowing his movements, with the all-important portal in the corner and hundreds of books covering the walls. It was the perfect study for him, a place he would be comfortable.

As yet, only Stefyn had the ability to open the portal. *One day I'll be able to make a portal,* thought Lourdan, filled with anticipation. He had access to immense, well-stocked libraries in two worlds. Libraries were his favorite places, and he would enjoy the hunt for that particular knowledge as much as actually gaining mastery of the spell. Stefyn wouldn't share his knowledge, but he'd found the information somewhere, and so would Lourdan.

When he did, he'd create a gate they could both walk through, a portal that could sustain itself, as the records at Pasanabira said the old masters were able to do. The most powerful high priests were jealous of their knowledge and always took their secrets to their graves. Lourdan reasoned they must have written something down for their own use. At a priest's death, all the papers and books in his library were taken to the monastery at Pasanabira. Of course, it would be in a secret code if the information existed. That was one of the first things he'd learned as an acolyte, and all his own work was written in code that only he had the key to.

But he would find the information and unlock it. He loved nothing more than a good puzzle and he would have all the time in the world to work that one out.

He turned back to the mirror, seeing the reflection of a handsome, young man with dark, curly hair, someone Lourdan thought he should know, but didn't. Superimposed over the young man's image was the profile of an immense minotaur. Since his remaking, he'd been beset with myriad conflicting memories and no longer recognized himself. Both the man and the minotaur were true reflections, and both were seen when any child of Tauron viewed him.

He now knew he'd been born to a fairly prosperous

family in the Valley of Mal Evol, east of Mal Evol City. He had demonstrated some skill at healing and had been accepted to train as a leash for the Hounds of Tauron. His training had been complete and he was about to gain his own coven when he'd begun to demonstrate the ability to sense and wield both earth and water.

He now remembered all of that—and having his past back didn't mean as much as he'd thought it would.

It was as if it had happened to someone else. Since regaining his memories, he'd realized his life before the priesthood didn't matter, just as Stefyn had told him. What did matter was everything that had happened *after* the remaking. Only with the sacrifice of his old life could he have been reborn as Lourdan.

Now he was unstoppable, both as a sorcerer and a warrior. He had his gifts, his ability to wield Tauron's magic with nearly as much skill as Stefyn. He was given a powerful staff to amplify the magic of Aeos that he was able to use. The god had named it Glaüdt when he bestowed it upon him. The staff enabled Lourdan to combine the two widely different magics, something he suspected Stefyn couldn't do. As a defensive weapon, he could use Glaüdt the same as any normal staff, and he was adept at disarming and killing an opponent with it. He rarely needed to do that anymore, though. Even barehanded he was a better fighter than nearly any warrior of Tauron, and they all knew it.

To counterbalance his slight build as compared to those born in Serende, Lourdan had been given a bull koudah, Brëcht, a rare beast that looked like a dragon with no wings. Instead of flying, the koudah ran on two immense hind-legs. The creature would enable him to outrun the legions when he led them to battle, a mount few in the legions could ever control or hope to ride. Brëcht was so dangerous that only Lourdan could approach or ride him. The koudah handlers were terrified of the creature, which allowed them to perform only the most basic tasks of feeding and grooming him.

If all went as planned, within three weeks Lourdan intended to mount an invasion and take the city of Braden from the goddess. Once he controlled Braden, the rest of Neveyah would fall. He grinned, thinking that with Brëcht to carry him, the legions would be hard-pressed to keep up with him. He would never allow them to forget who it was that controlled the beast, and who also controlled them. Control was everything.

Composing himself, Lourdan walked out of the portal room into the dark passageway. To the right, at the far end of the corridor, stood the heavy door leading to the dungeon and the altar room that would soon be his domain.

Casting his mind out, he sensed Dalgek waiting for him above in the conservatory rather than the dungeon. Turning left he went up the long, narrow, sloping corridor to the private, residential area of the keep. He came to a small door and stepped though, his eyes adjusting quickly as he emerged into the bright daylight of the vast, glass-enclosed room. "Honored Dalgek. I see you're well-prepared for the day's work, as always."

"Your Worship." The enormous minotaur greeted him formally, bowing low. Four lesser minotaurs knelt beside him, their foreheads touching the floor. "These priests await your bidding, as do I. This way, your mightiness. When you're free later, I have some other news that will require your attention. But it can't be dealt with until you've established control of the throne. I must remind you—the throne proved deadly to the two priests sent to take Lork's place."

He was led to a small door concealed under a stairwell. Dalgek stood back to allow Lourdan to enter.

"Remain here."

With Glaüdt to light his way, Lourdan entered the narrow, sloping passage, one cared out of the bedrock. After spiraling downward for a long time he came to another door, identical to the one at the top.

The chamber was lit by a brilliant white light, originating in the clear crystal of the throne and he blinked as he emerged the long passage. He gazed at the immense skeleton trapped within and the hairs on his arms stood on end, as the elements rode invisible currents.

He stood in a river of power.

Awed, he saw the immense throne had been hewn from a massive shaft of crystal ribboned with marble. It had been carved in the shape of a gigantic oak tree, its delicate branches swaying above the seat, moving as if in the wind. Static charges sent occasional lightning bolts high above to the canopy of the throne. The room was alive with the faint, discordant music of a thousand crystal leaves rustling in the unseen breeze made of magic. A few motes of dust hung sparkling in the air, riding the currents.

Stefyn had assured him that he bore enough blood of D'Mal in his veins for the throne to recognize him, and he had to trust his lover was correct. Clearing his mind, he walked to the throne, and placed both his palms against the crystal beside the skeleton, speaking the words Stefyn had taught him, meaning them with all his heart. "The blood of the keepers flows through my veins. I was born to care for you for all my days. Allow me to tend the soil, allow me to guide the people."

Locked within the stone, the skeleton god turned to face him, its sightless sockets scanning him, recognizing him, though not as having the blood of the keepers in his veins. The god saw he had not a drop of the blood in him. He also saw the taint of the Bull God was now upon him and, unknowing, this child of Aeos lived a lie.

He was dangerous.

Still, even though the healer was as much a prisoner of Tauron as the god himself was, the man before him had removed the poison and had the most crucial task yet to complete. Although he'd been radically changed since the day he cured him of the poison, this man was the enabler, the prophesied one who would open the way for the Hero Foretold. This was the sign the god, Ariend, had waited for. The end of his captivity loomed.

I will accept you.

Lourdan shivered as the words echoed in his soul—he hadn't been told that would happen.

Lourdan sensed the god scrutinizing him as he walked to the foot of the long stairs leading to the seat of the throne, following his passage. The empty sockets observed as he climbed each step. When he stood at the top of the stairs, he looked down through the crystal seat of the throne, seeing the bony face regarding him. He turned, knowing the god still stared and sat.

As if he'd been blind before, Lourdan's mind opened and visions of all kinds, both mundane and mysterious, inundated him. He saw the land, scarred and dying as if it had been poisoned, felt the deep sadness of the god within the throne. He sensed the god stirring and soothed him, promising to make the land verdant again.

He cast his mind out toward the gap, where a wall of mist prevented him from seeing all the way to the city of Braden. Stefyn had told him of the misty barrier known as the great shield. It barred his magic-sight but Lourdan saw that it lay well beyond Mal Evol City, near to where he knew the Temple city of Braden was. He sensed something beyond the barrier, but couldn't see what it was.

The barrier of gray fog had been raised at the end of the war by Aeos, keeping Stefyn from knowing her plans. It meant he had no control of the legions when they ventured beyond it, forcing him to rely on erratic generals. Thus, no large army had gone beyond that barrier since the last Great War.

Toward the west, in several round pockets, he could sense nothing, as if each blank spot had been shielded from his view. Those foggy, gray patches stretched along the River Morte toward the Mountains of the Moon. Stefyn had warned him of those vague, gray scars in the fabric of the valley. They were of a similar opaqueness as the great shield. It looked as if the renegade, Lork, had been unable to complete the destruction he'd attempted. Lourdan decided he'd have to visit each of them personally, to see what they hid.

Getting accustomed to the way the visions presented themselves one after the other was difficult, but eventually, he gained some control and the stream of information slowed, letting him see more with each glimpse. Lourdan cast his awareness wide, seeing what the exiled nobles in Mal Evol City did, how their slaves tilled the scarred land, and what herd beasts they raised.

He cast his mind further, glancing over the small frontier settlements of the elderly bulls too old to fight, graybeards who lived wild, hunting in packs to feed the legions at the keep. At the edge of his vision, the sod huts of a few more ambitious younger wounded veterans now settled along the edge of the gray barrier on the frontier of the gap, claiming it for Tauron, just inside the shield. He reflected that those hardy souls were far more valuable than the disgraced courtiers who reluctantly did penance in the more civilized parts of the valley nearest the Serende Wall, forcing their slaves to toil, attempting to carve a society from the wilderness.

He'd soon put a stop to that nonsense—those pampered nobles were there because they'd failed Tauron in some way. They'd been given the opportunity to start a new life, but stubbornly clung to the old ways, trying to hang on to the grace and nobility of Serende.

They didn't understand the meaning of exile, but they soon would. No court balls, no fripperies—nothing but simple, hard work was what these courtiers were supposed to do, and they would do it, or else. There would be no slaves, either. Plenty of lands lay fallow, waiting for the freed slaves to till on their own behalf, and freeing them would gain Lourdan a great many loyal followers.

Those wounded men on the frontier at the edge of

his sight—they were tough, old bulls, grateful for the opportunity to own land and thus gain a wife, visibly remade sons of Tauron every one, and battle hardened. Their children would be the first generation of legions born in the valley, the first sons of Tauron to consider the valley their true home. They were the men upon whose shoulders the new society would be built, and their example would lead the others.

Once his curiosity had been satisfied, Lourdan pulled back, his mind spiraling in on the throne where he sat, sensing Stefyn's mental caress as he separated from the link.

Dalgek and his priests bowed as the door to the passage down to the throne room opened, and Lourdan walked through it. "Your mightiness. Praise be to god—it has accepted you."

"It has indeed," said Lourdan. His mind felt confined after the vastness of the throne.

"Now you have control of the throne, I must tell you of news I received this morning—reports of a great wall that has arisen far to the west beyond the barrier, near the Horn of Misery."

VALLEY OF SORROWS

Chapter 22

"We can't risk trying to make another length today," John said quietly to Edwin as they had a quick meal. They were stopped at the second length they'd accomplished after closing up the city. "I'm done in. I can't concentrate and I don't see how you can. It takes too much chi, and this stretch will be the area Lourdan will test most closely."

Frustrated, Edwin shook his head. He wanted to deny it, but couldn't. "You're right, but this puts us really behind. We've lost four days. We don't have a clear timeline anymore—two seasons means nothing now. Zirik said time flows differently in Serende. That accounts for why they could always throw so many warriors at us, but it also means we only have one season, not two, and we've nearly wasted it all. We're really cutting this close." He struggled against his urge to rant about the situation.

John knew how on edge Edwin was, but couldn't offer him much comfort. "Let's, at least, ride on to the next place and make camp there. We can get started as soon as it's light enough, and if we work until the light is completely gone, maybe we can get an extra length built every day."

Edwin agreed. "It won't make up what we've lost, but it'll have to do. As Friedr is always telling me, we must work with what we have."

John gathered the group and explained what they intended. With no further discussion, they pushed on to their next destination.

They found a copse of firs which sheltered them from the wind and rain somewhat. However, the heavy winter rain made their camp a chilly, dismal place. The sentries walked the perimeter as much to stay warm as to watch for trouble. Wrapped in heavy, woolen cloaks, Zan and Lenn sat talking by the fire. Zan's eyes were drawn to the east, and Mal Evol. "Something tells me we're working on borrowed time now."

Lenn shivered at his words. "I fear you may be right. Everyone in Mal Evol must know about the wall by now. Someone will be sent to stop you, and it'll happen soon."

That evening, Lenn assigned the rotation for watches, categorically refusing to allow the four mages who were building the wall to stand watch. Surprisingly, John became every inch the offended military commander, demanding to stand his watch.

Edwin quietly prepared supper for the group, covertly watching as the scene unfolded. Feeling rather entertained by it, he grinned widely as John stood in the younger man's face, shouting. "I've stood watch every night on every mission I've ever undertaken for more years than you've been alive. I won't shirk my duty just because I'm older now."

"I mean no disrespect, and would never demean you in such a way. Neither you nor anyone else on your team is incapable of standing a watch. However, your work requires that you be fully rested. You'll make better speed tomorrow if you have a full night's rest." Despite fearing he'd made a misstep, he remained firm. "If we're attacked, my men and I will deal with it, but tonight and every night hereafter you will rest as much as you can and conserve your chi."

John looked like he was going to explode. Lenn forestalled him with a raised hand. "Sir. No other mages have the ability to do what you four are doing—I most certainly don't. This is far more important than any task the Temple has ever undertaken. Clearly it takes all your chi to accomplish it. Allow us to do our job and we'll ensure you can do yours."

Hearing the ruckus, Friedr limped over and intervened. "He's right, John. We didn't do nearly as much today as we could have if we hadn't stayed up all night picking over the bones of that mindbender. Stop being such a bully." He winked at Lenn.

For a moment, John stood silent. Then he grinned wryly. "I was out of line. I apologize. You're right, Lenn. My worst failing is I always feel I have to do everything myself. If you never learn anything else, learn this: don't fall into that trap."

Lenn grinned. "I understand, sir." He moved off to the other side of the fire, feeling more than a little out of step in the rarified company he now traveled with.

That feeling disappeared as Zan dropped down beside him once again, handing him a cup filled with soup while Edwin handed cups around to the others. Friedr passed around the bread and cheese, making jokes and setting the group laughing. "John knows you're right. We've just gotten used to fending for ourselves." He grinned. "I'll sleep like a baby, knowing I don't have to get up and freeze my backside in the middle of the night!"

Lenn smiled back. "I'm sorry about your dad. I heard he was killed. Whatever it was that happened to your father, it's left its mark on you, my friend."

"Yes. I suppose it has." Zan had prepared himself to have to discuss it and was glad to get it out of the way. "We couldn't save him and we nearly lost Friedr."

His features fell into their now habitually grim expression. "There were just so many of them. We wouldn't have survived without our swords and their ability to magnify our spells."

Lenn shook his head. "From what I saw today, I can't imagine how they could have beaten you."

"Having John in the link is what enables us to create the shield and the wall."

Lenn nodded. "Before we were called out of Aeoven, John had the top rank of all the duelers."

"I'm not surprised." Zan's thoughts turned inward, seeing the battlefield where he lost his father. "Here's the thing—we couldn't have built this wall with my dad in the link. He'd been given the elements of water and earth, but he was a true healer and his elemental skills were curative. He was unable to use them for battle so he couldn't draw the kind of power in those elements that John or Edwin can. He certainly couldn't move large amounts of earth the way Edwin does, although he could restore vast tracts of land to health, using his healing skills to manipulate the tiniest of organisms." He met Lenn's eyes. "That's what we were doing there. It was a healing journey, just as the Temple let everyone believe. But it was to heal the land, to cleanse the soil. We were trying to stop the Bull God's poison from leaving the valley and taking all of Neveyah."

Lenn's eyes widened. "That seems daft. Pardon me, but it does."

"I know. It *is* crazy when I think logically about it. But *that* was my father's skill—we did it one cell at a time, rather like we're building this wall, healing and shielding as large a patch of soil as we could, and then moving on to the next. Then we had to fight for our lives." Zan shrugged. "We managed to break the spell on the valley, but it cost us dearly."

Lenn sighed. "Your father paid the price with his life. He was a great man." He clasped Zan's shoulder. "But now you're going to see to it that his sacrifice wasn't in vain. He would be proud of you. The wall you're creating and the shield that protects it—I've never seen anything like it. The very look of it chills my blood. You say it takes very little effort to make, but it's because you're able to see both sides of the magic that gives you four the ability to create something so lethal and beautiful. No one else could do this though we all wish we could."

Zan didn't know what to say. "The wall is mostly for show. Edwin's shield is the true work of art and it's what takes most of our chi. Even without the visible wall, nothing could cross it. But this way, they can't see us, either."

"The world will be talking about this for generations to come, and they won't even know a lake is on the other side. The moat is half of the beauty, but the people of Neveyah will only know the boring side."

>>><<<

The next day the team managed to build one more stretch than they normally did before settling into camp in the cold, misty rain. Dampness driven by gusts of wind had everyone feeling the chill. They sat hunched around the fire sipping hot soup, wrapped in their heavy cloaks. John and several of the squad took special care of the horses, making sure they had a temporary shelter.

The attack came just after midnight. Two raggedly dressed men charged the camp and were immediately killed. A third man hung back, away from the campfire, thinking he was well-hidden. Lenn's night vision was as good as Edwin's, and he spotted the man knocking an arrow. He cast a cat-zapper to disable him, and while the man was still on the ground twitching, the squad quickly trussed him up.

With a sword at his throat, the man admitted that he and his brothers didn't want the wall to pass through their land. "It ain't fair. Our family's been here longer than there's been a Temple. We ain't gonna let you take our land."

A large soldier stared down at him. "Ferol—I remember you. You were given a large tract on the other side of the River Fleet. We were through here a week ago and you boys were making ready to move out then. What happened to change your mind?"

"Didn't change our minds. Never intended to do it, did we? You cutting us off from Mal Evol City can't be allowed. It's the only market for what we grow. Ain't no other place as will buy turnips most years and that's all will grow here. Don't know how to farm nothing else. Teller said you'd come this way soon enough. We figured we could end it now." Ferol grimaced, struggling against the rope that held him. "Didn't count on that bloody wall of black evil going up so fast. Has to be the devil's work, just like Teller said."

John emerged from the shadows. "If you can grow one thing, you can grow another, so don't try to play the ignorant hill-man with me. I know you're lying." He turned to the squad. "This man knows Teller, so he knows more than he's saying. We'll have Zan question him."

Lenn looked down at the prisoner and grinned. "This could be fun after all."

They dropped him in front of Zan, who immediately delved him. He'd barely begun searching for the spells that bound the man when Ferol's eyes rolled up in his head. Suddenly he spasmed, and died. Edwin poured a healing spell into him, to no avail.

"Danhk!" Friedr's expletive cut through the darkness. "He's gone. Save your chi, Edwin—he's well beyond our reach." Shocked, the three healers stared at each other.

John swore violently, his words making even the hardened soldiers blanch. "I told you, Friedr—this is how these people work. The next one will have to be treated like you did Graylor. We'll put him to sleep before he knows what's happened then Zan can ferret out the spells that bind him before he wakes."

The four mages had difficulty going back to sleep but finally did, and woke up the next day rested enough to do their task.

VALLEY OF SORROWS

Chapter 23

The first major attack came in the wild lands along the Falls Creek, well to the east of the River Fleet. The four mages had no idea a battle had ensued until they emerged from the trance to find two dead minotaurs and many of their own soldiers severely wounded.

Friedr linked with John, who drew healing chi through Riverbinder and channeled it to him, healing the two with the worst wounds. Zan and Edwin drew enough chi through their own swords to handle the rest of the injuries, which were minor, and then turned to disposing of the minotaur corpses.

Edwin said, "Thank Aeos these two didn't have any poisoned blades. We need to conserve our chi for the next length of the wall, so we'll have to bury these corpses the hard way. But we can bury them together in one pit." He took a shovel out of the wagon. "I'm pretty much out of chi." He tossed a pick-axe to a husky soldier named Borlam, who caught it by the handle, grinning. "Who else is uninjured?"

"Just me and Mage Lenn, sir." Serrel was a large man from the far north, with a heavy barbarian accent.

Zan, Serrel, and Lenn got shovels and set to work alongside Edwin and Borlam.

As they dug, Edwin said, "I wondered when our luck would run out. They know we're here and now we're going to have to fight for every step of the way."

Lenn winced. "They were tougher than anything I've ever fought before. We were lucky there were only two of them and they weren't prepared for me flinging magic at them," said Lenn. "They must have figured we were just soldiers and you were easy pickings.

Lightning's not my best element, but I'm getting pretty good with cat-zappers. It stuns them well enough so I can get in a few good whacks. The next bunch that pisses me off is going home with their tails on fire even if Garran does insist it's bad form unless you're outnumbered. They've no call to attack us—they're in *our* land."

Edwin agreed. "Fair doesn't count, when it comes to getting this wall finished, so use whatever skill it takes to do the job."

Zan glared at Edwin, and said, "But don't use fire, unless you absolutely have to." Lenn nodded uncertainly. Zan explained, "If you use that element John will go battle-crazy and he'll be useless. He can't help it—it's something that happened during the war." Understanding dawned in Lenn's eyes. The four continued shoveling dirt to one side, enlarging the hole.

Edwin sighed. "You're right, Zan. I wasn't thinking about anything but expediency and I forgot about dad's problem." He looked over at the two corpses. "I think these fellows were just scouts, sent to see what we were doing. They didn't report back so the next group will be larger. You'll have to be prepared to yank us out of the trance."

"How can I do that? The noise of the battle didn't even penetrate—if you didn't hear that ruckus, how can *I* drop you out of it?"

"You know that magic jab we use when we're teaching shielding?"

Lenn shuddered. "Ugh. I hate it."

"We all do. I despised Aeolyn for it when she was tutoring me." Edwin chuckled. "But it'll get my attention, and once I'm out of the trance, the others will follow. We'll likely still have enough chi to take care of any attackers short of an army at that point."

"Do you think you and Zan could do that air-thing you do and scout the area once you've regained a little chi? It's a lot more accurate than regular scouting, and I don't want to be surprised by any more minotaurs. I hate being ambushed."

"Of course. But we'll have to eat something first. At least, I will. We'll try to scout with air-magic more often. I suppose I've been too preoccupied with…things that may be happening in Aeoven. Feel free to remind me." Edwin paused his digging and looked at the hole. "I guess this is large enough. Let's roll these boys in here and move on to the next stop."

Darkness had fallen. John and Edwin had gone to their blankets, glad to have dry tents to protect them from the weather. Friedr sat talking to Zan and listening to the rain hissing in the fire. They paused as sounds of a skirmish at the perimeter of their camp shattered the quiet of the night. The noise died down as quickly as it started, and was followed by the voice of a soldier calling for Lenn, who used his magic to bury the corpses.

"Rats from the sounds of it," said Zan. "That's the second group tonight."

Friedr agreed. "Rats are probably the easiest for Lourdan or D'Mal to locate and use to harass us, in this part of the gap."

Lenn approached the fire, leading a soldier who bled profusely. Zan said, "Friedr, I believe it's your turn."

Chuckling, Friedr rose and healed the wounded

man. Sitting back down, he said to Zan and Lenn, "I suspect we'll have a lot of practice healing minor injuries from here on out."

Handing Lenn and the soldier each a tin cup of hot soup, Zan said, "Rats are vicious. But your squad handles them with a minimum of fuss."

The soldier returned to his post and Lenn sipped his soup, enjoying the warmth of the cup. "I think tonight is just the beginning. I'm doubling the sentries. From now on everyone in my squad is to sleep geared up and ready to fight."

Friedr nodded. "We've all had to do that at one time or another. You don't rest as well, but it's better than being caught unprepared. I don't mind sleeping geared up."

Lenn asked, "Zan, could you scout to see if any minotaurs have moved into our area since Edwin looked earlier?"

Zan sent his senses out, scouting the area. "Not within my range. Several more packs of rats are prowling the area. I'll look again before I go to bed."

"Good. You four can still sleep unarmored. You absolutely must be well-rested." Lenn caught Friedr's look. "If I think it's too dangerous, I promise to tell you. But for now, we can handle the rats."

Friedr nodded. "I'm getting soft, what with having a dry place to sleep, and all. I suppose I should enjoy the luxury of having guards, and just let your squad get on with it."

Lenn sensed his former weapons instructor's bitterness, thinking his angst was probably more about his crippling injury than anything else. "The squad is proud to be a part of this, Friedr. Not one of them is complaining or shirking their duty. These men and women are career soldiers and will remember guarding you four while you raised this wall as the highpoint of their time in the militia."

VALLEY OF SORROWS

Chapter 24
Lourdan

Lourdan emerged from the portal in the barracks. Hard on his heels were seven squads, giving him seventy new soldiers to add to the five hundred he and Stefyn had already sent over the course of two days. His boot heels rang on the stones as he strode between the lines of soldiers to Dalgek, who awaited him with scarcely concealed impatience. The priest bowed. "Your Worship. I have everything arranged, exactly as you commanded. We're ready to leave as soon as the last man is through the gate."

Lourdan couldn't see any other option. Ten more companies were on their way to the portal in the Serende Wall, but it would be two weeks before they arrived at Braden, and he couldn't wait for them. "How far has that accursed wall grown since I was first notified?"

"Perhaps twenty leagues. I sent out scouts, but they haven't reported back."

"How long before they have us completely cut off?"

Dalgek grimaced. "Less than a week if they continue spending magic at the rate they are now. Their goddess must be taking an active hand in this. There's no other explanation."

"No doubt you're correct. I'll have to look for myself, and see what I can do to stop them. Failing that, we'll have to stall them until the bulk of our forces arrive." Lourdan turned and strode through the connecting wing of the keep, walking quickly toward the throne room. Dalgek followed the requisite one step behind him, with the difference in the length of their strides causing the much larger minotaur's gait to become a dainty scurry, in his effort to remain the correct distance behind his boss. Lourdan said, "Have you discovered how the construction of this monstrosity got so far advanced before we heard about it?"

"The area is mostly unpopulated. It's because of the magic shield they raised at the end of the war— people don't like the way the land out there feels, so they stay in the better part of the valley. Aeos has constructed this thing well on their side of the valley, where we wouldn't see or sense it. Our spy, Teller, sent a message informing me of it, as did several old bulls living out there, but, as I wasn't in Mal Evol City, I didn't get the news until the day I informed you. But my under-priest, Jennec, immediately acted."

"What did he do?"

"As you know, the indigenous people of Mal Evol are not permitted to own weapons or learn to fight. With no legions available, Jennec sent a retired beastmaster, Thorken, to slow them down."

"That makes some sense, although I can't imagine what a beastmaster could do."

"He did make an effort. There are relatively few large beasts in the gap, and no water wraiths at that end of the valley. Thorken was forced to resort to thunder-cows. He used his ability to gather the beasts west of Mal Evol city into one large herd, and then turned them on the priests of Aeos."

"Thunder-cows?" Lourdan stopped short, forcing Dalgek to stop suddenly to avoid stepping on him. "God preserve me."

"Exactly. It didn't go well—apparently the priests

of Aeos have a strong beastmaster of their own. This priest snatched control of the stampede away from Thorken, who was our best. The stranger turned the herd back into the lands around Mal Evol City, but until the herd disperses it's making supplying the city difficult." Dalgek fell silent, flinching under Lourdan's gaze.

Lourdan's words fell coldly into the silence. "You understand that the people who live in the city serve Tauron and must be fed regardless of whether or not your constabulary gets a few well-deserved shocks. I will not have food shortages causing unrest. Assign more guards, but get the food into the city. Am I clear?"

"Yes, your worship. It will be done as soon as I leave your presence."

"Good. What of this incompetent beastmaster who allowed such a thing to happen?"

"He's dead. The thunder-cows were mainly diversionary. They did stall the priests of Aeos until he found a better beast to set on their trail, a chimaera. However, their beastmaster was able to counter him. Thorken was suddenly wrenched out of the chimaera's mind and went mad. His son was forced to kill him to protect the family."

"A chimaera—now *that* was creative." Lourdan began walking again, Dalgek obediently trailing one step behind. When at last he spoke, Lourdan's voice was unruffled although his words were firm. "There *will* be a properly trained, indigenous fighting force here, created from the new sons of Tauron born of this valley. You and I will see to their education, training, and remaking." They arrived at the door to the passage that led to the Throne of Stone and Bone. "You may wait here for me. The throne is a bit...capricious. I need you back at the altar in the church in Mal Evol City, so from this day on, I think an under-priest can handle the duties in the dungeon here. I'll reside here to ensure he doesn't develop delusions of grandeur as Lork did."

Dalgek shuddered. "Yes...unlike the first two unfortunates, Truuk had only just entered the room. I'm sure he was startled to find his insides so suddenly on the outside."

"Surprising, I'm sure. But at least, he was expendable. Fortunately, I'm able to exercise some degree of control over the throne and through me, the Highest is still able to govern the combined Worlds of Tauron."

"It is indeed fortunate, your worship."

Dalgek's sincere lack of ambition made Lourdan nauseous. He smiled as he closed and locked the passage door behind him. Any other priest would have known what was going on in the gap long before it had gotten so far advanced, despite it being on the other side of the veil. On the positive side, there was no need to compel Dalgek's loyalty. That had to be good for something.

Despite his lack of creativity, Dalgek would do well enough now that Lourdan had taken control. He could go back to offering up sacrifices and converting the children of Aeos to the worship of the Bull God, two things he was good at.

Lourdan snorted. *Sending a herd of thunder-cows to stop the goddess. If it weren't so ludicrous, I would weep.* He came to the end of the dark passageway and entered, closing the door behind him.

When he emerged from the throne room, he was

silent. Though he was still unable to see beyond the veil, the soil had told him the wall still grew, inching toward the Horn of the Moon. The area was remarkably devoid of people, but he'd seized the minds of a group of old bulls, minotaurs too elderly to be of use in the army and who were hunting in the area, diverting them to attack the priests of Aeos. He'd also found several pockets of rat-people at varying distances and did the same.

Striding back to the barracks, he ground his teeth in frustration. Those old fellows wouldn't stop the Temple, nor would the rats. But they would slow them down, hopefully enough that he just might be able to meet them before they cut the valley off completely if he left now with the troops he currently had at the keep.

But they would have to travel at a quick trot.

He had to somehow make his small force do the journey in three days, or be sealed in the valley forever. He would have to find a way to save Neveyah for Tauron—only the strong survived. He'd proven he was stronger than the Circle of Six, and now he would have to be stronger than the priesthood of Aeos.

VALLEY OF SORROWS

Chapter 25

Constant attacks by roving bands of rat people slowed the team, although Lenn and his men took care of them. In spite of the incessant rain, they still managed to get what they thought of as their quota done each day. Now they were closing in on the Horn of the Moon and would have the wall finished by the end of the week if all went well. Every day the wall rose higher, swooping further upward to meet the top of the Escarpment, just as it had at the Horn of Misery.

The only problem was, the higher the wall, the more time it took. The heavy rain was a nuisance, filling the moat as fast as it was excavated and making a morass of the earth upon which they sat. But once again, the low clouds hid the top of the wall and the Horn of the Moon, just as they had done in the south.

The group was slowed nearly to a crawl. They traveled one of the most rural paths in the gap, one with only two farmsteads located on it, both empty, but offering a welcome shelter from the weather. In many low-lying areas the track was in terrible condition, muddy and rutted, making it difficult for the team to pull the wagon with any speed. And without the wagon, Friedr would have been stranded as the mud made treacherous footing for both the horses and men. "We're still moving faster than I can walk," said Friedr, trying to find something positive in their predicament. He grinned at the grizzled older soldier, Reni, who rode beside him. "It pains me to admit it."

"Well, crippled or not, I wouldn't want to have another duel scheduled against you, just so you know." Reni's deep chuckle rumbled. "The last time they put me up against you, I ended up wearing my arse as a hat, and that was just you and a practice blade, with no magic. You might not be as nimble as you were, but I expect you're still deadly."

"If an enemy is kind enough to get within my arm's reach, I likely am," Friedr replied. "This staff Edwin made me is much longer than the usual healer's staff, and I've discovered it has other useful properties. It's become my weapon of choice."

"It's quite the rat basher," Reni agreed, making everyone riding in the wagon laugh. "You broke the skull on that poor thing with no effort at all."

"Rat Basher—I think Reni just named your staff, Friedr." Edwin's snickers floated back to the others, who followed as the wagon lurched through the wind and rain.

"It's as good a name as any." Friedr laughed and to the others he appeared in good humor but, in reality, nothing seemed to divert him from the cold and damp. When he'd been able to walk, his body heat had kept him warm in the worst of conditions, but now, riding along like a sack of turnips, he shivered constantly, feeling every drop that worked its way down his neck. He drew his hood closer around his face, looking up with gratitude when Lenn layered another cloak over him. "Thank you. I used to have a little fat to keep me warm. But I lost it when I was so ill."

Lenn nodded and remounted his horse, riding beside the wagon. "We can't afford for you to get sick. You're the only one who can use that sword."

When the wagon became stuck in a low, muddy bog, John and Edwin climbed down and each took a bridle, encouraging the horses while Zan and several others pushed from behind. Eventually, they were through the marsh and able to go a bit faster.

Watching all the drama from the safety of his perch on the wagon, Friedr thought that at least driving the wagon gave him something to do. He seldom allowed his frustration at being crippled to show, but it was there, lurking under the surface along with the nagging worry that his wife would find him repulsive once she saw his horribly scarred leg. Since the day he woke up in the cave with his life in tatters, the fear that Aeolyn would turn away from him had been slowly taking root, always in the back of his mind.

On top of that, he felt guilty for looking forward to seeing his children. Every time he thought of them, he remembered that Edwin's premature baby had died, and his son was living with Aeolyn. His friend had become silent and withdrawn, and never mentioned the situation, but it was clear he hadn't forgotten. And now that Friedr was a healer, he knew what could go wrong and feared for his own unborn child, wondering how he would deal with such a thing.

Edwin startled Friedr out of his circular thoughts. "Let's stop here. It's as good a place as any to raise the next section of the wall."

>>><<<

Shocked by the magic jab, Edwin dropped out of the trance, leaping to his feet and pulling Friedr upright. Zan handed Friedr his staff and they set to work, helping the squad kill the band of six minotaurs that had ambushed them. The section of wall was unfinished, standing half as tall as it should be and jagged.

John knocked the feet out from under his foe with a water spell and slit his throat. Edwin tripped a minotaur and stabbed him through the heart. Two converged on Friedr, seeing him as weak. Friedr's staff cracked one across the skull so hard the bones broke—a loud, snapping sound. At the same time, he sliced his other attacker with Dragonstorm, gutting him. Zan ran the prone minotaur through the heart.

As soon as it had begun, the melee was over. Gazing down at the fallen minotaurs and back to Friedr, Lenn said, "You're a demon with that staff in one hand and your magic sword in the other. The enemy hasn't got a chance against you. No one does."

Friedr snorted. "I don't want to give one of these fellows the opportunity to poison me again."

Friedr, Zan, and Edwin healed the wounded soldiers, while John stood with Lenn, examining the corpses.

"These men are old warriors. They aren't armed for war. They're armed for hunting." John's quiet comment got the others' attention and soon everyone stood around the bodies.

"How do you tell, sir? They all look alike to me." The soldiers echoed Lenn's question.

John held up a spear. "This is how they hunt. Spears are good for bringing down food, but not for fighting in close quarters, which is what just happened. These are old bachelors. See how grey they are? You can tell they're unbonded by looking at their clothes. Their jackets are roughly stitched together from several rams' fleeces. They're utilitarian clothes made for warmth, not protection in a battle. If they were bonded, their women would have made them with an eye to beauty. If these were going to battle, they'd be wearing heavy leather jackets made from thunder-cow hide and breastplates."

"It felt like they weren't in control of their minds." Zan's words drew a nod of agreement from Edwin. "I don't know who controlled them, but they weren't thinking for themselves."

John agreed. "Lourdan must be at the keep. We've no time to waste. We must finish up here and get on with this as quickly as possible. As fast as those minotaurs can run, we have three days, if we're lucky."

With his magic, Edwin scooped the soil out from under the bodies and covered them, removing all traces they'd ever existed. With that done, the four went back to finish the wall, completing that and two more lengths before it grew so dark they couldn't see.

VALLEY OF SORROWS

Chapter 26
Lourdan

Lourdan felt the change as he and his army passed through the shield that marked the border between Tauron's Mal Evol and Neveyah. He'd long wondered what lay beyond the veil, and now he would find out.

It neared midnight, and they camped there. Many things had hampered and slowed them, delaying them by a full day, everything from all four packs of hunting dogs dying of an unstoppable parasite on the second day, to a roaming herd of thunder cows blocking the path of his army.

That had been rather humorous, watching the lads get zapped as they attempted to shoo the stubborn herd out of his path. The absurdity quickly wore thin and every second's delay chafed. Lourdan had finally resorted to dropping into the thunder-cows' minds the way he did his koudah—but the multi-layered herd-mind had been too alien for him to be effective. He'd been unable to find the leader's mind and it had held them up for several hours.

Unlike Stefyn, Lourdan preferred the legions to function in full control of their own minds. He knew his men wanted to kill him—it was nothing personal, it was just how it was. They actually respected him, as far as commanders went. He ate the same food, and his tent was the same as theirs, with no extra frills, and he could kill any one of them with his bare hands.

His personal guards were bound by layers of spells and were completely his. They kept the area around his koudah clear whenever he was mounted, although that was usually not a problem—the touchy beast terrified the rank-and-file.

Lourdan was eating the standard breakfast of jerky and waybread when his scouts brought him word that the strange ramparts had nearly closed the gap. Not only that but a small wagon guarded by a few soldiers traveled toward the exit that remained, headed for the escarpment.

Somehow, Lourdan knew the wagon must be carrying the mages responsible for raising the wall, and also any magic relics that enabled the building of it. He leaned out of his tent, shouting orders to strike the camp.

Turning back to the scout he said, "What did you see? How wide is that gap?"

"P'raps five leagues, maybe more."

"Five leagues! Tell me exactly what was in the wagon." Lourdan wolfed his food in two bites and picked up his helmet, as the scout described what he'd seen.

"There was only four soldiers in the wagon, and many covered barrels. Two small horses pull it, and less than four fists of guards follow." The guard spoke carefully, trying to hide his provincial Gordec accent.

"So, less than twenty guards. They're confident in their success. Did they have anything that looked as if it might be a holy relic? Some magic tool that might enable their goddess's work?"

"P'raps under the canvas. Seems as though it was covering a lot of gear for a small group like that. Stands to reason they got 'em, though. The wall's going up mighty fast."

"How far away are we at the speed we've been traveling?"

"I'd say half a day."

"What? That won't do! We'll have to do better than that, or they'll have locked us out of Neveyah forever. I want whatever magic tools they're using. We'll have them, and we will secure the last gate out of this valley." He jammed the helmet on his head and walked outside. While his men broke down his tent, he saddled his koudah. By the time he was astride it, everyone was ready to depart.

Lourdan raised Glaüdt, magically enhancing his voice so it was heard by every soldier. "We run to that damned wall! Kill the priests of Aeos and bring me their holy relics!" With that, he settled Glaüdt in the special sheath just before his stirrup and spurred Brëcht, who leaped forward, setting a grueling pace his legions struggled to keep up with.

VALLEY OF SORROWS

Chapter 27

Friedr's wagon had arrived at a place several leagues from the Horn of the Moon, having stopped short of their intended destination. Just as at Wellesbridge and the last segments at the Horn of Misery, the final two spans would take twice as long as the regular sections. They would also require the largest expenditure of earth-magic for scooping enough soil and compacting it to create the wall.

The group agreed that the excessive number of attacks since leaving Braden meant Lourdan was aware of how close they were to boxing him in and was planning a major assault. He would be desperate to stop them completing the barrier. They'd broken camp in the dark, and as the day lightened it looked as if he might have that opportunity. Despite hurrying as quickly across the uneven, marshy terrain as the horses were able, they weren't quite to the first stop of the day when Lourdan's army was spotted.

Edwin and Zan scouted as far as they could with their air-magic, discovering the enemy at the limits of their range. When they told the others, John said, "There's nothing we can do to stop them, so we'll just have to work as fast as we can."

"It won't be fast enough." Edwin calculated what they had to do, and how long it would take them. "They're strung out in a broad front. Even if we skip the wall and only raise the shield, some will slip through before the second length is done. But if we can just get that part up, the rest will be locked out and we'll deal with whatever we have to."

"Of course, we won't have any chi." Friedr exhaled

heavily, clearly unenthusiastic. "Here we go again, doing it the hard way."

John said, "Edwin—I have a journeyman I'm supposed to be training in more than fighting rats. Lenn is as gifted as any of us. With his chi to boost us, I think we could, at least, raise the shield along the entire remaining gap before they get here. It would enable us to have the range we need to build the shield all the way to the Escarpment, and once it's up, you could make the wall as fancy as you want because they won't be able to break through. We'll have enough power to do it right with only one attempt."

"If he's willing, it would be the perfect solution. Ask him, now."

John called, "Lenn! This is it. But we have to move quickly. Lourdan is approaching with a small army at his back, and they're running." He climbed down from the cart before it had fully stopped, running to Lenn's side as he dismounted. "We just have one tiny problem. This last gap is too wide—we don't have enough magic to do it."

"What are you going to do? Can you hold them off with your blades? They're pretty powerful."

"No. The enemy has a weapon that can counter three of our swords—perhaps not Riverbinder, but certainly his weapon is familiar with the other three. Edwin has a plan to enable us to do it, but it won't work unless we can find some more power. You have to be in this with us."

Lenn stared at him, nonplussed. "What? I can't link—I'm no healer, and I certainly don't have the strength of magic you do. My blade is just a piece of sharp steel."

Edwin arrived at their side. "I can draw you into the link. If we did that, would you be able to let go of your magic and allow me to use it? I'd like to show this overlord just who he's dealing with—that Aeos is the true and rightful power in Neveyah. We *have* to finish the shield before he gets here."

John agreed. "You're as strong with fire as Friedr is. It would be enough to boost us. Otherwise, I don't think we can do it."

Despite his obvious doubt, Lenn conceded. "I'll do what you need me to do, but I have no idea what to expect. All I have to offer is my chi and my element of fire, and you're more than welcome to use them."

Edwin clasped his shoulder. "You'll want to use your sword as your focus. You may or may not be able to sink completely into the trance, but I guarantee you won't be prepared for what you can see and feel—the healing trance is quite different from anything you've ever done. I warn you—the physical sensations are almost overwhelming, but we won't let you lose yourself."

While they were talking, Zan eagerly searched the approaching horde, hoping for any sight of Lourdan. He found it, but it gave him no comfort—there was no sign of his father in the grim soldier who led the charge against them. And the beast he rode...it was utterly terrifying. He watched the warrior who rode with his faceplate up, urging his legions to fun faster. Resigned, he admitted to himself he'd known there wouldn't be. He watched as Lourdan lowered his faceplate, becoming a minotaur entirely clad in silver.

While Edwin explained as much as he could to Lenn about what to expect and what he would ask of him, John took the squad to one side, issuing orders. "Reni—use the archers first to pick off the leaders. Do what it takes to keep them off our backs. We're going to give it all we've got and span the last of the gap if we can do it before they're on us."

Reni nodded. "We'll get you the time you need."

Zan's eyes refocused as he pulled his senses back in. He and Friedr dismounted from the wagon. The sounds of Reni issuing orders, getting the bows strung and the archers into positon, punctuated the otherwise silent morning.

Friedr didn't wait for his chair. Ignoring his pain, he dropped to the ground, as did the others. Lenn sat between John and Zan, holding his sword the same way the others did, despite its lack of magic. He realized that it did make a good focus for him to concentrate on as he tried to clear his mind.

John said, "Use your grounding and centering exercises. Once you're on the edge of a working trance, we'll pull you in." Immediately the four healers settled into the trance.

With nerves as taut as wires, Lenn forced himself to remain calm as he saw in the far distance on the eastern horizon a dark shadow that shouldn't have been there. He cleared his mind, sinking as far into a working trance as he was able, priming the elements as if he was preparing to make glass, his usual task for the Temple.

He felt a cool, soothing presence as Edwin entered his awareness, gently drawing him deeper into the working, and the world faded. The only thing that mattered was the magic and Edwin Farmer.

The world suddenly opened before Lenn, earth and sky and spinning stars. *I'll never be the same,* he thought, drawing a sharp breath. *I will never be able to explain this.*

He forced himself to remain calm despite the momentary terror he felt when Edwin took his chi, fearing he might panic and run. At Edwin's request, Lenn raised his main element of fire and offered it to him.

Edwin took it, spinning it into the matrix.

The power surge provided by having the fifth mage in the link took Edwin by surprise. Desperately, he clung to his sense of self, fearing he'd lose control of the elements, and lay waste to the surrounding countryside. Sensing Edwin's panic, his father soothed him, helping him regain control. Once he had the magic firmly in his grasp Edwin rapidly began weaving the spell, working faster than he ever had before.

Erotic sensations washed over Lenn—the power of the magic in a far greater concentration than he'd ever felt before. Friedr spoke in his mind, calming him, reminding him to buffer himself. He tried, but the combination of the magic, the vision, and the power was nearly too much for him. Zan took the time to layer a heavier buffer over him.

With the extra buffer the sensations diminished and as they faded, Lenn saw a light born of magic. John's voice spoke in his mind, "The light is your guide. Follow it."

Focusing on the glimmer, Lenn fell fully into the spell. He had become part of the earth and sky, suffused with a sense of oneness with the starry universe. Now he was able to see Edwin's work clearly, observing from outside his body, able to see the elements and the auras of the mages he was linked to.

Edwin's sword drew the elements from every man in the circle, drawing them out as if they were threads, weaving them into a spell different from any Lenn would have created. It occurred to him that each mage really did think differently.

With some surprise, Lenn recognized the four elements. It had never occurred to him to wonder what they might look like, and now he was intrigued. Even more fascinating was the mysterious, indistinct element at the edge of his vision.

Gradually he noticed John's sword drawing those misty strands from the natural world, forming it into a ghostly substance. That eerie element flowed outward to the two swords of power held by Zan and Friedr, which behaved like magnetic poles, drawing in and amplifying the ghostly component, then channeling it back to Edwin's sword.

All four of the battle elements were combined with the mysterious fifth, creating a river of power, eddying around and through the group, flowing and spiraling into a gigantic vortex that disappeared into the mighty sword, Leviathan.

The mystery of the fifth, ghostly element absorbed Lenn. He had to know what it could be and he followed it, getting as close as he was able. Finally, he understood that what he saw was spirit, healing chi. At last, he understood *why* empathy was the most powerful of the magics. *Healing chi binds the world together. The elements form the world, but healing chi gives shape to the elements.* His joy in this revelation made him want to weep.

The spell was a living thing, growing and twisting, and still Edwin kept adding to it. Eventually, the construct covered the sky above and the earth below—the spell was the world and the world was the spell. Lenn's eyes were blinded by the beauty suspended before him, waiting for the final coil, the one last thing to make it solid....

Just when Lenn thought it couldn't get any larger, the world gave a sudden twist and shudder, as Edwin released the spell. A living fountain of power cascaded toward the sky, and to the mage-gifted it was as if the sky lit up from horizon to horizon. The air shimmered as the shield settled into place.

Nervous, and wondering if it was going to be the end, Reni watched as the five mages dropped to the ground in a circle and immediately seemed to fall into their working trance. Time passed, seemingly an eternity for the soldiers who shifted nervously, watching the strange, dark cloud hanging low and crawling rapidly across the ground to the east of their position.

As time stretched on, they began to make out individuals in the horde that approached. "Several hundred warriors at least," said Reni. He lowered his spyglass.

"Holy Aeos...how are we going to defend against that?"

Reni wasn't sure who said it, but he wondered the same thing. He became aware of a faint drumming, the sound of hundreds of pounding feet, disturbing the quiet of the morning. The earth trembled with their approach. "They're almost here." His mouth went dry. "Archers—make ready." Arrows knocked, the archers took aim. "Come on lads...get that shield up." He urged the mages, knowing they were working as fast as they could.

Suddenly he felt the hairs on his body rise and four furlongs to the east of where the team sat, the air shimmered and seemed to solidify as the spell took hold. "Blessed Aeos—they did it."

The main force of the enemy was only half a league away. Once again Reni raised his spyglass to see the oncoming army. One of the minotaurs stood out above all the others, drawing every eye. Clad entirely in gleaming silver, his face was completely covered by a wicked-looking bull's head helmet. He was mounted atop a strange, huge, dragon-like beast, towering over the legions. Reni had seen a picture of a creature like that in a book, as a child.

Behind him, Nathen said, "A koudah! That one's riding a koudah—there haven't been any in Neveyah since the war!"

The minotaur in silver was the only one mounted, riding just behind the front line, where he could direct his troops.

"What are they waiting for? We need that wall up." The speaker sounded nervous.

"Shut it, lads...you're safe now. The legions can't pass that shield even without the wall." Reni's voice cut off the mutters. He gradually noticed that his skin felt prickly—he'd been around battle-mages all his life and had never before felt such a strange sensation. It was like a thunderstorm was brewing. "They're raising earth-magic, and it's a *big* working if I can feel it."

"Big magic," said Nathen. "Even I can feel it. This is...disturbing. Look at their swords—they're glowing, even Lenn's. Only his is different, darker."

Connie J. Jasperson

Reni agreed. "Until today, his blade was just a bar of steel. Now? Who knows."

The mages continued to raise earth-magic, holding it in preparation for some large working. Through the haze of the shield, the Temple squad observed as the broad line of frontrunners met the leading edge of the barrier and were repulsed, falling back, writhing on the ground, their clothes smoking. As the leaders were repelled by the invisible shield, the silver-clad minotaur raised his staff, reining up and halting the legions' advance. Standing in his stirrups, he appeared to examine the shield.

With both hands, he raised his staff. A large, deep-purple stone set into the top of his staff glowed brilliantly, nearly blinding those who observed it. Through squinted eyes the squad gazed in shock as a shaft of amethyst-colored light shot from the crystal, playing across the barrier and then rebounding onto the enemy's force. Several minotaurs burst into pillars of flame as the reflected light touched them, panic scattering the others. The mounted leader fought to control his beast, which trampled several soldiers unfortunate enough to be near him.

Something about that sole mounted enemy terrified those who observed him. Perhaps it was the creature he rode, or maybe it was the way the other minotaurs seemed to avoid contact with him. Whatever it was, the Temple squad had no doubt that if Edwin's team had not managed to get that shield up when they had, they wouldn't have survived the meeting.

Nathen shuddered. "If this priest serves D'Mal, what must *he* be like? Aeos save me from ever finding out."

"Yes, indeed," said Reni. He too gazed at the minotaur.

Nathen stared at him, caught unaware that he'd spoken his horror out loud, and even more surprised to see agreement reflected on the faces that surrounded him.

Abruptly the earth shifted. The Temple squad staggered and fell to the ground as the earth moved. A great line of soil lifted, tearing itself from the growing rift, a small mountain range rising to block their view of the minotaur horde. "Holy Aeos...gonna kill us all...."

Reni ignored the mutterings of the Temple soldiers as they regained their footing. The relentless noise of the rending earth rose to a thundering crescendo.

Lenn was assailed by myriad emotions as Edwin created the most flamboyant display of earth-magic he would ever live to see. He attempted to follow some of it, but the enormity of the working boggled his mind, and he couldn't keep up with the rapid weavings. Overwhelmed by the sheer physicality of the spell he clung to consciousness as well as he could, praying he'd survive the experience. His magic flowed from him, all the elements now, drawn from his body as Edwin's sword, Leviathan, channeled forces he'd never imagined could exist. Overawed at the majesty of Edwin's creation, he wept with joy and elation.

"Look!" The Temple soldiers stared as the soil continued to rise until it lifted completely away from the earth and hovered a moment, mountains in the sky, stretching north and south for leagues along the last open stretch of the Gap. The thundering noise had stopped except for the sounds of some dirt falling along with a few boulders, into the rift from which it had been torn.

Slowly at first, and then rapidly, the earth fell into place on the western side of the vast trench, well within the shield. The earth shuddered with the force of the plummeting soil and rock falling into place. Loud grinding sounds and deafening groans shook the ground under their feet as the hills of soil were compacted into the black ramparts joining seamlessly to the wall they had finished the night before. Soon, the new wall was firmly anchored high on the sheer cliffs of the southernmost point of the escarpment.

Silence reigned on the Temple side of the wall, broken at last by nervous chuckles.

"Our lads were showing off for our visitors. Makes them seem a little more human." Reni's sardonic comment drew jittery laughter from the others. "That was pretty flashy. It shook me up good and proper."

>>><<<

The Temple group opted to camp where they were. With the shield and the wall now raised they were as safe there as anywhere, and the five mages were too exhausted to travel. Rats and other beasts occupied the area, but the squad would handle them.

Rain fell, trickling down Lenn's neck, but he didn't notice. He sat slumped against the lone oak tree in the field. On the other side of the wall, now concealed from his view, he knew the rain added to the groundwater filling the deep moat which now stretched the length of the gap from horn to horn, dark and serene. His eyes turned back to the others with whom he'd shared the most significant moment of his life, feeling a sense of kinship.

"You did well. I knew you would." John Farmer's hands shook with exhaustion as he handed Lenn bread and cheese. "I'm sorry I couldn't prepare you better for it. We didn't have enough time."

"No. It's okay. It's one of those things no one can explain."

Patting Lenn's shoulder, John moved off, cracking jokes with the squad.

Edwin sat down beside Lenn, leaning back with his eyes closed. "Thank you," he said, exhaustion coloring his voice. "You made it possible. But it was too much power and I nearly lost control of it." He opened his eyes and met Lenn's, who was surprised to see sheepish glee. "I always wanted to do something flashy and spectacular like that. We're not supposed to show off with our gifts, so I've tried to behave in front of the squad. But that was more fun than anything I'll ever do again—it was wild and on the edge of being out of control."

Lenn laughed. "I feel the same way. Thank you for drawing me into it. I'm not sure I learned anything I can use, but what a ride."

Once again Edwin leaned back and this time, he dozed off. Lenn just admired the wall, while Friedr lay stretched on his bedroll under the lean-to nearby, snoring. In the periphery, Zan paced, staring at the wall, wrapped in his cloak and consumed with his dark thoughts.

Lenn listened to John joking with the squad. He grinned, thinking about Edwin Farmer. The man had made a grand statement with the flamboyant way he'd raised the wall. Usually, Edwin did his work with an

Connie J. Jasperson

economy of effort, conserving his chi for the next spell, but this time, he'd made a spectacular display of power, doing it just for the one named Lourdan. He'd spent every last bit of chi he had, coming close to burning out his gift in his efforts. And then he'd been as proud as a novice casting his first successful spell—somehow that endeared the normally somber man to Lenn.

The drizzle stopped and the afternoon turned sunny although a chill clung to the air. After they had finished eating, Edwin, Zan, and John took to their bedrolls, taking a much-needed nap.

Perhaps it was his imagination, but Lenn thought the final section of the wall shone blacker and more deadly than any other. The jagged, razor-sharp shafts set into the top refracted rays of rainbow light when the sun came out in the afternoon.

"You should get some rest, lad. You're as tired as the others. Don't tell me you're not—your hands are shaking." Reni pointed Lenn toward his bedroll. "Sleep now. Your work is finished for the day. This is rat-country, so we'll keep guard while you boys rebuild your magic strength."

"I *am* beat, I admit it. But I just want to look at it. I'll never be a part of anything as great as that again. I want to remember this day."

VALLEY OF SORROWS

Chapter 28
Lourdan

Lourdan stood in his stirrups atop Brëcht, examining the vast black barrier built of magic that had risen before his eyes. Behind him, the legions stood silent. If he'd arrived even five minutes earlier, he'd have been able to overrun the mages who sat in a circle holding swords, points to the ground, as posed as a scene from a child's book. Their Temple slaves stood guard, the circle of five priests holding them in mindless thrall, no doubt harvesting their chi to power the working.

He was unable to approach the fortification because of the magic shield. Within half an hour of his arrival, the black monstrosity was seamless. From where he sat, he could sense with his earth-magic that it was anchored high into the escarpment, deep into the earth, and connected seamlessly to the rest of the incredible black ramparts that now sealed the gap.

He was cut off from Aeoven and the evil that lurked there. The blood-sucking, vampiric Temple of Aeos that held the lives of the suffering people of his homeland had won before he even had a chance to deal with them. The wall gleamed, black as polished obsidian, with jagged, razor-sharp shards set into the top, glints of sunlight reflecting off them.

Without a word, he turned the koudah south, following the shore of the rift that separated him from the wall, trying to sense how the energy barrier worked. Now he was driven to see the entire length of the construct, to search for any possible weaknesses. It was made of three parts: the visible wall, a wide, deep moat, and a disturbingly effective force-field that guarded both the wall and the trench before it that even now filled with water.

One of those three components must have a flaw at some point, and he would find it.

He sensed Stefyn's frustration through the tie that bound them. Lourdan's wrath grew, but unlike Stefyn, he channeled it into grim determination.

He'd been compelled to obey Stefyn's commands. Stefyn was, in turn, constrained by the generals who'd insisted that Lourdan spare the few legions he'd been able to assemble so they would have the strength to fight. Thus, they were hamstrung by the military geniuses in Stefyn's court who wouldn't hear of an untried youth like Lourdan running the war his own way. Lourdan saw in Stefyn's mind the thought that those generals would pay the price, and smiled.

None of their informants had mentioned the invisible barrier, so it must be a new thing—a spell of that magnitude must have been set by the goddess herself, to protect her priests. Therefore, it was likely he wouldn't have been in time no matter how fast they ran. He spoke through the link to his lover. "Stefyn...calm down. Tauron has her on the run. She's desperately defending her borders now, instead of attacking. Desperation is a sign of weakness. There will be a flaw in it somewhere. We'll do this methodically. Consider this—if I recall, it was Khalduk of Gordec who argued most strenuously for a measured approach. This gives you the leverage you needed to impose martial law in Gordec. You've been looking for a reason to do that, and this is your opportunity."

Stefyn responded, calmer and once again able to

think clearly. "You're right. His incompetence has been proven." Stefyn's laugh was gleeful. "As has Mohrec's… the province of Nuruk shall feel the weight of his failure." With his rage diverted toward more immediate targets, he said, "You'll find a way around the Temple. We will succeed, no matter how long it takes." He dropped out of the link, intending to deal with his generals.

Lourdan felt his absence almost as an ache and yet was relieved to be free of the burden of Stefyn's precarious temper. His lover was the Highest and paid a terrible price—the god was too frequently entwined in Stefyn's mind and his sanity suffered for it.

"Very well." Lourdan spoke into the silence. Another way out of the valley must exist, and he would find it. He would set his people free from the horrors imposed on them by the goddess, no matter how long it took. *Braden is their weakness. That city is now the only way out. They'll have to face me there.*

He spurred the koudah to a gallop, forcing his legions to run as they should have before the morning's fiasco.

As they would do whenever he needed them to, and to hell with sparing them. They were born to be spent, and he had been born to spend them.

Lourdan raised his faceplate, enjoying the sting and burn of the cold rain on his face as he and his legions raced toward Braden.

Chapter 29

After leaving Arlen, the team drove the horses hard. They rose well before dawn on their last day of traveling and rolled into Aeoven at mid-morning, finding it a changed town—bustling and as loud as Arlen. "I feel like a bumpkin again," said Edwin, making the soldiers Garran had assigned them, laugh. "I'd never seen a cobbled street until I saw Armat, which I thought was quite grand. Then I saw this town and understood what a real city is." His nerves were strung as tautly as a harp, but he managed to disguise it under a tight, professional smile.

The five mages parted with their squad at the end of the street.

Lenn embraced Zan, saying, "Good luck, my brother. I must go and see my grandmother, and let her know I'm back. Don't forget to invite me to your bonding!"

"If Anna will have me, of course, I will."

Friedr turned the wagon down Rose Street, pulling up in front of Edwin's house, setting the brake. There was no hitching rail, but John told the horses to stay put until he returned.

When Edwin arrived at the steps of his home, he found the door locked. "Are they perhaps at the infirmary?"

"I meant to tell you," his father said, taking Edwin's kit from him. "We have to keep the doors bolted at all times. It's the only house in Aeoven that must be kept locked, and that's for the protection of everyone *outside* of it."

Edwin reached up, feeling for the key on the ledge over the door jamb. He inserted it in the old lock, turned it and the door swung open. For a brief moment, Edwin saw the woman who was his wife—the woman he'd left when he departed on the quest months before. Her back was to him, and she rearranged the figurines on the mantel. She looked so familiar that, for a moment, joy soared in his heart.

The change in her was immediately evident when she turned and saw him. There was no recognition, no joyful reunion. Instead, exasperation flashed in otherwise dull eyes. She snapped, "What? More visitors? I don't want any more healers. Can't you people just leave me alone?"

Somehow he managed to get through that moment, feeling as if he'd walked into a stranger's home. His father stood beside him, with Zan and Friedr subtly lending him support. Halee came in from the kitchen her eyes alight with relief at the sight of them. Taking Marya's arm and leading her to a chair, she said, "Marya, these men are our guests, and we're glad to see them. This is Edwin and John, and their friends. Surely you remember John—he's my husband."

Marya's face crumpled, like a child who'd been scolded. "I'm sorry. So many strangers all the time, it's confusing. How will I know the one? The baby killer...."

Feeling as if he were in a dream, Edwin said, "We need to talk to Dane so that Friedr can get home."

Halee embraced John, and then Edwin. "We only just finished breakfast—there's plenty left. He and Anna are in the kitchen. I'll take care of Marya while you talk to him." Her eyes took in the changes in the three younger men and then her husband. She gripped John's hand, holding it as if she would never let him go again. "John—I've missed you something terrible. Why don't you tell Marya and I what you've been up to while they talk to Dane? You look like you've been having fun."

At first, Dane struggled with the truth of what had happened to Christoph, unable to believe it. Their bonding had been tempestuous, but Christoph had been the love of his life. Edwin shared his true-dream with him, lowering his barriers and allowing Dane into his mind. Afterward, Dane was completely devastated. Zan did what he could to help him accept that it couldn't be changed, explaining what he'd seen when they faced Lourdan in the race to close the Gap.

"Lourdan is not Chris. He carries a sword and uses Tauron's magic as a weapon. He rides a terrible beast. The minotaurs fear him. Christoph is dead, just as his ghost told Edwin." Zan held his cousin, letting him cry himself out. Tears streaked Anna's face and she put her arms around them both.

After Dane had pulled himself together, he, Zan, and Anna went down the street to his house, to give Edwin and John a chance to settle back into their home. Dane promised he'd be back the next day to help. "I just need a little time to deal with this. But if you need us, come and get us. She has to be watched at all times."

Edwin reassured him that he and his father would take care of Marya.

Disturbed by the profound change in Marya, Friedr

had gone home, but not before insisting that Edwin stop by his house later to see Jonny. "As soon as you decently can. He needs you too."

"I know. I'll stop by this afternoon."

With the house relatively quiet, Halee led Edwin up to his study in the attic, where his possessions had been moved. In his absence, the attic room had completely changed. Half of the attic now boasted walls and a ceiling. A real wooden floor had been laid over the old, rough planks, making it a comfortable, quiet place to work, or even an extra bedroom if needed. He'd always intended to make it into a proper room, but had never gotten around to it.

Halee watched his face carefully. "When they realized the extent of her illness, Rall and Kalen went ahead and finished this room for you, after they repaired the damage in the kitchen."

"I'll have to thank them. I can see why I've been turfed out of Marya's room." His bitterness was impossible to hide. He gestured to the new walls. "I'd have gotten it done eventually, but...under the circumstances this is for best. It's one less thing to worry about." He looked at his desk, placed under the small window where he'd always meant to put it. Marya's portrait, drawn by the assistant colorist, a lightning-mage named Elner, sat there, a picture of a woman who no longer existed except in Edwin's memories.

"Are you all right?"

Halee's concern both irritated and consoled him. "No. But I'll get by." His smile was forced, but at least, he'd managed one.

Sighing, she patted his arm and went downstairs.

Edwin got his gear put away, and then changed out of his leathers into comfortable clothes, feeling disoriented. He stared out the small window, attempting to cope with the fact Jonny wasn't there to welcome him.

He went back downstairs, carrying his favorite green cloak, intending to put it on the pegs by the back door where it would be handy. It was difficult getting his mind around the changes in Marya—she wasn't the same person at all, not even remotely. His wife had been funny, quirky, and a bit disorganized, but unfailingly kind and gentle. The woman who wore his wife's face was antagonistic and paranoid.

Concealing his consternation, Edwin greeted her, but she struck at him with the fire poker as he passed through the sitting room. Avoiding her blow, he grabbed her arms pinning them to her side.

Marya shouted, "Go away. You're a healer! I can tell by the markings. I don't know what you're here for, but I don't need you mucking around in my head too!"

Halee came running and took the poker. She led Marya to the sofa, telling her to sit down and behave. "You promised to be good! He did nothing to hurt you."

Marya began crying and apologized, but it was clear she didn't know what she was apologizing for.

The visiting healer, Lorana, wasn't there and when Edwin asked where she was, he was told she'd gone to the infirmary to give him a chance to settle in, before coping with a stranger in his home disrupted his life even more.

As if his wife wasn't a stranger.

Halee had given up everything to care for her, and

Edwin was more than merely appreciative—he was indebted to her, and to everyone else whose lives had been thrown into chaos by it.

By noon Marya had undergone a complete behavioral change, almost manically happy, chatting with Edwin about someone named Angel, behaving as if she hadn't tried to hurt him only an hour before.

She insisted on helping John make the stew for that evening's dinner, which turned into a tantrum when she wasn't allowed a knife. "I wasn't going to hurt the baby! I love her!" She burst into tears and ran to Halee, who soothed her. Edwin cast calm on her and Marya settled down but was soon in a state of high excitement again.

John peeled the vegetables which Marya slid into the pot, counting each vegetable as they went in. Halfway through, she lost interest and wandered into the sitting room, with Edwin observing her from the doorway.

Standing with his back to the kitchen, he heard his father breathe a sigh of relief, listening as John looked in cupboards until he located his favorite cooking knife. The familiar sounds of his father assembling the stew comforted him.

Edwin knew his dad was covertly watching him. The sounds of John making bread, measuring the flour into the large bowl, were interspersed with brief pauses, and he could feel his father's eyes on him. He was fully aware of his father's jittery nerves, casting calm on him and receiving a small smile for thanks.

John said, "She can't help it, Son—even as heavily medicated as she is, she radiates the madness and anyone sensitive is affected by it. I've good barriers, but not as strong as yours."

Still in the kitchen doorway, Edwin watched his wife repositioning the pillows and knickknacks obsessively. "I'm a good mother," she said to a doll, which at first he thought was Jonny's. She picked it up, hugging and kissing it. "You're a good baby, a good, good girl. I wouldn't kill you."

Seeing her arranging the doll and its clothes, Edwin felt as if he'd fallen into a nightmare he couldn't wake from. She looked up, seeing him standing in the doorway watching her. "Are you still here? This is Angel. She's my baby. She doesn't like strangers, either." Despite the medication and spells, her emotions surged wildly and he felt her madness pressing on his barriers. Calming himself, he sensed the dampening field Lorana had placed on her that morning had begun to fade. Subtly he reinforced it, seeing immediate improvement as Marya settled down, sitting by the window rocking the doll.

An elderly woman's voice spoke from behind him. "I had to let you see it for yourself. I can keep much of it at bay, but this is what you'll have to cope with every day and every night for the rest of her life." A frail, white-haired healer stood in the dining room, her face lined with loss and years of carrying heavy burdens. "She must be watched at all times, for her sake and the safety of others."

"You must be Lorana." His words felt flat, uncivil. "Forgive my inability to be gracious. I'm not myself today."

There was genuine compassion in her eyes as she greeted him. "Yes, I am she. And you're in shock. You need time to come to terms with this terrible change in your life."

She was easily the strongest healer he'd met, the embodiment of competence and power and her compassion soothed him. With his healing sight, he followed her as she layered several spells he'd never seen before over Marya, watching the stress in his wife's face ease. She began to show real enjoyment as she played with her doll, the first he'd seen her demonstrate since his arrival home. "The problem with these spells is they fade quickly and must constantly be maintained. But they're useful in this sort of situation."

Watching Marya with her doll, Edwin's veneer of calm shattered. Rage sparked in his eyes and he turned his face to the wall, hiding the fury that consumed him. His fists clenched and unclenched and he burned with the desire to hunt down and kill the mindbender who'd dared to do this to his wife. With sheer force of will, he buried those thoughts, concentrating on what he had to do to get through the next few days. How having a mother who was so mentally ill would affect Jonny had to be his main concern now.

When he turned back to Lorana, her bright eyes were commiserating with him. "Yes. I know that rage well. You're a lot like me, young man. You'll always be angry, but you'll channel and use it to do what must be done to protect Neveyah." Lorana patted his arm. "You bear the mark of the avenger behind your ear, as my husband did. Don't let vengeance destroy you. Your son's welfare is the most important thing to take into account now. You are his rock, his anchor—you must always be there for him."

The rain had stopped and Marya wanted to go outside to the garden. Lorana urged her to put on a cloak, which she refused. Ignoring his wife's fussing, Edwin gently tied the cloak around her, saying to Lorana, "You're right about Jonny. If you don't mind, I'm going to go and see him now."

"This is a good time. She'll be easy to manage for a while yet today."

Edwin passed through the kitchen, cheered by the familiar sight of bread rising and his father and stepmother cleaning the kitchen. He excused himself to go to Friedr's house.

Halee smiled. "Jonny's doing well, but he misses you. I go to see him every day and put him to bed every night. He'll be so happy to have you home to do that."

VALLEY OF SORROWS

Chapter 30

Jonny was beside himself when he saw his father approaching the front door of Friedr's house. He raced down the walk, screaming, "Dad! Dad!" as he leaped into Edwin's arms. He clung to his father as if he'd never let go. His son surprised him with how many words he had and the way he used sentences. His weeks with Aeolyn, playing with Freylin and Rynne had improved his language skills immensely.

Aeolyn and Friedr met him at the door, concern in their eyes. "Please don't take him home yet. He's safe here, I promise. We love him, and he's no trouble at all." Aeolyn put her arms around him, holding him and Jonny. "He's happy enough here and though he misses you, he's terrified of her."

Edwin looked at her, numbness stealing over him again. "Of his mother?"

Aeolyn nodded, holding back her tears. "She is…oh, Edwin, I'm so sorry. He'll be fine here for a few more days, just until you can get things straightened out."

He glanced down at Jonny, who tightened his grip on his father. "Dad. Fix Ahmah," Jonny said with absolute confidence. "Sick." His happiness and confidence his dad could heal his mother and make everything normal again brought Edwin to tears.

He told his son, "Uncle Zan is home now and he'll help Mama a lot, I'm sure of it." With all his heart he prayed it was so.

"Unca San," Jonny agreed, laying his head on his dad's shoulder.

"I missed you too," Edwin said. He closed his eyes,

forcing himself to concentrate so as not to be overwhelmed by how his son had changed while he was gone. The relief he found in holding him was agonizing in its intensity.

Pulling himself together, he asked Freylin to find a good book for them and sat reading to the three children, with Jonny on his lap. He read for an hour but then had to return home.

He was grateful that Friedr and Aeolyn loved Jonny and wanted him with them, but it killed him to have to leave his son behind. Jonny didn't seem to mind, running off to play with Rynne. Fearing his son had suffered emotional damage from all the changes forced on him at such a young age, Edwin looked into his awareness. He saw the boy had been worried, but his little mind was at peace now his dad was back, sure he would mend everything. He didn't want to go where his mother was, and accepted that his father had to leave him.

"Don't worry, my brother. We'll keep him happy, and we'll see you tonight when you come to help put him to bed." Friedr's rough embrace heartened him.

Aeolyn said, "Friedr tells me Zan may be able to help Marya. I hope so—I miss her like crazy. But Halee has become a dear friend to me, a model I aspire to. She's visited twice a day, helping me get the children home from the nursery and also when I put them to bed." She squeezed his arm. "See you after dinner?"

Edwin let himself out the kitchen door, walking up the alley through the heavy, cold rain. As he closed Friedr's gate, he saw Dario approaching down the alley, stopping at Edwin's back gate, waiting for him.

Dario clasped his hand. "Hello, my brother. I heard

you arrived back this morning. I'm on my way to see Kalen. Garran probably told you about my wife. Bekki is dead."

Edwin nodded. "He did. Words fail me. How are you getting on? Do you need anything?"

"Mikel and his wife, Sari, keep me going. Kalen helps too." The older mage's eyes were haunted. He wasn't the fiery mage he'd been when Edwin last saw him. "Edwin—think of the good times, and don't let the bad destroy the memories."

Edwin nodded, comforted by the man he didn't really know well, but who'd lost the woman he loved. "I'll get by."

"When things are resolved here for you, the others in our group have some plans we want to share with you and Zan," Dario said. "The information Zan peeled out of Graylor in Braden, and two dead bodies that turned up in the crafters' quarter here recently have given us an idea of who we're actually looking for. The dead man and woman are tied somehow to Cayne's murderer. That person is responsible for Marya's situation."

Edwin felt better, having a solid plan of action. "Good. Ferreting out mindbenders is my true task for the goddess, one that may not be accomplished in our lifetime."

Dario nodded. "Mine too. If you need anything, I'm here for you." He turned and walked up the alley toward Father Rall's house, where Kalen now lived.

Edwin unlocked the gate and entered his back garden, carefully relocking it behind him. He found Marya soaking wet, sitting in the garden with no shoes on, idly stirring the chilly mud with her fingers.

"Marya, aren't you cold? Where are your shoes?"

Instead of answering, she lobbed a handful of mud at him and ran up the steps to the laundry porch, just as Halee came out. "Marya—I only turned my back on you for a minute. Where are your shoes?"

"He stole them...he stole them...my armor too...."

Wiping the mud from his face, Edwin realized she was talking about Stefyn D'Mal, and shook his head, trying to clear his mind. "I'll find her shoes. They must be here somewhere."

"Lorana was called to the infirmary, but she'll be back soon." Edwin could hear the unspoken *I hope* in Halee's voice as she led Marya into the kitchen. "Let's get you cleaned up again, shall we?"

After a bit of searching, he found his wife's shoes. One was in the chickens' water trough as if she'd thrown it there, the other had slipped off her foot and was lodged in the mud of the winter-barren vegetable plot. He scraped the mud off and took them up to the laundry porch, setting them in the wash tub. "I found her shoes," he called to Halee. "I'll just clean them now, so they can dry."

"Good. We're nearly done in here," replied his stepmother, as she toweled Marya's rain-damp hair dry. "There you go, Marya! All clean. Now we'll just get your shirt changed and then we'll have tea."

"I don't want tea. Why is that man still here? Is he a healer?"

"Yes, he's a healer. He's my son, so he lives here."

"But I don't know him...what if he's the one...what if he's the one who killed that baby? I don't need a new shirt. I like this one."

"No one killed a baby here, dear. And you do need

265

a clean shirt. This one's muddy. I'll just wash it, and then you can have it back." Halee was endlessly patient, even when Marya elbowed her in the ribs with her struggles.

Edwin paused and closing his eyes he cast a spell of calm over his wife, relaxing as she stopped resisting and allowed Halee to put a clean shirt on her. With both her shoes cleaned, he set them on a shelf to dry and went into the kitchen. Talking cheerfully with Halee about the building of the wall, he poured boiling water over Marya's tea, steeping the leaves of chamomile, silf, and sativa. When it was brewed, he poured it into her favorite cup, stirring honey in just the way she liked it. As he did, he thought in an offhand way that before her illness she'd very likely compounded the very herbs that now helped to calm her.

John returned from the husbandry complex where he'd stopped in to visit with his former journeyman. "Walther has the entire program under control. He has four new novice vets, now, too."

Halee kissed John's cheek. "Father Rall is looking forward to your return to the novice water-mages on Lunaday, and they are too. All of them are excited to see you again. They've been working on a surprise for you. I think you can relax and enjoy being home now."

"I haven't told you—I have a new journeyman. Lenn."

Halee laughed. "I hope you're being nice to him. You were pretty hard on him in the arena."

John blushed. "I was in a bad mood that day. He and I get along well, and he'll be a good liaison for the militia. I'll have more time to spend with my wife, you lucky thing."

Edwin said, "Aeolyn tells me Jules is going to be your permanent assistant, taking Christoph's old job."

Halee nodded. "He just can't quit, no matter how often he threatens. And he's been walking with no canes at all for the last month. Carrying a buffer has really eased the damage to his joints. Henley has improved immensely too. By the time he went to Armat, they were both sparring with the seniors in the morning weapons group."

With one eye on Marya, who held her doll, rocking it, Edwin said, "I noticed Henley was looking pretty spry when we saw him in Braden. I thought he must be carrying the buffer the way I showed him."

John washed his hands, put on an apron, and looking in the stewpot, he stirred it. "Things smell good in here." He put the raised loaves of bread in the oven, saying, "It won't be long before dinner. When the bread comes out, we'll eat."

Edwin observed his parents in the kitchen, smiling inanely despite his now familiar sense of numbness. It was all so strange, so disorienting, trying to find some sort of domestic normalcy amidst the chaos of keeping Marya safe. Everyone talked brightly as if nothing was wrong, yet they were ready to leap out of their skin. Her madness affected everyone despite the sativa tea laced with silf, a situation he'd never come across. It was clear the silf didn't completely cut her off from her gifts. He wondered what would work since the silf was ineffective.

As the afternoon wore on, she grew fidgety. Edwin hovered over his wife, watching her every move.

Lorana came back from the infirmary, with more medicines. Dinner time neared, and Marya became more agitated, despite the increased layers of spells and the herbal teas. She became enraged when Edwin wouldn't allow her to move the fireplace screen and add wood to the low fire that burned in the sitting room.

She threw a figurine at him, which broke against the wall when he ducked. She snatched at the broken shards, trying to cut her own arms, but he caught and held her. He was too quick for her to be able to injure herself, but she flailed at him, slashing his cheek and drawing blood.

Hearing the struggle from the other room, Lorana came running, casting a spell he was unfamiliar with, and Marya's behavior instantly calmed. The white-haired healer quickly took care of his cut, and Edwin went back to watching Marya. He handed her the doll and helped her find all the clothes for it, once again wondering if he'd slipped into a nightmare.

Night had fallen, and the house on Rose Street was quiet. Edwin lay on a cot that had been set up in his room under the eaves in the attic. Staring into the darkness, his head spun. He maintained a ward over his wife as if he was standing a watch—he couldn't be in the house now, without it. Below him, in what had once been their bedroom, Marya slept soundly under the influence of a layered sleep spell, combined with herbs, and Lorana slept on a cot nearby.

For the last few weeks, as he finished his quest, Edwin had known his wife had suffered a breakdown. He'd also known it was caused in part by what she had suffered in Mal Evol, mindtraps triggered by the death of their baby. He'd understood she was mentally ill but had been unprepared for the way it changed her.

Naïvely, despite the letters from Halee, Dane, and Lorana, and even though Garran had warned him, Edwin had been convinced that his wife would be fine, with the proper care.

He'd been wrong.

The woman he'd come home to was a stranger, a child possessed of an unpredictable, violent temperament, at times striking out in anger when she was denied things she could hurt herself with. There was no beauty in her features—they'd become coarse and dull, devoid of that elfin spark of mischief and wit that had been so uniquely *Marya*.

He still had trouble comprehending that she didn't recognize him. He was just another of her keepers.

Alone in the dark of his attic room, tears burned his eyes as he faced the fact his bonding was forever changed. He tried to sense his wife's presence the way he'd always been able to, but there was nothing, no subliminal connection. He'd been unable to sense it since the days after Christoph's…death.

Now he knew why. Their bonding was broken.

What he'd seen when he looked into her mind frightened him—a dark madness that wanted nothing more than to consume her. A small part of her still fought against it, struggling to survive against the evil, the part of her soul that was protected by her vows to Aeos. His shoulders shook as he forced himself to consider the fact even Zan with his tenacity and ability might not be able to solve what was wrong with Marya.

Lorana wanted to take her back to the special infirmary where other healers whose minds had been damaged by the mad priest were able to live as well as possible under the circumstances. They were watched at all times, medicated, and layered under heavy spells.

Now, reluctantly, Edwin knew that if Zan was unable to help her, it would be the best thing he could do, both for his wife and for his son. It would be the only way to give Jonny a normal life. Having made the only decision he could live with, tears scalded his face and he gave in to them, weeping off and on until dawn began to lighten his room.

Wearily, he got up and went down to feed the chickens, doing the chores he'd always enjoyed, going through the motions with less feeling than if he were a rag doll.

Leaning against the fence surrounding his chicken run, he stood with the feed bucket held slack in his hand. He heard the rattling of pots in the kitchen, and through the window he saw Halee laughing as his father prepared breakfast. From outside looking in, they looked so normal, so much like any happy family, yet they weren't, and his wife's madness was a blight on them all.

Gazing up at the window of his wife's room, he saw the curtains open as Lorana began the morning routine, preparing Marya for the day.

What the future would be like now, he couldn't even envision. Somehow he would deal with his life, one day at a time.

VALLEY OF SORROWS

Chapter 31

In the dark of early morning, Zan sat at the table in his barren bachelor apartment, reading. It felt odd to be back, but on leaving Dane's house, Anna returned with him to his rooms. She and her mothers had prepared dinner at Dane's house, and when he and Anna left, the two women remained with Dane helping him come to terms with the truth of what happened to Christoph.

Now, at least, he was grieving normally. Dane didn't blame him for placing Chris under a truth geas, but a part of Zan would always believe he'd caused his father to make such a terrible choice.

Zan smiled as he thought about the previous evening and the passionate, amazing woman he loved. Dozing lightly, for most of the night, he held her, marveling at the blessings Aeos had bestowed upon him.

He tried to work quietly, so she could sleep. They had a busy day ahead of them, despite the fact he'd only arrived in Aeoven the day before.

When he and Anna had arrived in his apartment, he'd found a long letter from Lorana under his door, along with a sheaf of her notes, briefing him on what to expect, and how she had approached treating Marya. He'd glanced at them briefly and left them for the morning. Anna was more important just then.

But, after hearing what Dane and Anna had told him privately, he was terribly worried and couldn't really rest until he'd read the case history.

Lorana's letter read,

"I know you've just returned, and

under normal circumstances, I would
never press you when you're grieving and
in the midst of planning your father's
memorial service. Abbot Forli from
Hyram Temple tells me you might be able
to help me assess the damage done to
Marya Farmer. I would like you to meet
me at the Farmers' home tomorrow
afternoon, for you to evaluate her for
yourself, and to support Edwin as we
develop a plan for her long term care.
Bring Anna, and it will appear to be a
social occasion, old friends having tea."

The bulk of Lorana's case-notes and her
commentary were detailed and very helpful. In her first
notes, she had written that the episodes of madness did
not seem random.

"The one positive thing is that when
she was his captive, Tauron's high priest
was unable to break the geas which binds
the vows the clergy of Aeos all take,
although it is evident he tried."

And later:

"It appears as if someone is
tampering with her because each episode
has occurred when she returned from the
infirmary."

Another entry:

"We carefully checked the credentials
of the people who were on duty, including

the cleaning staff, but so far we've found no one who hasn't taken the vows to serve Aeos."

And yet another:

> "Now it's muddied. I can't see the pattern, and if there is a coven of Tauron's acolytes embedded in Aeoven, it will be difficult to find them, with the influx of new people being resettled here. Still, we must keep searching."

A slight sound alerted him to Anna's stirring. Soon she stood behind him, her arms around his neck, kissing his cheek. He sensed spikes of love and concern for him and pulled her onto his lap, resting his cheek against her hair as he thought about Marya's condition. "We're to go to Edwin and Marya's today," he said, finally. "Lorana wants us to have tea with Marya, and while she's diverted with your exceptionally delightful company...," he kissed her, "I can assess the damage. Later, I need to go to Dane's and help him with planning Chris's memorial."

She kissed him soundly. "I'll go with you to Dane's too. I'm taking the rest of the week off except for my time helping with Marya, to be with you. But there's something we need to do this morning after we have breakfast in the dining hall, where you'll be seen by all to be dining with *me* so none of the other girls will think they can poach on my territory."

"Oh? What would that be?"

"We need to register our bonding today so we can get a house, or we'll be stuck in the bachelor's quarters for who knows how long, as houses are going fast with all the refugees needing good homes. We need our own kitchen so we don't have to eat in the dining hall."

Zan's heart leaped with joy and then settled as he thought of their conversation of the previous night. "But what about your dream of a formal Temple bonding? Only last night we talked about how you've dreamt of your bonding day all your life." He wanted nothing more than to register their union but was unwilling to deny her the day she'd always envisioned.

"*This* is what I really want. Having you in my life is what makes me happy, and I don't see any point in waiting for a big party when what I really want is right here." She kissed him, setting his heart thumping. "We *are* together—let's register it and let the world know we have more than an arrangement between us. This morning when I heard you rustling your paperwork out here, I realized I want nothing more than to wake up to that sound every morning." Her arms tightened around him. "This way, we'll get our names on the list and be assigned a home of our own."

"I admit I *would* like to be bonded now." His heart lightened at the prospect of having her in his life forever. "Until we're assigned a house, these rooms will have to do. Indeed, it will be a home simply because you're here. But, I think your mothers will miss you. You moved back with them when you left the novice barracks, so that tells me you're very close, as I was with my parents. I never really left home until I became a healer, you know."

"Yes, but they love *you* too and care deeply about Dane. They only want us to be happy. Let's send a messenger to everyone and let them know what we're doing this morning. They can meet us there at ten." She stood up, kissing the top of his head. "Since we'll be busy later, I'm sure my mothers will pack my things for me, and help us carry them here. Besides, Dane will agree with our decision. He wants a grandchild too."

Zan had no words. He gave her his answer in his embrace.

Friedr's homecoming had gone much more smoothly than he'd expected. Aeolyn had taken one look at him and said, "I hope you hurt the bastard who did that to you." The day had been utter chaos with the children unable to play outside, but they'd managed to have fun anyway. Edwin's obvious turmoil, both times he'd come to see Jonny, had made Friedr feel like weeping, but he managed not to embarrass himself or Edwin. On his second visit, after he'd gotten Jonny to sleep, Edwin had said very little other than a few pleasantries, but it was apparent his situation was worse than they'd hoped.

Then, after the children were in bed, Aeolyn had proven to Friedr that he wasn't as crippled as he feared. The memory of their intense reunion left him smiling all through breakfast while the children tried to be on their best behavior for him. It had lasted nearly five minutes until Freylin accidentally kicked Rynne with his fidgeting. She promptly struck at him with her spoon, landing a glob of porridge in the center of his forehead. Wide-eyed, Jonny stared, clutching his favorite blanket.

"Manners, you two!" their mother said, in the tone of voice no one ever disobeyed. The meal progressed in a normal fashion after that.

"Thank you for a lovely meal, children. I've missed having breakfast with you," Friedr said as they climbed down from the table to take their bowls to the kitchen.

Freylin said, "You're welcome, Dad. We missed you too."

"Welcome, Da." Rynne was so serious.

"You welcome, Unca Fweedah." Jonny grinned, a perfect miniature of his father.

Seeing Rynne toddling behind Frey with her bowl made him realize how much they'd grown and changed in his absence. Jonny followed, carrying his bowl with his blanket dragging the floor behind him. The baby quilt his mother had made before he was born was a piece of his old life, a thing that brought him comfort, and wherever he went, his 'bankie' went too. The boy became inconsolable if he had to be parted from it, so Aeolyn had to wait until he was asleep to wash it.

Rynne's little voice tugged at Friedr's heartstrings as she ordered everyone around. She sounded like a baby version of her mother. She'd learned to walk in his absence, as he'd known she would. She had so many words now, far more than Jonny, who was several months older. When he'd left, she'd had none. "Clean you mess, Da,"

"Yes, dear." Friedr carried his things to the kitchen one-handed, making two trips. Knowing they'd grown and seeing it were two different things. The din of his children who now played in their 'fort' under the dining room table was only slightly less than that of an attack by minotaurs, but he enjoyed it immensely. He settled down to read the stack of reports that waited for him, some from Kalen Rallsson, who was once again the

Temple armsmaster, but most were from Darlen, who had several patients he wanted Friedr to examine.

> "Abbott Forli tells me you have dealt with other cases such as these, where the patient was far from a healer at the time of the accident and the bones were set improperly. If you think you can help, I think we should try to do it as soon as possible. I would like to have you on my rounds with me on Lunaday if it's convenient."

Friedr wrote a reply, saying he'd see him first thing Lunaday morning. That would give him several days before he had to go back to work. He needed to spend that time with his children and wanted to be available to help Edwin through the next few days.

He'd only read through the first of Kalen's reports when a knock on the door sounded. Leaning heavily on his staff, Friedr limped to the door, to find a messenger, a novice fire-mage named Kia. When he opened the door, the dismayed expression on her face as she saw her former armsmaster so crippled was plain. "Oh! Sir—I heard you'd returned, but no one told me about...." she snapped her mouth shut abruptly, trying to cover her astonishment. "Welcome back. This is from Zander Christophson. I'm to wait for your reply." Tears of sympathy filled her eyes.

"Thank you, Kia. How did your studies with Garran and Kalen go? They were my weapons instructors too," Friedr said, trying to ease her shock. "Don't worry about me, I'm fully healed now. I was injured, but can still defend myself quite well.

Remember, I'm a master with this staff, although I'm unlikely to be set upon by thieves here in Aeoven."

"Garran is very strict, but I learned a lot from him. Kalen is really fun, 'cuz he's a lightning mage. Sir, I didn't mean to be rude when I first saw you. It must have been a terrible battle if they were able to wound *you*," she said, with the frank honesty that twelve-year-olds were famous for. "I hope you killed them dead. Was it beasts?"

"Yes, they were beasts all right. And, I got a few licks in." He repressed a laugh. Everyone always said something to that effect when they first saw him now. "Just a moment and I'll give you your reply." He quickly wrote "We'll be there" on the back and sent her off.

Before she left, she said, "We need to work on your sword-arm, sir. You've not been able to practice much while you've been journeying. I know you're a healer and all now, but someone will think they can beat you in a mage-duel because you're injured. So...let's make some time for it, okay?" She looked at him challengingly.

"That's a good idea, Kia. We'll do that next week, I promise. Now that I'm going to be healing full-time, I'll need a regular sparring partner, so thank you." As he closed the door, Friedr grinned, thinking she had the makings of a weapons master herself.

Aeolyn came into the sitting room, her otherwise slim figure round with her advanced pregnancy. "Who was that? Is Marya...?"

"It was Kia. She's on messenger duty in the bachelor quarters today. This is good news, dear one," he said, hugging her with his free arm. "Zan is having his fondest wish come true this morning at ten. We're to meet him and Anna at the registry and witness their bonding."

"Thank Aeos, for this respite from the misery. We need some joy," she said, leaning her head against his chest. "I haven't known what to expect next, the way things have been. Poor Edwin, his life went to hell in his absence." Her dark eyes were full of worry. "We'll have to hurry, if we're to be there at ten," she said. "Children, let's get cleaned up. We have a little visit to make, so we need you to be on your best behavior." She bustled off to the kitchen.

"Ow! Stop it. Ow!" Frey howled as Rynne tried to pull him out of their fort by his hair. "Dad! She put jam in my hair!"

"Rynne! He doesn't need your help." Friedr tried not to grin at their antics. "Here, let's get your hands washed."

"Sawwy, Fway." She did look contrite. "A hug." There was indeed, jam in Freylin's hair, and Rynne's jam-sticky hands had more than a few bright red hairs stuck to them.

"Don' be sad. I put da toys 'way fo' you." Jonny patted Frey's shoulder, and turned to the toy basket, his blanket draped over his shoulders.

Freylin accepted the hug from his sister and dashed his tears away. "Thank you, Jonny. Can you help me wash my hair, Dad?"

"I can do that, Son," agreed Friedr. Right at that moment, he'd never been happier, despite the commotion in his home.

Sending her best wishes, Lorana remained with Marya while the others walked to the Registry. The bonding was performed by Jules Brendsson, who noted the changes in the three young men, with sadness. The ceremony itself was simple—only a few vows, and the formal registering of their union in the book. In Jules's mind, the symbolism was important, which was why he volunteered as the registrar. Both the bride and groom were already sworn to Aeos, so he had no real need to set the geas of fidelity on them, but the act of swearing faithfulness and constancy before one's friends and family was an emotional and binding thing. Each time he facilitated the ritual, he remembered his own bonding day and it brought him closer to the memory of his wife.

Connie J. Jasperson

Chapter 32

"San! San!" Jonny's cries of joy alerted Edwin to his guest's arrival. "Dad! San an' Ahna!" He stood on the sofa, looking out the window, pointing down the front path. "I ope de dor?"

"Okay, Son. Yes, you may open it," Edwin lifted Jonny down and unlatched the door for him. "Halee—Zan and Anna are here."

"I'll take Jonny back to Friedr's to play with Rynne and Frey," said Halee, worry lines tight around her eyes. "I'll return right away. He doesn't need more confusion than he's already had."

Edwin nodded. "I think that's best too. I didn't realize...I should have let him go home with Friedr after the bonding party. He didn't really want to come here."

"I know. It's taken us a while to become used to it too."

Earlier that morning before breakfast, Edwin had a long, difficult discussion with Lorana.

"I'm sure you've noticed how her madness affects you, and every healer she comes into contact with." Lorana gazed at him with sharp, brown eyes. "My staff in Farmington is specially trained to care for healers in Marya's situation. They're minimally-gifted healers, so they aren't affected by empathic surges. We currently have seven patients there, but I can comfortably house and care for up to twenty."

"I need to hear what Zan says before I make a final

decision."

"Of course. I would feel the same way. But, I warn you—she is dangerous. Or perhaps I should say she's poisonous as she is now. You're a fine healer and have the ability to keep a dampening field on her, but you'll have to give up your practice to remain here all the time and your son won't be safe around her. If Zan is unable to resolve this, you must make a decision, and do it soon. I have to return to my other patients, all of whom are in just as much need of my care as your wife."

All Edwin could do was shake his head, as if denying it would make it all go away.

"Halee needs to return to the job she loves, and you *must* get your child back to as normal a routine as possible. Today, after Zander's visit and assessment of her, we'll put together a plan for caring for her. Once I see what he's able to discover with regard to the tampering that was done, we'll know how to proceed. And, my dear—you won't be in the link when Zan is evaluating the damage. You're not able to be dispassionate. The rest of us can handle anything Zan may need in the way of supporting magic during that phase of this."

Edwin had agreed, knowing she was right, but his hesitation was impossible to disguise.

After the first treatment of the morning, Marya's demeanor had been nearly normal, although she still behaved toward him as if he were a stranger. If not for the ever-present doll, an outside observer would see nothing wrong. By the time he'd returned from Zan's bonding ceremony, her disorientation and erratic moods had begun to surface, and even the heavier spells did little to calm her for long.

Still, her tea was dosed with silf and sativa, which would make her more likely to be agreeable for the afternoon.

Returning to the kitchen, he found his wife staring at the wall, the one she'd set on fire. "They're in there, you know." It wasn't the first time she'd said that, nor would it be the last. She was obsessed with the wall and with killing whatever it was she thought lived within it. She looked at Edwin. "Fire is the only way. They have to die or they'll kill us all. They killed a baby in this house and blamed it on me."

Edwin didn't know what to say. "Marya, we have guests." He deftly led her to the sitting room. "Zan and Anna are here." Smiling professionally, he handed her the doll and helped her get herself seated.

"Where is that child?"

"He's visiting elsewhere. He won't be back today." Edwin was miserably aware that bringing Jonny home for a visit had been a mistake. Marya had stared at him, following his every move. The strange look in her eyes as she gazed at Jonny troubled Edwin. He'd been forced to keep him away from his mother, which was no problem as the child avoided her, dogging his father's footsteps everywhere. Several times she'd asked Edwin who the child was, and why he was there. "He's my son, come to visit me," was his reply. His heart felt leaden, yet shattered.

Now she said, "More guests? There are too many people here already. Do I know them?" She tried to rise, to go back to the kitchen. "Guests need food."

Gently Edwin guided her back into her chair. "Yes, you know them, so don't worry. Halee made plenty of sandwiches and we'll have tea with them. You haven't seen Zan in a long time so this will be fun." Edwin forced a smile and she settled back down. "Dane will be coming to our little luncheon too."

"I don't know those people. This house is full of people I don't know and it's not right." She glared at him. "It's not right!"

Halee returned, bringing Friedr with her. Soon they were all seated, pretending they were at a party, although until her tea took effect, Marya glared suspiciously at everyone but Halee and Lorana.

Underneath the small talk that was carried on around them, all the healers but Edwin had linked, following Zan, observing as he delicately scarched Marya's subconscious mind for the tell-tale loops he knew were there. Edwin had the distinctly unfamiliar feeling of being overlooked, keenly aware of how patients and their spouses must feel at his hands.

He'd never felt so alone, so helpless, or so close to panicking.

Afterward, Marya and Anna sat in the winter-barren garden while Zan and Lorana discussed what they'd found with the others.

"She has indeed been tampered with, several times recently. There are many small traps set in her mind, all of which are poised to be sprung whenever one is unraveled. I was able to remove the two most recent loops, but they'd already done their intended damage, springing the core trap." Zan gauged Edwin's reaction. "The central snare has been there since her captivity, and is wrapped around the geas binding her to the goddess, preventing it from working to keep her safe from tampering. It's so complex and deeply embedded that I suspect Stefyn D'Mal was guided by Tauron himself when he set it. It's been in her mind all along, waiting to be triggered either by an event or perhaps by an acolyte of the mad priest."

Lorana said, "How bad is it? It's too deeply embedded for me to fully see it. I know I can't unravel it."

"I think I'll be able to help resolve some of this for her. But you have to understand that I won't be completely successful. Because it's so intricate, I need some time to think about how I want to go about it. And I'll need the support of the four swords. We'll do this tonight if everyone is agreed." He clasped Edwin's shoulder. "I promise that if it looks like my trying to remove the central geas will kill her, I'll stop."

Lorana said, "And even if he can free her mind, her heart has been seriously compromised. Surely you see how it races all the time. She has suffered as much damage as if she were poisoned."

His expression more grim than ever, Zan agreed. "That damage, my brother, is irreversible. If she *is* freed, she doesn't have many more years, so you must make the best of what you have."

Edwin's face crumpled. Despair burst from him and for a time, he was unable to speak, barely able to breathe between gasping sobs. At last, he said, "I'm sorry. I think…I knew…but I didn't want to believe. I hoped maybe...you could…." His step-mother held his hand, and his father hovered beside him as if to shelter him. "Garran warned me, but I somehow thought she'd be like she was when we rescued her all those years ago, shattered, but mostly sane. I didn't realize...but when I saved her, even Aeos said she couldn't undo it all. I should have understood what she meant then."

Zan gave Edwin a chance to pull himself together. "I was able to do a little just now, so she'll be far more obedient today, and less inclined toward hurting herself."

"Thank you," was all Edwin could muster. Hearing his worst fears confirmed, he now struggled to stay focused, to keep himself under control. "I know what has to be done now, for Jonny's sake, if you can't resolve it. He'll be able to come home to stay."

Lorana patted his shoulder. "I know what it's like to let go of the love of your life while they still live. Either way, you have a hard road ahead of you, but you have the will to do it."

Edwin looked down, not wanting to see the sympathy in their eyes, his anger rising once again, polluting his spirit. He forced himself to use his calming and centering exercises while the others discussed treating the splintered woman who was his wife.

He looked up when Lorana spoke directly to him. "Edwin—in the event this fails, the safety of the community has to be considered. If Zan is unsuccessful, I want to take her to Farmington on Lunaday. That gives you four days to come to terms with this."

Edwin nodded, ignoring the winter that now settled in his heart. His head dropped to his hands and he bit back his sorrow. "Did I really rescue her when I took her back from Stefyn D'Mal? Or did I just condemn her to a life of misery?" Once again his shoulders shook, and his father held him as he sobbed until he had no tears left.

Chapter 33

Night had fallen. Edwin's dining room was filled with people, all of them there for one purpose. The table had been taken away, and extra chairs brought in. Marya sat in a comfortable chair in the center of the room, surrounded by those who loved her. She was awake but under heavy sedation, both magic and herbal.

The group that now encircled Marya Farmer included the seven most powerful healers currently working in the temple. Every other mage in the room besides the healers had, at least, one small star for healing and would be drawn into the link once the healing had been done. They would contribute their spirit and element to the permanent shield that would be layered over her and tied off.

Zan was going to try to undo a god's work.

Father Rall and Halee observed, each making notes for their own offices. Anna had joined the link as a journeyman observer, taking the official case notes for the healers. Beryl, who was the Dean of Healers at the college, Arne Sorensson, the head of general healing, and Darlen, the head of surgery at the infirmary would be assisting and observing. It was their intention that Zan would be officially raised to adept regardless of the outcome, as he'd proven his skills and abilities many times over. Lorana made the seventh in the circle.

Rall believed the battle about to be waged in Edwin Farmer's home was the true battle against evil.

Everyone in the circle had prepared for the task, opening themselves to the goddess and asking her guidance.

Zan reached for them mentally and the older healers were impressed by the power of his presence within the link and his calm assurance. Arne whispered to Rall, "Zan is the master. I'm now the student."

When the healers looked at John's sword, Riverbinder with their healing-sight wide open they saw lines of force emanated from it, not only connecting each of the swords in the circle, but also passing through and connecting all the healers who were in the link.

Darlen whispered to Lorana, "No wonder the sense of power is so strong—the normal link has been multiplied far beyond what it should be, and then the sword magnifies it again."

Marya sat docile, glassy-eyed, and completely unaware of her surroundings. Zan spoke, his comforting voice asking her what she remembered about the days leading up to the day she gave birth prematurely to her baby daughter. Each time she answered a question regarding a specific memory Zan loosened and dissolved a small thread in the tightly twisted knot of magic bonds in her mind.

Finally, he came to the day of the miscarriage. "Do you remember where you went that day?" Zan layered a new spell that soothed Marya, making her feel safe, distancing her from the event.

"I was terribly sad about Christoph's death and horribly worried about Edwin and the others. I went to the midwife for my weekly visit...she was away on a house-call and so was Denys. Saw her new journeyman.

Everything was fine…very healthy…her assistant was new."

"Who was this assistant? Do you remember her name?"

"Nora. I'd never met her before. But she had come from Derry to be with her daughter who is a new novice healer," Marya's voice was sleepy. "She was very nice. She delved me and told me I was carrying a daughter. I knew I was carrying a girl all along…."

Halee and Rall looked at each other and nodded imperceptibly. The elderly midwife, Olivine, had died from a sudden heart attack two days before Marya's miscarriage. She'd been assisted by Denys Erynsson, a journeyman healer for the previous two years. He hadn't changed his profession and had been raised to adept. So far as Halee knew, until the recent influx of people from Braden, Aeoven was so small, it had only needed the two midwives.

There had been no new novice healers from Derry or any other southern town in the last year. Quietly Halee stood up and went to the sitting room where she composed a note to be sent out to all the Temples. It was only a clue, but now they knew the miscarriage was no accident.

When she returned, Zan was still gradually unraveling what had happened and with each successful answer, he was able to untangle a loop, releasing it safely.

"I agree, that was odd," Zan was speaking, having moved on to another memory. "The seneschal's crew doesn't usually have time to bring the firewood inside the back gate. But you say this lady was very kind to you."

"She'd heard I'd just had a baby who died only a few days before, and she was trying to help me," said Marya, tonelessly. "I told her my father-in-law would do it but she insisted."

"Did she touch you, to help you up the stairs or anything? Just to be polite, I'm sure," Zan probed the maze of loops, gently loosening the one associated with this memory.

"In the garden...I felt faint. She helped me into the kitchen." Marya fell silent. Zan had reached the core of that particular knot.

"Do you remember what happened later that day?"

"Yes. I heard the voices in the chimney—they frightened me. They went away when I built the fire to cook our dinner. Once the fire was going, the smoke killed them." Marya shifted uneasily, and Zan stopped his probing and moved away from that loop for a moment.

"The voices in the chimney, what did they say to you?" Zan gazed at the loop he wanted to ease, knowing he would have to be very gentle about it.

"They said...they said...." As Marya faltered, Zan loosened the knot, not unraveling it yet, but just holding it ready.

"What did they say," he gently probed.

"They told me to kill my son." she stared, glassy-eyed as Zan gently relaxed the loop. "They said my baby was lonely and needed her brother to be with her, but I made them leave."

"You were brave. You didn't listen to them and you made them go away." He now loosened another loop in the tangle.

"I was relieved. I kissed my son and then I went to

bed." Her breath became more rapid as she remembered the evening. "I wondered where my husband was. He should have been there to kill the voices, but he wasn't. So I thought perhaps they'd killed him. I heard the voices in the chimney again. They were so loud they woke me," She spoke as if viewing the scene from a distance. "They were going to kill my family so the baby wouldn't be alone."

"What did you do next?"

"I went down to the kitchen. The voices were everywhere, even in the walls. So I built a fire but this time, it didn't work. It wasn't big enough—I had to keep adding to it." She shuddered as Zan released the loop.

"Did the larger fire stop them?" Zan's attention was now on the central web of the geas.

"No. John came and put the fire out with his magic before I could kill them." She sighed. "Then I couldn't get to them. I tried to break the wall with the ax so I could get to them...so my father-in-law could see them. I wanted to tell him about them, but they wouldn't let me."

"Who wouldn't let you?" Zan paused, hovering over the tangle.

"The voices. They were everywhere. I couldn't make them stop, and they didn't want me to tell. They sealed my lips. I couldn't tell the truth, even when Lorana tried to heal me." Now Marya showed signs of being visibly upset. "I tried, but I couldn't."

Forced to simply observe, Edwin held his breath, and Lorana soothed him. Zan layered yet another sense of wellbeing into Marya's mind.

"What happened after that? Do you remember?"

The tightest tangle lay within his reach, but he dared not touch it until she answered his question.

"I realized I was dangerous. I didn't know the fire had gotten out of control until John put it out. When I saw what happened to my kitchen I was frightened," her voice faltered, but she kept speaking. "I knew then something had happened to my mind and I thought it was something Stefyn had done when he... when he..." She fell silent, unable to speak.

Zan saw he would have to find a different way for her to speak about the memories embodied in the loop in order for it to be loosened. He decided to take a different approach. "You tried to kill yourself. Do you remember why?"

"I was dangerous."

Delicately he eased the tension on the tendril. "Why were you dangerous?"

"They said to kill everyone. I would find myself with the knife in my hand. I couldn't think of any other way to protect them." She shifted in her chair and shuffled her feet as if to get up. Lorana placed the thought she wanted to stay, and she sat back, still tense. Marya's face betrayed her agitation, but Zan had been able to loosen the knot just enough. Now he was able to completely untangle it. With the removal of the central geas, the rest of the unraveling went much easier.

Somewhere around three in the morning, Marya lay on the settee, sleeping peacefully, finally free of the many-layered geas which had been set on her.

Zan said to Lorana, "Now our task is to build the shield/barrier around her that we discussed. In this, Edwin will be the leader. We'll build it as we did the ward on the wall, using all the elements she doesn't have the ability to use, tying it off to her life-chi so it won't fade. The elements and spirit of all those at this table will be woven into it. She'll never again be without a barrier. No Hound of Tauron or even Lourdan will be able to break her barrier and affect her mind ever again. Father Rall, Abbess Halee—are you willing to lend us your spirit?" At their nods, Zan mentally reached out and drew Halee and Rall into the link.

As the sun rose, Edwin sat beside his wife, holding her hand as she slept. Tears of joy and exhaustion had dried on his cheeks, but he didn't care. His wife was returned to him, and it was all that mattered. The misery of the last months finally fell away from him. For the first time since Christoph's death, Edwin felt something akin to happiness.

Edwin had dozed off when Marya woke to find him there next to her. Gasping, "Edwin, you're home. I dreamed you'd come home and you really are here!" She sat up and threw her arms around him. "Oh, my dear, it's been hard, but now you're home." She began to cry. "I was so worried. We don't know what happened to Chris, only that he's dead."

Gathering her to him, Edwin said, "It's been a long hard journey, but now we're home."

Sobbing, Marya said, "The baby came too early. She died. But at least, I got to hold her for a day."

"I know, love. I know." He kissed her forehead and gently wiped away her tears. "They told me in Braden. I'm so sorry I wasn't here with you, but now I'm home."

VALLEY OF SORROWS

Chapter 34

The line outside the seneschal's office in the city of Aeoven had moved rather quickly. Lindie D'Orman found herself filling out the form and getting the key for her shop faster than she'd expected, given the level of bureaucracy these people seemed to enjoy. "Is there plenty of storage in this shop? A good attic, perhaps?" She wanted a good-sized, dry cellar, but didn't want to draw attention to herself by asking for one.

The overly-bright woman at the desk said, "Yes. The attics there are large and finished inside. Plus, all the shops in that row on Commerce Street have large, dry cellars if you need more storage. The upstairs living quarters are quite spacious in these older buildings. Just like when you lived in Braden, if you have any problems or anything needs repairing, let us know and we'll get someone over right away."

Linette went back outside, to where her brother waited with the wagon. "It's down this street, second from the end, on the right. It should be fairly large."

Her brother flicked the reins and the wagon pulled away from the curb, the rattle covering the sounds of their low conversation. "It better be large—we have to tithe forty percent of our profits just for the privilege of earning a living. Tell me again why I have to work in the bakery?" Teller scratched at his newly grown beard. "I wish you'd let me shave, or, at least, cut my hair."

"Stop whining. We have a shop at no cost out of our pocket, and a place to live, just like Oran did in Braden. We don't have to buy anything—in a pinch, the Temple will even provide us with basic food and clothes, boring and ugly though they are. As for shaving—perhaps you'd like to be recognized by your former customers?" Linette looked sideways at him. "Maybe you'd enjoy being questioned by Temple assassins. Those mages in Fleetside were quite curious about you. So you're a baker now."

"What did you tell them my name is?"

"Telly. We're Lindie and Telly, just like when we were kids. We'll keep it simple and easy to remember."

Teller tried to get past his disgruntlement and failed. "Why did you kill Oren? He ran the family shop, which allowed us to do our work freely."

"Not this again. Oren deserved it." Her eyes were hard as she added, "People who don't do their tasks should be wary, don't you agree? And you will do exactly as you're told, my dear little brother. You've drawn attention to yourself and used your second chance."

"What do you mean my 'second chance'? I did nothing except tell the minotaur under-priest where she would be that night. He wanted a healer and I showed him where to find one."

"Then why were those mages interested in you? The day you were gelded and ejected from the priesthood in Mal Evol City was your first chance. Dalgek should have offered you up on the altar that day. He would have if you weren't my brother."

Teller's look of horror was gratifying. Desperately he turned the subject away from the one day he couldn't bear to remember. "That healer—they were interviewing every patient from that day, not just me. And I wasn't the last one. She saw several others after me. The under-priest didn't take her until it was dark."

"Telly, Telly...you don't get it. You raped a child

and brought shame on our family—the healer with those mages recognized immediately that you'd been gelded. They also know only one sort of crime warrants that punishment. You're only getting this chance because you're all I have left, thanks to that monstrosity of a wall." She snorted. "But you won't get a third." She was lying. He was crucial to her plan, or she would have let the Temple have him back in Fleetside.

Teller flinched under her glare, wondering if her madness would resurface.

She remained calm, with her usual acidic demeanor. "Between Oran's laziness and paying both his tithe and my own I've lived hand-to-mouth for long enough. You'll work in our bakery, Telly, just like when we were children, and you won't complain about it. I have a task for our god here, and you're going to help me do it."

"You keep saying this, but you don't explain yourself. What work can we do now? We're cut off from the church."

"We're cut off from the chancellery, but not from god. Our task is what it's always been—weaken the Temple of Aeos and force the goddess to kneel before Tauron as her rightful husband. That won't ever change. I've been successful at my work so far and I've remained hidden, unlike you."

"I was always successful at spreading the truth in subtle ways. God knows my heart and soul belong to him, even if you don't understand that."

She smirked at his expression. "Your task is to pretend to be a good son of Aeos and enable me to do my work. Oren had a task and he failed. Our new task is clear: we must raise an altar to Tauron, right under their noses. The shop they've so generously given us has a cellar, brother dear. All we need is a congregation."

"Here in their holy city? Are you nuts? This place is far more dangerous than Braden. There are mages and healers everywhere."

Teller's astonishment drew a nasty chuckle from his sister. "Fortunately, they're clearly marked, so spotting them is no trouble at all. Flashy armor, disgusting tattoos—they stand out wherever they go."

He said, "You're right about that, but still, this is dangerous. The reason we've been successful in the past is we worked from the shadows. To do this correctly will involve many tasks, all of which could draw their attention. Just acquiring the suitable vessels for the purification ritual will be difficult. I've been a rag-and-bone man, so I know about acquiring things, but here I have no contacts. I'll have to obtain them from the enemy without knowing who to trust."

She waved his concerns away. "We'll achieve what no one else has ever done. You and I are going to do what we do best—use our gifts to discreetly sell the truth with every loaf of bread. Tauron is the one true god. Only through strength and sacrifice can a person see the kingdom of heaven. Aeos has allowed her people to become weak, and they don't understand sacrifice. We'll rectify that and bring the people of Neveyah to Tauron, one convert at a time." Her eyes were alight as she added, "We're going to save this world."

Buoyed by the power of her conviction, Teller replied, "I pray you're correct that we can do this without being discovered. They've won this battle, but the truth must eventually prevail. Only when Aeos kneels before her rightful husband will the balance of the worlds be restored. On that day, Tauron will reign over all the gods with the Queen of Heaven at his side."

Warmth lit Linette's harsh features, an echo of her once youthful beauty. "That's why I didn't turn you over to the Temple last week, Brother dear. You understand what we have to do to bring this about and you have the gift of persuasion. I can't do this alone."

Teller halted the wagon in front of an empty shop. "Is this it?"

Linette looked at the paper. "Yes. We can unload in the alley. There's supposed to be a stall back there for the horse, in the wagon shed. It says there's a community pasture, two streets over."

Teller nodded. "The market quarter here is laid out like every other Temple town. They aren't very imaginative. But at least, one knows what to expect."

Linette hid her smile. The little voice that was her constant companion said, *Ah, but does your dear little brother know what to expect? I doubt it.* Wild laughter echoed in her mind, and she had to forcibly stifle the urge to laugh along with it.

Chapter 35

Zan let himself in at Edwin's back gate and saw Marya seated at the table in the garden, shelling walnuts. "You look like you're having fun," he said. "I'll sit here with you and wait for Edwin."

"Before you ask, feel free to delve me and have a look inside my head too. I know you need to. Christoph would have done the same." Humor lit her features, her pale skin nearly translucent in the winter sun. "Dad's keeping me busy. We're making fruitcakes for Holy Day gifts, but he won't let me do anything fun for fear it'll wear me out. Did you and Anna get a house yet?"

Zan chuckled. "Houses are still being allocated to the refugees, so no, not yet. Maybe next week. We're fine where we are for now. We eat with Dane anyway, so we don't really need a kitchen." Zan reached for her wrist and his dark eyes took in her pallor. Her faint pulse was too rapid, but they were unable to slow it. He sat opposite her, casting a strengthening spell on her.

Halee came down the back steps carrying a bowl, a chopping board, and a knife. "Hello, Zan. How's Dane today?" She sat beside Marya. "Edwin will be out in just a minute. He's helping Jonny hang the last garland over the front door." She dumped dried fruits out of the bowl onto the board, chopping them. "I'm not much of a cook, but John seems to think I can't ruin these!" She scooped them into the bowl.

Marya and Zan laughed.

"Dane is doing well, much better now. He'll be back to work after the New Year begins. He's making pies for Holy Day and shooed me out of the kitchen. Anna is working at the infirmary, and I wanted to see

Marya before Edwin and I went to our meeting."

The back door opened, and Jonny came down the steps, followed closely by Edwin. At the bottom, the boy ran to his mother. "Ahmah! I hanged it! Come and see!"

Patting her daughter-in-law's arm, Halee said, "Go and enjoy the decorations with him. I'll finish cracking the walnuts."

Zan stood up and came around the table, helping Marya up. "You feel stronger today to my senses."

She laughed. "I'm surrounded by the best healers. Even Dad keeps casting little spells my way. I have energy today, and that's good." Grinning, Edwin took her elbow, helping her up the steps, following her inside.

Zan sat back down, opposite Halee. "Despite her permission, I didn't want to snoop too much in her head. But everything we did is still protecting her."

Halee let out a breath she didn't know she'd been holding. "Good. I wasn't worried exactly, but not knowing the identity of this priestess of Tauron worries me."

Zan's expression darkened. "We're going hunting today, after our meeting with Kalen. How's Marya coping? She seems cheerful, but she's had a lot to absorb, and I sense a great deal of confusion and sorrow underneath it all."

Halee had finished picking the nuts out of the shells and standing up, she tossed the shells onto the compost heap. "She's had a hard time understanding what happened. She has no memory of most of the last three months, so for her it's like the baby died only days ago, and she's devastated about Christoph. She's grieving for the baby as any normal woman would, but she finds happiness in the small things again." Halee smiled warmly. "Yes she's not well, but Marya is resilient. I have my daughter-in-law back, thanks to you, Zan. You've no idea what that means to me."

>>><<<

Kalen Rallsson ushered Edwin and Zan into his study. It was rather like a war room, with a large table in the center, and shelves filled with books and rolled up maps around the perimeter. Moran was seated at the table, poring over maps.

Edwin had always thought that Kalen looked just like his dad, Father Rall, must have looked as a younger man. Both were exceptionally tall men with white hair that fell well past their waist, and both had icy blue eyes. But where Father Rall was a water-mage, his son Kalen was a lightning-mage and their augmentations were radically different, as were their personalities.

Once the greetings were out of the way, Kalen sat and gestured for them to be seated. He said, "Many things have happened during your absence, some of which you're aware, and some I need to tell you."

Edwin sat opposite of him and grinned. "I'm listening. Dad won't tell me anything that might disturb me, so I have to get my information from Garran or you."

Kalen chuckled. "That's John's way, all right. You're aware your father was attacked? It was instigated by the same person who killed Cayne, and is also responsible for Marya's breakdown."

Edwin and Zan both nodded. Edwin said, "I only know what Halee has told me because dad refuses to discuss it. Since the attack didn't actually kill him, he claims it's nothing to worry about."

"We'll get to why that attack is still relevant after I explain what happened two months ago. The first of two healers disappeared. The first one, Yllene, was on a two-week journey and is believed to have vanished from the town of Fleetside. Because she was in a town, she had no guards. Fleetside Temple was not yet finished, so she was detached from Braden Temple's infirmary, and there was some confusion because of that. The Abbott in Fleetside, Noli, was in the final stages of building the Temple there, so he had only minimal staff. He said the girl had a habit of forgetting to let them know when she was called out, but always checked back in."

Moran took up the story. "I was in Braden at the time and was sent to look into her disappearance. When I checked the calendar to see the last day she was actually seen by a patient, the kidnapping must have happened just days after Christoph fell."

Kalen said, "Yllene is a young journeyman just out of the novice barracks, and hasn't been heard from since. We've received no demands for ransom, so if D'Mal took her, you know what that means."

"Yes. She's gone to the altar and nothing was left to send back to us." Edwin's anger surged, but he buried it. "I knew Yllene well. I trained her in barriers. And the other missing healer?"

"A senior adept, Bekki, also missing from Fleetside. Because she was bonded, she had been given a temporary posting covering Ylene's circuit. It was to last two weeks at the most."

The news stunned the two healers, leaving Edwin speechless. Zan said, "We were told Dario had lost his wife, but not how."

"This is where it really gets complicated, so bear with me." Kalen leaned forward, speaking low. "While you were finishing up near Wellesbridge, Moran returned to Braden from clearing the Gap. The day he arrived back, a dead woman was found just outside the eastern gate. She'd been dumped there during the night."

Moran said, "It was Bekki."

Zan shook his head as if denying it would change it. "Garran implied her death was natural."

"That's the official story. He probably felt you had enough on your plate with constructing the wall and everything else." Moran continued with his story. "I could see that she'd been taken into Mal Evol, most likely to the Shadow Castle. Scars on her body indicated she'd been ritually broken. Somehow she'd survived that. They probably intended to return her to us alive as one of their bizarre warnings, but somewhere along the line she died."

Kalen said, "As always, they left her where her corpse would be found. Her body was deliberately arranged as a message to the Temple."

Moran said, "One bit of information I've gleaned about Tauron's priesthood, is that part of an acolyte's path to full priesthood involves making ritual sacrifices. It also involves demonstrating certain skills regarding their magic. Breaking the will of prisoners and binding them as thralls is one of their tasks and is one way they maintain a grip on their nobility. To break a priest or priestess of Aeos and leave them alive is considered an almost impossible feat. Such a thing can only be done by an extremely powerful mage."

Kalen pulled out a piece of paper and consulted it. "The minotaur you met on your travels, Zirik—his comments provide the key to the person responsible for Bekki's ultimate fate. I've been thinking on what he said about the difference in the way time flows between Serende and Neveyah. If you add in his cautions that the new Overlord had been successful in completing his sacrifices as an acolyte, only one person could have been responsible for what happened to her directly after her kidnapping.

"We know this man has the abilities of a gifted healer, so he has the skills necessary to do what was done to Bekki. He was also on the path to the priesthood and had to make several ritual sacrifices to prove his worthiness."

"Lourdan." Edwin fought down nausea at the thought.

Zan sat silently, his somber features giving no clue as to his true thoughts.

"Yes." Kalen tapped his fingers, thinking. "I believe Lourdan broke the geas binding her to Aeos, turned her to Tauron and in the process, destroyed her. As far as I know, other than Baron D'Mal, only Lourdan has the kind of strength in empathic magic that would be required to facilitate the ritual and leave her alive."

Edwin forced himself to assume the detached, clinical mental state he maintained when working with seriously ill patients, separating his logical mind from the emotion generated by the revelations he'd just heard. "How did two healers vanish and why didn't the Temple know sooner?"

"In both cases, by the time we realized they were

gone, we were in the midst of the uproar of the evacuation. That meant we were limited in what we could do to look for them."

Zan asked, "What of the younger healer? Yllene."

"We believe she's dead, likely given as an offering to their god. As I said, we've heard nothing about her fate. If they'd managed to break her on the altar as they did Bekki, they would have made sure we found her corpse." Kalen shrugged.

Moran's bondmate, Piers, had been ritually sacrificed a year previously. Grief marked him, but he was detached and professional. "It's a fear tactic. They can break us and want us to see the evidence of that fact. This is why the Temple must be extra vigilant in guarding our healers. Any coven embedded in our population could get at them, and even though they won't have D'Mal's knack for mind magic, they'll have a connection to Tauron. Sacrificing a healer or battle-mage on the altar to their dark god is their sure way into whatever they see as heaven."

Moran looked at the clock. "Dario and Mikel should be here any minute. They can explain more about this to you since they've been handling the investigation. We'll hear what they have to say, and then walk the city and show you how to sense for mindbenders."

Chapter 36

Edwin and Zan sat at the worktable in Kalen's study, with Moran, Dario, and Mikel. Kalen unrolled a map of Aeoven, setting weights on the corners. "This is the updated map of the market district. As far as the seneschal knows, every refugee family who had a shop in Braden now has one here in Aeoven. The shops and houses marked in red are the ones newly occupied by refugees from Braden and elsewhere in the gap."

Dario unrolled his own map, updating the few he didn't already have listed. "I'll make sure you and Zan have copies of this," he said to Edwin.

Kalen turned to Zan. "I'll requisition copies of the transcript, but would you tell us exactly what Graylor told you about the mindbender who was known to be here in Aeoven?"

Zan complied.

When he finished, Dario said, "The other man Graylor spoke of, Teller—his trail led me to Fleetside. And now I hear Anders suspects the junk-man knows something about Bekki's kidnapping. But apparently I'm too close to that situation, so I'm off the case." He sat back, seething.

Moran said, "You *are* too close to it. It's only been a few weeks and you've not had a chance to come to grips with your grief. Noli will deal with Teller if he's still in Fleetside." His voice was firm, showing none of the emotion he must have felt. "I know how you feel. No one knows it better than I do, but we can't let vengeance get in the way of justice. We who bear the rune have an extra obligation to Aeos and to justice."

Dario winced. "I know. I know you've all lost as

much as I have. Forgive me." He attempted a smile and forced himself to return to the main subject. "Anyway, Linette is a fairly common name. We found two friendly-girls with that name at the Weaver's Rest and several well-established older women who were living here before the influx of refugees, and who knows how many there are now. The friendly-girl who is missing from the Lantern, which is a much seedier place than the Weaver's Rest, and who was connected to Cayne was also named Linette. She may or may not be dead."

Zan asked, "We need to consider how Graylor told us the woman he called Linette hides herself. This is the capital city of Neveyah. It's run by the Temple, so mages and healers are walking around town at all hours, yet none have ever sensed her presence."

Kalen nodded. "Unfortunately, followers of Tauron here in Neveyah are careful. However, every now and then a convert repents and turns themselves in to the local Abbott, which is the only way we ever find them."

"Linette will be drawn to other followers of Tauron so we may find her by finding others less clever than her," said Edwin. "How do they worship their god? Do they have meeting places?"

Kalen stood up, pacing again. "What the few of their altars I was unfortunate enough to see in Mal Evol all had in common was they were usually below ground. It has to do with being in the womb of the earth. Even the large Chancellery in Mal Evol City is built so that the actual temple is two levels below the ground."

Edwin said. "Tauron's followers are cut off from their center of worship. What would we do under the same circumstance? Let's assume Tauron's followers will be forced to set up their own altar now they've been denied access to the valley. They should follow the same pattern, don't you think? So it will be underground. Which shops and houses lack basements? That'll narrow it a little."

Zan's pencil made a scratching noise as he took notes. "I wonder about this Linette that Graylor spoke of—could a woman have the duties of a priest? She must be known among those followers of Tauron hidden in our population."

Kalen considered Zan with some speculation. He said, "That's a good point. Tauron withholds magic ability from women, as they're responsible for rearing children. Strength of magic and ability to wield it is crucial in their society. Only the strongest mages can gain status in their temple hierarchy. However, we've heard that some of their most respected scholars are women. Perhaps they can become priestesses in that way."

"Graylor claimed he was a full priest, and yet he'd never been remade as the minotaur priests are. It seemed like he was a member of a new sect, and she would be too." Zan thought for a moment. "We have to realize that the last two generations of people in Mal Evol have been raised to follow Tauron, and people who still follow Aeos are hidden, but they may not trust the remade clergy of their new rulers."

The six mages bent over the maps, checking against other blueprints from the seneschal's office and making notes.

Half an hour passed. Kalen stood up and stretched. He said, "What I want to do now is divide ourselves into two groups of three, splitting Edwin and Zan.

We'll show you how to recognize what you're sensing. And then, as quickly as you can, you have to learn everything there is to know about this city and the people in it."

Edwin and Zan nodded.

"Zan—you, Moran, and I will begin by walking the crafter's quarter." Kalen picked up the weights and re-rolled the map. "Using your ability to link and wind-speak, you'll stay in contact with Edwin, who'll be walking the market with Dario and Mikel. Having a pair in our group with the ability to link and use air-magic is the one advantage we have in this fight and I intend to exploit it to the fullest."

Chapter 37

Snow and slush made the streets of Aeoven slippery. Few shoppers were out, so shopkeepers were willing to be generous. Edwin and Zan were pictures of nonchalance, no different than any others braving the post-holiday weather. Well into their first month of duty as part of Kalen's team, the two were linked, searching for any sign that the mindbender was present. However, they'd found nothing out of the ordinary, and Kalen had begun to believe the mindbender they were looking for was no longer in Aeoven.

Their duty was technically a battle mage's task, but they were dressed as off-duty healers, wearing the standard green cloaks that marked them as being no threat to anyone. Edwin and Zan strolled through the market, stopping at each stall and shop, sometimes making a purchase. Their audible conversation revolved around the drapes Zan was making for his and Anna's new home on Lilac Street. Their house was on the far end near the river, with their back gate across the alley from Friedr's.

They stopped at a new shop, one that sold silk and other fine cloth. Zan's eyes lit up as he saw a bolt of rich, intricately woven, midnight-blue material. The sign read, "Linen Damask."

"Ooh. This is reversible. It'll look as good from the outside as in." Zan examined it closely. "It's stout enough for upholstery."

Edwin hid his boredom. "Is that what you're looking for?" His mind wandered, itching to be done with their tour of the market, but they still had several more streets to cover. "It should keep out any drafts, and no one can see through it, so you'll have privacy."

Zan's current obsession of furnishing his new home was conveniently in line with their new responsibilities. However, he had a tight budget and took bargaining seriously, which amused Edwin.

"I don't know. It's exactly what I want, but I'm sure it's too expensive." Zan turned to the shopkeeper. "Sir, how wide is this fabric? If it's the right width for my needs, I may want four lengths."

Edwin gazed out the window, listening to Zan bargaining with the shopkeeper. In the weeks since their return to Aeoven, the shopkeepers had come to know them well and liked Zan. He was a sharp haggler, a skill they appreciated.

The negotiations were approaching the conclusion. The shopkeeper held up a length of the material. "You'll never find better, not in this town, even though you bargain like a mercenary."

"Business is slow during this weather, and I have a limited number of coins. This beautiful material is gathering dust when it could be earning you the coins that remain in my purse. I can offer you nine coppers for each length," said Zan. With ten coppers equaling silver he was perilously close to not having enough money for the material.

The shopkeeper demurred. "You're right that business is slow today, but not so much that I must sell at a loss. I can accept one silver for each of the four lengths, but not a copper less. This came all the way from the weavers in Moreton."

"Ah, but you were in Braden when you originally

acquired it, so it wasn't rare at the time, and you got it at a good price. However, you did have to cart it here with the rest of your stock, and that's worth something." Zan fell silent, mentally counting his coins. "Agreed. Four silvers, if you can deliver it to my home."

"My son will deliver it. Where to?"

Flushed with his victory, Zan gave his address and paid the man.

As the door closed behind them, Edwin laughed. He said, "You know you're as bad as Dane. Right?"

"I know, but I was raised in a nice home and I want to live in one. Anna doesn't sew and I do." Zan shrugged. "Where to now?"

"We should walk to the boot shop at the end of the street. We can pretend to window shop. Then we'll be done with our circuit for the day."

"A good idea. I'm out of funds now."

Edwin grinned. "So the rest of our tour should go quickly."

By the time they reached the end of the street, both men were feeling hungry. Edwin said, "There's a bakery. 'D'Orman's'—must be refugees from Braden. The name is one you'd hear down that way. I don't think we've been inside there yet. Let's see what they have. I'll get us a snack since you're impoverished now."

"Thank you for taking pity on a man down on his luck, kind sir." Zan's mimicry of an old beggar they'd healed in Widge made Edwin chuckle. "Now that you mention it, we do our own baking. I suppose we haven't had any reason to go inside there."

The bell over the door tinkled as they entered. "It

smells wonderful in here." Zan's stomach rumbled as he spoke, causing them to burst out laughing.

The glass case was filled with specialty baked goods, things Edwin had only seen in Arlen and Braden. "I love those cream-filled things. Remember that fancy bakery we stopped at? I'd never had anything so good."

Zan agreed. "I could eat myself fat on them."

A man of about forty entered from the back, drying his hands. His voice, when he greeted them, was more like a boy's than a man's, but it was pleasant, with a slight accent that marked him as from the Gap. "Greetings, healers. What can I get for you today?"

Edwin bought two of the cream-filled pastries, handing Zan one. "You know, I think I'll take a dozen more if you have them. My family would love these, and I should make sure this lout's wife has a treat too."

Through the link, Edwin said, "He's been castrated. There's only one crime warranting that punishment."

Zan realized he was staring at the man. Quickly he said aloud, "I'm a lucky 'lout' to have a friend like you taking care of me. This is a fine bakery. It reminds me of a place we stopped at in Braden. The family who ran it came out of Mal Evol city. Apparently they had a bakery there before the war, S'Rylien's. Did you know them? Madame S'Rylien was proud of her family's heritage."

"I wouldn't know anything about the bakers of Mal Evol City, other than our father had once been one," replied the man, who seemed a friendly person. "My sister and I were born in the valley but have little memory of it. We left when the war started and were raised in Braden. Our recipes came from our father, who learned from his father. "

"Who does the baking here?" Edwin looked around. "This is the finest bakery I've ever been to, better even than Madame S'Rylien's."

"My sister does all the baking," replied the man. "I don't have the knack she does, so I run the front."

After a little more small talk, the two men left the shop carrying their purchase in a paper bag.

Once out on the street, they walked down to the boot shop, still sensing for anything unusual. Then they turned back toward the square where Temple Boulevard met Commerce Street.

Edwin's steps slowed, and he came to a stop. Speaking low, he said, "It feels like someone with healing empathy is working nearby. But it's muffled. I don't know how or why."

Sensing the faint discordance, Zan cast his awareness out. "Now that you mention it, I sense it too." He cast his awareness inside the shops around them, finding nothing out of the ordinary.

"Someone with a strange signature is definitely working with the healing side of magic, but I can't narrow down where, exactly," replied Edwin. He turned around, pretending to be searching for a particular shop.

Zan agreed. "No. I can't sense where they are, other than somewhere at this end of the street. It's a large area, but...now it's gone."

Edwin said, "Whoever they are, they were well-shielded, which is why we couldn't locate them. They have an unfamiliar style of magic so we know it's one of Graylor's ilk. Once I locate it, I'll have to examine their shield more closely to take it down. But I don't know where it was. It felt spread out over too broad an area for me to pin down."

Throughout the mental conversation, Edwin and Zan maintained smiles, apparently discussing nothing of import. Through the link, Zan said, "We need to see Kalen."

John stood in the kitchen, peeling vegetables and talking, detailing his plan for the militia. His journeyman, Lenn, sat at the table, taking notes. "Father Rall used his influence and got this on the agenda for the final day of the conclave, so we have no wiggle-room. They have to agree with it on the first vote, or we'll be sunk until the summer conclave."

"So we have to summarize it and also write it out?" Lenn kept writing as he talked. "The conclave is nearly over. Just getting the summary written in such a short time will be a challenge. Are you sure we have to provide them with the full proposal in detail?"

"Yes. Even though the majority of the Abbacy will only skim through the summary, they have to be able to *claim* they read the whole thing. Halee has assigned us several scribes so we'll have a copy of the plan for every voting member. We need to have the proposal in their hands two days before it's heard, so they can't say they weren't informed."

"That gives us three days to write it out, and two for the scribes to make all the copies." Lenn looked up. "We won't get much sleep this week. We can't work on this when we're supposed to be teaching novices how to use magic. We'll each lose half a day of work time, there. Is this how this sort of thing is done all the time?"

"Not usually." John paused to slide the vegetables

into the pot.

Lenn finished writing and set his pencil aside. "There—I have it all organized in an outline form."

John sat down opposite him, glancing over the outline. "Good. Let's get as far as we can before Marya wakes up, and Halee and Jonny get home. If you stay for dinner tonight, we might be able to finish the summary after Jonny goes to bed. We could start writing the formal proposal tomorrow."

Lenn brightened up. "Your supper looks far tastier than what the dining-hall is offering tonight." He glanced toward the sitting room where Marya dozed on the sofa under a colorful knit blanket. "But will it be too much for your daughter-in-law? She looks so frail."

John shook his head. "She enjoys having company. We'll make sure she doesn't over-exert herself."

Both looked up as the door to the back porch opened. Edwin entered, followed by Zan.

Greeting Lenn, Edwin opened the cold-cupboard and set the paper bag inside. The healer was far more cheerful than Lenn had ever seen him. "These are cream-pastries, for dessert." He grinned at Lenn. "Don't worry. There's enough for everyone—I bought a dozen. We need to see Kalen about something, but we'll be back." The door closed behind them but opened up immediately as Edwin stuck his head back in. "I almost forgot. Zan and Anna are staying for dinner, so toss an extra spud or two into the pot." He ducked out again.

Grinning, John stood up and reached into the vegetable bin, setting several more potatoes and carrots on the cutting board, along with an onion.

Lenn looked from John to the back door. "Is it like this all the time here?"

"Pretty much. That's why soup is usually on the menu." John glanced at the cold-cupboard, anticipation in his eyes. "Cream-pastries are a treat from the old days. We must have gained an old-style bakery along with the refugees from Braden."

Chapter 38

Linette entered the bakery kitchen from the cellar. Her clothes were dusty and she was exhausted. Shielding her work from any mages that could be passing by had depleted her reserve of chi.

She quickly dusted herself off and washed her hands and face. Donning an apron and a clean bandanna, she began measuring flour for the next day's baking, setting the kitchen up to immediately start in the morning.

The back door opened, and Teller came in. "Here are the eggs. The hens we were given are laying well despite the cold. I've got the kindling stacked and ready for tomorrow morning." He set the egg basket down on the workbench. "We've had very few customers today, thanks to the weather, but one greedy fellow bought all your cream pastries."

"Good." Linette nodded. "I've done as much as I can downstairs for now. It's taken me longer than I hoped, but everything is in place. Once the altar is consecrated, we can begin cultivating the seeds we've planted in the community here."

Teller sat at the table watching her work. "I know you're still unhappy that I was unable to find golden ewers. But I acquired the finest brass ones I could get without drawing attention to us. They were expensive but were the largest I could find. Apparently some people use them for decorations. Trying to make their tiny rooms look special, I suppose."

His sister said nothing, so he added, "I'm glad a copper bathtub was acceptable to you because the only other option was a common laundry tub. Large ewers and ceremonial founts are not easily sourced here. I have no connections in this town, but from what I can tell there's no market for those things." His lips curled in distaste. "They don't purify themselves before entering their goddess's presence."

"You said all that yesterday." She covered the bowls of flour with towels, and looked at the sourdough starter, adding some flour and water.

Her work done, she sat opposite him. Linette's gaze had grown disturbing whenever her eyes fell on him and now was no different. "Brass and copper will do to begin with. It was the best we could find and took all our coins. All that remains is the consecration of the altar. You'll have to arrange for a proper sacrifice. Frosday night would be the perfect time for the ritual of consecration." Linette watched her brother's features carefully. "I'm not talking about a beloved dog or the finest sheep this time. It has to be a true, fitting sacrifice."

Teller stalled, not sure what she was asking of him. "Frosday...why so soon? I may not be able to find anything of value on such short notice. And where will you find a priest so quickly?"

"The first dark moon of the new year occurs on Frosday," replied Linette. "I cast the bones this afternoon when I finished setting the final stone. The auguries are that the hour just before dawn on Frosday will be the most auspicious moment this year. The days are just beginning to lengthen, and with no moon, Aeos's influence will be diminished." She paused, tapping her fingers. It was a recent habit that annoyed Teller. "And a *thing* won't do as a sacrifice. To properly consecrate this chapel, it's crucial that we provide the god with a worthy sacrifice. A rare, unique gift, one such as you regularly found for Dalgek."

Teller didn't want to understand. "This town is crawling with mages. Surely there's no need for me to run such a risk anymore."

"A child. We need a child for this."

He tried to conceal his dismay, searching for a way to convey the dilemma such a request presented without triggering her rage. Carefully he said, "There are no street urchins or beggars anywhere in this town. I haven't even seen any pickpockets here. Given how heavily the Temple taxes the merchants, you'd think there would be a large population of homeless people, but there are none. Not even among the addicts. And we've no priest to celebrate the offering." Teller stood, planning to go back outside to finish his chores.

Her voice was cold and demanding, her expression implacable. "I know that's the segment of society where you found most of the gifts you supplied Dalgek with. But even if there were candidates in that population here, an unwanted beggar-child wouldn't be good enough. This is the most crucial ritual in the life of this altar. The offering must be cherished or it isn't worthy. Tomorrow you'll find me that gift, or you will *be* that gift." She rose, intending to go into the shop.

Dumbfounded, Teller tried to absorb what he'd just heard. "*You* are going to personally perform the ritual? But you—without magic women can't be remade priests." He stepped back from her, knowing she teetered on the edge of insanity and would reject the truth. Still, he had to say it. "We must wait for a proper priest. It's written that the one who would preside over the altar must have endured the altar. You've never undergone the remaking. You've never experienced the altar."

Madness looked out of her eyes as she rounded on him. "Who else is there? An unmade priest with no balls? You lost your horns and your magic the day they castrated you."

Teller's features crumpled. "Don't talk about that day...don't...you have no idea...augh!" He pressed his hands to his face, his shoulders shaking with silent sobs.

Linette snarled at him, rage at the humiliation he'd brought on her family all those years before robbing her of her precarious sanity. Raising her hand, she focused her will and regressed her brother's awareness, plunging him into the moment of his unmaking, watching as he collapsed to the floor, writhing and shrieking, clawing at his own throat, desperately trying to kill himself. Her face was a rictus of evil as she held him in the memory, replaying it again and again, intensifying it until he no longer had a voice.

She drew chi from his agony and terror, luxuriating in the feeling of having plenty after the hard afternoon of expending magic in completing the altar. Sated at last, she said, "You keep forgetting something crucial, Brother dear. Despite the fact I only have Aeos's magic, I'm a full priestess. I've studied in Serende. I'm all that's left of Tauron's priesthood here in Neveyah, thanks to that bloody black wall. I'm the High Priestess of Neveyah and my altar will be where Tauron's kingdom enters this world." She let him out of his memory and waited for his sobs to subside. "I require a worthy sacrifice. You will get me a child. Tomorrow."

Shuddering and unable to speak, Teller nodded.

"We're all there is to bring forth the new era of Tauron's dominion over Neveyah. New traditions are necessary to bring it to fruition. I have no under-priest to serve me as yet. You'll assist me, and if I must, I'll draw chi from you. You'd best make sure the offering is healthy enough that such a thing is not necessary."

Chapter 39

The scant snow and slush had disappeared for the most part, and though the weather was cool, it was sunny and dry. Edwin was home early and cooking supper, while Marya and Halee sat at the kitchen table, sewing on quilt blocks. They laughed about Zan's obsession with home decorating, trying unsuccessfully to keep their voices down so John and Lenn could work in the dining room.

As the afternoon progressed, Jonny grew restless and noisy, running from room to room.

"Outside, Gandad. Pease?" John looked down, seeing his grandson's hopeful expression.

With his paperwork spread all over the big table, his grandfather tried to be patient with him. "We can't right now. Uncle Lenn and I have something we need to finish, but tomorrow we'll be able to play."

"Aw. Sawwy." Jonny sat on the floor, trying to amuse himself with his blocks.

Halee set her needlework down. "Jonny, why don't you and I go and see if Freylin and Rynne can go to the children's garden with us while it's still light out? That'll give granddad a chance to finish his work. When we come back, your dad will have supper ready."

Marya smiled wistfully. "That sounds fun. Frey is probably feeling the same way as you are, Jonny." Thanks to Edwin and Zan's continual efforts at healing her, Marya's heart was slowly gaining strength, but she tired quickly and was mostly housebound.

Jonny could hardly contain himself while Edwin

dressed him in his coat and hat. As soon as his mittens were on, he hugged his mother. "I be back soon, Ahmah."

Halee and Jonny walked down the alley, entering Friedr's garden through the back gate. Jonny raced up the steps and stood waiting for his grandmother.

Aeolyn and Halee sat at the picnic table adjacent to the sandbox, watching the children digging in the damp sand. "This was a good idea," said Aeolyn. "The weather has been so bad, and they've been cooped up in the nursery all week. Friedr is on duty in the infirmary tonight, so I was just about at my wits' end."

Freylin ran up to the table. "Can we play hide and seek? We won't go far."

Aeolyn said, "Stay close. Rynne and Jonny can't count very well yet, so play fair with them."

"I promise." Freylin turned and raced back to the others.

The two women chatted, listening to the children's laughter as they played their game. Freylin's voice drifted on the afternoon air, telling Jonny, "Touch each finger, right? Count one-two-three. We'll hide."

"Ahwight."

Halee and Aeolyn laughed as Jonny repeated 'one-two-three' about ten times before shouting, "I find you now!"

After a while, the children's voices grew quieter, and they could be heard discussing a bug of some sort. "It's a beetle." Freylin sounded quite sure of himself. Soon they were chasing each other around the low bushes.

A cold fog had begun rising near the river, lending

a mysterious quality to the late afternoon. The sun was low on the horizon, tinting the winter haze pink. Halee said, "They should sleep well tonight, as hard as they're playing." She laughed as the three children raced past them and around a shrub, trying to catch a squirrel. "Jonny has been feeling cooped up too, now that the excitement of Holy Day is over."

"I hope they're getting a little tired." Aeolyn rolled her eyes. "I've some work for Rall that needs to be done tonight. He wants it before the conclave opens tomorrow's session."

"I have work to do tonight too." Halee felt a tugging at her sleeve and looked down.

Jonny stood at her elbow, his face serious. "Gamma. A man tooked him."

Halee's mind seemed to freeze. She forced herself to say, "A man took who?"

"Fwey." Jonny pointed toward the path that wound through the Mages' Quarter. "He tooked him."

"He put a cloth on Fwey's mouth," Rynne said, her little eyes round with fear. "Fwey bited him."

Aeolyn leaped to her feet, but Halee put her hand on her arm. "He put the cloth on Frey's mouth?"

Rynne nodded. "Fwey dint like it."

Aeolyn pulled away and ran to the path. "Freylin! Frey!" She ran first one way and then the other, calling her son's name, becoming hysterical as her calls went unanswered. "Freylin!"

Halee grabbed her, forcing her to listen. "Aeolyn. Frey's not here. He's been kidnapped. We're wasting time. We need to get Kalen's special group out hunting for him. Now!"

Without speaking any further, the two women

swept up the children. Panic fueled them as they raced to Kalen's house.

Chapter 40

In their private rooms over the bakery, Linette gazed at the unconscious boy. "There's a bruise on his face. He was to be brought here unmarked."

Teller quailed under her glare, raising his bloody hand. "He nearly bit my fingers off. Despite that, I managed to get the spice into his mouth."

"You roughed him up in the process. Just for that, you can heal your own hand." She delved the boy, healing his bruises. "What's his name?"

"His mother called him Freylin."

Linette held the boy on her lap. Bemused, she stroked his coppery curls and looked closely at his clothes. "Freylin…he's precious. His mother dressed him with care. Look how neatly she made this coat. And his cheeks—so rosy and sweet." She held the comatose child to her breast, cradling him. "He's like a doll come to life." She gently examined his teeth and looked at his eye color. "He's four, maybe five years old."

Teller's hand throbbed, but he didn't ask her to relent, knowing it would do no good. Instead, he said, "He's a large, heavy doll. I thought he was older than that. He talks well for his age."

"Help me get him downstairs. I have a room prepared to house offerings."

The room was just off the bottom of the steps. It looked like a normal bedroom, but with no windows and an iron-bound door that could be barred on the outside. As he carried the boy inside, Teller avoided looking toward the altar that occupied the center of the cellar.

The room held a bed, a rocking chair placed beside a lamp, a few books, and nothing else. Teller handed his sister the child and Linette sat in the chair, rocking Freylin as tenderly as any mother.

Teller asked, "Won't he need some toys? What if he wakes up?"

"No. He's going to sleep now and forever." She kissed his cheek, cuddling him, marveling at his perfection. "He's of barbarian ancestry, so he's tall for his age. Look at him—red hair, blue eyes—definitely from the far north. You chose well." She looked up at her brother, happiness in her eyes. "You'd best get prepared now. Tonight will be long, and you have many prayers to offer if we're going to open the way for Tauron."

Unsure of what to say, Teller nodded and backed out of the room, closing the door.

She kissed the boy's soft cheek, cuddling him. "I love you so much, Freylin. I'm going to save you from a life of misery, and make sure you go to heaven while you're still sweet and precious."

Softly, Linette sang a lullaby.

>>><<<

Teller knelt before the altar, ashamed of his nakedness. He'd cleansed and purified himself, but he never allowed anyone to see his mutilation. Still, it was written that the servant should appear before the god with nothing to hide.

His thoughts were dark and scattered, making it nearly impossible for him to concentrate. A woman performing the ritual, assisted by an unmade priest...they'd be fortunate if the god didn't strike them dead for such blasphemy.

If Tauron could manifest within Aeos's holy city at all.

Desperately, Teller tried to conquer his doubts. If only he had the use of Tauron's magic. He could still sense it, but was forever barred from touching it, a punishment as harsh as...the other. He knew the Temple priests roaming everywhere couldn't sense the bull god's magic, but Linette's use of Aeos's magic to shield the chapel had the possibility of drawing attention.

He wondered, did she have the focus to do such an involved ritual properly? She'd reminded him that Graylor had instructed her, and technically he'd been qualified to perform the rituals if any of those new Aeos-born priests were.

Teller despised Graylor for the role he'd played in his unmaking, but if he had been trapped on their side of the wall, surely that cold man would rein Linette in. Only Dalgek or Graylor could force her to see reason when the madness had command of her. She'd proven the day before she was once again more than half mad, when she had...she had....

He pressed his hands to his eyes, weeping for the loss of his manhood and his magic. When his sister was in the grip of her insanity, her cruelty had no bounds.

His lips trembled, as he pulled himself together. God only knew how this was going to go. What if her entire plan was a product of her insanity? What if her audacity was as blasphemous to Tauron as it seemed to him?

He had no choice and would have to deal with the consequences, as the god willed. Teller cleared his mind and put the matter in Tauron's hands. Pressing his forehead to the floor, he began the prayer-spells, chanting, his voice soft and hypnotic. His heart rate slowed as he fell into a near-trance, but without the magic he could only hover on the edge of the reverie, unable to grasp what he could see.

With sheer force of will, he buried his doubts, concentrating only on success, convincing himself that his sister's altar would be acceptable to the god of darkness.

Chapter 41

Friedr paced, leaning heavily on his staff. His barbarian accent was pronounced when he burst out, "Why am I being kept here? I should be out there searching for my son. I'm lame but not incapable. He's out there somewhere. I have to find him!"

Father Rall rounded on him. "Settle down, Friedr. This isn't about your lame leg. I know you're frantic, but I won't have you out there leaping to conclusions and making rash judgements. What is needed is a rational approach. Have faith that we'll find your son. In the meantime, your wife and daughter need you to calm down and support them."

For a moment, John thought Friedr was going to explode, but instead, he went to the table where Rynne sat with Jonny. Several toys were on the table. Friedr picked up a carved pony, staring at it.

Both children were unusually quiet, watching the adults. Aeolyn stood at the front window, peering through the curtains and Marya stood beside her with her arm around her shoulders.

The front door opened. Everyone looked up hopefully as Halee entered, followed by Jules Brendsson. She said, "Kalen and the special group are scouring the market now."

"Why the market?" Father Rall asked.

Halee replied, "Apparently Edwin and Zan got a whiff of a mindbender down at the end of Commerce Street near the boot shop yesterday. But when Kalen and Moran went back they sensed nothing. Neither did

Dario and Mikel. Kalen was planning for the group to return tonight, to try to home in on it."

Friedr said, "A mindbender? What would a...?" He broke off at Rall's headshake and glanced at the children.

Halee continued, "Edwin and Zan know what they're looking for." She handed a list to Rall. "Here is the list of mages searching the other neighborhoods tonight. They know they need to report to you here."

Jules laid his hand on Friedr's shoulder. His voice was comforting, fatherly. "Beryl is on her way here to be with the children. She'll scan their awareness for what they can remember about the man."

"Beryl understands children." Friedr nodded, wondering if he was having a nightmare. "I don't want my daughter and Jonny scarred by having witnessed his abduction."

Jules looked at his notes. He said, "A healer will accompany each search party. They'll truth-read each householder and sense for children at every home. Darlen will accompany my group, and Dane will accompany Gorden's group. We'll begin knocking on doors as soon as everyone is assembled. Each group will return here as soon as we've cleared our section. With as many searchers as we have, it shouldn't take long."

Rall said, "John and Halee, you're searching with Jules. The messengers are all alerted to the need for speed tonight."

The front door opened again and a white-haired healer entered. Immediately she crossed to the children, sitting down and picking up a toy. "Hello," she said to Rynne. "I'm Beryl. What kind of game are you two playing? Farm animals?"

With Beryl keeping the children occupied, Friedr stood up, hobbling to Rall's side. "We five need to speak in the kitchen. Now." His glance indicated Jules, Halee, and John.

Once they were all in the kitchen, John shut the door behind them. Friedr said, "What's the connection between my son's abduction and the possibility of a mindbender in Aeoven? I have a right to know why my son was kidnapped."

Feeling ill, Rall capitulated. "You do have the right to know. Mindbenders sometimes take street-urchins and other vulnerable people to use in their rituals. With the valley of Mal Evol sealed off, we've been expecting the worshippers of the Bull God who're hidden in our population to surface. Certain rites involve children."

"Rituals…! No. Not my son." Friedr blanched and sat down, hard. "Aeos, please. Not that."

"Friedr," Rall's voice commanded his attention. "Mindbenders use Aeos's magic. The streets are crawling with our people, all of them with their senses wide open. We'll sense this creature and find your son."

"It's my fault. I murdered Graylor's children." Friedr looked at John, guilt and helplessness stark on his angular features. "Now one of his kind has taken mine in payment for my sin."

Rall, Halee, and Jules fell silent, not sure what to say.

"You did nothing of the sort!" John moderated his voice. "Graylor himself doomed his adopted children when he set that filthy geas on them." He put his hand on Friedr's shoulder. "Freylin was not singled out because of what happened in Braden. He was likely taken randomly. There are no homeless here, no street children for an acolyte of Tauron to prey on. Freylin was a child playing and had strayed out of his mother's sight. It could have been any child."

"But it wasn't just any child. It was my child."

>>><<<

The search crews had all departed. Rall and Beryl played with Jonny and Rynne, building a fort with blocks.

Friedr sat with his wife in the sitting room, clenching his jaw to keep from screaming. He put his arm around her, as much to receive comfort as to give it. Aeolyn leaned against him, her arms wrapped around her belly as if holding her unborn child protectively.

Both parents watched Rynne obsessively as she played.

Marya sat at Aeolyn's other side. She picked up her friend's cold hand and held it. "Edwin will find him. I promise."

Chapter 42

Six figures crept through the shadows, swathed against the rain in the dark garb of the Temple Assassin, their features and augmentations disguised behind black bandanas, and wrapped in cloaks the color of the night. Their ebon armor was specially bespelled to enable them to remain unobserved, the finish absorbing light rather than reflecting it. When they reached the place where the path to the market split, they stood in a group.

With their consent, Edwin drew Moran and Kalen into the link. Zan brought Mikel and Dario into it. The four men staggered, unprepared for the experience, although they'd been warned.

Reeling, Dario pressed his hands to his eyes. "How do you live like this? I see too much…it's like seeing out of all your eyes as well as my own." Mikel and Kalen echoed his startlement. Moran stood silently, sifting through the images.

Zan laughed. "We don't live like this. It's a tool we learn to use when needed. Ignore what everyone else is doing and concentrate on seeing only through your own eyes. As you gain control, those images will become peripheral. Speak by thinking your words, like I'm doing."

It took several long moments for the four battle-mages to become accustomed to hearing and speaking with their minds, but they soon got the hang of it. Sorting out what they were looking at was more of a struggle.

Edwin grew frustrated at the time it took to get coordinated. "I wish we'd had a chance to work on it before now. Linking isn't easy to just dive into."

Zan agreed. "At least, you all have some minor healing ability, or we wouldn't be able to do this."

Mikel said, "Yes, but I'm only able to heal minor wounds when a companion is injured. I can't sense the patient, and it takes all my little bit of healing chi to do it. I have to resort to potions, bandages, and splints for anything more than a scratch."

The others agreed. Kalen said, "It takes all my chi to cast a minor sleep spell."

Zan said, "Still, it's enough for this. That's all we need."

After more than a few minutes of disorientation and scrambling to regain visual focus, the others were able to move despite the distraction. With all six finally in communication and walking without stumbling, they divided into two groups.

Edwin and Zan began searching each property using their gift of air-magic. Silently they walked the street on opposite sides, pausing in front of darkened shops, most with lights on in the upstairs living quarters. They didn't linger long in any home, glancing around only briefly. Once all the people were accounted for they moved on. The hours grew late, and gradually the windows darkened as lamps were extinguished and people went to their beds.

Dawn approached, and an icy rain fell. The group was gathered under the awning of a darkened bakery, sheltering from the weather. Hidden in the shadows, they were nearly impossible to see, shrouded in black.

Still connected by Zan and Edwin's link, they conferred mentally, ensuring the street remained silent.

They had returned to the west end of Commerce Street.

Speaking through the link, Edwin said, "I know we've been through the market three times and found nothing. But something is off and I want to know what it is. The strangeness is here at this end of the street."

"Yes," Zan agreed. "It was in this neighborhood where we sensed a strange vibration the other day. Everything feels awry to my senses here."

"You're right," Kalen said, "but we'll need to change into regular armor if we intend to search during daylight. We never wear black where we could be recognized."

"I feel certain we'll find him in this neighborhood." Edwin's frustration rippled through the link. "I know it."

Because the brief flash of a mindbender's presence had occurred near the bootmaker's shop, they thoroughly examined the premises. The bootmaker and his wife were sleeping, with their infant daughter in the cradle beside them. His home and his cellar contained nothing that didn't pertain to his business.

Zan's mental voice was wry. "I'm glad he's not involved in this. I have a fondness for his footwear— they're much finer than Temple boots."

The others stifled their chuckles.

Looking at his list, Kalen noted, "We're at D'Orman's bakery. Lindie and Telly, a brother and sister from Braden. It was empty when we were here earlier, but perhaps it warrants a closer look."

Moran said, "I sometimes went to D'Orman's

bakery in Braden. But it was run by a man named Oren S'Elwyn. He'd been a troublemaker but had settled down by the last time I had anything to do with him. As I recall, he inherited it from his uncle who was the original owner."

Kalen examined the list again. "There's no mention of an Oren S'Elwyn as a tenant here."

Edwin thought for a moment. "Zan and I were in this bakery two days ago. The man behind the counter had been castrated. When I heard his voice I delved him, but saw it had been done long ago."

Kalen was not the only one who winced at that image. "We all know why that particularly unpleasant punishment is exacted."

Zan said, "He's no longer a danger in that way."

Mikel's mental voice was as soft as his speaking voice. "Correct me if I'm wrong, but when I read the transcript of your interview with Graylor, I thought he said one of his accomplices was a man who'd been cast out of the priesthood for raping a child."

Zan thought back, picturing the conversation. He replayed the memory, sharing it with the others.

Kalen's thoughts revolved around the name. "Teller…Telly…it could be. Teller is on the list of people in Fleetside to be revisited by Noli's people."

"He could be here instead. It's chaos in Fleetside right now, and so many new people arrived here in Aeoven during the last four weeks that he could easily be one of them." Dario firmly quashed his surge of emotion. "But Graylor implied he didn't have a large enough gift of empathy to be a leash. If Telly is the rag-and-bone man, Teller, then Lindie could be…Linette. She could be the woman Cayne was involved with."

Edwin said, "This is what I remember of our conversation with the baker on Odensday." He shared the memory. "I sensed no ability for either empathy or the elements."

Dario shook his head. "That doesn't mean anything—he was a priest of Tauron, so he must have had the gift of Tauron's magic at some point. We can't sense those gifts, and we don't fully know what they are, other than they can move things with their minds like you can."

"True, but if they castrated him, they might have stripped him of his gifts too." Edwin tried to remember what magic he'd seen from the two minotaur mages he'd fought.

Dario's mental voice was grim. "If this baker is our quarry, we'd better hope so."

Moran said, "When I viewed your memory a moment ago I saw that you asked this baker if he knew Madame S'Rylien. He neatly dodged answering it. S'Rylien's bakery was on the other side of town from D'Orman's, but if he truly *was* a baker in Braden he should have known them. Braden's community of expatriates from Mal Evol was close-knit and proud of their ancestry, to the extent that their children's marriages were frequently arranged to preserve their culture."

As one, the group turned toward the still-dark windows. Once again Edwin and Zan carried their spirits inside the shop. Despite the fact that dawn was only an hour away, no one stirred in the kitchen. The banked coals in the large oven's firebox slowly cooled. Ghosting up the stairs to the family quarters they saw the beds were still made, indicating that no one had slept there.

No fire burned in the sitting room fireplace.

"Bakers are usually up and working long before dawn." Mikel focused his attention on what was on the worktable, seeing nothing set up and waiting for the day's work. "The other day, you said the mindbender seemed shielded. Could something like that be at work here?"

"It did feel muffled, which was why I only caught the edge of it," Edwin agreed. "But what I find even more intriguing is that, on closer inspection, it feels like there's no basement here."

Kalen peered at the list. "Why would this shop have no basement when all the others do? The last occupant was a wine merchant. It's listed as having a full cellar with shelves for storage, and a finished attic."

"A wine merchant would have a large cellar." Edwin sent his senses on the wind, carrying the others and passing through the immaculate kitchen. "My earth sense tells me there's a basement here." His eyes, when he returned to his body, were alight with anticipation. "I'm being blocked from seeing it." He used his air-magic to examine the kitchen again. "There is no closet behind this door. But it *is* where the cellar entrance should be." He returned to his body and his eager blue eyes met Kalen's. "Let's see what lies beyond that door."

Pulling out his lock picks, Edwin unlocked the shop's front door and used his air-magic to silence the bell over it. He waited as the others followed him in, closing the door behind them.

In the bakery kitchen, the six men gathered before the door that had to lead to the cellar. Slowly Edwin turned the knob. As he did so, a strange thrill coursed through him.

"Wait!" Zan's mental caution halted Edwin's hand mid-turn. "Something is going on down there—something bad. Pray to Aeos we're not too late."

Edwin agreed. "It's definitely our mindbender." Together, Edwin and Zan layered empathic barriers into the elemental shields the others bore. "There—you four should be safe from her empathy."

"We'd better hope she's alone." Dario's worried tones caused the others to pause. "If she has elemental mages as thralls, they'll likely be the age of our younger novices. They'll die too. Be prepared."

Edwin and Zan's hearts sank at the thought.

Kalen's mental voice was calm but firm. "We take no chances. We'll go down one at a time so we're not all jammed in the stairwell."

Chapter 43

Teller felt his sister's presence beside him. He chanted the offering prayer as Linette placed the unconscious child on the altar, unclothed as was required. Bowing, she stepped back and knelt, pressing her forehead to the floor. Her voice joined his.

Teller's doubts resurfaced and his awareness widened, which shouldn't have happened. He tried to regain his focus. It was just…women were barred from the altar. He didn't know how Linette's goddess-given healing magic could possibly be acceptable to Tauron.

And then there was the problem of his inability to fully enter the trance. He was distracted on too many levels and, therefore, unfit to serve. His sister was unclothed—it was wrong, almost incestuous, but he could probably get past it. But knowing she would see his mutilation also interfered with his ability to focus.

He had to put the distractions aside. His full commitment to the ritual was imperative. If the god wasn't satisfied with their devotion, he would destroy them. Through sheer willpower, he managed to shut out his doubts, relaxing enough to hover once again at the edge of the reverie.

Linette's lowered eyes concealed her glee at having manipulated Teller to where she wanted him. Suddenly, she rose.

Teller cried out, "No! You must remain obeisant!"

Boldly she placed her hands on either side of her brother's head. Abruptly, control of his body was ripped away from him.

Linette couldn't hide her exultation, laughing aloud. Against all odds, her plan had worked and now, for as long as Teller lived, Linette would be his leash. The prodigious abilities he'd been forever barred from using were now hers, along with the knowledge of how to use them. This moment of power was the true reason she'd saved his otherwise worthless hide. She now had full use of the abilities she needed to enable the rituals.

Power crackled around her and she basked in the sensation.

"Hah! And Graylor said I was unfit to be a leash." Linette laughed again, a wild cackle. "You should never have doubted me, Brother. Now we begin the true ritual. Now is the advent of the Bull God!" She knelt beside him. "Sing, Brother. Sing the welcoming prayer to our god."

Shunted to a corner of his mind, Teller could only observe and obey. His voice joined hers in chanting the invocation.

As the prayer of welcome ended, Linette rose to her feet. In her hands, she held a bronze knife with an amethyst embedded in the handle, which she laid on the altar beside the boy.

Raising her arms in supplication over Freylin's small form she offered him to her god. "God of fire and darkness, giver of life and death, I freely offer you all I am and will ever be. My body is your vessel. Enter this vessel and through me, receive your gift." Filled with the power she'd robbed from her brother, she spun the germinal spell of offering.

Her entreaties met with silence.

Again Linette opened her heart to Tauron, beseeching him to enter her and receive his gift.

Yet again the god didn't make his presence known.

She stood, looking at the child and the knife which

stubbornly lay untouched by the hand of god. Tears of frustration burned her eyes. After all her work, the god had found fault with her. Bowing her head, she said, "Great Tauron, I'm unworthy to make this offering, I know. I am but a frail woman. But I'm all that remains of your children here in this savage land. I'm the only one strong enough to do this for you, to open the way for your advent into Neveyah."

She knew she'd done everything correctly. Her altar room was exactly as it should be. It was furnished with the finest benches, enough to seat twenty worshippers. The precious child who lay on the altar was physically perfect and still so innocent. He was the finest gift she could have acquired anywhere.

All that was needed was for the god to accept her sanctuary and then she would fill those benches for him.

Her mind spun, wondering where she'd failed. Teller must have been right about that one thing—she hadn't been tested on the altar. Perhaps the god's silence was a test and she had to pass it.

It was more likely that Tauron was barred from manifesting by the goddess. They were in the heart of Aeos's city. It made sense that he couldn't materialize there unless a way was opened for him.

Although she loved the child, she would have to perform the ritual without Tauron's guiding presence, and she would have to do it with no faltering or mistakes. *Show no weakness,* she counseled herself. *If you show any weakness, you will fail, and to fail is to die.*

Linette picked up the knife and raised it high above her. "I can do this for you, great god. I shall open the way."

A slight chill at her back alerted her to trespassers. Turning she saw a large group of black-clad Temple mages bearing down on her with swords drawn. "Blasphemers!" Raising her hands, she drew forth the stasis spell from Teller.

There were too many targets. Stealing the secret trick Teller had perfected, which was a force-net, she cast the stasis spell widely, halting the group. With the enemy unable to advance, she managed to snare the nearest of the intruders, one who'd dare draw his blade in her sanctuary. Alive with the power, she bound him with one hand, gagged him, and held him suspended off the ground.

Simultaneously she used her own empathic magic to cast a web of pain at the others. "You walked into my trap of your own free will, assassins. For that, you must suffer." She laughed. "I feared I wouldn't have enough strength to open the way, but my god has provided me with you." She turned to the one she had snared. "Your pain will replenish my chi." Raising the knife, she slashed at his exposed abdomen.

The amethyst knife glanced off the intruder's armored belly, but his sword arm had been raised at the moment he was caught, revealing the unarmored place of weakness. With all her might, Linette thrust the knife in deeply, twisting it.

Tears of silent agony ran down his face, and the room seemed to spin...he couldn't get his breath...couldn't breathe...blessed darkness closed in.

Chapter 44

Before they entered the stairwell, Edwin said through the link, "My mage-sight is still barred from seeing what we're entering. It's a fog to me. It feels like several people are there in a largish space, but I can't see it."

Kalen nodded. "Remain silent and spread out when we reach the bottom. Once I give the signal, be prepared to fight in close quarters. If Freylin is there, protect him at all costs."

Agreement rippled through the group. Edwin pulled the door open, revealing the steps to a cellar, stairs that ended in a short, dimly lit hall. What sounded like women's voices drifted up, rhythmic chanting in an unfamiliar language.

Kalen entered the stairwell. Dark and silent as shadows, the five followed him one at a time, creeping down the dark, narrow stairs. Once in the hallway, Kalen motioned them forward.

His eyes widened as he emerged into the altar room. Through the link, they saw the room was crowded, with an altar in the center. Benches were arranged in rows around it, but only two people were there, both stark naked. Freylin was lying on the altar, also unclad.

Zan was the last to enter, arriving just as the priestess turned. The cellar erupted in noise as benches fell over and the priestess began screeching unintelligibly. She cast an unfamiliar spell that rolled off the barriers he and Edwin had layered over the group. A strange, humming force field rose between the woman and the others. Ducking back into the shadows, he hid.

Zan peered around the corner. To his horror, he watched as Dario was caught in some sort of spell and raised off his feet. Slashing at him with her knife, the woman cursed in a foreign language as her blade glanced off his armor. Her eyes were vicious as she stabbed Dario beneath his arm, where he was unarmored, impaling him, twisting the knife.

He could see the others were halted where they stood, unable to press through the barrier. Each one tried desperately to break through the strange web. The naked man who knelt by the altar suddenly jerked to his feet. His eyes were unfocused as if he was in a daze. Suddenly lightning shot from the baker's hands, stabbing everywhere.

But it was not the magic of Aeos.

Lightning rolled off Edwin's shields. He struggled to get to the altar, barred from it by the unseen force, and by lightning. Through the link, he said to Zan, "She has us caught in some kind of barrier...I can't get to Freylin."

Still not sure what to do, Zan crouched at the foot of the stairs, the only one of them not caught by the barrier.

Zan felt Edwin frantically poking at her barrier, trying to bring it down. Answering, he said, "There must be a weakness. Every shield has a weakness."

Kalen and Moran were rooted in place by her barrier, unable to reach Dario to help him.

Still in the shadows Zan observed, trying to decide what to do. Just behind the woman, he could see

Freylin. His small chest rose and fell as if he was sleeping.

Zan said, "Keep her attention. I'm going to get Frey." Crouching low and moving in the shadows just outside the light cast by the candles, he sidled behind the others, angling until he was on the far side of the altar behind the mindbender and her thrall.

Slowly Zan reached out, covering the child with his cloak and picked him up. Extending his shields closely over him, Zan said, "I have him shielded."

Via the link Kalen said, "Get him out of here—take him home. We'll meet you there." To the others, he said, "Use whatever means to finish this now."

Instantly Zan obeyed, racing through the lightning which rolled off his shields, leaping overturned furniture, and running up the stairs.

Edwin cast water, slipping it under the woman's feet, causing her to stagger. The barrier went down and the spell holding Dario also failed.

He fell to the floor and didn't stir.

The four converged on Linette and the mage in her thrall, their blades flashing.

>>><<<

Shunted to the corner of his mind, Teller watched as his magic was torn from him, lightning shafts cast with little care, flung wildly at the intruders. "Not two spells at once!" He tried to get her to hear him. "You're wasting the power, burning through it like that. Be sparing, or you'll...oh, god." His nerves screamed as his already low reserve of chi was depleted.

Ruthlessly Linette drew chi for the two spells from her brother's life force. No matter how he tried, Teller was unable to get her attention.

A black-clad figure passed to the right of Teller, leaping over the benches, clutching something large and heavy to his chest, under his cloak.

Frustration nearly choked Teller, but with his sister in control of his body he was unable to speak aloud. "Stop him! He has the child!" His mental cries went unheard and the figure disappeared up the stairs. Every nerve in his body screamed as if he was on fire.

As the thief disappeared up the stairs, water sheeted across the floor, knocking Teller off his feet, and the stasis spell went down. He regained his body, and disoriented, he tried to see what had happened, but he was blind. He could hardly breathe, but as the pain diminished he began to regain his vision.

As his sight returned, he saw his sister lay beside him on the floor in a pool of water, stunned. With an economy of motion, a short, dark-eyed mage ran her through the heart.

Teller was almost glad when the tallest man's blade sliced through his neck. The cold, ice-blue eyes were the last thing he saw.

>>><<<

Kalen looked down at the headless corpse, wiping his sword. Moran pulled his blade from the woman's chest. They both turned toward the altar where Edwin knelt beside Dario, seeing the healer was tranced. Mikel knelt beside him, holding Dario's hand.

Removing their bandanas, Kalen and Moran knelt beside them, praying for Edwin's success.

After a long time of trying to find some spark of life, Edwin leaned back. "It's no use. He's gone. If I'd been able to get to him sooner, I could have saved him."

"I'll miss him." Mikel tenderly wrapped Dario's cloak around him and covered his face. "Before Bekki came into his life he used to get me into so much trouble—you have no idea."

Edwin's words were thick. "I remember it well. He had a knack for mischief."

"She changed him, settled him down. Her death hurt him deeply." Mikel's voice was rough.

Kalen felt the weight of his ever-present grief. "So many deaths can be laid at the hands of those two: Dario, Piers, Bekki, my son Ivar, and Cayne. Who knows how many others?"

Moran said, "At least Dario is with Bekki again." His own eyes were moist. "I could almost envy him."

"Don't say that," Mikel's reply was muffled, as he wiped his eyes. "Yes his time here is over, but you still have much to accomplish."

Kalen said, "Let's get Dario's body to the Temple. I hope Zan made it back to Friedr's safely."

Edwin closed his eyes, sending his spirit out, scouting Friedr's home. "He did, but Freylin...it looks like there's a problem."

Chapter 45

Friedr's house was silent, despite the fact he and Aeolyn sat at the kitchen table, unable to sleep. Lenn stood guard at the front door, and John the back. Rall paced before the fireplace.

Halee had taken Marya and the two children home. "Rynne can stay with us tonight. The searchers have found nothing, but Kalen's team is still looking. They're the ones who'll find him if anyone can."

Just after dawn, the front door to Friedr's house burst open and Lenn ushered a black-clad figure in. "They found him!" Friedr moved quickly, trailed by Aeolyn and Beryl. John followed behind.

Zan laid Freylin on the sofa. Removing his mask, he said, "He's been drugged." Everyone gathered around the child.

"Where are his clothes? Has he been—" Aeolyn pressed her hand to her mouth, unable to say it.

Zan laid his hand on her arm. "No. He's unharmed in that way, but I can't tell exactly what they drugged him with."

Beryl knelt beside him. "His breath smells like daze-spice...and sativa. They were clumsy and overdosed him." Linking with Zan, she delved Freylin. She looked up at his worried parents. "He'll recover. We'll stay with him to make sure. He'll wake sometime this afternoon and likely won't have any memory of the experience."

Friedr fought back tears of relief, leaning on his staff and holding Aeolyn with his free arm as she sobbed for joy. "Thank you, blessed Aeos. Thank you."

John said, "I need to get a message to Halee and

Marya that he's been found. Where are the rest of your team?"

Not wanting to alarm the others, Zan stood up. "They were still busy when I left. John, Father Rall, we need to talk somewhere private."

Beryl said, "You do that, Zan. Friedr and I can handle this."

>>><<<

Aeolyn had taken Freylin up to his bed, and she and Beryl sat in his room.

Edwin entered Friedr's house, followed by the others. Zan looked up and saw Dario wasn't with them. His eyes met Edwin's, seeing confirmation of his worst fear.

Rall seated them in the dining room. His sharp eyes missed nothing. "You have much to tell us."

Exhaustion and grief threatened to overwhelm Kalen. "You're right, Father. Dario has gone to Aeos's Great Hearth. But we removed both the mindbender, Linette, and the man known as Teller." Pulling himself together, he gave a detailed account of what happened, occasionally asking the others for confirmation of a point he was unclear on.

Friedr had his notebook out taking notes, as did Father Rall.

Rall asked Edwin, "When you encountered this magic barrier, what did it feel like to you?"

"It was like nothing I've ever run into. When we fought D'Mal, his shields were different, hard to detect, but incorporating enough of our magic that I could find the ties. This woman had a mage in her thrall, but he wasn't in control of his gifts, and her barrier hummed.

"Their mental union was similar but different from

Graylor and his thralls. Teller was an unmade priest. Somehow, they magically barred him from using his gifts of Tauron's magic, probably at the same time he was punished for the crime of rape. His sister was able to use his abilities the way mindbenders usually do, but their bond was twisted." Edwin shook his head at the futility of it all.

Zan agreed. "I sensed she was completely insane, so leashing her mind to a priest of Tauron apparently didn't work the way Graylor's thralls anchored his."

Rall looked up from his notes. "I've always wondered if a minotaur could be returned to the physical state of a normal man."

"Unfortunately, he wasn't normal, although he may have been saner than the woman." Edwin shuddered. "If the process of the Remaking is as much of an ordeal as we've heard, I can't imagine what being unmade would be like."

>>><<<

Edwin entered his bedroom. It was mid-morning and despite having had no sleep his parents had left for work, taking Jonny and Rynne to the nursery, trying to bring some normalcy to the children's day.

He was more than tired. The events following Frey's kidnapping had worn heavily on him.

Marya lay dozing, her frail beauty never failing to move him. He lay down beside her, and she stirred, snuggling closer into his arms. Edwin sensed that before they left, his parents had made sure she drank the medicinal tea, and her heart was beating more regularly. She was still exhausted, though. The uproar of the night before had taken a toll on her fragile reserves of strength.

He knew Marya had been terrified for Freylin, but also for him. She'd handled it well. Nonetheless, it had been too much for her.

Closing his eyes, Edwin delved her, strengthening her, ensuring she would wake rested.

He lay wide awake, lost in his thoughts. He had to make some crucial decisions. Marya's health had to be considered so he couldn't take her back to the farm in Markett as he couldn't use magic there, or his healing gift.

But he could ask for a post in Armat. It was far away from the stress of Aeoven, yet close enough for regular visits. Henley was Abbott there now, and the Temple was just large enough to have a small infirmary attached to it.

Armat Temple served a sleepy farming community that was spread over a wide area along the River Rangle. Most healers wanted to be posted in larger towns and rarely stayed longer than a year.

Dario's death underscored the dangers of his life in Aeoven. His wife had been through more than enough as it was. He had to ensure that Marya had nothing to worry about.

Mikel was without a partner, but Zan could work with him. He'd know that Edwin's decision was for Marya and would agree it was necessary. Kalen might argue but would accept his choice.

His dad and Halee would understand. They were still newly-bonded and it would do them good to have some time to themselves. But leaving the practice he'd built as a healer…that was the thing giving him pause. He loved what he did, and he'd been away from his patients for half a year as it was.

Edwin's thoughts ran in circles. He had to choose. He didn't know how much time he had left with his wife and he wanted her to see their son grow up. Their life in Aeoven was killing her.

His own mother had died too young. He'd been nine when she perished and he didn't want Jonny to go through what he'd experienced.

At last, he came to a decision. He would apply for the position as the senior healer for Armat Temple. It would take a few months to organize, which would give everyone a chance to get used to the idea.

With the decision made, he was finally able to relax and drifted off, holding Marya as she slept.

VALLEY OF SORROWS

Epilogue

"No...I like this chair over there, after all." Marya pointed to the place where the chair had originally been.

"You say that now, but later...."

"That will be then." She giggled.

Laughing, Edwin put the chair back.

He looked around the small sitting room of their new home. It was slightly larger than a bachelor apartment in Aeoven, in that it did have a small kitchen and a large covered porch facing the shared courtyard. "These rooms are really quite pleasant—a lot smaller than the house in Aeoven, but perfect for the three of us."

"Everything is close and easy to get to," Marya agreed. "I like that we can eat in the Temple kitchen on days when you're too busy to cook. It's just across the garden."

"And I like that the garden is just out the door, with no steps for you to climb." When Edwin applied for the post, Henley had understood Marya's health was precarious and made sure that their rooms would work well for a semi-invalid.

The town was peaceful and quiet, a pleasant change from the bustle of Aeoven. Through the open door, birds could be heard, hopping from branch to branch, along with the sounds of the Temple's flock of chickens. Sheep and horses occupied a fenced meadow just beyond the Temple. The air was filled with familiar sounds that took Edwin's mind back to days on the farm in Markett.

The burden of worry and grief he'd carried for so long seemed to lift away as he realized he had nothing to do but enjoy the day with his family.

Hand in hand Edwin and Marya walked out to the courtyard that all the permanent residents shared. Jonny followed and immediately asked if he could dig in the garden. Edwin found a spot where he couldn't damage anything, and the two sat on a high-backed bench watching him, laughing at their son's running commentary as he entertained himself.

Marya said, "Jonny will miss Freylin and Rynne's company. And also little Hilde—she's so sweet, with that fluff of red hair."

Edwin agreed. "But Henley's grandson visits regularly and there are children in the village near his age. He'll meet them Lunaday when he starts in the nursery."

"And Aeolyn will bring the children when she and Rall have business here." Marya laughed. "Rall's going to tear his hair out, traveling with three children."

Chuckling, Edwin agreed. "But, Freylin will move from the nursery to school at the end of summer. He'll stay home with Friedr when his mother travels, then. And Rall loves it, or he would find a different assistant. Aeolyn handles it all beautifully and keeps Rall organized the way he likes it. I think she's on the high road to an abbacy."

Finally voicing the concern she'd kept secret, Marya asked, "What about you? You were being mentioned to take Arne's place as head of general healing. You've taken a post that could be filled by any competent senior healer."

Closing his eyes and leaning back, he put his arm around his wife's shoulders. "I have everything I've ever wanted. And I can't imagine a more relaxing place to raise Jonny." He chuckled as another thought struck him. "Besides, I'm the boss in the infirmary here, with no traditionalists second-guessing me."

Marya relaxed, sensing the honesty behind her husband's words. "You're going to have to smarten up a lot of journeymen."

"They'll get used to it. There's no need to waste magic on things that can be cured by other means."

"Well, your first journeyman victim is supposed to arrive on Restday." Marya giggled. "He's in for a surprise the first time you two get called out to heal a cow. Until you get a vet assigned to you, it's just you, your journeyman, and the life of a village healer."

"Maybe so. Mages should learn humility early in their careers, in my opinion." Edwin grinned, thinking about the differences between his new post and the one he'd just left. "Especially healers. It's too easy to be arrogant, which gets in the way of compassion."

He leaned back, closing his eyes, enjoying the feeling of having Marya resting beside him. The afternoon grew warmer, and the future stretched before him, as bright and as happy as it had seemed when he first fell through the portal all those years before.

APPENDICES

EXCERPT FROM THE BOOK OF LIFE

In the beginning, there was only the void, and the void was barren of life. Nor did any element exist there no fire, no lightning, no earth, and no water. All was as it should be, and the void waited.

Two spheres from beyond the void approached each other, as gently as bubbles blown in the breeze. When they touched, a new sphere was born. And in the void, new spheres appeared until ten new worlds had been born.

The Father and Mother were pleased and admired their work. Then began the great unraveling, and they surrounded the spheres of their children in a protective cocoon that they called the universe.

In the center of the universe, a star flared into existence. The day glowed with the light of the star, the physical manifestation of the Almighty Father. The ten worlds revolved around Him, one touching the other, and all was well in the universe.

The universe grew strong. In the night sky, the Mother cast a myriad of stars and set the moon to illuminate the dark. The moon was the physical manifestation of the Mother of All.

No longer did the spheres create new worlds when they touched. Instead, where they touched, gods were born. Upon awakening, each god made the choice to be male or female, and in this way, the spheres were divided, five worlds for the gods and five worlds for the goddesses.

For the long time of their childhoods, the gods and goddesses shaped their worlds, creating the lands and waters. Each world was different and yet similar, as were the deities who formed them, and each admired the handiwork of the others.

As they grew to adulthood, the deities began to populate their worlds with diverse peoples, whom they considered to be their children, and all were content to live in their worlds, and the universe was at peace.

And the gods and goddesses were five each, and these were their names in the order in which they came into existence:

Meren, god of the Water World Aquas, and his wife Grete, goddess of the Woodland World Alrunne.

Olod, god of the Sky World Geminis, and his wife Oriane, goddess of the River World Danus.

Priscis, god of the Winter World Morovi, and his wife Delhine, goddess of the Summer World Erendi.

Berrin, god of the Grasslands World Sanuvyr, and his wife Feylyn, goddess of the Ice World Chysat.

Ariend, god of the Mountain World Cascadia, and his wife Aeos, goddess of the Verdant World Neveyah.

All was as it should be. Eons passed in harmony until once again, a sphere appeared. From whence came this sphere, none of the deities knew, nor did the universe. Nonetheless, they welcomed this new world, and when the new god was born, he chose to be male. They called him Tauron, and in his childhood, he created the Arid World of Serende. All was well until Tauron grew into his adulthood and realized he alone of the gods had no mate.

At first, all the deities agreed if he had come into existence, then surely another goddess would come to be his wife. Tauron listened to their counsel and was patient. But as the eons passed and no new goddess was born for him, he became miserable in his loneliness.

"Why did you create me only to leave me alone?" Tauron often asked of the universe, but he received no answer, for the universe had not created him. Yet he was beloved, and the other deities made much effort to ease his loneliness, to no avail.

And the eons passed.

With the passage of time, Tauron became ever stranger, jealous, and cruel. The other deities began to fear and avoid him. He became even lonelier, and eventually, he descended into madness. He demanded abject worship from his people to ease his pain. As the eons passed, he realized he was alone and would always be so unless he could find a wife worthy of him.

In his obsession, he decided Aeos should be his wife. "She is the youngest of the gods other than me. She should have been mine."

Thus, it was in the guise of seeking counsel, he went to Ariend's mountain home of Cascadia and sought him out. During the feast Ariend set before him, Tauron took him by stealth and surprise. Tauron sealed Ariend alive into the haft of a spear carved from Ariend's own mountains and thrust the spear deep into the earth of the world of Cascadia.

Aeos, seeking her husband, could find him nowhere. She was distraught and sought the help of the other deities. The other gods and goddesses did not know where Ariend could be and knew something had happened to him, for he would never have abandoned his wife or his world and his children. They searched for a thousand years but did not find him.

Though all the deities came to Aeos's aid, one only pretended to search. Tauron was occupied in a different way. He added league after league of Cascadia to his own world and at last took Ariend's own beloved people, subverting them and making them into creatures lower than beasts. What once had been a gentle, clever, and scholarly people now were voracious and filled with an unquenchable hunger, mindless and violent. Tauron was filled with joy as he looked at his improvements to Ariend's people. "They were too full of pride before. Now they are as they should have been."

When Aeos saw what Tauron had done to Ariend's people, she knew he was responsible for the disappearance of her husband, and she searched the land. At last, she came upon the crystal and marble spear that had been thrust into the ground, creating an immense crater. There she found the skeleton of her husband Ariend embedded in the haft, arms outstretched and face raised to the heavens. Upon touching the crystal, she felt his heart beating and knew him to be alive. "Mother, Father, see what Tauron has done to my husband! Help me to save him, I beg of you!"

The Mother of All wept to see her son in so terrible a place. "My daughter, I must remain to hold up the sky, but the Almighty Father hastens to your side. Though many long years will pass, this evil deed will be made right. I have foreseen it."

Her father came to her side and wept upon seeing Ariend. "My daughter, it pains me, but I cannot interfere in this, though I wish it were not so. This tragedy must play itself out."

The other deities counseled Aeos to take the valley for her world and thus protect her husband until she could find a way to free him from his prison. The oldest brother, Meren, said, "Ariend still lives. There must be eleven worlds and one God for each. Tauron has added half of Cascadia to Serende and still attempts to take it all. He has subverted Ariend's people and made them into less than beasts. We must seal our worlds so none can cross the barriers, else Tauron will be the only god in the universe and our people will be abused in the same, cruel way." And the eight gods and goddesses sealed away their worlds.

Aeos did take all of Cascadia that Tauron had not yet gained and sealed the world of Neveyah from him. Then she ceded half of the combined worlds to her Father to ensure the balance would not be disturbed, and he guarded the land and people most carefully, for there must be eleven worlds, one for each of the eleven deities. Together, they nurtured the two worlds, weeping with sorrow over the fate of Ariend's people at the hands of Tauron. Each did what they could to mitigate the peoples' suffering, though they were not able to completely undo Tauron's work.

Aeos named the crater Mal Evol, which means Valley of Sorrow. For three thousand years, she guarded her husband and the spear that entombed him, ruling Neveyah and Mal Evol with love and a gentle hand. Aeos bequeathed great magic to a few of her people so they could withstand Tauron's hordes. She also gave the valley to one of her most trusted servants and instructed him to build a castle around the haft of the spear, saying, "When the blood of your blood sits upon the throne, you will have knowledge of everything that lives in the land of Mal Evol. Ariend will accept you and the blood of your blood to guard the remains of his world."

Thus, the trusted servant and his sons gave their lives to the carving of the throne.

Once more, Tauron began pressing Aeos, saying her husband was surely dead, and she must wed him and cede the other half of Cascadia to him to right the balance, as there must be one god for each world. She refused saying, "My husband lives. The Almighty Father is a god and worthy of the care and keeping of the eleventh world until my husband can be freed from the prison of your making." Tauron at last went away, weeping and descending ever deeper into madness.

Thus was born the enmity between Neveyah and Serende, the land of Tauron, the Bull God.

And in the world that he named Ariend, the Almighty Father planted the seed of the vine from whose line will come the Hero Foretold, the One Who Takes Back All.

Time and Calendar of Neveyah

Each year consists of 365 days and is divided into four seasons: Winter, Spring, Summer, Harvest, and one Holy Month.

Each season consists of three months, making twelve months that equal 28 days each, plus a Holy Month. Harvest (Autumn) and Winter are separated by the Holy Month of 29 days. The actual winter solstice falls on the first day of the month following (on the first day of Capricas). This is a month sacred to the Goddess Aeos, Goddess of Harvest, Hearth, and Home. It is a time when people travel to visit family and simply take time off for a small vacation, often taking two weeks to do it. On the day that falls between last day of the Holy Month and the first day of Capricas (called Holy Day,) each family holds a ritual feast in their home. It is a feast of thanksgiving and prayers for the New Year. Every four years, an extra Holy Day is added to the calendar and the day is a festival day all across Neveyah. Such a year is called a Long Year, though it is really only one day longer.

The months and seasons are as follows:
Capricas, Aquas, Piscus   (Winter) Begins on actual day of Winter Solstice
Arese, Taura, Geminis   (Spring)
Lunne, Leonid, Virga   (Summer)
Libre, Scorpius, Saggitus   (Harvest)
Holy Month   thirteenth month, stands alone on calendar, ends day before the winter solstice
Holy Day   Bridge between old year and new, belongs to no month, a day of celebration

Days of the Week -

1. Sunnaday—Minimal business is conducted; each family's tasks for the Temple as a whole are completed, such as chopping firewood, quilting, making clothes, and preserving food. The members of the temple clergy assemble in work gangs to accomplish these tasks from which they all benefit.
2. Lunaday
3. Tyrsday
4. Odensday
5. Torsday
6. Frosday
7. Restday – no business is conducted, and only minimal work is done on farms and other places where some work must be done seven days a week. This is a day for people to spend with their families or to pursue their personal interests.

Prominent members of Edwin Farmer's Family Tree

Aelfrid Firesword, founder of College of Warcraft and Magic
Biann D'Braden – 1st abbess and founder of Braden Temple
Iain Farmer
Liam Farmer
Wynn Farmer - *Mountains of the Moon*
John Farmer – *Forbidden Road, The Wayward Son, Valley of Sorrows*
Edwin Farmer–*Tower of Bones, Forbidden Road, Valley of Sorrows*
Son – Jon Farmer

The Prophecies of Neveyah

Abbot Devyn D'Mal to the assembled clergy at Mal Evol Temple in the year 3215

"Keeper, you must save the remnant of my children, for when the end-times are upon you, you shall be barred from the valley of poison and beauty. The wall shall stretch from Horn to Horn and shall be the sign that none from the Valley of Shadows can enter the golden land. The eternal youth, the Lost One, will take the City of Gloom and those of my children left behind will suffer unto the third generation. He stands on the wall and gazes on the golden land, unable to enter."

Mother Lera to the assembled Clergy at Aeoven in the year 3229

"Hark now! The advent of the Bull God is upon us - he comes to claim his bride. She rejects him, and his mad desire is thwarted. Still he claims the dowry as was promised. The verdant lands shall fall to the Bull God and shall become a wilderness of thorns. Seek the hero who will hold safe the Heart of Neveyah. Take the Heir down the Forbidden Road and shroud him with the light of truth. Now comes the Hero from the lands of the Almighty Father; from his line shall come the one who will take back all. From him shall come the Hero Foretold who will triumph on the day of redemption."

Father Rall to the assembled clergy at Aeoven in the year 3254

"The storm rises in the lands of Neveyah, though it does not bring its wrath fully for yet awhile...when falls

the Beloved Hero into darkness, then will the storm's wrath fall upon Neveyah. The children of the Bull-God answer the call that rides on the wind. The light of truth remains shrouded beneath the Throne of Stone and Bone. The cradle of the rightful heir lies obscured by the truth. Let the Hero go to the Shadow Castle to seek the hand of her whom darkness has claimed. The moon is dark - In stealth seeks the hero for the window to the Tower of Roses; in stealth he unbars the door to the forbidden room. Four heroes depart and five return; yet the battle is not won, but only the first skirmish. The Beloved must fall to darkness ere the light of truth is restored to the Shadow Castle! Blood and tears reign in the Shadow Castle until the Hero Foretold comes to restore the scion to the throne."

<u>Edwin Farmer to his companions on the Holy Quest in the year 3254</u>

"The verdant springtime lies coiled beneath the surface of the shattered lands, waiting for the call of the Beloved, to set it free. The Beloved Hero falls to darkness; he sows the poisoned seed across the shadowed land, yet will he rise up to set free the land of Mal Evol on the day the land takes him home. All will see the fruiting of the land of the Living Shades. This will be the sign; the day of redemption is at hand."

Father Rall to the assembled Clergy in the year 3259

"The Dark God laments his betrothed, she chooses him not. The hordes of the broken lands despoil verdant Mal Evol. Now send the heroes four into the land ruled by the Throne of Stone and Bone. Should the treasured one be lost to darkness, those left to walk in the light must flee down the Forbidden Road. Treasured and Beloved, beware the voice of reason. Long days of darkness shadow the realm. The poisoned land flowers, but death walks amidst poison and thorn. When blooms the land again, the day of redemption is at hand. Four heroes journey to bring forth the spring, but balanced on the edge of reason is the outcome.

Edwin Farmer to the assembled Clergy in the year 3260

"Now begins the quest in earnest. Send now the heroes four to the Shadowed Land. Beware! Beloved, the true task for which you were born begins. The storm rages, the door opens upon the field of battle, in grief recall the Forbidden Road. The Beloved Hero will rise on the day of redemption. Mist and shadows shroud the truth, but the Hero Foretold shall one day set them free. "

Edwin Farmer to the assembled on the battlefield in Mal Evol in the year 3260

"My Beloved Hero has fallen. As has been foretold, he shall sow the poisoned seed, and the garden city will fall to him. Darkness falls upon the shadowed land. Long years of suffering and pain lie before us at his

dread hand. Yet, when comes the Hero Foretold, the Beloved will rise up and free the land. On the day of redemption, you will know deliverance is at hand when poison gives way to spring. Seek now the Forbidden Road, lest you be lost also."

Zander Christophson to the assembled at Braden Temple in the year 3260

"The end days are upon us. As has been written in the stars the Garden City must fall. Let your heart be eased, Dark Knight. Your beloved rests at my Hearth. He has earned his place in heaven. Now must the Companions aid the Father and the Son in building the wall which cannot be breached from Horn to Horn. The Elder Warrior and the Dark Knight must gather my people and lead them to the Holy City, all lies ready for them there. In less than two seasons the Lost One will lead the hordes of Tauron to the gates of the Garden City. He stands on the walls unable to enter the golden land, and the broken children of Mal Evol stand behind him. In his grief he sows the poisoned seed, a vain effort to recreate the verdant land. This must happen before the Throne of Stone and Bone lies broken and the Mountain God is free of his prison. The One Who Takes Back All shall right the balance of the worlds."

VALLEY OF SORROWS

Connie J. Jasperson lives in Olympia, Washington. A vegan, she and her husband share five children, a love of good food and great music. She is active in local writing groups and is an active member of both NIWA and Pacific Northwest Writers Association,. She is a founding member of Myrddin Publishing Group. Music and food dominate her waking moments.

When not writing or blogging, she can be found with her Kindle, reading avidly.

You can find her blogging on her writing life at: Life in the Realm of Fantasy:
http://conniejjasperson.wordpress.com

Myrddin Publishing Group
www.myrddinpublishing.com
~~~

More great books from every genre await your reading
pleasure!